THE BRITISH PUBLIC WITH THE SUN BANG IN ITS EYES.

ONLY A "TRY ON" FOR A KISS.

Angelina :—"WELL, HENRY, IF YOU ARE GOING TO SEND ME A BRACE OF GROUSE, DON'T KEEP THEM TILL THEY ARE BAD BEFORE YOU LET ME HAVE THEM, AS YOU DID THE LAST TIME YOU HAD A DAY'S SHOOTING."

Henry :—"BAD! YOU DON'T MEAN TO SAY THEY WERE BAD?"

Angelina :—"YES, THEY WERE AS BAD AS—WELL, AS BAD AS A KISS FROM A PERSON YOU DON'T LIKE."   [*Gets one from a person she does.*

AWKWARD AND LUDICROUS MISHAP TO A MARKET-GIRL IN BRITTANY.—THE BOTTOM OF HER PANNIER FALLS OUT AND HER DONKEY RUNS AWAY.

A SCENE IN BLACK AND WHITE.

[Our friend Buskin, still on the look out for novelties, was determined not to be rivalled by any number of Indian dancers. "Why go to the expense, my boy, of sending to India, when all you have to do is to have the girls blacked?" But he met with his difficulties.]

Buskin.—GOOD HEAVENS, MADEMOISELLE! HOW IS IT YOU HAVE **NOT** MADE UP *A LA NAUTCH?*

Première Danseuse.—NO, MEESTER BUSKIN, I VEEL NOT. I VEEL PAINT MY EYEBROWS, BUT I VEEL NOT BLACK MY FACE. I VEEL NOT MAKE MYSELF VON FRIGHT. NEVARE!

THE WOMAN

WITH THE YELLOW HAIR:

A Romance of Good and Bad Society.

———•———

BY THE AUTHOR OF "CHARLEY WAG,"

ETC., ETC.

————————

WITH TWENTY-FOUR ILLUSTRATIONS.

————————

LONDON:

PUBLISHED AT THE UNITED KINGDOM PRESS, 28, BRYDGES STREET,
STRAND.

SOLD BY ALL BOOKSELLERS.

PREFACE.

———o———

It was after a protracted course of milk-and-water novel reading during a severe illness, that the author of this Book formed the rash determination of trying to write a story, in which, honestly, and without exaggeration, he would endeavour to picture life as every man knows it unhappily to exist, but as none of our novelists dare to draw it.

That he made a great mistake the writer does not for a moment deny; but that he has found many thousands more readers than he ever expected, he gratefully declares, and gladly takes this opportunity of thanking them.

The writer has heard this book called "low," "vulgar," "coarse," and "indecent." In refutation of these slanders, he can only beg of those who have not read it, to read, and judge for themselves.

———

DEDICATION.

TO

HER MOST GRACIOUS MAJESTY

LAIS,

ONE OF THE QUEENS OF "BOHEMIA,"

THIS

HISTORY OF A SISTER,

IS DEDICATED BY

HER MOST OBEDIENT, HUMBLE SERVANT,

THE AUTHOR.

CONTENTS.

———o———

FIRST PORTION.

CONTENTS.

THE WOMAN
WITH THE YELLOW HAIR.

THE BRIDGE OF SIGHS.

CHAPTER THE FIRST.

THE BEGINNING AND THE END.

UPON the night of a general holiday, when the illuminated London streets were as light and crowded as at noonday; when all loyal citizens and true Englishmen were re-

joicing, a man diee miserably and alone in a Whitechapel garret—unknown—uncared for: meanwhile the rest of the world went on re-rejoicing.

So does it fall out that there are ever some amongst us who are in sorrow: ever is there a death's head grinning at our feasts. The self-same day Romulus is made general and

Remus degraded to the ranks. This morning the prince is waiting to be crowned, another less fortunate gentleman to be hanged;—the mob outside prepared to cheer either. To-night Medora is a bride, and Molly an outcast; one falls asleep to dream that the world is all bliss and barley-sugar, the other awakens to find it hard, uncharitable, stony-hearted. Medora goes on smiling and dreaming; Molly, wrapped in her rags and her misery, flies, despairingly, Bridgeward!

Meanwhile, reader, you sit and laugh; I crack my small jokes for your entertainment. Our story " stops the way."

CHAPTER THE SECOND.

A BACHELOR'S PARTY IN THEIR CUPS.

IT was half-past one o'clock in the morning, and everybody had had quite as much as was good for them. In fact, the supper-party had become a good deal too noisy. The room above had hammered on the floor, the room below had banged at the ceiling, the rooms on either side had for the last half-hour kept up a duet of indignant remonstrance, without in the slightest degree quelling the riot.

Mr. Maurice Cheveleigh was giving what he called a quiet little supper in his chambers, in Foot Court, Holborn. There was a young cornet in the Guards, and a very haughty swell from the Home Office, three ladies from the ballet of Her Majesty's Theatre, the scene painter from the Apollo Saloon, a comic singer, and the editor of a religious newspaper. Mr. Maurice Cheveleigh was in a government office, and had a salary of ninety pounds a-year, out of which he managed to spend three hundred. When he gave a party he did it in style. The table and floor were strewed over with the *debris* of a sumptuous repast,—lobster shells, empty champagne bottles, half-emptied game pies, and a broken salad bowl. The room was full of tobacco smoke, one gentleman was making a speech without any listeners, another was attempting " Beautiful Star," on the post horn, two were quarrelling, one was asleep, and the rest of the company were singing a chorus; whilst, over all, was heard a loud and continuous knocking from above, below, and on both sides of the apartment.

"Ladies and gentlemen!" bawled Mr. Maurice Cheveleigh, who was the orator upon the occasion: " I think that before we break up this very pleasant party——"

"Nobody's going to break it up, Maurice," interrupted Jack Ochre, the scene painter. " We're not going away for hours yet."

"Nothing," continued the host, " would afford me greater pleasure——"

"Oh! we all know that," broke in half-a-dozen voices. " You don't want to get rid of us. Here's Maurice's jolly good health, with musical honours!"

"Only, what I would suggest," began Cheveleigh, during a momentary cessation of harmony, " is, that we don't make so much noise."

This proposition met with general disap-proval. What had they come there for but to enjoy themselves? It was just like him, always to begin grumbling if anyone spoke above his breath. He was a nice fellow to give a party. Were not the chambers his own? Very well, then, had not he a right to do what he liked in them?

"Chorus, ladies and gentlemen, and let them have it hot."

They did let them have it to a pretty tune, too, so that the whole tenement rang again.

"This is infamous!" ejaculated the old gentleman who lived underneath, and who had gone to bed with a sick headache about four hours ago, and been unable to get a wink of sleep. "This is infamous!" he repeated, sitting up in bed, and apostrophising the reflection of his night-cap tassel, which bobbed at him in the looking-glass as though it perfectly agreed with him, " and not to be borne," he added, shaking his head at it savagely; and with determination he jumped out of bed.

"Well, Perks," cried the old gentleman. indignantly, addressing a person who was stumbling up stairs in the dark, " what the devil do you mean by this disturbance?"

Now Perks was a little feeble old man with gin-and-watery eyes, convivial by nature, but depressed by circumstances. He was the husband of the lady who had charge of the chambers, and was in his married life ruled with a rod of iron. He usually lived in great retirement, was a porter in the city by day, and spent what he earned by " over-time" in getting helplessly intoxicated round the corner at the " Hand and Heart," until such time as he fell with his nose in his tumbler, which being considered as a sign that he had had enough, he was carefully propped up outside the door by the potman to come round again, and take himself home.

Upon this particular occasion Mr. Perks had taken himself home with many lurches, and by a somewhat circuitous route, taking the gutter once or twice in his way, and lying down in it to rest himself, so that when he did get home at last, and had managed to open the door, after fumbling twenty minutes on the wrong side for the keyhole, he had rather a tumbled and ghastly effect in the dim candle-light.

"What the devil do you mean by this disturbance?" repeated the exasperated tenant.

"Nice goings on, you horrid little wretch!" a shrill female voice screamed from the landing above: " nice goings on in a respectable house, with nobody but a poor weak woman left to be put upon, and insulted by the likes of *them*."

The *them* must have had reference to the young ladies from Her Majesty's Theatre.

"Wh—at's the row?" asked Mr. Perks, making violent efforts to stand up straight and speak plainly.

"What's the row?" repeated the old gentleman, as a fresh outbreak of vocalisation, mingled with a wild fantasia on the post-horn, took place above. "Why, that's the row, which that infernal young man and his black-guard associates have been kicking up ever since I went to bed. Are you going to put an end to it, Perks? or are you going up to join them? Which is it to be?"

"What am I to do?" asked Perks, very faintly.

"Go and kick them out!" said the old gentleman; and as though the operation was as easily performed as suggested, he retired into his apartment, after having made it, and went to bed again.

But it is all very well talking of kicking half-a-dozen obstreperous individuals down stairs—everybody is not born a Samson. Mr. Perks was a mild man, strong in *morale*, but weak in action; and he didn't see his way clear.

At that moment a policeman's heavy boots were heard upon the pavement of the court outside. Mr. Perks straightway summoned the gallant constable, and emboldened by his presence led the way up stairs, Mrs. Perks propping him up, and the Perks's servant, a dilapidated female of spare and bony aspect, who looked as if she never went to bed, forming a pleasing background to the group, as she winked, and blinked, and bobbed her nose in the candle behind them. As they entered the room a quadrille was going on to a whistling accompaniment. The post-horn having become incoherent through injudiciously mixing his liquors, had retired from public life, and was going to sleep with his feet on the table.

The fun by this time had grown furious, and every window in the house was clattering in its frame. The ladies by this time had lost all that chilling *hauteur* and restraint which are so opposed to conviviality, and which we so frequently encounter in the higher walks of female society. Kitty Mortimer was smoking a cigar, and Lizzie Gibbons was introducing pirouettes, double shuffles, and entrechats into the quadrille, that would have brought the house down at Her Majesty's, while Polly Davenport, who had become boisterously playful, had broken a couple of wine glasses and the host's pipe, and torn Miss Mortimer's black lace flounce off her crimson satin, in the very first figure. In short, there was no absurd nonsense about any one; they had come there to enjoy themselves, and meant to do it.

CHAPTER THE THIRD.

DRUNK AND DISORDERLY.

"TAKE him up!" said Mr. Perks, pointing out Mr. Maurice Cheveleigh, and immediately beating a retreat behind the constable.

"Eh!" said the person indicated; "what's the matter, old gentleman?"

"Everything's the matter, Mr. Cheveleigh, sir. It's disgraceful!" cried little Perks from round the corner.

"It's abominable!" cried Mrs. Perks.

"It's shocking!" added the Perks's servant, dabbing herself in the mouth with the candle, and extinguishing the light.

"It won't do!" said the constable, as a clincher.

"Why do you allow men to bring such creatures here, Mr. Perks?" cried the good lady. "You know the landlord wouldn't like it."

"Come, come," interposed Cheveleigh, "none of that. You know I won't have my guests insulted."

"Pretty guests!" cried the good lady, giggling hysterically.

"Well, Mr. Perks, what have you to say for yourself?" continued the delinquent, without taking any notice of their remarks. "Who objects to my noise? If anybody does, let them come up and try and put us out." After which he slammed the door in the faces of the deputation, and, double locking it, played a defiant blast upon the post-horn, whilst the rest of the company gave three cheers of derision.

"I'd better go and get help," said the policeman, "if you want to turn 'em out, though I don't exactly know that it's legal." So saying, he departed in search of a comrade, and presently returned with a couple he had found round the corner, and who willingly accompanied him upon the information that there was "a deal of drink stirring."

Meanwhile the party in Cheveleigh's rooms held a council of war as to what should be done. The ladies were for going away quietly; Cheveleigh was not anxious for a row; and the rest of the company came to the conclusion that the *soiree* had been prolonged to a sufficiently late hour, and that they had better go. So everybody got ready to start, the host intending to accompany them. As it turned out this was the worst thing they could have done, for you see our friend the policeman had brought round his two allies under the impression that they would have some refreshment for their trouble; so when they saw the company departing, it is not to be wondered at if they felt a little savage.

"Now, then," cried the first policeman, "move on there, without any row."

"Who's making a row?" asked somebody, of course. The somebody being Charley Bux, of the Guards, who had lately performed upon the post-horn with such startling effect, and who was anything but sober.

"Move on, there!" roared the policeman, giving him a push.

"Keep your hands off!'

"Move on?"

"I shan't!"

"You shall!"

"Take that!"

Nobody could ever tell how it came about, but everybody was wrestling with somebody else in another moment. In another moment a rattle was sprung, more policemen came up, and three of the party, Mr. Bux, Mr. Cheveleigh, and the haughty swell from the Home Office, were being dragged along to the lock-up house, whilst the rest of the company, more or less excited and noisy, followed behind. When they reached the police station the three prisoners were taken inside, and the door slammed upon the rest of the procession.

"What's this?" said the officer on duty.

"Drunk and disorderly, and 'saulting the police in the execution of their duty. That's the ringleader (pointing to Bux), the other two helping him."

"What are they?" asked the inspector.

"Rum lot — swell mob, by the look of them."

"Why, you infernal——" began Mr. Bux.

"None of that here," interrupted the policeman, who had hold of the speaker, giving him a vigorous shake.

"Search him!" said the inspector. "What's that?"

"Somebody's silk handkerchief, sir."

"Somebody's! Damn it! why, it's my own."

"You need not criminate yourself, young man," said the inspector, sternly. "Lock him up."

"Lock me up—lock me up!" cried Bux, much exasperated. "Mayn't I send for bail?"

"I shan't take it for you—the others can." And so they then conducted Mr. Bux to his cell, the constable inquiring whether he would like to write home, because if he would he was sorry to say he couldn't; and whether he would like a light, in which case he feared Mr. Bux could not be accommodated, as it was against rules; further adding, that he was exceedingly grieved that Mr. Bux could not have a cell to himself, but that he had no doubt he would find a drunken sweep, who would be his companion, very excellent company; further adding, in confidence, that the gentleman alluded to was in for biting off a man's ear, and was of an uncertain temper.

Then Cheveleigh and his companion, having communicated with their friends outside, were, after some little preliminaries, liberated on bail.

"I shall go home to bed," said the heavy swell from the Home Office, who, with a crushed hat and a torn coat, looked anything but "heavy."

Most of the company agreed with him about their ultimate destinatioon, and general handshaking ensued.

"Well, I shan't," said Maurice Cheveleigh, who was at all times of a roving, restless turn of mind.

"Who says making a night of it down the Haymarket?"

Nobody said anything favourable to the suggestion, and Cheveleigh, wishing them good night, lighted a pipe, hailed a cab, and went there by himself.

———

CHAPTER THE FOURTH.

"THOSE CREATURES!"

"TO the Haymarket!" The Haymarket, where midnight is noonday — where roses are carmine—where there is much drinking but little thirst—where the same faces pass and re-pass each other every night, and all night long with the same threadbare badinage, the same senseless joke, the same dreary, weary smirk on the thin cracked lips. Where the grey-haired old rip is chucking the brazen-faced child-woman under the chin, twisting his wrinkled face into a sickly smile.

It has gone twelve—put up your shutters, respectable tradesman! Get you home, honest people! Stop your ears, Pity! Turn away your head, Mercy! Clench your hand, Charity! We are among the outcasts—" the ulcers and incubuses of society"—the rouged and ragged, flaunting tawdry—pretty faced and tastefully dressed;—in short, among "*those creatures!*" and we are come to find your husband, madam, your brother, or your son, whichever it is that you have been sitting up for so patiently these many hours. Be of good cheer, dear lady, he is in right merry company, and in no hurry to get home to you. Be not hard upon him when he comes in; you know he has a sufficiency of your society any day, and he is now amongst such jolly fellows, and such pretty women. Aye! they will be pretty, you know, some of them, with their audaciously bold faces, much prettier than you are. Besides, you know, boys will be boys, and the good world smiles not unkindly upon their innocent gambolling.

Here am I, in the garish gaslit market, in the hostlery of the "Blue Posts," hob-nobbing with the respectable father of a family. The hope of the same house is but a few doors off, in at Bob Crofts', with some one who wears a pink bonnet, and uses the worst of language. When he is tired of Bob's he will go to Sally's, and then to Rose's, and will keep on drinking and swearing, listening to, oi repeating, some of that vast store of the unprinted literature of England. He intends, perhaps, to be virtuous to-night, and so will go home very drunk about four, a. m., under the guidance of a philanthropic policeman, who has a prospective half-crown in his mind's eye.

If he intends to be wicked——But here my publisher taps me upon the shoulder, and exhorts me sternly to cut it short.

You read the newspapers and the police reports. You are aware of the existence of the bedizened pariahs. They pursue not their profession for the love of it, but for bread—to keep life in them—as the only resource left. Granted they must live, then, somehow. It is, my friends, the Head and the Hope of the respectable family who support them. Why not? They hold up their heads in society with the best of us: the world condemns them not. Should an obscure scribe dare to wrestle with the world? No—it is not the man but the woman who sins. Bring her out and stone her! Hoot at her! Drive her off! Move her on, policeman!

Where to?

What odds! Out of sight—from the kennel to the gutter; from doorstep to dung-heap; from the dark arches to the river; from the river to death; from death to batter madly, hopelessly, imploringly, at the closed gates of heaven.

Move her on!

Where to?

To anywhere, policeman. No—not to the workhouse. They won't let her in there!

———

CHAPTER THE FIFTH.

PARIAH'S PARADE.

THEY were moving her on that morning, with a vengeance!

The vestrymen had been importuning the magistrates upon the subject. The chair intended to put her down. His worship had made up his mind to the same result. And the police, as the cant phrase runs, had had "the office given them."

When the police have had the office given them, I should advise you, if you have a tattered coat or gown, my poor brother and sister (and, alas! it is your only wear, I know), I should advise you not to get into their way. It is not unlikely that you might get yourself into trouble, and into the wrong box. You might find yourself next morning face to face with his worship, who will stand none of your confounded nonsense, listening to an account of your outrages upon a forbearing and gentle body of men (like all the Z division are, to my certain knowledge), which you do not clearly recollect.

You are surprised that your memory should so fail you, until you hear that you were in a disgusting state of intoxication, which, knowing that you had not tasted bit or sup all day or night, you wonder at. It is not unlikely that if you try on any of your confounded nonsense, giving the lie to the worthy officer, who is unfolding the dire history of your manifest atrocities, you may presently find yourself "waiting for the waggon," and that you may go away to jail, and get your hand in on the mill for a week or so. And serve you right, for you should not be poor and ragged, hanging about the streets when you ought to be snugly tucked up in the soft warm bed you have not got. Shame on you! Hi! police!

When Maurice Cheveleigh lounged into the Haymarket, pipe in mouth and hands in pocket, Z 3003 was asserting his authority under the following circumstances:—

Frances was talking to Tilly upon that engrossing topic, the opening of the Leviathan Casino, which had just been licensed in the face of the strongest clerical opposition ("Bigotry beaten to the dust," and so on, vide posters of the period). Frances had bought a new gown for the occasion,—"A yallar silk, dear, with lace flounces."

"Mine's a ble-ue," said Tilly, with what is commonly believed to be a patrician accent. "Double skirt, and trimmed with be-ugles."

"Now, then," roared Z 3003, who felt no interest in their little details; "go inside or move on!"

But Frances wanted to know what they were doing that was illegal.

"I'll show you, double sharp," replied the zealous officer, and he would forthwith have obliged them with the requisite information, had not Maurice come up opportunely, and pacified both sides. As they desisted immediately, Z 3003 left them with a few words of advice. Another woman was standing there, perversely in the middle of the pavement; but this one was wise—she recovered her feet after the policeman's gentle push, and, without a word, slunk timidly away.

There was a crowd at the corner, round a drunken man huddled together on a door-step. A sympathising stranger was endeavouring to persuade him to get up, but the "overtaken," well knowing that faith could not be put in those legs of his, was proof against argument.

Up came the master mind, Z 3003, put the crowd on one side, and shook the drunkard by the shoulder.

"Gerrup!" said the policeman. "Where do you live—do you hear?" And he shook him hard, but he shook nothing out of him.

"Oh! he'll tell him—he's so persuasive," sneered the crowd, derisively.

"Don't you hear the gentleman is asking you a question?"

"Clever man, Z 3003, aint he?"

"Embryo inspector, I should think!"

"Do you want a night's lodging, some of you?" asked the object of this playful satire, which interrogatory caused a dead silence.

Z 3003 pursued his inquiries—"What's your name?"

No reply.

"What's your name?" with another shake, this time shaking a hiccup out of him.

"What do you say?" asked the policeman, severely.

"I think he says it is Gough, sir," suggested Cheveleigh.

"Don't speak so loud!" expostulated a by-stander; "he mightn't like it to be known at Exeter Hall." At which the mob laughed immensely.

Of course the end of this little scene was, that the drunkard was taken to the station-house and locked up. After which Z 3003 went upon his rounds, picking up a case every now and then, until he made up a baker's dozen. Firstly, he boxed the ears of an inoffensive, ragged little blackguard, and took him into custody for howling. Then he bore off a seedy foreigner, whose offence consisted in not being able to explain his innocence in English. Then he took up a wretched woman, who swore she was "a doing nothink," and her still more wretched companion for helping her. Sometimes the mob cried out, "Who takes 'black mail?'" which words signify a prostitute's bribe to the police. Sometimes they cried out "Shame!" as Britons will do sometimes when they see the strong bullying the weak; though, for that matter, the weak are often enough in the wrong, and quite unworthy of the Briton's sympathy.

Besides, you know, the police are always in the right. Don't the newspapers prove it?

When he became weary of watching this zealous officer, Cheveleigh betook himself to the bar of Thompson's public house, where he was surprised to find the editor of the religious newspaper, and a couple more of his friends, drinking and smoking, and apparently as fresh as though they had just begun the evening.

———

CHAPTER THE SIXTH.

A SERMON IN THE HAYMARKET.

STILL further, to Cheveleigh's surprise, who should they presently discover, in a quiet corner, smoking his pipe, than Jack Ochre, the scene painter, who had bidden them all good night a couple of hours ago.

He was in conversation with a very miserably dressed young person.

"Hollo, Jack!" roared the editor.

"Hollo, Ochre!" roared the other two gentlemen.

"By Jove!" ejaculated Cheveleigh, "he's in ladies' society."

"Tableau of Joseph forgetting himself," said the editor.

"Who's your shoeless friend, Jack?" whispered Cheveleigh, taking him aside. "I'm very sorry to see this, you profligate giant. I'm afraid you're leading a gay life unknown to your family."

"Whose business is that?" quoth Jack Ochre, blushing the colour of his huge red beard; for Mr. Ochre took great pains to establish his reputation as a woman hater, and despiser of petty dissipations.

"A craven heart sheltereth itself behind a bulwark of bombast," remarked Mr. Cheveleigh, sententiously. "Knowing thyself to be in the wrong, oh! my friend Jack, wherefore dost thou not confess thy fault, order in a fresh tankard, and purchase thy young friend a better pair of shoes?"

"Do you know who she is?" asked Jack, regaining his good humour.

"Not the honour," replied Cheveleigh.

"Yes you have," said the other. "The woman who was dressed so magnificently one night at that dancing place in Holborn, who took us up to the Haymarket in her own brougham."

"Good heavens!"

"Yes. I met her just now in the street, she recognised me, and began to cry and to smear her face with her dirty paws, in streaks, as you may see; and she said, in her own peculiar grammar, 'Oh! I is so wretched, I wish I was dead, I do; I owes my rent, and would have drowned myself, but I knowd they would pull me out agin; and I should have pisoned myself, only I know they wouldn't sell me nothink. Oh, dear!' and etcetera. So I advised her, as there seemed to be so many hindrances in the way of her departure for another world, to try and put up with this one of ours for a little while longer. Then she went on to say that she was hungry and thirsty, at which you will be surprised. And I thought, that had I been a charitable person —which I rejoice to say I am not—and had I been possessed of half-a-sovereign——But I am approaching the fabulous. Having nothing, I gave it, and was thanked accordingly."

This wicked liar, I feel convinced, reader, *had* given her half-a-sovereign, for all that.

One of the company feeling, what he called peckish, a general move was made in the direction of Scott's Oyster Rooms; and here they called loudly upon Randle for more and more dozens, until daylight, with a sodden face, peeped in over the blinds, and leered upon the revellers.

And now out of the Market and to bed. Weary, dead beat, and more than half drunk, our young friends turn homewards. The editor and his two companions lived westward. Ochre and Cheveleigh offered to accompany them for a short distance up Piccadilly. At the pump, by St. James's Church, they halted to say good-bye. As they were talking, something tattered, and frowsy, and hideous, in the semblance of a woman, shambled up to them, and begged for alms.

"Go to——" roared the editor, naming the ultimate destination to which, I have no doubt, any parson would have prophesied that the whole party were rapidly journeying.

"Oh! do please, gentlemen," whined the phantom.

"Yes, do please, gentlemen!" cried Ochre, with an energy that startled the party, and made the poor petitioner stare in stupid surprise. "Make up a subscription of a penny each, and I will give two-pence—you won't miss it. Any of you would give six times the amount to the gaudy Jemima and magnificent Matilda, who don't want it; but here's a poor wretch starving, for whom you won't take the trouble to pull your hands out of your pockets. You may be begging yourselves some day—you know you ought if you had your deserts, and were not overpaid by deluded employers. Here's a chance to help a fellow creature. Make haste, the recording angel is balancing his ledger for the night. Where are your dirty pennies?"

So they gave the sum required, laughing and applauding Jack's eloquence

"God bless you, sir," cried the phantom.

"Trash!" said Ochre. "Be off with you, and don't try it on again to-morrow, because it mayn't work so well."

"Jack, you're a good fellow, upon my soul!" said Cheveleigh, as they walked away together. "If ever I have to take to begging I pray that I may meet you."

"Unliklier things than that," returned the other,—"unliklier than the begging, I mean."

"You're a good fellow," continued Cheveleigh, "and one I am proud to call my friend. I know I am becoming helplessly drunk, but I sincerely hope not maudlin."

"I'm sorry to contradict you, Maurice, but I think you are making a fool of yourself. It's not your fault, I know, and arises from an incautious amalgamation of alcoholic stimulants. Good morning—take care of yourself —don't run foul of Z 3003, or you may get into the papers. Thank God I am not a householder, so you can't send and disturb me for bail if you get locked up again."

CHAPTER THE SEVENTH.

NELLY RAYMOND.

VERILY I hope the reader is not disgusted with Maurice Cheveleigh. At this moment he is far from looking his best: his boots and hat are dusty: he is sodden, tumbled, and tipsy, and is scarcely the sort of person you ladies would pick upon for a hero. But do not be too hasty: to-morrow morning, when he is washed and brushed, and freshened up with soda and brandy, he will be quite another man. You will find that he is young and handsome, with light curly hair, and large, bold, blue eyes. You will find that he is a high-spirited, roystering, careless, open-handed, warm-hearted young fellow—a little too wild and a deal too generous to get much credit with the "Heavy Respectabilities" of this world. So do not be too hard upon our young friend, for he will retrieve his character to-morrow I'll be bound.

I do not believe that he had more than one enemy in the world at this period of his life. This was, of course, the person of all others whose good-will it would have been to Mr. Cheveleigh's interest to possess—no other than the head of the government offices where he was clerk. Mr. Parchingby had more than once taken offence at certain little ebullitions of misplaced jocularity which had emanated from his junior. He was aware of the fact of Cheveleigh having frequently mimicked and ridiculed him in the office. He was furious at the offhand style in which the young man was wont to receive his reproofs. Once they had met upon neutral ground (they were both upon a holiday trip) at an hotel at Paris, and the senior had been much humbled by the junior, owing to the former's ignorance of the French language.

Besides all this, it happened, too, that once upon a time there dwelt in that Papistical and Bohemian suburb, Brompton, a certain lady who was beautiful, though lowly born—a stylish creature, who rode in the Park in her brougham, with a little ugly dog lolling out its tongue and ogling you from the window, and who, though she bore not his name, was a considerable item in Mr. Parchingby's expenditure, and perhaps stood him in a good deal more than the Mrs. Parchingby (by special license) he kept in Russell Square. And to this Brompton beauty did the audacious junior at one time (let us hope unknowingly) presume to pay his court, until, one night, the protector and the lover met upon the same hearth; high words ensued, somebody was turned out of doors, somebody deserted, and two men, hating each other immensely, met with a low bow next day at the official desk, and argued an hour about an overcharge of twopence in a contractor's account.

"I don't mind much how soon I am in bed!" said Mr. Maurice, reflectively, as he walked along the streets smoking his last pipe.

Just as he reached the corner of Foot Court, and was turning up the narrow passage by the "Hand and Heart," a young girl, coming in the opposite direction, ran against him, and hastily apologised.

"Oh, sir, I beg your pardon."

"I beg yours," said Cheveleigh. "I hope I haven't hurt you. See, you've dropped something. Allow me!"

He picked up a book which had fallen from her pocket, and opened it.

"*Lockhart's Life of Scott,*" said the gentleman, much amazed. "You don't mean to say you've been reading this?"

"Yes, I have," replied the girl, taking it from him. "It's very interesting."

"Not so interesting as the *London Journal,* or *Reynolds's Miscellany,* is it?"

"Well—no. It's drier."

"Oh, it's drier," said Maurice. 'And, pray, who was Scott?"

"Scott! Why him as wrote the story in the *Journal* about Queen Elizabeth and Amy Robsart."

"And Lockhart?" asked Maurice.

"Oh, Lockhart," replied his new acquaintance. "Lockhart? It doesn't say who he was."

"And so you like the *London Journal?*"

"Yes, I prefer it to the *Herald.*"

"The *Morning Herald?*"

"*Morning Herald!*" she repeated, with a laugh at his ignorance. "The *Family Herald,* of course. But I can't stay here talking to you, sir. I've got to be at my work."

"What is that?"

"Brush-drawing."

"What?"

"Putting the bristles into brushes, you know."

"Where do you work?"

"Why do you ask?"

"Because I'll walk with you, if you'll allow me."

"But it will be taking you out of your way."

"Not at all: my way is any way."

"I'm going to Providence Row, Finsbury Square. That's where I work;—and I have to be there by eight o'clock. I got up early this morning, and thought I would come out for a walk. What time is it now, sir?"

"About seven."

"Oh, I shall have lots of time."

"Don't let us hurry then. Suppose we sit down somewhere upon a door step."

"How absurd!"

"Absurd you call it. A hard stone and a cold crust, with the woman I love, is far preferable to——"

"Don't talk such nonsense. What a funny fellow you are."

"You flatter me, Miss. And why?"

"Asking me about the *London Journal,* and coming out of your way to walk with me."

"I think we've been having rather an eccentric conversation for this early hour in the morning, and considering that we never met before," said Cheveleigh. "But I'll tell you why I'm coming with you, if you'll keep it a secret."

"Certainly."

"And not tell more than a dozen of your most intimate lady friends, with injunctions not to tell more than a dozen of theirs——"

"What is it?"

"It is because I love you."

"Don't do that—I don't like it!"

She disengaged her waist, which he had encircled with his arm, and looked very angry.

"Don't you believe in love at first sight?"

"No, I don't believe in your love at all,

sir. Please to leave me alone. I am only a poor girl, and you are a gentleman. I wish you would not talk like that—I am not what you take me for."

" Don't say I have offended you, my dear. Make it up, and let us be friends. There, I won't do so any more."

" You promise."

" I swear."

" There is my hand then."

" And you'll forgive me ?"

" I never was angry with you. No, I don't mean that. Be quiet, or I'll scream out."

Mr. Cheveleigh, profiting by the loneliness of the street, had kissed her.

" I must say it," cried he, " although it offends you, and you leave me on the instant, you are the nicest and the prettiest girl I ever saw in my life."

Although Mr. Maurice bore the character of a proverbial flatterer, yet in this instance there was indeed ample ground for his enthusiasm. A rosy, golden-haired girl, whose laughing blue eyes, pouting lips, and flushed cheeks, seemed to bid defiance to the stifling atmosphere of the crowded workshop where she spent her days, and the squalid and unwholesome garret where she slept at night. Plainly and poorly dressed, but still so graceful in her then worn shawl and common cotton frock— so blithe-hearted and gay, though her life must needs have been of the hardest—so gentle-spoken and modest, though so used to the buffetting of a coarse, rough world, she might have been likened to some wild roadside flower which had sprung up among the weeds and briars, and grown alone in beauty, surrounded by a wilderness of rubbish.

They walked along the streets chatting of many things ; of her work, of her employers, of the country and green fields ; of Heaven knows what other incongruous matters, foreign to the time and place, until at length they reached their destination.

" I work up here," she said, " and I must wish you good-bye."

" Give me one kiss before you go. The smallest in the world—just for the name of the thing. And before you go, may I ask who my pretty companion is ?"

" My name is Nelly—Nelly Raymond."

" And a very pretty name it is. When shall we meet again ?"

" Oh, I don't know—soon."

" Soon. But when ?"

" You don't want to see me again. We shall meet accidentally, perhaps. Good-bye."

" But I say——"

" I must go—good-bye !"

And away she ran. Mr. Cheveleigh ran after her to the end of the court down which she had vanished, but could see nothing of her.

" Well," said he, reflectively, " this has been rather an unprofitable hour spent. I don't know, though ; not more so than the rest. Good-bye, my little fairy! We shall never meet again, I suppose, and so I'll take myself off to bed. It's almost time !"

He had almost forgotten the little brushdrawer by the time he reached his own door ; but she was thinking of him, and continued to do so at intervals throughout the day, her busy fingers meanwhile working on mechanically.

At the same time were the thoughts of another woman closely connected with, though totally unknown to her, occupied with the same subject. While severed by the barriers of society—living, as it were, in two different and distinct worlds, and yet bound together in their dearest hopes and affections—crossing and recrossing each other in the paths of life, ever at variance and opposed, ever unknown to each other, yet sisters still. So shall we meet them in this history. So shall we find them—beautiful, rich, and happy ; poor, deserted, miserable !

What means that scene upon the " BRIDGE OF SIGHS"—who are the actors ? Years hence, one sister passes thus upon her way ; a wretched outcast, crouching in the shade, looks curiously upon the Woman with the Yellow Hair, whom, years ago——

But we anticipate our story.

CHAPTER THE EIGHTH.

ONLY A MOTHER'S LETTER.

WHEN our young profligate got into his sitting-room, the broad daylight was streaming in at the window upon a dreary scene of riot and disorder. He looked at it all in great disgust, and then began to undress slowly, with his eyes shut. Presently he looked at himself in the glass, and saw a very haggard, sallow face, which made him mutter " Fool !" as he turned away moodily.

He was just going to get into bed, when he perceived a letter lying upon the dressingtable. It had come during the late festivities, and he had put it away to read when the company was gone. It was *only* a letter from his mother.

He opened it now with perhaps a feeling nearly akin to shame and remorse, and I should not wonder if he blushed a little.

His mother wrote in French : she was a Frenchwoman. What she said was this :—

" My own dear, neglectful, cruel child, am I never to see you again ? Has your poor mother, living here alone and so sad, these many months, no place in your heart ? Can you not spare me a little moment ? Will you not rob your dear friends of a few brief hours to spend with a poor sick woman who so loves you ? I have been very, very ill, and am still so unwell as to be unable to leave my room. I am left quite to myself, though the house is full of company. There is Mr. Hadget, the London attorney, money lender, thief catcher, or whatever he may please to call himself. There is also a choice collection of rustic seducers and beer-drinking louts always at your father's table. It is with such people that he now spends his whole time. I spend mine in my room on my side of the house, little troubled by this agreeable society, save when the chorus of their horrible songs, or the roaring of their coarse voices as

ALONE IN HER MISERY.

they sing or quarrel, come up the stairs in the middle of the night, and wake me trembling.

"I would not write thus, my own dear Maurice, did I not feel so sad and lonely. Oh, for some dear one to whom, your poor mother could confide her griefs, and sorrows, and secrets. Maurice, my son, I have a *a great—a dreadful secret to tell you*. One which I dare not trust myself to write—one which my heart tells me I dare scarcely confide to you in words. It can be told only when holding your hands in mine, my dear boy—leaning my head upon your breast—lying at your feet.

"My God! I am talking too fast; I am feverish and excited!

No. 2.

"I love you, Maurice, my dear child. Your mother kisses you! I send you a little money. Come to me without delay.—LOUISE."

The letter enclosed a five-pound note. The son put both into his pocket, and sat down upon the edge of the bed to think. It was not a pleasant occupation. A whole year had elapsed since he had been home. Not that it was at such a distance, or that he had lacked the means or opportunity. He had been to Paris, and he had been to the Isle of Wight; had been to visit his friends; had been feasting, and tippling, and making love this year past, wasting every night with the most worthless company, but he had not had time to go and see his mother. Had it been Frances, now, or Tilly, or Kate, or Lou, or any one with no claim upon him, it would have been very different. He might have fallen in love with any one of these fair young damsels; have given up everything on their account, have made every sacrifice for their sake. Such would have been quite natural and in the regular course of things; but how could you expect him to do so for a mother? Her very letter, there, so full of tears and love, laying bare the heart of an unhappy, slighted woman, is tossed on one side, and is forgotten, to be found and read by her dear child upon his return, sodden and stupid, from his graceless debaucheries.

Oh! mothers, mothers, ever is it your fate— ever will it be so! Nurse the dear little ones; cuddle them closer and closer; hug them to your tender bosoms! keep them as long as you can. Alas! it will be no great while, at best! They shall desert you for their dolls and rocking-horses; they shall go out into the world and forget you. There shall spring up rivals to you, in little, meek-faced chits of girls, and conceited boobies of boys, who shall bear off your children in triumph, and you shall weep and lament unavailingly. You must leave him, then; you must not obtrude your presence upon your rival's household. Do not poke your old nose where you may get it pulled. You have become a mother-in-law— a bugbear—a nuisance. Get you home, foolish old woman, and cry; there is naught else left for you!

The more our young profligate pondered over his conduct the longer he sat, there, upon the side of the bed, swinging his leg in time to his thoughts, the less excuse could he find for his neglect. He began to feel very much disgusted with himself. At last he rose, and taking a *Bradshaw* from the bookcase, began to look for the next train.

"It's no good bothering about it yet," he reflected. "I can't catch the first, and there is lots of time before the second."

So he got into bed, and was fast asleep in three minutes.

Anon the Perks's bony handmaiden put her grimy head inside the door, and gazed upon the sleeper.

"'Ow 'andsome!" whispered the ancient virgin to herself. He was the finest, handsomest, richest, kindest gentleman she had ever known, and had inspired her gentle heart with a sort of platonic affection. "Oh, how proud I should be of him if I was his mother!" she thought. "I wonder whether he has one!"

She sighed, and went away, shutting the door to, noiselessly, behind her, afraid of disturbing him.

CHAPTER THE NINTH.

A VERY NICE YOUNG MAN.

IT was late in the afternoon when Maurice awoke. A very sober-looking, orderly young gentleman was standing by the bedside, who asked him, rather severely, whether he meant to waste all the rest of his life in slumber.

"By Jove!" retorted the profligate, "it's the only time I don't waste." And he raised himself and scratched his aching head, mournfully.

The sober-looking young gentleman said, "You're about right, there;" and then sniggered complacently, and stroked his chin, as though he had been very witty.

"Did you see the letter I left for you?" he asked. "It was from your mother, wasn't it? I found it under the grate, where it had fallen, I suppose; unless you thought you had read it, and threw it there. Your head aches, I see. I hope you were not very drunk last night?"

"I was sober when I went to bed this morning," said the other, peevishly.

"This morning? Bless me! you're killing yourself. Is it a bad headache?" And he laughed again, as though he had made another joke.

The speaker was Maurice's cousin, who shared his chambers with him. But Mr. Ernest was a very different sort of man to Mr. Maurice. He was at the same office, but much higher up. He had different tastes and different companions. He had not joined in the festivities of the previous evening, having been, instead, to a ball at a lady's house in Baker Street, and returned after the supper had concluded. As frequently occurs, the great difference in the tastes and opinions of the two cousins formed the main prop of their friendship. Had they both been possessed with the restless, wandering temper of Maurice, they must, of necessity, have worn one another to death in a fortnight. Had they both been of the reserved and taciturn disposition of Ernest, they must have had a third party constantly in their company to break the long, dull nights of silence which they would have passed together in body and apart in spirit—each hugging his own hate within his breast.

"Look here, Ernest," said his cousin. "Where are you going to spend your holiday?" (They were both on leave of absence for a fortnight from their office.) "I am going home. You must come with me."

He then explained briefly, the contents of his mother's letter. Ernest soon made his mind up. He had formed other plans, but the proposed trip would come cheap. He was a careful young man, and did not like wasting money; so, before the day was over, an express train bore them away from London to the estate of Maurice's father, Sir John Cheveleigh, of Skearcrowes Hall, Yorkshire.

In these days of rapid travelling one must not waste much time in description; so, as they set off upon one line, we must bring them by another to their journey's end.

"Confound it!" cried Maurice, a dreadful thought striking him as he placed his foot upon the platform at the terminus. "I ought to have gone to the police-station. What ever will be the consequence?"

CHAPTER THE TENTH.

STRANGE COMPANY AT SKEARCROWS.

THE proprietor of the great rumbling, ill-built, half-ruined tenement known as Skearcrows, was standing at the dining-room window this evening, listening to the moaning of the wind among the trees of the shrubbery, and waiting for his son's arrival, or rather for his servant's return, having sent the latter with a tax-cart to meet him, and bring home some brandy from the railway station.

He was a stout old gentleman, very red in the face, and rather asthmatic. In his youth he might have been handsome, even noble-looking. He had a very red nose now, rather inflamed eyes, and but two or three black stumps of teeth, left here and there in his jaws. It were as though a glorious sun of gin-and-water had gone down in his face, tweaking his nasal organ by the way. He was dressed in a seedy suit of black, and wore an old battered hat pressed down tightly upon his straggling silver locks. He was not the sort of old English gentleman I would have liked to introduce into my story, but, you see, this history is taken from life, and you know I must not distort nature.

Ah, me! where are those fine old country squires one reads of in novels?—*which is their county?*

He had not to wait long, for the tax-cart was even now turning the corner of the avenue which led to the house, and after jingling and jolting awhile helplessly among the ruts and stone heaps, came to a sudden halt before him.

"Hallo, father!" cried Maurice.

"Hallo, my boy!" responded the old gentleman. "Who's that? Ernest? Glad to see you. I say, you didn't leave the brandy behind, did you?"

Assured to the contrary, the next matter for consideration was the safe disposal of the horse and trap. This could not be effected without a light, so Sir John began to roar out for the attendance of his retainers, the servant whom he had sent with the cart having been left behind to walk, as there was only room for two.

"Cursed skulking scoundrels!" remarked the country gentleman, having put himself out of breath without causing any visible effect. "I'll discharge the lot."

"Shall I go and look for some one?" asked his nephew.

"No, no—never mind. Perhaps we can find a lantern somewhere. Confound the door, when's it going to be mended?" and the old gentleman stumbled about in the inner darkness of the stable, until he discovered the object he was in search of. After which, and much hard swearing, consequent upon the dampness of the matches, absence of a halter, and dearth of provender, the horse and vehicle were safely lodged, and the three gentlemen entered the house, carrying the brandy.

It was a dark, dismal-looking place, inside, imperfectly lighted by the cracked lamp in the hall. Grim faces stared out at you from blurred old paintings upon the walls. They were "the ancestors," old Sir John was wont to observe, with a chuckle; "and a damned trumpery lot too; not worth their weight in firewood, any man jack of 'em!"

I think he was about right, too; and, indeed, were it not for what is called "old associations," I myself should have much preferred a pretty wall-paper.

While Ernest was disposing of his coat and hat, Maurice inquired after the health of his mother.

"Eh!" said Sir John. "All right, I believe. Why?"

"I thought she was ill," said the son.

"Ill!—no: not that I know of," replied the father. "Who said she was?"

"She told me so."

"Told you so, eh? Absurd mawkishness! She's always ill, according to her account. Likes to be creeping on the fire-back all day—never going out—never seeing or speaking to any one."

"Where is she?" asked the son,

"Where is she, eh? Where ought she to be?" retorted Sir John. "At the bottom of the table, doing the honours of the house to the gentlemen I choose to invite? Not she! She's too high and mighty for that. We're too low a lot for her ladyship. Bah! Come to dinner, boy!"

Dinner had been announced, in the middle of the old gentleman's speech, by a very pert-looking, showily-dressed young woman, whom you might have taken for a servant, had it not been for the gay ribbons in her cap, and the sparkling rings upon her fingers; whom you might have taken for a lady, had it not been for her bold speech, bad grammar, and black nails.

"All right, Kitty," said the country gentleman. "We're quite ready."

He led the way into a large oak-panelled room, where a table was laid for dinner, at which a gentleman was already seated, sharpening one knife upon another. Three other gentlemen stood round the fireplace. One was a very withered, shrivelled-up old man, with scanty grey hair upon a little ugly head, almost swamped in a great coat collar, which seemed to be providentially kept down by his big ears. Next to him stood a hulking giant, in top-boots and spurs, who was about twenty years old, but whose face, bronzed by sun and drink, might have belonged to a man of thirty. The third was a red-faced and rather shabby man, dressed in rusty black, and wearing a dirty white neckerchief, and a huge bunch of keys dangling from his fob. But it was the gentleman at the table to whom the attention of the cousins was unaccountably and involuntarily directed. He was a hard-featured, middle-aged man, with a grating voice, beetling brows, and large wolfish teeth, which, owing to a convulsive twist of the lip to which he was subject, showed like those of a snarling dog. He was above the middle height, and strongly built. His hands were very large, and the fingers long and bony; and in them was observable something of the restlessness of his grey eyes—something of the ugly twitch of his lips. He wore spectacles.

It is a pleasant idiosyncrasy of some comic authors to depict the wearers of spectacles as a guileless race; as though a weakness of sight must be necessarily wedded to simplicity and greenness, when everyone knows that blindness is one of the most frequent results of youthful dissipation. For my part, among the number of profligates I have known (which, for their sakes I grieve to say is not small), the greater part have worn glasses. It surely cannot have been that these wolves in sheep's clothing adopted spectacles as a blind. I have known but one professed Atheist, and he was a mean-looking man, in barnacles, who would have been the worst person in the world to have *posed* for Ajax.

"My nephew, Mr. Hadget," said Sir John, introducing Ernest to the gentleman at the table. "Mr. Piper," indicating the shrivelled old man. "Young Tom Piper," pointing to the giant. "Mr. Ganders," with a motion towards the person with the white neckerchief. "My son, Maurice, you all know. Kitty, let us have another plate, and bring the soup in."

"Has pretty Kitty had her dinner?" asked Mr. Hadget, looking up slily, as he felt the edge of his knife.

"She'll have it presently," replied the host, very sharply; at the same time, as it seemed, kicking in Hadget's direction beneath the table.

"But won't Miss Kitty join us?" the other pursued, smiling, and unconscious of the pantomime, whilst the young men looked on wonderingly.

"No, no! Hold your tongue! Help the soup," the host said, hurriedly, winking, and frowning at the speaker.

The pert young woman of the ribbons had luckily not heard this little dialogue. When she had set down the soup, she flounced out of the room, and was seen no more.

CHAPTER THE ELEVENTH.

ONE IS WEEPING, WHILST THE REST MAKE MERRY.

ANYTHING new in town, sir?" asked Mr. Ganders of Ernest.

"Nothing that I know of," he replied.

"Who won the Cesarewitch?" asked young Piper.

"I don't know, I'm sure."

"Confound it! I should have thought you'd have brought it down," cried old Sir John. "But I sent Bob Sawder to ask at the station."

"They must have had the telegraph an hour or two ago," said Ganders.

"Didn't you go near there, Mr. Hadget?"

"No, I didn't," said Hadget. "I've told you so before."

"I'm open to lay odds against 'Greased Lightning' yet," cried the host.

"Pooh, pooh!" said Hadget. "I fancy 'Sphynx' and 'Day's Wonder,' myself."

"Day's Wonder! Bosh!"

"Come, then, Sir John, what will you lay against her?"

"I'll give the odds."

"And I'll take you—in quids," replied Hadget, booking the bet. "We shall see who knows most about it, when Bob comes back."

"Will you do the same with me, sir?" asked the giant, of Hadget.

"Don't bet with that boy, sir, for heaven's sake!" broke in Piper *pere*, in a shrill, reedy voice. "What's he know about betting?"

"You leave me alone, old gentleman," retorted the giant.

"Hold your noise, you villain! I'll give the odds, Mr. Hadget, if agreeable."

"Quite agreeable. 20 to 1, isn't it?"

"30 to 1, you mean," returned the other.

"Yes, 30 to 1," said the host; and the bet was booked, young Piper grumblingly refusing to have anything to do with it.

"So there's nothing fresh in London, eh, Ernest?" said Sir John, after a pause. "How's business getting on?"

"As well as can be expected, sir," replied his nephew.

"I've heard great accounts of your ability. You're what's called a 'light,' aren't you? Is Maurice one?"

"Not at the office," said Maurice.

"You're a night light, I think, Maurice," said his cousin, kindly.

"Takes after papa, eh?" chuckled Mr. Hadget. "A little wild."

"In my boyhood——" suggested the father.

"Gad, it's been a long boyhood—almost got into another childhood," said Mr. Hadget, cackling cheerfully.

"Fine women in London, I reckon!" cried Giant Tom, leaning back in his chair, with his hands in his pockets, and leering like an ogre. "Dresses theirselves up a bit spicy, I reckon."

"What's that scoundrel saying?" cried Father Piper again.

"Talking about the London gals, daddy."

"London gals! God bless my soul! Is the world come to an end? A miserable creature, with half a year's life in him, to talk so, when he should be thinking of his coffin! Pass the wine, poor boy! pass the wine, and don't fill your own glass. You've had enough, already, I can see."

It was an odd conceit of the poor old gentleman, that this hulking giant of a son was weak and ailing. He never spoke of his offspring without a sigh of compassion for his shattered constitution, and was in the habit of calculating how long he (the father) would live after he had seen his son comfortably interred. During the course of that particular evening, some little incident occurred which led him to discover his son's shortness of sight. The old man seized upon the information with avidity, and cried out, slapping young Piper on the back, "You're growing blind. Dam'me, he'll want a dog and string in a year or two." And then, all through the rest of the night, he kept on calling his son's attention to objects at some distance, and comparing the difference in their sights, with great apparent satisfaction to himself, but with many groans for the other's premature decay.

"What's your opinion about the present

Ministry, Sir John?" asked Ganders, by way of changing the conversation.

"Can't say," rejoined the gentleman addressed, who was at the moment consulting his watch, and fidgetting for Bob's return.

"Can't understand Palmerston's tactics myself," pursued Ganders. "There can be but one solution——"

"He must have got drunk," said Sir John, reflectively.

"Lord bless me! do you think so?" cried Ganders, aghast.

"He couldn't have been all this time walking home. Perhaps he's come."

Mr. Ganders seeing that Bob Sawder and not the Premier was the subject of interest, became silent, and drank hard out of revenge. He was a "vet" of the neighbourhood, more celebrated as a toper than a horse-doctor, to whom the host owed a long bill.

What claim the Pipers, father and son, had upon Sir John's hospitality, it would be difficult to tell. When a grey-headed, disreputable, godless old man, with just enough money or credit to enable him to entertain his guests, is yet shunned by all good society as some moral bugbear, he is apt to get round him some queer company. Thus did old Sir John Chevelelgh, a gentleman born, and a man of property, as rumour said, feast and drink with Hadget, the low London attorney, Ganders, the drunken horse-doctor, Father Piper, an independent gentleman, of questionable antecedents, and son Piper, half jockey, half horse-dealer, half poacher, and wholly a blackguard.

The bottle circulating freely, the company got very merry until broken in upon by the arrival of Bob, with the name of the winner of the race.

"Was it 'Greased Lightning?'"

"No it worn't."

"Then what, in God's name, was it?" cried Sir John.

"Mr. Sweep's mare, 'Day's Wonder,' won it by a length, 'Ginger Cocktail' second, and 'Dust-up' a bad third."

"Oh!" said Sir John, with a very long face, "I owe you thirty, Hadget."

"Well, father," cried the young giant, "pity you didn't leave me alone, isn't it?"

"Hold your noise, you scoundrel!" cried Mr. Piper, presently, when he had recovered a little from the shock.

"Lucky guess of Hadget's," thought Ganders, and at the same time began to wonder whether it was possible that he had got the information before he laid the wager.

While they were talking Maurice had quietly left the room in search of his mother. He found her alone in her bed room, in the other wing of the house. There was no other light than the fire, which shone full upon her as she knelt upon the ground, her head resting on her arm, her arm resting upon the sofa, her soft hair streaming over her shoulders. At a first glance you might have taken her for some young girl, so slim and graceful was the outline of her figure. But presently she raised her face, and then he saw the great and awful change a few brief months had wrought in her. The face he could once remember so beautiful, was now hollow-cheeked, and pinched, and careworn; the hair he remembered, so black, glossy, and luxuriant, now thin and streaked with grey. The beautiful woman, the dear, kind loving mother, who was so proud of the curly headed little boy long years agone, whom he could recollect coming like a flood of sunshine into the sombre cloisters of the old French school, where he was educated, whom he could see now, as she was in their old garden among the flowers, —in their drawing-room at Paris, with all the lights, and music, and dresses,—at a hundred other times and places, all gone never to return.

She knelt there now, unthought of—uncared for, sobbing alone in her misery. The brutal merriment of the sots below occasionally breaking in upon the otherwise unbroken silence. Where was her husband? Where was her son—the only being in the world whom she had left her to love and cherish? He had just torn himself away from the table, his face yet flushed with wine and smelling of tobacco-smoke, to come and "do the dutiful." That is the phrase you young men use, I believe. And does it not mean shamming affection and love for the purpose of wheedling more pocket-money out of the old people? And do not the stupid old creatures, grateful for the sacrifice of your valuable half-hours, bring forth the scanty purse, and send you away rejoicing with the money in your pocket that would have done for sister Jane's allowance, which she never gets; would have bought the little dainties mamma doats upon and denies herself; would have kept the impudent tradesman, with the unsettled bill, from off the door-step?

Maurice, repentant, remorseful, stood looking upon the mother he had neglected. A moment sufficed to bring back to his recollection so much that he had long forgotten. He saw her now, with her pale, sickly face, and felt that she was going from him—that she was dying there alone, while the rest made merry.

"Mother!"

She had half risen at the sound of his voice, with a frightened look, then with a smothered cry, fell sobbing on his shoulder.

Had he just come! How long he had been. How she had waited for him! How well he looked! How handsome he had grown! How proud she was of him! To pat him on the head, to fondle him, and lovingly caress his curly hair; to lean her cheek against his; to listen to his soft voice telling the lies he inwardly blushed for; to hold his hand tightly in her own; to think him all that was good and kind, and brave, and noble, was but what every good mother does—is it not? It is what you, you foolish woman, think of your worthless child Jack, whom you succour and comfort when papa has turned his back upon him. Jack is not, in your eyes, what he is in mine, and in those of the rest of this charitable world. You will never know him for the fool and knave he is. What odds?—what loss?

Late into the night the mother and son sat talking over old times. She asked him what he had been doing in London, and whether he had many friends, and whether he found the evenings dull in his lonely chambers. He answered as near the truth as a son could answer who led a wicked life and loved his mother.

When they got to talking of old times, she told him of something of which he had never heard, and she herself had nearly forgotten. And she told him, amongst other matters, of a town in the sunny south of France at fair time; of the stalls crowded with bonbons, painted saints, and cheap nick-nackeries; the streets, with village maidens, in white caps and wooden shoes, and their red-faced swains, in blue blouses. Then of the shows, Polichinelle, and the circus, the dancing girl, and the clown of the ring—not a painted, whiteened fool, but a tall, handsome man, with flashing eyes and white teeth, with pointed moustache, and small white hands. A lighthearted, gay fellow, turning summersaults gracefully, with a "Hoop-la—aie! aie!" A surly, cold-blooded, cruel wretch, with an iron will and a whip of steel— a whip to threaten with, aye, and sometimes to cut with, too, right into the flesh of the shrinking girl, in the scanty skirt, spangles, and burst boots. Then she told him of an English "milor," with kind words, and plenty of cash. Then of a flight, by night. Of unavailing pursuit, and rest and happiness. Then of the metamorphose of the poor dancing girl into the grand lady. All which history was true —his mother the heroine, his father the hero.

Late into the night, the mother and son sat talking. She had not been so happy for many, many weary months, she told him.

The pert Kitty broke in upon them, at last, to know whether her services were required by the lady.

"No, no; not to-night," the French lady replied pettishly. She spoke poor English, and preferred to converse in her native tongue, as she had been doing during the evening with Maurice.

"That woman!" she whispered, when Kitty had flounced out and slammed the door. "Her presence tortures me—kills me!"

"Why, mother?" he asked, surprised.

"She is—she is —— Never mind! She has more influence with the master of the house than I have. Why should she not? What right have I to complain? Maurice!" she cried eagerly, and drawing him closer to her, whilst in her eyes he saw a kind of shrinking horror that was dreadful to look upon— "Maurice, I have a fearful secret to tell you, if I dared—if you would not despise me —— "

"Sir John would like to see you, sir, and says that he will be glad to see my lady, too, if she will honour him."

It was Miss Kitty who brought this message, and delivered it with much pertness.

"Go—go, my child. Good-night! Kiss me. Good-night!"

Maurice met his cousin upon the stairs, who was on his way to bed, profoundly bored by the conversation below.

"They have been asking for you. Your father could not think where on earth you had got to. Some of the gentlemen are the worse for drink. I don't care about any more myself. It's ridiculous to sit up late in the country, so I'm off to bed. But don't put yourself out on my account."

———

CHAPTER THE TWELFTH.

SOMETHING ODD IN HADGET'S SMILE.

BY the time that the company separated to go home, or to bed, the small horns were growing larger. It was getting on for half-past three by the clock in the hall, yet old Sir John and his attorney still sat over the bottle in the dining-room. They were both rather drunk. Old Cheveleigh was dozing off to sleep, and Mr. Hadget was soliloquising.

"Fine picture of yours, that, Johnny," said he, puffing at his pipe, and staring at an oil-painting over the mantel-piece. "John Cheveleigh, when he was a young man, and before he became a landed proprietor. John Cheveleigh, Esq.—rogue, thief, and teller of untruths. Here's your health, little boy in the big collar!" and he drank to the portrait. "Maurice is something like what his father used to be, but without the hang-dog look about his jaws."

"You're a low brute," responded his companion. "Take a bone, and lie down!"

"And what is my worthy friend? what is the honourable gentleman who has just spoken? An arrant old rascal—that's about his figure!"

"Who says so?" cried the other.

"Ah!" replied Hadget, smiling. "Who, indeed? Who but the magistrates of the County of Middlesex, the Governor of Cursitor Castle, and the gentleman who horse-whipped you for selling the race at Newcastle, and the young man who was fleeced of his money in one of the West-end clubs, in the year—the year you went to church last—anno domini half-a-century ago, you sinful old man!"

"I could hang you, anyhow!" growled the other.

"But I could cut your throat first!"

"How!"

"How—with one of your own razors, and a twist of my wrist."

The two men looked at each other: the ugly smile dying out of one man's face, had birth in the other's, with twice its hideousness.

"I could," said Hadget pleasantly, "but I won't, because we are such good friends, and I love you so. Good night, my venerable friend. God rest your grey hair! Go and say your prayers, and sleep your drunk off."

They separated, and the smile returned to their faces when alone—in Cheveleigh's case giving place to an uneasy, suspicious look over the shoulder, and an anxious glance at the fastening of the door: in Hadget's, to an ugly scowl, and a tight clench of the teeth. Then again breaking out, as he stood at the dressing table with the razor-case in his hand, and listened.

He looked in the glass, and saw the Devil smirking at him, to whom nodding familiarly, he put out the light and went to bed, and to sleep, as placidly as a new-born babe. Then a cock began to crow, and presently it was another day.

CHAPTER THE THIRTEENTH.

PRETTY GOINGS ON.

THE next day, and the next, and the next, passed over in much the same fashion as days usually passed over at Skearcrows. The sick woman fretted herself unavailingly in the dreary loneliness of her sick chamber: the rest of the household continued to make merry. As a rule, the gentlemen got drunk over-night, and rose about noon the next day, having partially slept off their libations, to drink cyder, bitter ale, or soda water, as restoratives to their shattered nerves. Old Sir John, who, with a deranged stomach in a morning, was as moral in his precepts as any one could have desired, prophesied the downfall of the establishment with much solemnity, usually winding up his discourse by assuring any person who might be listening to him that "that sort of thing" wouldn't do, and straightway ordering in his first instalment of drink for the day, set to afresh.

The London attorney was by no means a favourite with the servants of the house. There was but one member of the household whom Hadget did not treat as an inferior, to whom he was always very polite, flattering, and conciliatory. It was she of the ribbons and jewellery—she of the bold eyes and brazen face, who was in favour and authority. Hadget called her the Rustic Pompadour. "And how is the bewitching Kit—the enchanting Phillis?" he would say to her. At which encomiums the sportive nymph would toss her head disdainfully, bidding him call people by their proper names if he wanted to speak to them.

"Fair Flower of Earth!" Mr. Hadget would continue, ecstatically, and, poking his lean arm through Maurice's, point to the woman's retreating form, and say, "What taste your father has!"

But the young man, disengaging himself hastily, frowned, and walked away, as though the subject were distasteful to him.

Pleasure was the chief object of every one in this strange household, with but one exception—that of the sick woman who moped alone up stairs. Sometimes her son spent an hour or so with her; but there were some races coming off within a few miles of the house, and more than ordinary merry-making going on, so that he could not be always dangling at his mother's apron strings.

During the race week there were pretty goings on at Skearcrows. Much eating, and more drinking. Every evening the same debauch; every morning the same moralising. Maurice called it a jolly life. Ernest shook his head, and sighed, and though he partook freely of the creature comforts, seemed to be ill at ease in this bad society.

The sick woman up stairs went on moping.

One day returning from some pleasure-party

Maurice found a packet of letters waiting for him. They had been forwarded by Mr. Perks, who had found his address after a deal of inquiry. Maurice had forgotten to leave it.

As he broke the seals and read them one after another, the young man's brow darkened, and he bit his lip. One was a notice from the landlord to leave at the end of the quarter, and a request for the immediate payment of six months' back rent. Another announced the death of his tailor, and informed him that Mr. Togman's executors would like the three years' bill settled. Another said, that the amount of bail forfeited by his non-attendance at the police court, had been paid by his security, who would thank him to refund as soon as possible. There were others equally agreeable. Above all, an imperative summons from his office, commanding him to report himself immediately, and explain certain inaccuracies in his accounts.

"Good God!" cried Maurice, "what am I to do?—what does it all mean? I must go to town to-night!"

CHAPTER THE FOURTEENTH.

HOMELESS.

HE knew not what excuse to make at home. A few hasty incoherent words—a promise to return shortly, and he was in an hour's time tearing along in an express train to London. What was he to do? He was awfully hard up, and did not like to ask his parents for more money.

He thought about it in the train; and as he walked slowly to Foot Court. It was such a disagreeable subject to think about, that he gave it up, and was whistling blithely when he reached the door as though he had nothing on his mind.

He stopped suddenly, for there was a woman crouching on the door-step, her face hidden in her hands. The wind fluttered her thin shawl—she had no covering on her head, and the cruel rain beat down upon her wet and tangled yellow hair.

It was not such an uncommon sight surely, to see a miserable, friendless, homeless, hopeless wretch, huddled away in a dark corner waiting for Death and Rest. Why should he stop to wake her from her stupor? Would he have the vision of a worn, wan, hopeless face to haunt him in his dreams? Hold! Nay, he has touched her head, and recognised with an ejaculation of surprise, Nelly, the little brush-drawer he met that morning, on her way to work, a week ago. What was she doing there? What strange fatality had brought her to that spot?

Oh, dear! oh, dear! oh, dear! she was so wretched, so wet, so cold,—and oh! she wished that she was dead!

But, Nelly, I shall want you for a heroine, and cannot spare you yet awhile.

Maurice stooped down, trying to soothe her; but for a long while she would not be comforted, would continue obstinately sobbing. At length procuring at a late closing public house some hot brandy-and-water, he prevailed upon her to sip a little of it.

The liquor reviving and stimulating her to be more communicative, she presently told him that she had had a dreadful quarrel with her mother-in-law, and that the unfeeling woman had so prevailed over her father as to induce him to turn her penniless out of doors, not giving her even time to put on her bonnet.

There are always two sides to a story. But why should not this be the best side? It was that of a pretty girl—sufficient reason for Mr. Maurice's warm espousal of her cause. He agreed with her that it was a shameful proceeding, unnatural and illegal. However, there she was, and there she could not remain in the cold. Would she go back home with Cheveleigh, and let him try to set matters right? No—no—no; it was no good. Here she shivered and said she felt very ill. Ill! good heavens! what was to be done? His rooms were in that very house, the door-step of which she sat upon.

Would she come in?

Brush-drawers and the like, earning from six to ten shillings per week, have not perhaps all the fears and scruples about society's good opinion, you, gentle reader, may entertain. Nelly, remarking upon the darkness of the entry, stepped fearlessly forward as Maurice shut the door behind them.

"Take hold of my hand," he said. "Take care you do not fall. That's all right. Wait till I find my key."

He opened the sitting room door, and striking a match, lighted the lamp and kindled a fire, with the girl's assistance. While thus engaged she had found time to glance at the pictures on the walls and peep into the bed rooms.

"Do you live here alone?" she asked.

"No; but my friend is out of town."

"Which is your room?"

"Ours?"

"What do you mean?"

"Are you not going to stop here?"

"Where?"

"With me?"

"Can you give me a night's shelter? As your friend is not here, will you let me have his room? I shall be so grateful."

"His room! Yes—ah!" and Maurice whistled.

"You are offended with me," she said, taking his hand, and looking up wistfully into his face. "Never mind. It was rude of me to ask you. Thank you all the same. I'll go."

"No: look here, Nelly."

She was near the door. She stopped.—"What is it?"

"You can't wander about the streets all night—something might happen to you."

"Never fear. I can take care of myself: I'm used to rough people."

"No. But, look here. Have some supper."

"I'm not hungry."

"Yes, try a little, after all my trouble. Have the arm-chair. That's it. Let me take off your boots; your feet are quite wet. The kettle is boiling; — have some wine and water."

The least drop in the world, she would take. He mixed it, and gave it to her by the teaspoonful, amid much giggling.

A neighbouring clock struck Two.

"How wrong of me to keep you up like this. How dreadfully late it is. I must be going."

She rose as she spoke, and began to arrange her shawl.

"Where are you going to, Nelly?"

"I don't know, I'm sure. Somewhere."

"Why should you go?"

"I must go, some time, I suppose."

"Why?"

"Why? How foolishly you talk. Because—because——Oh! I don't know."

"Why not stop with me, Nelly?"

"Do you want a servant?"

"Not exactly; but I do a mistress."

"I'm sorry I stopped. Open the door, please. No, I must go. I'm very much obliged for your kindness. I shall be always grateful. There are so few kind to me, I am not likely to forget. Good-bye. I'm sorry you said what you did. It has hurt me more than I can tell you; but I thank you; I do thank you, very much. Good-bye!"

Why did she burst out crying violently, and bury her face in her shawl? He caught her hands in his.

"Nelly, don't cry like that. You must not go. I am sorry to have hurt you. Forget I said so, dear Nelly."

"No, no, I cannot forget. Good-bye."

She was turning to leave the room, when she staggered, and would have fallen, had he not caught her.

What was the matter?

Oh! nothing. A glass of water—nothing but a little giddiness—nothing but a swoon.

He laid her, speechless and insensible, upon the sofa. To sprinkle her face with water, apply smelling-salts, which were luckily at hand, and chafe her cold hand between his, was all he could do; and, in so doing, to call upon her in great terror to wake up, was perhaps not unnatural under the circumstances. She came to presently, but felt very weak and poorly. Maurice asked if he should fetch a doctor, but this she refused. After awhile, he gave her a bed-candle, and asked her to sleep in the spare room, and not think of going.

She said "Good night!" to him, smiling faintly, thanked him again for his kindness, and, leaving him, kissed his hand.

Then Mr. Cheveleigh lighted a pipe, and, stirring the fire, sat down in moody contemplation thereof.

"If any fellow I know were to get hold of this," thought the young man, "I should never hear the last of it. What an infernal fool I am!"

More smoke, and another stir at the fire.

"This sort of thing is all very well in a novel, but when it comes to real life—Oh, you know, it's damned absurd!"

Violent puffing for the next five minutes.

"Virtuous, forsooth! Turned out of doors at one in the morning, without a bonnet; found sitting on a door-step in the rain—is willing to go alone to a fellow's chambers, but is virtuous."

A dig at the fire and extinction of the pipe.

"I can't believe it!"

THE WORLD WITHOUT AND THE WORLD WITHIN.

CHAPTER THE FIFTEENTH.

"MOCK MODEST."

MAURICE CHEVELEIGH was a man who made it a rule never to dwell on disagreeable subjects. It is what many persons do. Jolly dogs, up to their eyes in debt, and without a care in the world. Just such a light-hearted fellow owes me fifty pounds, and I don't believe he ever gives it a thought.

With Maurice the worst of it was, if he banished one unpleasant train of thought from his mind another immediately supplied its place.

No. 3.

"There's that infernal office. I suppose I shall get the sack," he thought.

Then changed the subject.

"I wonder how I am to pay my debts."

Then changed again. Back to Nelly this time.

"Poor little girl, I hope she is not going to be ill."

Then again,

"What a fool she must think me. But still, what could I do else? Well, nobody will be the wiser if I don't tell them."

I dare say, after all, Maurice was no worse than many other young men. Though one is not accustomed to see much profligacy represented in the costumes of the second half of the nineteenth century.

Look at our literature, look at our drama. Could anything be more moral? Does a wicked lord endeavour to seduce a peasant girl, she overwhelms him with virtuous eloquence, and makes him feel ashamed of himself. We applaud her, and hiss him. Does a woman meditate the commission of a frailty, right-minded female friends argue with her, and plot and scheme for the abasement of the villanous tempter. Does she, in spite of all their good advice, go wrong, she goes so very wrong, and leads such a life of subsequent misery and remorse, that one comes away terrified and improved by the picture of her sufferings. In our novels and our plays the wicked ones always get the worst of it—as they ought.

But in real life! Ah me! Can that be Miss Flora Fitzclarence who impersonated the noble-minded peasant girl that scorned the noble lord's magnificent offer of a purse full of metal buttons in exchange for her virtue, I see dining with her protector at Blackwall, and half-tipsy before the dessert comes? How sick she must feel of acting the bride at many mock marriages, knowing no one in the world, off the stage, who would make an honest woman of her. Is that the noble-minded hero who was about to marry the peasant girl when the curtain went down, that I know leads so profligate a private life, and is by turns figuring in the Insolvent Court or Crim. Con. trials? Is that the grey-headed judge who was, I see by yesterday's newspaper, so hard upon the Whitechapel Don Juan that, they say, quite keeps Mother Crow's infamous house agoing?

Everywhere we turn, are we not the witnesses of vice and depravity? It is the talk of every man, yet all men ignore it. Do all our novelists write for boarding-school misses and Sunday-school teachers? Is it because they all lead such happy domestic lives in the bosoms of their own virtuous families, that they forget what is going on outside the domestic circle? The very name of harlot you start back at, or skip over, affrighted and ashamed, when you find it any where but in your Bible. Go on, Josephs and Pamelas, the world is right, and I am wrong. If the monster exist in our city, let us gag him, and hide him away—stamp upon him, tread him into the ground before company; behind their back, why then——

Why, then, when no one is looking it doesn't matter.

As that disgraceful profligate, Mr. Maurice Cheveleigh, still sat ruminating in his lonely room, the lamp began to smoke for want of pumping, the fire went out with excess of poking, a neighbouring clock struck three, but he had not yet made up his mind.

"I could not turn her out of doors again on such a night—could I? Ill as she is too. There's nothing left for me to do but to go to bed—to my bed. Ha! ha!"

And he laughed in a ghastly fashion, trying to make himself believe that he thought it very funny.

But he didn't.

CHAPTER THE SIXTEENTH.

BED AND BOARD "FOR NOTHING."

WHEN Maurice awoke next morning to the sweet music of the Perks's servant's voice, he sent that gentle maiden into the next room to inquire after the health of his visitor. And the Bony-one, who by the by was not the least in the world startled by the visitor's sex, came back presently with great concern depicted on her unwashed face, and said that she had found the girl very feverish and ill, but had persuaded her to take a cup of tea.

Upon the receipt of this intelligence the host's countenance lengthened somewhat as he began to cast about him for the means of escaping from his present dilemma. He had hardly bargained for a sick lodger when he asked Miss Nelly to stay with him. Who could tell how long her indisposition might last. It might be serious. She might die there! Whew! the bare idea made young Cheveleigh shiver. However, there she was, and she was ill and must be attended to. Maurice was always one of the softest hearted, most reckless kind of fellows that ever lived, and wanted but a better bringing up to be the hero I would, as his historian, have wished him to be. So he told Miss Perks to run for the doctor, and, knocking at Nelly's door, bade her lie still and not excite herself.

Bolusout, M.D., came presently from round the corner, felt the patient's pulse, looked at her tongue, and wagged his head profoundly. After which, and other cabalistical pantomime, he departed, promising to send a mixture, and informing Mr. Cheveleigh in an impressive whisper, that "we required quiet and repose," but that he had ultimate hopes of "our getting over it." The "we" did not include, as you might suppose, the doctor, the patient, Maurice, and the Bony-one, but referred only to Nelly.

Alas! WE suffered much, the "mixture as before" was repeated over and over again. WE were in high fever and became delirious. Maurice sat night after night watching by the bed side. The Perks' servant proved herself to be a second mother, though she had never been a first. Bolusout, M.D., wagged his head and waxed more mysterious daily; yet WE went on suffering. At last, when WE were thin and wasted a change came, and WE grew better, and the delirium passed away, recognised and thanked our kind host who sat watching us.

"How long have I been ill?" a thin voice asked of him.

"A week."

"I thought it was since yesterday. How good of you to let me stop here. Whatever should I have done without you. How kind you are——"

"Oh! nonsense," Maurice interrupted her. "You must not excite yourself, the doctor says;" and he changed the subject hastily, for to himself he seemed not very kind or generous, and to be acting very like a fool.

During the whole of Nelly's illness nobody

had been admitted to the chambers. Several friends had called, who were in the habit of using them much after the fashion of an inn, except in the one particular of payment, but receiving the uniform reply of "not at home—not expected, and said no one was to wait," these gentlemen retired much disgusted, and muttering among themselves.

"Those Cheveleighs are horribly mean!" said one visitor to another.

"You're right there," his friend replied. "Don't overburthen you with their hospitality if you are ever obliged to go there to knock out an hour or so in want of better occupation."

"Never invited me yet," said Mr. Letchery, the editor of the religious newspaper, "I'll be hanged if they have."

And perhaps, thinks the writer, there was small occasion.

Nelly grew stronger every day. Soon she was able to go out in a little bonnet Maurice had bought her, and she had trimmed. But as she began to get well she became rather uneasy and anxious to be released from her present equivocal position.

She would have gone back to her old employment, but here she met with a refusal owing to her prolonged absence; and when she consulted with Maurice upon the subject, he persuaded her that it was ridiculous to continue toiling for a miserable stipend, insufficient to keep her decently clothed and fed.

"Besides, Nelly, I want to make a lady of you."

"To make a lady of me!" the girl exclaimed, looking inquiringly at her companion's face, which met her's unmoved as he guessed her thought and laughed inwardly.

"I wish you to learn some accomplishments, Nelly, to fit you for better employment. You shall have masters, and live in a little lodging of your own. You can work all the day, as I do, and in the evening, when you like, I will take you out to the theatre, and so on, and amuse you. Why should we not? You have no one in London to care for you, and I have no one that I care for. I like your company better than any other, and what should stand between us?"

"But, Maurice, I shall cost you a great deal of money."

"Not more than I can spare."

"But when you grow tired of my company, Maurice, what will become of me?"

"Better wait till then, Nelly dear, before you begin to think of it. You will be in no worse position than you are now, and more likely to get employment. Besides, I never shall tire, dearest, I swear —— "

And here he swore eternal constancy, et cetera. But ladies require a deal of persuasion to do what is best for them. One can scarcely credit it, but this young person made believe to wish to find some employment, at once, that would make her independent.

Maurice did not relish this desire for independence.

She would prefer, she said, some light employment which did not confine her too much. I fancy such places are much sought after, for

Mr. Cheveleigh professed to spend his entire days in trying to find one, without success. The lodging was taken, a quarter's rent paid in advance, and Miss Nelly established therein; where she spent her days reading novels which her friend lent her, and wondering when the situation would turn up.

In the evening they generally went out together to some place of amusement.

She was passionately fond of music, which led to Maurice persuading her to spend a portion of her day with a music master, and in practising upon a piano he hired for her during the time she was out of employment.

"That's a stunner you've got hold of, Maurice," said the editor one day, calling on him at the office.

"What do you mean?"

"Why, the yellow-haired girl I saw you with at the theatre. You were in the upper boxes."

"Yes; I had orders."

"So I thought. But who's your friend?"

"She's a stunner I've got hold of," said the other, laughing, and turning on his heel.

I know not whether all I have written here seems grossly improbable, yet is no portion of it imaginary. Such things happen every day in London, setting no one wondering.

All this while money matters were not looking up, as you will see; besides, there was a little unpleasantness at the office.

——

CHAPTER THE SEVENTEENTH.

ADVICE GRATIS.

ONE evening Mr. Maurice Cheveleigh went to smoke a pipe at his friend Jack Ochre's lodgings in the City Road. Mr. Ochre lodged in a single room, which served him by turns as drawing-room, dormitory, and studio.

It was an attic, and had once belonged to a photographer; but the landlady, an austere, right-minded woman, of a religious turn, and by name Macparing, had given the previous tenant notice to quit, as she said in consequence of the number and character of his visitors. Though here reports vary,—the photographer attributing his bankruptcy to the uninterrupted solitude which he enjoyed during business hours, owing to an unaccountable shyness and unwillingness upon the part of the public "to come forruds." He, however, took notice at his landlady's desire, and himself and his traps clandestinely off at his own, leaving some weeks' rent unsettled.

Mr. Ochre, however, "barring bad hours and tobaccy incessant," caused Mrs. Macparing little trouble. He was a scene painter at the Apollo Saloon, deriving much employment and tolerable remuneration therefrom. And he also painted pretty little subject pictures, which usually got refused, for want of room, at the Exhibitions, but were not unpopular with the pawnbrokers. Of an evening he read a good deal, and rarely stirred abroad according to his own account, yet was often met with at strange hours and places by his friends.

Mr. Cheveleigh had been asking for Ochre's advice upon some difficult matter. We can guess what, by Jack's reply—

"Leave the girl alone, man," roared out the painter, relinquishing for a while his pipe, to utter this oration. "Surely there are lost women enough upon the London streets, without your going out of your way to add to their number. If the girl be honest, for heaven's sake leave her so."

"Well, if I do, some one else won't."

"Haven't you done enough to damn yourself already? You're nearly twenty-six, I think. If not, try and discover some new and attractive vice. They've all grown very stale and hacknied with over-use. But leave the girl alone. Not because it would be wicked of you—you'd laugh at that argument—but why should you ruin her and drive her on the streets? You don't mean to drive her on the streets. Bah! what will you care what comes of her when you're tired! And you will tire. Is there not a fearful, inscrutable destiny which drags a woman down from the narrow rugged path of virtue,—drags her down, however she may wrestle and fight against it? It always was so. So give her up. Great God! let her go her way, let her go her way, and be an honest woman if she can."

"You're very warm, Jack."

"Well, I am; at least, I was a moment ago. Give me the tobacco. I forgot where I was, and whom I was talking to—I've been wasting my eloquence and your time. I apologise. You won't take my advice, of course (you would be simple if you did), so please to forget I gave it. Your good health!"

"I think I will take it though, Mr. Ochre, for the woman's sake," replied Maurice, with a slight sneer. "She shall escape! Let her be an honest woman—'tis a paying trade. Perhaps she'll marry. Let the church legalise her union with some base-born besotted brute, who'll bruise her face and break her bones. Let her sink to his level, 'as the husband so the wife is.' Let her perpetuate her species in the shape of future brutes, and live happy ever afterwards."

"Well, well, I shall not continue the subject any further," said Jack Ochre, burying his red beard in the pewter pot. And they began to gossip about literature and fine arts.

"What absurdity that Ochre talks about some things," muttered Maurice to himself, as he walked home. "I might be the greatest villain out, to hear him. What harm will it do the girl? Bring her on the streets. Ridiculous!"

On his way he met his friend Mr. Charley Bux. Where was he going? Would he take a cigar? Maurice was going home—that was Mr. Bux's road. "I say, Cheveleigh, who's that fair girl everyone is always meeting you with? I've seen you twice. It's an old friend, is it?"

"No, not a very old friend."

"What a fellow you are! I hope it is nothing improper?"

"No," said the other, with something like a groan; "it's proper enough."

"Law! then don't you think it's a great waste of time?"

"What?"

"Trailing about a modest girl."

"No, I don't, if it's amusing."

When Mr. Bux met a friend of his, next day, he told him the news.

"You know Maurice Cheveleigh?"

"Man in a government office?"

"Yes, the Bad Bargains! Well, he's keeping company with a dressmaker, and means honourable."

"By Jove!"

"Yes, the banns have been put up. They've been 'asked' twice."

"Well, I always thought he'd go to the bad. He has such low tastes. By-the-bye, will you make one of a party to go to the Lord Chief Baron's to-night? There's a new trial coming on. A young curate, who's up from the country, and living with me, wants to go and hear it. We'll drop in at the Argyll if the other's slow."

CHAPTER THE EIGHTEENTH.

GETTING INTO DIFFICULTIES.

PARCHINGBY was head clerk of Her Majesty's Bad Bargains.

The Bad Bargains is, as everybody knows, the best Government office to get into. The examination is something terrific, but the duties do not exceed long addition and letter-writing, with the aid of printed forms and a dictionary.

The general public know the Bad Bargains as an office where there is a deal of waiting (mostly in strong draughts), a deal of snubbing, a deal of disappointment—in short, as an office which it is better not to tackle.

Parchingby was austere and severe. A man of portly mien and few words; a man with a great waistcoat and no heart. A rigid disciplinarian, whose very vitals were red tape and sealing-wax. A wonderful man of business, with a constitution of cast iron, who came to his office an hour before the time of opening, and left three hours after closing time, and did twice as much work as anybody else, and was esteemed in proportion.

When Maurice came from the country he straightway reported himself to Mr. Parchingby, who received him with a frown.

"Why did you not return sooner?" said he.

"I only just received the letter."

"What do you mean? Where were you?"

"At home," answered Cheveleigh sullenly. He gave no further explanation, feeling indignant at the superior's insulting manner. But when he came to think it over afterwards, he saw what a bad impression his silence must have created.

"Very well, sir, since you have thought fit to come at last, perhaps you'll explain that."

Parchingby opened a ledger with a crash as he spoke, and pointed to something in it.

"Explain what?"

"That! Can't you read?"

It was a curious scene between these two men, both smothering their indignation, both talking calmly, if not civilly.

" Will you be good enough to be more explicit?" said Cheveleigh.

" Yes, I will. Through the grossest carelessness and negligence on your part, an overpayment has occurred, which I feel it my duty to report fully to the committee of management, at the next meeting."

" Anything else?"

" Yes, sir, this much," cried Parchingby, trembling with passion : " I shall recommend your dismissal."

" Anything else?"

" Leave the room, sir."

" Certainly. I should not have come had you not sent for me. Look here, Mr. Parchingby,—there has never been much love lost between us two since—since I took your woman from you."

" Sir, how dare you —— "

" How dare I? Fiddlestick! we're alone. You can report me, if you please ; you can get me dismissed, if you please ; but if you do, by God I'll give you the most infernal hiding you ever had in your life. That's all. Good morning."

If the hall porter, corpulent and cringing, who bowed, bare headed, before the white waistcoat of the chief, had only known how that chief had been bearded half-an-hour ago by his junior, would he not have chuckled inwardly?

How delighted we all are to see our superiors humiliated. What a shocking thing human nature is. Is it not?

This little affair at the office did not make Maurice feel very comfortable, as you may suppose. The unpleasantness about his mistake blew over after a little while, or rather subsided, and might at any moment have broken out afresh. It was a very trifling error after all, and one committed in a moment of forgetfulness ; but then, Parchingby was his enemy, which made it a very different matter.

Ernest prolonged his visit at Skearcrows by another fortnight, though he had written a letter to his cousin, in answer to a demand for his half of the rent due, saying that he intended to give up his share of the chambers.

Blue eyed Nelly, unmindful of the remarks which Maurice's idle friends were pleased to make about her, grew plumper and prettier daily. She had the softest, whitest hands now—nothing like what they were when she did the nasty brush-drawing work. She could play very tolerably upon the piano, and sang, with good taste and feeling, such small sentimentalities as at that time haunted the street organs. She was growing quite " the lady."

Jack Ochre, whose oracular wisdom had, among his companions, procured for him the title of " Wise Man of the East," was pleased upon several occasions, to express anything but a favourable opinion regarding the fair-haired beauty, in whose company he had occasionally spent the evening. But then, I am afraid, Jack was, at times, something of an ill-natured cynic, and always a professed woman-hater. Extraordinary, as it may appear, after the highly moral harangue, which we heard him giving to Mr. Cheveleigh, some time back, he took quite an opposite view

of the case, with Mr. Letchery, the editor, who argued with him the subject, and said, that if there was any seduction in question, it was upon the side of the woman, and that she was an artful, designing minx — feathering her nest, and selling her virtue upon the most advantageous terms.

Dear, blue-eyed, laughing Nell, let us own that they judged thee wrongly. So light-hearted, and merry, and clever, yet withal so virtuous, for thou wert virtuous, then, whatever they might say of thee,—however strange and inconventional was the life that thou did'st lead with thy good-natured good-for-nothing lover.

" What a fool I am," this same lover cried aloud, having reached his chambers about day-break one morning from a public ball, to which he had escorted Nelly. " What a ridiculous idiot I must appear to anybody! I am over head and ears in debt."

He looked ruefully at a long bill, which had awaited his arrival.

" Yet," he continued, " I go on dilly dally-ing. It must be decided this week—one way or the other. Either she comes to live with me, or she goes to—where she chooses. And how the deuce am I to get some ready money to go on with? Hadget will give none—I can never see him. It is no good writing home. By the lord! there's nothing left for it but Shylock !"

The bare notion of which dreadful alternative kept him wide awake for hours.

CHAPTER THE NINETEENTH.

WORSE AND WORSE.

WHEN a man begins to go down in the world, who is there willing to lend him a hand? Very few of us. We all have our foot ready to kick at him as he passes by. Does he weather the storm, and struggle back again to his old place, we are willing to forget his little misfortunes, and have a warm embrace at his disposal. When a woman falls, she does not so easily right herself. Her sex are as ready with the feet as we are ; but they do not often look over those sort of things. The sinner may repent ; but she is for ever outside the gate, and the footman has orders not to admit *the creature* upon any account.

Our young friend, Maurice, began to be overwhelmed with difficulties, as he was over head and ears in love with that blue-eyed syren. Going, as usual, tolerably late to his office, one morning, he found a gloomy shadow upon the faces of several of his fellow clerks. Dreadful official rumours were afloat. Those in power had determined upon reducing the establishment (there had been some unpleasant questions in the House about the expense, and so a dozen temporary clerks, including Mr. Cheveleigh, were dismissed at a moment's notice. However, our young friend's valuable services being deemed necessary, in a branch where he had been lent for a fortnight, to tie up and label superfluous papers, he was retained for another week, with orders to clear up such matters as he had left in confusion. You might have seen Mr. Cheveleigh up to his middle in documents of all sorts and sizes, sorting and labelling with great rapidity and apparent recklessness, during such portions of the day that were not consumed in lunching, surreptitious pipes, or social converse. "The Cheveleigh system," as this gigantic undertaking was always termed after its completion, must have been arranged upon a principle entirely his own,—no mortal man ever being able afterwards to find anything he wanted in any of the huge bundles, and, in some cases, it led to much angry correspondence with the perverse public, who, as usual, thought that they were not "being acted right by."

Although this volatile young man was as lively as ever, and seldom spoke half-a-dozen serious words together upon any subject, he was secretly very miserable and dependent. I believe that he was in the habit of groaning and weeping when alone, in a manner ridiculous to behold. His thoughts were ever centred upon one point of difficulty—what was he to do about Nelly? He could not give her up; but he could not afford to keep two establishments. Could he afford to keep one? Yes—for a mistress, but not for a wife. Why not a wife? Because it would then be requisite to keep up some appearance—to mix in society. And would society receive her? Scarcely. Who was she? Would she not require a character from her last place—besides the ring and marriage certificate? When he was owner of Skearcrows, and a country gentleman, could he introduce her to society? Would they not ferret out the "back numbers" of her history, and put her down for no better than she should be? Why should he marry—a young man with money at his disposal—(at present rather embarrassed; but that was another reason why he should not)—the heir to a fine estate, with he knew not what noble career awaiting him—to be tied down and for ever trammelled by an early marriage? Not that he should ever leave her. Why should he? He could always keep her—out of sight. A wife he could not—people must know that; and as for ceasing to love her, the thought was preposterous. Does not *amours* rhyme with *toujours?*

To which the writer responds enthusiastically, it does: and love is eternal; and one never gets sick of any one else; and there are no broken hearts and deserted women in the world!

When Maurice carried himself and his bad news home in the evening, he found Nelly sitting before the fire in his room. She usually went there first, lighted the lamp, drew the curtains, and made all look snug, and warm, and cheerful against his arrival. The dinner was served. It came from "The Plumes," in the court; and the young lady sat down, gaily bidding her lover help her, for she was very hungry. The lover, with a lugubrious expression of countenance, began to carve the steak.

"God help those who, being hungry, have yet nothing to eat!" said he, after a pause, with a view to improving the occasion.

"Or to drink either," responded the fair one, taking a deep draught from her tumbler. "What a fine parson you would make, Maurice. Let me smooth your hair down—behind your ears—there! Beautiful!"

Mr. Cheveleigh, relinquishing sentiment for the present, kissed his companion with his mouth full, and proposed a glass of wine. There were two bottles left, which he had brought from home, and he filled their glasses.

"Don't let us go anywhere to-night, Nelly. We'll sit at home."

"With all my heart," she said. "It's dreadfully cold, is it not? And it was raining when I came in."

"Ah! everything is miserable enough. Come and sit by the fire, Nelly; close by me, dear."

There was a long pause.

"Maurice, you're very dull to-night," she said at last. "Has anything happened? What ails you?"

"Not much,—but much may happen, Nelly. We may have to separate."

"Separate! Then, are you tired of me, Maurice?"

"Tired of you, Nelly! You know it is not so. I love you more than all the world—more than myself and my life; for what would they be to me were you gone? Dear Nelly, I would do—will do anything to please you. I will ever worship you, and forestall your every want and desire; your slightest fancy shall be law to me. Why should you doubt my faith? Have I not, these six months past, been devoted to you? Have I not given up my old friends, and my old habits? Do I not love you?"

The red embers in the grate shivered as it were, and crept together; the rain beat heavily upon the window panes, and the hurried tramp of a solitary pedestrian was heard upon the flags of the court below. No other sound, no other movement, save the throbbing of her heart against his hand.

"Dearest Nelly, when I first met you I was in a rather different position. I have since run into debt, one way and the other, not to any great extent it is true, and I could easily have got over it; but to-day I have lost my situation at the office, and shall probably be for some time out of employment. It will be necessary, therefore, for us to economise our means. When I asked you, some time ago, to share my lodgings with me, I was much better off than I am now. I will not ask you again, dear Nelly; and yet I cannot afford to give you all the little pleasures I should like, if we remain like we are. I will try my utmost to find you some suitable situation, and then—then we must part."

A squeeze of the hand and a low sobbing was the only reply.

"But, dear Nelly, it is very hard to leave you, to relinquish all the cherished dreams of happiness I have had so long nestling in my heart, to break the spell that has crept round my every-day existence, and—throwing away romance—to sit down to begin my life afresh. Dear Nelly, I will not ask you to make a sacrifice for me, the greatest that a woman can make. There are many other better, richer men than I am : you will easily find one, and as easily forget me.''

" I shall never forget you, Maurice—no, never!" she cried vehemently. " You have got yourself into all this difficulty for my sake. You took me out of the streets when I had no one to care for me. You have helped me to educate myself; taught me to look up to you, and rely upon you; taught me to love you very, very much. You are as good as I am, and a hundred thousand times better. Who have I in the world to care for me but you? Who else's good opinion need I covet? I shall never forget you, dearest; and I shall never leave you. If you are poor, I can love you poor; if you are rich, I can love you no more than I do. Dear Maurice, we will part no more : never again—never again!''

He strained her to his heart, where she lay weeping, her soft yellow hair brushing his cheek.

The fire went out altogether, and the lamp, for want of pumping, gurgled, and gave up the ghost.

___

CHAPTER THE TWENTIETH.

THE RICH LADY AND HER POOR DEPENDANT.

IT was half-past eleven o'clock, the time common people were going to bed, and genteel ones just beginning to think about spending the evening. Cabs and carriages were rattling up to Mrs. Falsetto's Baker Street mansion, and unburthening themselves of their fashionable contents.

" Nice lot you're got to-night, John Thomas,'' said a cabman, rendered bitterly ironical by the receipt of his legal fare. " Hope they'll be as flush when they leaves, for your sake.''

" A bob all the way's from Buckingham Palace, was it, cabby?" inquired a commiserating bystander.

" That's the aristocracy all over—that is,'' remarked a mechanic; and began to rehearse a little crushing oratory for next Monday's discussion club.

The carriages kept rattling up; the company kept coming; the gorgeous gentlemen in scarlet plush received them kindly, and handed them over to other gentlemen equally gorgeous and urbane, who, in their turn, delivered them up to more gorgeousness and urbanity; so that, in course of time, they were finally announced at the drawing-room door under singular distortions of their names.

That is old Lord Crowsfoot's carriage, the nobleman there was the action about which created so much scandal. That one belongs to the old Dowager Lady Shanks, whom his revered Majesty, George the Fourth, was so gracious to (she was younger then, and did not wear a wig), and got her husband a place about court, because — he deserved it, I suppose.

There were many other carriages besides; for Mrs. Falsetto was a lady of fashion, and kept the best of company. She was the widow of a banker, who had left her a plum, and her entertainments were very magnificent. She was a delightful woman—everybody agreed about that. She was the best natured woman in the world, that was equally certain. She was the most bountiful soul alive. She had built a church, though she never went to it ; and her name figured in large capitals at the head of every fashionable charity.

" Ah, my lord, how kind of you to come and see me.''

" Your ladyship is really too good. I never expected this honour.''

Thus she welcomed her distinguished guests. She had no great difficulty in gathering round her some of the bankrupt nobility !—high-born paupers, who lived on credit, and were not too proud to associate with a rich plebeian.

" My dear Drawler, this is, indeed, amiable of you to sacrifice your time to an old woman like me. How is it your lordship has an evening to spare?''

" Every moment of my life is at your service, dear madam,'' his lordship replied. He was a fair haired, pale faced, tawny, moustached gentleman, an officer in her Majesty's 8th Dragoon Guards — a very smooth-spoken gentleman, neither very witty nor very wise —just clever enough to be vicious, and rich enough to be forgiven for it. For the world is not so hard upon profligacy on a grand scale, as it is upon your cheap Lovelaces.

" Oh! you flatterer!" cried Mrs. Falsetto, laying her skinny hand upon his lordship's arm, and smiling at him bewitchingly, with two rows of the most natural false teeth. " What can you see in an old woman like me to care about?"

Perhaps, otherwise than as a work of art, there was little to admire in the rich lady's personal appearance. Her roses, her teeth, her hair, and her bust, were all by the best makers. Her eyebrows were her own, but they derived their glossy blackness from Mr. Langdale's marvellous hair-dye.

His lordship shook his head deprecatingly of her words, as though he would give her to understand that he thought her a perfect Venus, and knew very well that she knew it too.

" I want to introduce my nephew, Maurice Cheveleigh, to your lordship; but the bad boy has not thought fit to come and see me.''

" I think I met him at the rooms of a man called Bux,'' replied Drawler. " He sang a comic song, I think. He seemed a very jolly fellow.''

" He's dreadfully gay, I'm afraid; but it's the way with all you young men!" the lady continued, with a sigh. " His cousin, Ernest, now, is quite different—a perfect pattern of propriety. He's my man of business and general adviser.——Eh! what is it, Dorcas? how you made me jump.''

Lord Drawler looked up at the person thus addressed. At the first glance he saw nothing but a dark middle-sized woman, about twenty-four, with a plain face. Looking at her again more attentively, this time, she was still plain. Yet she had beautiful eyes,—large, dark, and sparkling. She had beautiful hair,—black, soft, and lying smooth as velvet on her tight braids. She had beautiful teeth,—small, white, and regular. Standing there, with her big eyes cast down, and her teeth covered by her compressed lips, her lithe figure half concealed by the black gown she wore, her dark face half hidden in the shade, he thought that she was very plain. Presently, when some one spoke to her, the big eyes lighted up, the white teeth glistened, the cheeks flushed, and she grew, beneath his eyes, slowly, more and more beautiful.

"Lady Crowsfoot wishes me to sing. Shall I do so?" she whispered to Mrs. Falsetto.

"Yes; and do your best."

"Who is that?" asked Drawler, watching her retreating form.

"That?" cried the lady with a laugh. "That's Dorcas Abbot, my companion. A poor, helpless, stupid thing—absolutely worth nothing; but I can't find it in my heart to get rid of her."

The person thus described at this moment began to sing, in a powerful and melodious voice, one of those beautiful airs which I have heard clever critics term "the spasmodic jinglings of the mountebank, Verdi." But Dorcas was not a clever person, you have been told, and she threw her whole soul into the performance, forgetful, as it seemed, of time and place; and as her rich voice rose and fell, it carried with it the attentive listeners, and sent a little thrill and flutter of delight through their hearts.

"Not bad, upon my honour," said Drawler. He would have asked her to sing again, but this the old lady overruled, as it was growing late, and the guests were rapidly departing.

"Don't be long before you come again to see me," said Mrs. Falsetto, languishingly.

She saw the last of her guests depart, smiling sweetly on his retreating form. Then, as the door closed, so the sunshine faded from her face, and she sat motionless, in thought, gloomy, and older by a score of years. The lines grew harder and deeper in her sallow face, and her rouged cheeks gleamed ghastly in the candle-light.

She was an ugly old woman, to say the best of her. She was a cross-grained old woman too, it would seem, for she turned her head with a jerk, and called out sharply, "Dorcas!"

The girl might have been thinking, for she did not answer for a moment.

"Dorcas," cried the lady, "are you deaf?"

"Did you call, ma'am?"

"Did I call! What a fool you are to ask such a question. Did you not hear me? What a fool you are! I wonder I keep you."

The companion made no answer, but meekly came to do her bidding.

"Help me up-stairs to bed."

Her mistress could be still more cross-grained and ill-tempered when it took her fancy. She grumbled a good deal as her companion helped to undress her.

"Bah! how sick I am of the stupid people!" Mrs. Falsetto said, wearily. "How I hate them all! They're glad enough to come though. No, they're not glad to come either: neither of my nephews are here. Take care to write to Mr. Ernest to-morrow. As for that boy, Maurice, he does not trouble himself much about me, the ungrateful young wretch! Dimples, you clumsy booby, what are you doing?"

This last was to her maid, who had hurt her mistress's head with the brush.

"There, go about your business, I don't want you. Dorcas will do. You grow more awkward every day, I declare."

As the process of undressing proceeded, Mrs. Falsetto's personal appearance did not improve. When her teeth were taken out and put in water, and her wig taken off and boxed up for the night, the rouge rubbed off, and the frilled nightcap put on, she was no beauty.

At last she was helped into bed, and the pillows nicely adjusted. As she lay down, the clock struck two. The companion was very tired and sleepy.

"Dorcas," said the old lady, "I don't feel inclined to go to sleep—read to me a little."

Without a word of reproach or remonstrance, Dorcas Abbot took up a book, and, seating herself beside the bed, awaited further orders.

"Go on! What are you waiting for?"

"What shall I read—this French novel?"

"Yes. Go on."

So she read on as calmly and quietly as though it were five hours earlier in the evening. The old lady listened drowsily to the sound of her voice, nodded, and caught her breath—then woke again and listened—started, jerked, and snorted; last of all fell fast asleep and snored.

Dorcas read on to this accompaniment—although she was unaware of the circumstance—read on mechanically, heeding not the purport of the words she uttered, her thoughts straying the while to distant scenes and places.

She stopped at last, suddenly. The old lady was dead asleep, looking very wrinkled and sallow, and hideous in her frilled night-cap.

The other woman stood by the bed, eyeing her askance with a swelling vengeful heart, and evil eyes gleaming beneath beetling brows.

"There is a year's life in her, at most," the watcher muttered; "a year at most. Sleep on, you cold-blooded, cruel wretch. It would be a charity to stop the breath that gives you so much pain to draw. I would not."

She laughed noiselessly, then crept away with cat-like tread to her attic.

She undressed herself, still preoccupied with her thoughts.

"Oh! God, how long must I live this wretched life!" she cried aloud, in her anguish. "How long am I to be this woman's slave? Oh! why am I so miserably poor?"

She fell upon her knees, and wept and prayed. Then rose again, slowly and wearily, and, clambering into the window-seat, sat huddled up and thoughtful, watching the first faint streak of dawn stealing over the sleeping city.

"How long shall I be a slave?" she repeated, between her teeth. "When will Ernest marry me, and take me away from here? Oh! how long shall my servitude endure?"

Day broke and found her still sitting there —still brooding over her wrongs. She had not closed her eyes when a sharp jerk of the lady's bell summoned the dependant to another day's humiliation.

IDOL WORSHIP.

CHAPTER THE TWENTY-FIRST.

"NOTICE TO CORRESPONDENTS."

BY the way, before we go any further, I ought to say a few words about the title of this book.

Would you believe it, reader (though for that matter, some of you must know it)—would you believe that the writer has been perfectly overwhelmed by letters from people whom he has never heard of in his life, and who make suggestions? They want the name of the book to be changed. They suggest others: they ask the meaning of the title—they ask what is to become of the

heroine—they object to yellow hair—they want to know what "yellow hair" means. "What makes you write of such a horrid creature, who cannot even speak gramatical?" says one lady, who does not speak very "gramatical" herself.

"Why yellow hair? Is that what people call carrots, or is it like hay?" asks one gentleman.

"Yellow hair is frightful," says a lady, who does not dot her i's, and who, the writer supposes, has black.

Dear readers, it would be impossible to please every one of the half-million who, my publisher tells me, buy this book.

THE WOMAN WITH THE YELLOW HAIR is no imaginary character, but a living, breathing woman, and objects to change her colour to suit anybody. So what am I to do?

CHAPTER THE TWENTY-SECOND.

THE GOLDEN-HAIRED GODDESS.

NELLY did not go back to her lodgings, except to fetch away her "things;" and thus these two loving hearts joyfully commenced upon a life of infamy, of base sensuality, and low, grovelling profligacy, — all which could have been entirely changed to virtue, and honour, and rapturous bliss, by one small circlet of gold, a printed paper filled in with two names and properly witnessed, and half-an-hour's ceremony in a church. Well-a-day, poor lost ones! the writer and the reader cast up their eyes in company. But let us still follow their career of sin and wickedness; for there is no doubt a stinging rod put by in pickle for the pair of them.

Those bundles at the office, I am afraid, were very imperfectly sorted next day. About an hour before the usual time of departure, Mr. Maurice Cheveleigh had washed his hands and changed his coat. At last, after yawning and fidgetting about for some time, he put on his hat, and, pleading urgent private affairs, walked himself off.

To the court, of course. There he found Nelly. She was sitting, as usual, by the fire; a book lay in her lap, which she had been reading.

"Why should we keep on these rooms, Maurice?" she said. "Are they not very expensive? I am sure one would be quite sufficient for us, at present; and there is one to let upon the floor above."

"My dear little housekeeper, we will talk it over. Economy is the order of the day, but not of to-night. I've got a surprise for you."

"Oh! What is it?"

"To-night is the first night of the Opera, as you may be aware."

"Oh, my dear, are you going to take me? How kind of you! But does it not cost a great deal?"

"Madam, expense is a minor consideration: I have got tickets."

"Tickets! What for?"

"For the stalls. You shall go like a lady. I have brought you a pair of gloves, and you can wear that dress you went to the ball in the other night. But, confound it ——"

"What's the matter, dear?"

"You've got no Opera cloak."

"But I shall not want one."

"Yes, you will. I like you to look to advantage. May I not be proud of you, and wish to make other people envious? Never mind. While dinner is getting ready, you look to your frock, and I will go and see to the rest."

Saying so, he departed; presently returning with three parcels—one containing an Opera cloak, another an Opera glass; and a third, a suit of clothes.

"I ordered the carriage at a quarter to eight, Nelly—a brougham, from the livery stables."

"Oh! Maurice, how extravagant of you. Why not a cab?"

"My dear, when we do things we do them in style. To-morrow we will turn over a new leaf. You shall keep the keys, and we will live in future upon kisses and bread and onions!"

So this happy, careless couple, spent their time in such small talk as this. I'm afraid he is not much like the heroes of other penny romances, though for that matter, I believe, that heroes, having taken off their cocked-hats and spurs, condescend to twiddle twaddle like the rest of us.

After dinner she began to dress. What an undertaking was this pretty woman's toilet—twice had she to run out for hair-pins, and other little wanting necessaries. How beautiful she looked, standing before the glass—her soft, wavy, golden hair falling upon her white shoulders. And when THAT FROCK WAS put on! when she stood encircled and fortified, as it were, behind a vast bulwark of half transparent, undulating, flowing, boundless, snowy floods of *tulle!* and when she stepped back for the glass, and placing a hand upon each of Maurice's shoulders, bade him tell her how she looked, who could have resisted the charm? Who could have done otherwise? Wisdom gets bemuddled, philosophy takes flight, and, moral restraint lets go her hold in the presence of such overwhelming loveliness. He fell upon his knees, worshipping her.

"You look like a queen!" he cried.

... that all?—nothing but a queen! Kings and queens are commonplace people enough to look at in their every-day hats and bonnets. Did she not look like a divinity—a glorious golden haired goddess!—the very ground on which she walked hallowed by her touch?

"I only want one thing now, to look like a real-born lady," says pretty Nelly.

What is it—give it a name? No need for that. Down the chimney flies a fairy—I mean in at the door comes the Perks' maid, bearing in her hands a beautiful bouquet, which Maurice had bought for her, and ordered to be sent home.

"Oh, how delicious!" cries the Perks' servant, ecstatically, poking her red nose into the flowers. "Oh! mam, how beautiful you do look."

Cheveleigh selected a camelia, and arranged it in her hair.

Was it not time to go? What time was it by Maurice's watch? He had not got his watch. Not lost it, she hoped?

"No, not altogether. It's with uncle Attenborough."

"Attenborough! I never heard you mention him before."

"He was taking care of my dress clothes, and, seeming hurt at my taking them away, I left the watch as a hostage."

"You mean you pawned it. Oh! Maurice and to buy these extravagances for me!"

"Why not for you, you good-looking, ungrateful woman? Give me a kiss!"

The carriage was waiting at the bottom of the court; it could not come nearer. Nelly put her cloak over her head, and tripped lightly down the pavement. Desperate poverty relinquishing its pipe for a moment, stared after the bright vision, awe-struck!

"What do you think of that?" asked the astonished court-folks of one another. She was made to charm and delight all beholders. Wherever she went she gained more and more admirers. Yet shall she gain still more. Think of her, you poor dirt-begrimed denizens of the squalid court! worship her while you may, soft-headed Cheveleigh! but the time will come when this shall alter, when the goddess shall be high above thee—unapproachable. Not yet awhile though; so while there is yet the sunshine, make the hay.

It was to Covent Garden that they went; Bosio sang. Could Nelly fail to be delighted? She listened to the rich melody of the singer's voice, spell-bound and entranced. She was very happy, and wet her handkerchief so with her tears, that she had to borrow Maurice's.

As they were coming through the lobby of the theatre, a man at the door bawled—"Mr. Cheveleigh's carriage stops the way." Maurice pressed forward with his beautiful companion on his arm. The crowd fell back on either side, whispering to each other their admiration of her. There were, among them, two of the men from the Bad Bargains. These stared stupidly at the girl, and nodded to Maurice. Two other persons saw them pass—Mrs. Falsetto and Dorcas.

"Look, Dorcas, there is young Cheveleigh. What a beautiful woman with him!"

Dorcas was looking at them; had seen them first. She made no remark upon Nelly's looks, but, "I wonder," said she, "whether he is engaged to her?"

"Dear me, Dorcas, how can I tell?" the elder lady cried, impatiently. "I don't know all his friends."

"He has no female relations but his mother, I believe," Dorcas pursued. "I wonder who that can be;" and went on wondering an hour afterwards.

Next day the two Bad-Bargain men had great news for their companions. Some one was pitying Cheveleigh's fate, in being discharged with so short a notice.

"Reserve your commiseration for those who need it. Cheveleigh has means of his own, you may be sure."

"What makes you think so?"

"You would if you had seen him at the Opera, last night, when they were calling out his carriage, and he was handing in one of the most magnificently swell women eyes ever beheld!"

"You don't mean that!"

"Yes, I do; ask Dudley."

This run on increasing in magnitude, like a rolling snowball, and got about the office. Perhaps not much to Maurice's dislike, when he came to hear of it.

As they rode away from the theatre, Nelly leant back in the carriage, and her brain seemed to swim round in a wild sea of fair imagery. She was very silent for some time. At last she spoke.

"Oh! how I should like to be an actress!"

"She shall be an actress, if she likes," cried Maurice, laughing, "and I will come the first evening to the gallery, and applaud till they turn me out."

"No; but seriously."

"Seriously—we'll think of it."

CHAPTER THE TWENTY-THIRD.

THINGS DON'T LOOK UP.

WHEN we have possession of that which we prize most on earth, when SHE is ours—ours only, exclusively, entirely (and such a case *is* probable, cynic and scoffer)—what need of the existence of the other mites, atoms, and units who make up the rest of the world? Away with them! what are they to us? We want no wiseacre's advice, no Solomon's noddle-shaking, no commonplace people, with their vulgar notions, to intrude upon us: no other companionship but that of the beloved one; no other tongue than hers. The honeymoon has just begun, and the bliss, which has been warranted eternal, scarce tasted.

Will it ever be different to this? Will the society of some of these despised atoms and units ever come as a relief to the wearisome monotony of the ex-beloved's omnipresence? The meanest of us have our allotted missions to perform. Perhaps some of these poor creatures were created for our especial enlivenment, so let us not be too hard upon them, brother!

But do not imagine for a moment that our misguided young friend, Maurice, required other society than that of the woman he worshipped. Yet, the first transports of passion cooled down, they began to think of other occupations than foolish billing and cooing. Mr. and Mrs. Cheveleigh moved into more humble and economical quarters up-stairs, where they got two rooms and partial attendance for eight shillings a week. Here was removed the most useful portion of the furniture, the rest being sold to a broker in the neighbourhood, who designated the superfluous chairs and tables "firewood," and grumblingly paid firewood price for them.

The "moving" took place upon the last day of the quarter. Maurice worked and drank beer like a labourer. A young man named Adams, and a connection of the Perks' family, was engaged to lend a hand, which he did whenever it was a question of emptying or replenishing the pewter pots. The Perks' servant having fallen down-stairs under a box, very early in the day, was incapacitated for further exertion, and pretty Nell, with her dress carefully pinned up to be out of the dust, and an old pair of gloves on to save her dear little delicate fingers, looked on, gave orders, and superintended the operations generally. At night, when the carpet was nailed down, the pictures hung up, everything in its place, and tea-things upon the table (they had had a pic-nic dinner, in the middle of the day, among the ruins), Mr. Maurice leaned back in his chair, and surveyed the arrangements with tranquil delight.

"It's not so bad, Nelly, eh?"

"No dear," said the lady, going on quietly with her tea.

"But, does it not look comfortable?" pursued the enthusiastic young man. "Nothing wanting. What *could* you wish for, Nelly, eh?"

"Well, I wish," said Nelly, whose mind was with her meal, "I WISH WE HAD SOME 'WINKLES!"

She entertained a partiality for this plebeian shell-fish, which deserted her not even in the days of her greatest affluence.

It would afford small amusement to the reader, I dare say, were I to chronicle the daily life led by this sinful young couple; yet Maurice always spoke of this as the happiest and most wicked portion of his existence! All moralists and good people must cry out indignantly at such a confession; yet, after all, did not these two live together as man and wife—with the same outward show of decency and decorum, in every way aping the married life, except, perhaps, in hidden squabbles, snappings, and loathings, sometimes attendant upon the licensed partnership; for here no bond or tie held them together; and did either tire of the other, and think that he or she could live independent, there required but a word to sever the connection and free themselves, without help of Judge or Jury, Church or State.

Maurice continued in his infatuation for the goddess. Little of the gilding wore off by his touch, and where it did, he fancied that fresh beauties grew in its stead. She was to be an actress—that was decided. The only thing that remained was to find a manager who would take her. Was it ever the ill-fortune of the reader to be obliged to hawk his talents (thinking he had got some hawkable) in the public market? It is only by so doing that you discover how overbearing, arrogant, and hard-hearted the patron can be—how truckling, mean, despicably self-depreciating, and timorous, the patronised can become. Shame on ye, Barrabas, publisher, of Paternoster Row, who didst in days gone by force the writer of these pages to dance attendance in your ante-chambers and lumber-rooms! Shame on ye, stuck-up company of hirelings and clerks, who didst mock my anxious looks, and turn a deaf ear to my inquiries! Shame on ye, porters and warehousemen, servants of the hirelings, who didst hustle me roughly and unnecessarily as ye passed by, or didst kick unmercifully the shabby hat which I had hidden away in a dark corner, to be ready to go bareheaded, into the PRESENCE.

Well, Nelly was to "come out."

Wonderfully expressive phrase of so many opposite meanings! With the middle-class Miss, signifying her first appearance as a marriageable young lady in the society of some thirty or forty people, in evening dress, at a friend's house; or, if of genteeler connections, five awkward minutes under the eyes of Majesty, to be followed by a life time under the eyes of nobody. With "those creatures," the pariahs, traviatas,—lost ones, "coming out" means what we respectable people would call being cast upon the streets,—means commencing "a walk," commencing to barter, body and soul, health, life, self-respect for the means of living, to prolong the misery. Nelly's notion of "coming out" was a brilliant entrance upon theatrical life at one of the largest London theatres to one of the most crowded of audiences, and with the most unbounded success. Such things occur now and then in the dear old imaginative novels. Maurice and Nelly had no doubt that they would succeed if they only knew how to go about it.

The company of Jack Ochre, with his big red beard and his dirty black pipe, was sought for, and obtained without much difficulty. Jack partook of dinner and a glass of grog at the court, and his opinion was requested.

Most unenthusiastic of men, he puffed forth volumes of smoke, but said little.

"Well, Jack," cried Mr. Maurice.

"What do you say, Mr. Ochre?" the lady chimed in, persuasively.

"Wait half a minute or two!" remarked the artist-philosopher; and, with this mysterious request for rather an indefinite allowance of time, he put on his hat and left the room. Returning in five minutes, he handed Mr. Cheveleigh a copy of the "Pot-house Pioneer," which he had procured the loan of at the "Hand and Heart."

"Do you read that paper?" said Jack.

"Very seldom see it," replied Maurice.

"So I suppose," grumbled Jack. "It's rather exclusive. Kept among the licensed victualling and dramatic circles. However, since your good lady is anxious to join the profession, perhaps it would be as well if you borrowed a number now and then."

"There are lots of advertisements here," said Mr. Maurice, reading; "but, hang it, these are all of celebrated people in search of engagements?"

"Not all," said Jack. "Allow me;" and he read aloud to them the contents of one of the columns. It appeared that there was an immediate demand for an entire company, and a good stage manager, for disengaged stars, and a living novelty; for a juvenile lady, ballet ladies, a sentimental lady, a lady characteristic dancer and a characteristic comic lady; for a good comic nigger, second low comedy, second old man, a good Irish comic, a utility, and many more. But to all these demands was attached two disheartening notæ benæs,—"None but first-class professionals need apply. None but sterling talent will be treated with." Still more dispiriting the intimation accompanying some, that no amateurs need apply. Amateurs are much in the same disadvantageous position with regard to literary or dramatic employment as the poor Irish with regard to domestic service.

"Well?" said Mr. Ochre, interrogatively.

"Oh!" said the hitherto sanguine couple.

"Do'sn't look lively?" said Jack.

"Not very!" said poor Nelly, smiling the faintest of smiles, and feeling very much inclined to cry.

"But, Jack," cried Maurice, smiting the table a great thump, "everybody must be an amateur to begin with?"

"That's true," said Jack; and, it being rather late, he took his depature without further remark, leaving Maurice and Nelly very silent and thoughtful.

"I don't like that Ochre," Nelly said, presently. "He do'sn't seem to take any interest in other people's affairs?"

"No—curse him!" cried Maurice, indignantly. "And yet," he added, after a pause, has done me a many kindnesses, and helped me when no other would!"

CHAPTER THE TWENTY-FOURTH.

AN ACTRESS AND HER CRITICS.

MAURICE went to bed over-night with a settled determination of doing something decisive in the morning; but, unfortunately, daylight found him still very unsettled as to what the something was to be. Father and son resembled each other in the habit which they both had of procrastination. When old John, or young Maurice, found themselves in a fix, they would shake their heads wisely, saying, "This sort of thing won't do, you know;" or, "Something will have to be done, you know;" and, having got this far, seemed apparently, to think that they had done everything which laid in their power, and that the evil would abolish itself without more ado.

About a week after his last visit, Jack Ochre dropped in one night, uninvited, to smoke a pipe. "Heard of any engagements, yet?" he asked.

"Don't know how to set about it," grumbled Maurice. "I've written to two or three people, and got no answers!"

"What, managers?"

"Yes."

"Ah!" said Jack, meditatively. "I don't think people answer those sort of letters, usually. Nobody ever took any notice of mine."

"What would you do then, Jack?"

"See them personally; and worry them, and tire them the way the beggars do. Nobody would give beggars anything if it were not to get rid of them."

"It shall be done!" said Maurice, with determination. "To-morrow I will begin."

"By the way," remarked Jack, "what is the lady's line?"

"Comedy, I should like," Nelly replied, mildly.

"What parts do you know?"

"What parts? Why, none at present."

"Ho! ho! ho!" laughed Ochre, coarsely; and Nelly blushed crimson.

"Why, Mr. Ochre?" she asked.

"Because the manager may want to hear what you can do before he agrees to giving you his humble twenty pounds a-week."

At this suggestion, Nell purchased two or three sixpenny plays at Mr. Lacey's, and began to study the parts of *Lady Teazle*, *Constance*, and *Mrs. Chillingtone*. These she rehearsed with Maurice, who pronounced her reading of each character perfect; and, with a view of affording others to judge of her abili-

ties, Maurice learnt the part of *Sir Edward Ardent*, in duologue of "The Morning Call;" and purchased for a couple of pounds the privilege of performing the piece with Nelly, at a private theatre, and of distributing two pounds'-worth of tickets among his friends.

The evening of the attempt arriving in due course, and the two pounds'-worth of tickets having crowded into the boxes of the dingy little house, in company with the friends and friend's friends of the other performers, also with tickets—for nobody ever thought of paying here. The curtain rose upon a short, sentimental piece, to which the audience listened not very attentively, cheering their particular performer, and laughing at the rest. After this came "The Morning Call." *Sir Edward Ardent*, Mr. Morris. *Mrs. Chillingtone*, Miss Arundel Howard (her first appearance).

When the curtain rose, *Mrs. Chillingtone* was discovered seated; but, thinking it would produce a better effect, and being by no means shy; for she knew very well, even if Maurice were not incessantly informing her of the fact, that she was a genius and a beauty; she advanced to the footlights, and read a letter which she held in her hand, in a ringing voice which was perfectly audible in every part of the theatre. The two pounds'-worth of tickets, of course, applauded with feet and hands until compelled to desist from fatigue; and even the rest of the audience, dazzled by the beauty of her face, the fire of her eyes, and the dash of her manners, contributed their mite of approbation, all which this golden-haired goddess took to herself affably, and condescendingly conscious that it was but her due, and smiling encouragingly upon the lookers-on in a manner delightful to see.

As for Maurice, to do him credit, it was no motive of vanity which led him to appear, but a desire to help and encourage the young lady by his presence; and he was so joyful at her reception, that he came upon the stage in high spirits, and scarcely thinking of the other side of the footlights, rattled through his part with such vigour and animation, as brought down repeated rounds of applause.

At the conclusion of the piece, Maurice rushed round to seek his friends.

"Well, well," he cried, quite out of breath, and buttoning his coat, "what did you think of it?"

"First rate!" quoth one, with enthusiasm.

"No end!" cried another.

"You beat Mathews!" cried a third.

"By Jove, Maurice," said Jack Ochre, "you did that wonderfully!"

"ME?" cried Maurice, too excited to be grammatical. "It's Nelly I'm talking of. Didn't she act like an angel?"

"Maurice, you're in luck there."

"What a fine woman!"

"What eyes!"

"What a neck!"

"What hair!. The right colour, eh?"

"No, but I say," said Maurice, "what do you think of her acting?"

"By heavens!" cried Jack, "I think her one of the prettiest women I ever saw."

"Most potent, grave, and reverend philosopher!" said the lady in question, curtsying low to Ochre, as he took his leave of them that evening at the court, " you have not afforded me the unutterable pleasure of hearing your sage opinion upon my merits."

" I fear, madam," Ochre replied, " that the pleasure must remain unutterable. Were I to give vent to the unbounded enthusiasm with which your merits inspire me, I'm afraid I should spoil you for ever."

" I don't believe you, sir; you're only laughing at me."

" Look at me: am I not serious ?"

" Well, perhaps you are. Did you like my acting ? Had I sufficient confidence ?"

" I thought so," Ochre answered, very quietly.

" Oh! Thank you. Good night."

They were alone upon the staircase, Nelly having gone to light him out. Maurice lay upon the sofa in the sitting room.

" Jack," she said, placing her little hand softly upon his shoulder, and smiling down upon him, " tell me, do you think I shall ever be a great actress ?"

" What a question! That must depend upon yourself, and the discernment of your audience."

" Do you think I am clever ?"

" Very clever."

" As an actress, I mean ?"

" I have not had sufficient opportunity of judging."

" But, by what you have seen ?"

" Why should you cross-examine me ? I am not everybody. My opinion can scarcely be worth the having."

" But I will have it!" stormed the beauty, stamping her foot.

" Well, then," said Jack, " no."

" Why no, Mr. Ochre ?"

" Because the part did not suit you. You were too forward—gave yourself too many airs for—for a lady."

" Thank you, sir. Ha, ha! It's very kind of you. Good night, Mr. Ochre. I am *very* much obliged to you."

" No, you're not; but you would have it. Don't be offended, Nelly."

" Offended! Ha, ha! the idea !"

She could not have been, although the door did slam to rather suddenly, and with a great bang. Offended at what *he* said—the idea !

" I suppose I've made another enemy, as usual," mused Mr. Ochre, left to himself. " Well, it cannot be helped! She deserved it, a conceited hussy! She's a woman, in short. Here's my pipe out, and I've no matches. Better not ring and ask her for one, perhaps." So saying, he put his pipe away, and set off for the City Road.

" Why, Nelly, dear, what is the matter ?" cried Maurice, in great alarm, as she entered the room, and, without speaking, threw her arms round his neck and sobbed. " Nelly, speak to me, my love: what is it—what *has* happened ?"

" Oh, nothing! Your friend," she sobbed, " Insult——Oh dear, oh dear !"

" Friend !—insult !" cried Maurice, growing hot and cold of a sudden. " Who ? What ? Ochre ? Damnation !"

" Stop, stop, Maurice! What are you doing ? Not that—I don't mean that !"

She clung to him only just in time. The impetuous youth would have dashed headlong at the foe, with a fierce determination of vengeance, and a perfect ignorance of the nature of the injury he had sustained.

Then Nelly explained what conversation had taken place between Jack and herself; and, having enumerated all his disparaging remarks, burst out crying again with renewed violence. Then it was Maurice's turn to soothe and comfort her. She was a good actress. She should be a great one, or he would know why. He felt an inward conviction that she would—that she must be famous.

" He said I was unladylike," sobbed Nelly, not yet altogether consoled.

And let me tell you, sir,—who are, I can see, inclined to run down my heroine as a weak, vain creature,—that I should like to know how your young woman,—plain, and conscious of it, though she may be,—would stand being called unladylike by some one whose opinion she valued. She values yours, now. Try it. It will open your eyes to one of Penelope's weak points, I'll warrant me.

Our friend, Maurice, was loud in his denial of Mr. Ochre's judgment.

" And I don't care twopence," cried he defiantly, raising the pretty yellow-haired one in his arms, and kissing off all traces of her tears, " I don't care twopence whether you're like a lady or not. You're like an angel; and that's what a many of them are not; and if angels are unladylike, why, all the better; and Jack's getting an ill-natured fellow, and had much better keep his genius for his pawnbroker's fine arts, than waste it in talking of what he does not understand."

With which opinion the writer coincides.

CHAPTER THE TWENTY-FIFTH.

NOW OR NEVER.

MAURICE began to see about the " something" in good earnest. After pestering and persecuting all his friends until he was universally voted a nuisance, he obtained two or three introductions to London managers. Upon these gentlemen he called and stated his case. Some were very polite, and some were not; but all were alike in their reply—they did not want another actress. Of the first manager Maurice requested an engagement for Miss Nelly as Leading Lady. You should have heard Buskin's laugh, opening his huge mouth so that the applicant saw half-way down his throat. With Rougynoir and the rest of them Mr. Cheveleigh was much less aspiring. He dwindled down to Singing Chambermaid as he got further east, and had half a mind to beg for a place in the ballet when he had travelled past Norton Folgate.

Very low-spirited he was, you may be sure, as he took himself and his bad news home to his anxious partner.

Poor Nelly! were all the dreams of future greatness to fall to the ground ? Meanwhile, in spite of repeated failures, she studied very hard at her stock parts, and at her music. A piano had been hired, and you might often have seen that soft-hearted female, the Perks' servant, upon the landing, listening, spell-bound, to the singer's thrilling notes.

Nelly came upon her unawares one evening in the twilight, and found her whimpering and smudging her nose with her dirty hand. She blubbered out, "Oh! do-ee, do-ee sing that piece again, ma'am. It's so like angels!"

Fallen angels, perhaps!

When Maurice was beginning to despair of finding her an engagement, it at once occurred to him that if the managers were to see the lady themselves, the matter might be settled in an interview, at her own terms. Acting, therefore, upon Maurice's advice, Mrs. Nelly dressed herself in the most bewitching of bonnets, the tightest-fitting gloves, and widest skirts, and prepared to take the managers by storm.

These potentates were much more civil to the lady than they had been to Cheveleigh. Some of them bade her recite, and applauded her performance vociferously. Some appointed a second and a third interview. One proposed a quiet little dinner at Blackwall, and one whispered strange hints about a brougham, and a villa at Putney; scarcely comprehending which, but knowing that it meant no good, Nelly flushed up at, and rejected indignantly. Finally, she was not engaged by any of them.

The young couple were sitting very mournfully one evening at the court, Nelly trying to read, but going over page after page with no idea of its meaning; Maurice trying to smoke an unlighted pipe, his thoughts meanwhile all astray. Most decidedly the time had arrived for that long talked-of something to be done. He had almost run through all his quarter's salary (a gratuity which he expected to receive, had not yet been awarded, owing to official procrastination). His father would not increase his allowance, wondering why he did not come home, if he was out of work. His mother's letters spoke of suffering and neglect, and entreated him to return. Nelly's case seemed hopeless. He was very much in debt. The fact was, that he must get some money somehow. But how? Weary of boring his friends. Everybody had long since come to the conclusion that Nelly would never be an actress, and had no talent, and that Maurice had gone mad about her.

He was turning these things over in his mind, when a knock at the door aroused him. A very warm and dirty little boy had brought a note from Mr. Ochre, marked "Immediate."

"What's he got to say, I wonder," Maurice said, opening it with secret misgivings.

"Apollo Saloon, Five o'Clock.

"Dear Maurice,—Bring Nelly in a cab, full gallop. Miss Fleshings has thrown up her part for to-night, as *Constance*, in 'The Love Chase.' Manager furious. I reasoned with him. I proposed Nelly. Bring her down. This is a chance not to be missed. I shall tell lies to him until she comes—contradict nothing. Dress is all ready. Curtain goes up at half-past six.　"JACK OCHRE."

CHAPTER THE TWENTY-SIXTH.

MORE OF HADGET'S ODDITIES.

IT seems very natural to me who love London, and have lived there all my life, that Ernest should soon tire of the pleasures of the country.

We cockneys don't understand them, perhaps. When we get to a fragrant meadow, or pleasant piece of pasture land, we straightway light our rank havannah, and squatting down, set to talking of the town life and scandal.

A very little of the green fields and buttercups go a great way with most of us, though we rave about them regularly towards the close of every "season."

But our good young friend, Ernest, had other reasons for wishing to get away. My lady readers will believe me when I say that he was heartily sick of the Skearcrows' society.

They were a bad lot.

Nobody in the neighbourhood visited there. Indeed, there were rumours afloat respecting the fascinating Kitty (she of the ornaments and mourning nails), which were scarcely creditable.

About twenty years before the date of this story, Sir John had come to Skearcrows, bringing with him a French wife, a little Frenchified child, a French lady's-maid, a French nurse, and all manner of French manners and customs, highly distasteful to the bigotted Briton.

As is the custom, I believe, in some rural districts, the parson, doctor, and neighbouring small gentry, called upon the new tenant, as soon as he was installed in his new residence, and paid their homage to him.

I have reason to believe that the parson, the doctor, and the neighbouring gentry did not meet with that courtesy which might have been expected from a rich, travelled gentleman. To an earnest, and, to my thinking, not unreasonable request from the village ecclesiastic, that he would head a subscription for the church steeple, and embellishment thereof with a new weather-cock, Sir John Cheveleigh was pleased to return a most insulting answer, suggesting that if the steeple were out of repair, it should be taken down altogether, and not renewed. The medical man was snubbed, and the small gentry systematically outraged, until at length nobody called upon the new people, nobody bowed to them, everybody affected to be unaware of their existence, and everybody watched them, pryed into their affairs, poked their noses into their private concerns, and canvassed their smallest movements with the greatest zest and enjoyment.

You know how some women love to dwell upon unpleasant subjects — how she will rake up old grievances, forgotten quarrels, and all manner of distressing odds and ends from the lumber-room of oblivion. When she buries her husband, or her child, or her dear friend, she will have them back, out of their graves, and put them through their last agonies as many times a day as you will hearken to her. Has she ever forgotten that frailty of yours—ever ceased to allude gently to the way you threw away her fortune in the speculation she suggested? Will the matter ever die until you bury it with her?

You can fancy what a field was opened to the gentle maids and matrons of the neighbourhood by the conduct of the new proprietor. Those games of cards on Sunday, the drinking, the swearing, the queer company; those strange females from town, who visited them—so objectionably good-looking and provokingly well-dressed, but whom any one, at a glance, could see were no better than they ought to be; how it was all talked over and commented upon at the little tea-parties.

Some ladies pitied his poor wife; some tossed their heads at the mention of her name. At the period when the events happened I described to you in my preceding chapters, the neighbourhood had given Skearcrows up to the undisturbed indulgence of its vicious tastes, and the household seems to me to have made itself pretty comfortable, in spite of the stern decree of excommunication pronounced against it,—seems, too, to have lived upon the fat of the land, in spite of the frequent predictions of its rapidly approaching insolvency.

One morning the postman brought a letter for Mr. Ernest Cheveleigh. It came from Dorcas Abbot.

It was a very prim, decorous epistle, written in a cramped, clerk-like hand, not at all like a lady's writing.

"Dear Sir,—Your aunt requests me to state that she would feel obliged to you for your presence at your earliest convenience. Hoping that you are enjoying yourself,—I am, yours sincerely,   DORCAS ABBOT."

Then came a postscript in quite a different style, scrawled hastily, and blotted sadly, which said :—"Dearest love, do not fail. Ever your own   DORCAS."

This must have been written after the first had been read and approved of by the old lady. What a deceitful proceeding!

"No unpleasant news, I trust?" said Mr. Hadget, who was present.

"Only that I must go to town to-morrow."

"So soon?" cried Hadget, as though it were his own house. He liked entertaining company at somebody else's expense. "Let's go to dinner, and make a night of it?" said he. "It's fearful weather out of doors."

It was a black and stormy night. A howling wind abroad; a pouring rain at intervals; then, thunder and lightning; then more wind and rain.

Now that her son had returned to town again, there was plenty of moping for the sick woman at Skearcrows. This was a night when few timid people would have chosen to sit alone. The invalid had pulled down the blinds, muffled the looking-glass and fire-irons, and crept into the darkest corner of her bedchamber, scared and trembling. When she was tired of waiting for the storm to subside, she fell asleep; and, covered up in a mass of garments she had hastily collected round her, looked like a bundle of dirty clothes waiting for the wash.

The usual night's debauch was going on down-stairs, and the monotonous sound of Sir John's voice, reciting some dull obscenities to his half-fuddled pot-companions, was occasionally heard during a lull in the tempest.

Perhaps Mr. Hadget had heard his host's stories before, and did not feel amused by them; for he had left the table quietly, and wandered in the gloomy house alone.

It was strange that he should take a fancy to visit that part of the establishment where the sick woman's room was situated; for his own chamber was at the opposite side of the building. A cautious, stealthy tread was natural to him at all times. There may have been no more than usual of the tiger in his creeping walk: there was no more than usual of the wolfish glare about his sunken eyes, as he peered in upon the sick woman, twitching his mouth, and exhibiting his gleaming teeth.

"Ahem!" he said. The sick woman slept on soundly. "How lucky!"

What was? He had the oddest ways about him—this humorous attorney. He took the light from the table, and, advancing noiselessly, passed it to and fro before the woman's closed eyes. Then, seemingly satisfied of the soundness of her slumber, he took a survey of the room. He visited all the drawers and boxes, plunging his hands round the sides, and groping in them, with the address of a Custom House officer.

"If she has it, it's about her." The eccentric gentleman regarded the form of the sleeper with a singularly ferocious look, saying this as though, if it were her heart he sought he would not have scrupled to have torn it out. From her face his eyes wandered round the room again, and lighted on her work-box : a common thing enough, with a cracked stag, in mother-o'-pearl, upon the lid. It was locked, but he hesitated not a moment. Placing it between his knees, he wrenched open the lid, and from it fell a mass of old letters and scraps of paper the Frenchwoman had treasured up, with a sprig or two of lavender.

Gathering them up hastily, he thrust them into his pocket, and replaced the box. But yet he was not satisfied.

"It's not among these," he said. "She's got it on her, or may I——"

He seemed as though he had half a mind to rifle her pockets. Indeed, he was stooping over her, when all of a sudden she began to struggle, and to cry out in her sleep —

"Maurice, my boy—my love, Maurice, forgive me! I am a sinful wretch! Your mother begs upon her knees : Maurice, my child, have pity on me!"

Quick as lightning he blew out the candle, lest she might wake and find him there.

But she went on, still struggling and talking in her sleep. The spy stood motionless, and drank in every word with greedy ears. Then, as she awoke, twisted herself into an easier posture, and fell off to sleep again, Hadget, stealing on tiptoe from the room, went down-stairs, chuckling in goblin fashion, rubbing his bony hands, and mouthing in a way most horrible to look upon.

"No need of it now!" he cackled to himself. "No need of it now. It's as I thought. THERE ISN'T ONE AT ALL."

NELLY RAYMOND.

CHAPTER THE TWENTY-SEVENTH.

WHO'S AFRAID.

THERE was no occasion for Mr. Ochre to have said that the "opening" referred to in his letter "was a chance not to be thrown away."

Pride had died a natural death long ago. Nelly thrust on her bonnet, tearing off a string in so doing. Maurice seized his hat. The little boy rushed down the court, squeaking, like one possessed, for a cab. In they jumped, little boy and all.

"Love Chase!" shouted Maurice, not knowing what he was saying.

No. 5.

"Where, sir?" said the cabman, astonished. On they flew. Nelly tried to scan over the part as they went along. Of course she did not understand a word of it, and when they reached the Apollo she could not remember the first sentence.

They found the manager waiting for them. It was just a quarter past six.

"This is her, eh? Do you know your part, young woman?"

"Perfectly." Maurice answered for her.

"Oh! that's lucky. Hum! Ah! Nice looking—fine girl—can't change the play—damned young hussy, Fleshings—pay her out for it. Go and get your things on then. Here, Mrs. Musty, dress this lady. Go with her, my dear, and look sharp." Thus disconnecting, talking, as much to himself as to the listeners, he pushed Nelly towards a dilapidated old lady who toddled up, and then walked away to abuse the carpenter.

As soon as Nelly was dressed, the stage manager stepped before the curtain and informed the audience, who were growing impatient, that the delay arose from the sudden indisposition of Miss Fleshings, to which information the public replied by groans and hisses. He then went on to state, that a young lady had kindly volunteered to perform in her stead, and that as it was her first appearance, he trusted they would encourage her by that kind consideration which they always awarded to budding talent, etc. etc., and so on, until his flood of eloquence getting entangled in a hopeless knot, he bowed and walked off in the middle of a sentence.

After which the British public there represented, flapped its great red hands together, and banged its boots upon the floor in token of applause.

By this time Nelly was dressed, the prompter rang up, and the play began. She stood waiting by his side for the cue. Bullyrag the manager was there scrutinising her dress and appearance, and bidding her take courage and speak up. Maurice was there trembling in every limb, by turns peeping at the book, and at the stage, and at the lady, and wondering how many thousand years it would be before her turn came.

"Don't be afraid, Nell," he whispered. "Now or never. You *must* be successful.".

But there was no "must" in it—only a great deal of chance, and a dread uncertainty which made her lover feel faint and sick.

Ochre, having seen her dressed, ran round to the gallery to applaud, and to bribe some little boys up there to do the same. Everybody was in a great flutter except one.

The person who apparently stood the least in need of encouragement, was the fair recipient thereof, as she waited with flushed cheeks and flashing eyes, stamping her foot with impatience. Truly, she was very beautiful in her tightly-fitting riding habit, her fair hair arranged to flow luxuriantly upon her shoulders.

"Can you laugh?" asked Bullyrag, anxiously.

"Yes, a little," replied Nelly.

"Go it, then!" he said, pointing to the book where her part commenced; and Nelly straightway laughed a long, thrilling, joyous laugh, which made the manager stare and gape again, for he had expected a faint, hysterical cackle at the best.

The novice was little daunted by the surging sea of upturned faces before her. She was sure of her words, and felt pretty confident of success. It takes a great deal to convince a person that he is not a genius, when he has made up his mind that he is. If Nelly had failed, she would have attributed it to the brutal ignorance of that indiscriminate beast, the British public. But it was not to be so. The British public flapped its hands, and banged its boots, and took kindly to the pretty woman.

Some half-dozen discontented people hissed at the conclusion, because they were friends of Miss Fleshings, or because they could not see,

or for some other reason; most of the audience applauded; while some did neither, being too eager to get on their hats, and run out after beer.

Maurice was in ecstacies. He caught her in his arms as she came off. Was she not the loveliest, cleverest, most fascinating woman ever born?

Bullyrag was less enthusiastic, and more calculating. He had made up his mind to engage her at half the salary Miss Fleshings had received. He argued, for some time, about the irregularity of the whole proceeding, Nelly's want of stage knowledge, and the number of his staff. At length, he closed with her for forty shillings a week, which, he assured her, would ruin him. This sum wanted, as the reader will find upon calculation, just eighteen pounds and ten shillings adding to it, before it reached the sum Mrs. Nelly had dreamed of some months before; but still, her engagement was so fortunate, so unexpected a happiness, so like a miracle indeed, that she could scarcely believe in its reality. The ladies of the company stared at her as rudely as women can stare at an interloper of their own sex, and criticised her attire, when she had changed the theatrical trumpery for her own pretty bonnet and mantle; but the goddess was little abashed, and bowed quite stiffly to the low comedian, who came up with a little compliment upon her talents. Poor second-rate people! who will you be, and who will she be, two years hence? It shall be found in the future chapters of this history.

"Poor dear love! she is quite tired," Maurice said, caressingly. "Let us go home to supper."

"Yes, Maurice,—let us go home."

"Stop a moment," said Maurice. "I wonder where Jack is all this while."

Indeed there had been so many things to think of, Jack had been quite forgotten.

CHAPTER THE TWENTY-EIGHTH.

WHAT EVERYBODY SAID.

HE turned up at the moment. "I've just written a few lines for the 'Pothouse Pioneer,'" said Jack, "and sent them to a fellow on the paper, who, I know, will dress it up, and get the paragraph in to-night. They publish to-morrow."

"How kind of you to think of it, Jack," cried Nelly. "How can I ever thank you! But you are such an old friend of Maurice's, he must thank you for me, for I cannot find any words half strong enough for what I feel." And she pressed his hand warmly in hers, while her big blue eyes filled with tears.

"Tut, tut!" said Jack, looking down upon her, thinking how beautiful were those big eyes, how eloquent the silent grip of her fingers, and that perhaps she had some heart after all; and, as for being vain, had not a woman with such beauty and talents a right to be proud of them, and to expect homage and admiration at the hands of such every-day, commonplace clowns as himself? Would he have a woman to be without pride? Was he justified in saying the mortifying things he had said to her? A nice namby-pamby, unnatural piece of goodness he would have a woman to be, had he his way. Oh! he felt that he was a fool, and was heartily ashamed of himself.

"You will come and have supper with us, Jack? It's very rude of me to call you Jack, but Maurice does, and may not I? May I, Maurice?"

"Aye, aye!" cried Maurice, shaking Ochre by the hand; "no one is a friend of mine who is not a friend of Jack's."

Without more ado, they left the theatre, and took a cab home, stopping by the way to order unlimited oysters and stout for supper. When these delicacies had been duly discussed, and a brew of grog set before each gentleman, out of whose tumblers the actress took homœopathic refreshment in a teaspoon, the conversation finally settled, without interruption, upon the wonderful events of the evening.

"There was a great deal of applause," said Maurice.

"Yes," said Nelly, innocently, "particularly in the gallery."

"That was a good sign, I thought," Maurice continued. "Once please the gods—eh?"

Maurice thought himself very sharp. If he had a fault, it was being a good deal too knowing.

Perhaps Jack thought it best not to say anything about himself and his troop of boys, so he changed the topic by drinking Mrs. Nelly's good health, and wishing her every success; in which toast Maurice joined him, standing on a chair, and hurraing so vociferously, that the other unsympathising inmates of the house, who had gone to bed, were heard knocking below and on either side of the room; a demonstration which induced Mr. Ochre to light his "home pipe," and get up to take his leave.

But he did not depart before the couple had thanked him over and over again; and, Nelly lighting him out asked, archly, whether she had acted like a lady upon this occasion; to which the painter responded by bowing low, and craving forgiveness for the freedom of a serf in daring to dictate manners to a queen. In reply, Mrs. Nelly, with a graceful sweep of her arm, and a tolerable accent, said,—"La reine vous pardonne," offering him a pretty hand to kiss, which Ochre, clumsily enough shook instead, and so they parted.

"That Ochre is a very good fellow," said Nelly, reflectively, when she had rejoined Maurice. "But it's a great pity he is such a bear. Why does he not get polished up a little? Does he dance?"

"Jack, dance!" cried Maurice, laughing at the idea.

"How I should like to see him try," cried Nelly. "Wouldn't he tread upon his own toes—so?" and the pretty, graceful woman tried to make herself look awkward, in the most delightfully ludicrous manner imaginable.

Jack Ochre looked in next day.

"Here's the paper," said he, "and here's the paragraph."

Then he read the notice of the first appearance in London of a very piquante and promising young actress, at the Apollo Saloon. It prophesied a great and glorious career of the debutante; then praised the management of the "spirited lessee;" alluded casually to the effective scenery, and concluded with a slap at the leading gentleman, just to give force to the praise of the actress.

"The worst of it is," said Ochre.

There is always a worst, somehow.

"What is it, Jack?"

"They've printed the name wrong."

So they had. It was Waymond, instead of Raymond. Such mistakes are not unfrequent in such cases, and few notice them, except the injured party.

It happened, however, by some fortunate chance, that a great literary celebrity, who writes in a weekly illustrated paper, under the title of "The Mooner at the Pubs," happened to be present at the debut, and complimented Mrs. Cheveleigh in the highest terms.

I suppose that several millions of insignificant individuals never read these important notices; or, if they did, not knowing Nelly, forgot all about it next moment; but the small world in which she lived read it, and were much impressed thereby.

And then it was that everybody began to remember how they predicted her success from the very first, and how they had over and over again argued themselves black in the face, refuting the faintest idea of the possibility of a failure.

––––

CHAPTER THE TWENTY-NINTH.

A FLAW IN THE DIAMOND.

NOW had the celebrated Miss Fleshings only minded her p's and q's, and played her cards properly, I have no doubt that Bullyrag would soon have been at her feet again.

He was very much attached to her, I'm certain. She, however, was a spirity creature, very high and mighty, and all that sort of thing.

"The idea of employing that woman! Putting her in my part—a mere novice—a— I don't know what all. It's scandalous! What they can see in her is more than I can tell!"

It's odd; but one professional never can see what anyone else can see in any other professional. Luckily for pretty Nell, a good many saw a great deal in her, and she gained in public favour daily.

Certainly the salary was rather small. Nelly did not tell the other members of the company how small it was. Very properly she kept all these second-rate people at a distance, and taught them to know their places. Nor was Maurice more communicative with his friends, who were led to believe that she was starring it at a huge weekly salary.

To tell the truth, her acting was nothing

very wonderful, but she was a monstrous pretty woman, and that goes a long way. Besides, she had an extraordinary amount of assurance, and the British public likes to be insulted by its favourites.

There was one person in the world besides Maurice who thought her a genius. This was the simple handmaiden at the court chambers.

"Oh, mam, how beautiful you do it! Oh, my goodlings, me! how ever you can think of it all, it do surprise me! Do'ee, do'ee do that bit again."

Nothing loth, the yellow-haired would repeat the scene she had been rehearsing. She frequently dressed up in her finest clothes, and acted to the Bony-one, who sat the while with her mouth wide open, bluebottle catching.

There was a mystery enshrouding that servant of the Perks'. People said she was Mrs. Perks' sister, but that she was a very inferior woman, and not fit to associate with the rest of the family, who had been genteel, and seen better days. The Bony-one had never been genteel, had never seen better days, and never would see them, most probably, in this world; as there are a many of us, my lady, who never do; who go on, hoping and hoping; whose ship is always coming in, is continually being "spoken," but never reaches port. Not that Miss Perks hoped for much. If she had, what could it have been for? What was her ambition? Permanent out-door relief from the "House." It couldn't have been more. She had never known what was meant by luxury, or ease, or happiness, or pocket-money. She had never read a novel, or tasted pine-apple, or had a sweetheart. Once, in her wild youth (forty years ago), she went half-price to the play. She spoke of it now confusedly, and looked back at it, as at a sort of dream. One day, she tasted the dregs of some lemonade and sherry, which she found in Cheveleigh's rooms. She called it "heavenly!"

So time wore on, and Nelly promised to become a popular favourite with East-end audiences. Then must follow an engagement in the West—thunders of applause, and a princely fortune. Surely that was not too much to expect. Meanwhile, Bullyrag would not go beyond the forty shillings.

It was a source of great comfort to Maurice that Jack Ochre was engaged at the same house as his dearly beloved; for behind the scenes there are many petty jealousies and mean squabblings, but very few friendships. It was a fine sight to see how all those poor second-rate women affected to look down upon the Beauty, just like a plain and shabbily-dressed virtuous woman turns up her nose at a magnificently attired traviata she catches her good man ogling. The pretty woman had snubbed the rest of the company to such an extent, that they were not generally anxious to cultivate her acquaintance. Thus it was that she became very intimate with Jack.

Sometimes she mounted into Mr. Ochre's painting-room, and watched him manufacturing distant scenery, costly interiors, gloomy cells, and dazzling dells for the forthcoming pantomime.

"What do you think of that?" he asked, one day, pointing to one of these works of art.

"Capital! You are very clever, Jack."

She was standing close to the scene which she affected to admire. I believe this style of painting looks best at a distance. I have, also, my doubts whether she knew much about the fine arts, or could have told what the daub was meant for, had she been pressed hard.

"Clever, you call it?" Jack said, with a laugh. "You're so fond of chaff."

"That's very unkind of you to say so, Jack. You know I meant it."

Then she pouted.

"I wish Maurice was as clever as you."

"Maurice is a swell. You wouldn't have him be everything. He'll be a baronet some day."

"What's that to me?" she answered, with a passionate stamp of her pretty kid boot; "that won't make me a lady."

"Do you think there's too much green about this?" Ochre asked, pointing to the canvas.

"No! I don't know—I'm no judge."

"Why, my dear Mrs. Cheveleigh, I'm sure you have a great deal of good taste and discernment."

"Why?"

"Because you discovered my talents."

"That's just like you, Mr. Ochre; you're always making fun of me—you are—you know you are. I don't know what I've done to make you hate me, but I'm sure you do. I've always tried to please you, for—for—Maurice's sake."

Here she burst out crying, and, sitting down among the cobwebs and paint pots, quite reckless of her *moire antique*, sobbed passionately.

Ochre went on for some time, seeming not to notice her. Then she began to cry a little louder.

"What's the matter, Nelly?"

"N-n-nothing," sobbed the lady.

"People don't cry about nothing. What is it?"

She made no answer, only her grief increased twofold.

"Mrs. Cheveleigh — Nelly! Don't, for God's sake! I beg your pardon. I'm a horrible beast. What have I said—what shall I say?"

"Say! I don't want you to say anything," she suddenly cried out, springing to her feet, and sending the paint pots flying. "What have you done? You've done nothing, of course—nor said anything. I'm a fool—that's all! I wish I was dead!"

She swept from the room after this outburst, laughing shrilly, and was in boisterous spirits all the rest of the evening.

That night, after Nelly had been called before the curtain amid thunders of applause, and was coming off blushing and palpitating, Maurice was waiting for her at the O.P. wing. The young man felt very proud of her.

"What a beautiful woman she is!" he was thinking. "What a splendid actress! And it was I who made her so. Her name is in everybody's mouth. If she had not met me, she would never have been heard of."

Here the golden-haired goddess interrupted him by stumbling over his legs, on her way to the dressing-room.

"Bother you, boy!" she cried, irate.

She had grown many years older than he was now.

"I never saw anything like your legs, they are always in the way."

He and his legs continued to be in the way of everyone all the rest of the night, and the stage manager hinted that behind the scenes was not a place to loll about in, whilst some one else roared out to him to keep that ugly head of his out of sight of the house. He was at the time poking it beyond the shade of a side wing, to catch a glimpse of his idol on the stage.

"Are you tired, dear?" Maurice asked, when the piece was over.

"Tired!" she exclaimed. "Tired of what?"

"Tired with what you've done to-night?"

"Oh! that? Yes, I'm tired."

"Shall we go home?"

"How you talk! I must get my salary, I suppose. I'll go and see about it. Sit there, and wait."

He did,—an hour. Ochre came up.

"Not gone yet?" said he.

"No," said Maurice; "I'm waiting for Nelly."

"You're a model for husbands, Maurice," Jack said, laughing. Then added to himself, "What a hussy it is!—what a hussy it is! What a shameful slut!"

CHAPTER THE THIRTIETH

CONTAINS BOB SAWDER'S BLESSING.

ERNEST CHEVELEIGH packed up his carpet-bag, and made elaborate excuses for his departure, which, however, were perhaps, unnecessary, and not needed, for his hosts and their servants had grown somehow unaccountably rather sick of his company; as hosts, somehow unaccountably but generally grow sick of us all when we stay too long with them upon our visits. It is true that they usually conceal their weariness; we seldom catch them yawning behind our backs, or nodding in our company; but they are, sometimes, mortally tired of us for all that. I have seen a whole family who have been listening in a sort of dull torpor, or struggling with an almost uncontrollable fit of the fidgets, whilst some poor, unconscious visitor has been chatting late into the night at their house, confident that he was wise, and witty, and entertaining, blind to the fact that he was keeping them out of their long-coveted beds. I have seen a whole family spring joyfully from their seats at the first hint he might make of his departure, find him his hat, assist him with his coat, and literally bundle him into the street in their impatience to get rid of him; then when the door was shut, thank providence for their happy release. But this is, of course, a very exceptional case.

Mr. Hadget assured Ernest that Sir John would be dreadfully cut up about his departure.

He might have been certainly; but he did not show it. When Hadget mentioned the circumstance to him, and suggested that he should entreat Ernest to prolong his visit, Sir John mumbled something which might have been mistaken for "good riddance," only I can hardly think he would have been so rude.

Perhaps the good young man's presence was a restraint upon the low company.

The Pipers and Mr. Ganders said "good bye" to him with a degree of heartiness which looked as though they would not break their hearts at his departure. Indeed, they offered to walk to the station with him, and see him off, with suspicious alacrity.

Old Mr. Piper was as anxious about his giant offspring as ever. He shook his head, and pointed to his hopeful son as they walked along.

"Breaking up, sir," groaned the old man. "Look at his poor shanks—look at the poor wretch's shanks!"

"What's the matter with them?" asked Ernest.

"Weakening, sir," whined the doting father: "giving in at the knees they are."

"I don't see what ails his legs," Ernest replied.

"No—no, because you're not accustomed to them. You haven't noticed them give way, or——" here Mr. Piper stopped, and stepped back a pace to look the other in the face, "you say so to deceive me, good young man—bless you—but I know it. My poor boy! Oh! my poor boy — he's—he's—fading fast away!"

"Now then, gov'nor," roared the delicate subject of these remarks, looking round, and mopping his head with a flaring pocket-handkerchief. "Move them baccy pipes o'yourn."

This was a delicate allusion to the paternal limbs.

Everyone could not have been glad that Ernest was going away. Bob Sawder, the ancient retainer of the Cheveleigh family (a blear-eyed old man, whom Sir John had brought into the country with him), was deeply affected at the railway station.

"God bless you, young gentleman! I shall never forget you. I don't want nothink to drink your health with in; I can think of you without."

Nothing was offered, so he went on,—

"You're the sort of young gentleman, sir,—excuse the liberty,—as I should wish to see Mr. Maurice more like, sir. The whole place is going to ruin, sir. If anything was to happen to dear Sir John,—which the Lord forbid! though he can't last long, going on as he does,—and Mr. Maurice wasn't to live long,—which heaven send he does!—we should see the estate come to you, sir. Them would be times, sir. God bless you, for a real gentleman? Might I kiss your hand, sir. Thank you, sir. It's very good and kind of you."

I think Bob Sawder was right. Mr. Ernest was a great improvement on the rest of the family. He was neither a drunkard nor a profligate. He took good care of what money he had, and spent it on himself in decent and orderly fashion, which was highly creditable to his good taste.

You would not have found him keeping a woman like his spendthrift cousin. First of all, because it would have been immoral; and secondly, because it would have been a foolish expense.

Now, that booby Maurice, in his blind and ridiculous infatuation, squandered his last shillings in adorning the fair person of the yellow-haired beauty, while he himself went about nearly in rags. Indeed, his old battered hat, and his worn-out boots, excited no small mirth among his companions, who remembered him such a swell in times gone by.

Ernest, on the contrary, was always exceedingly well-dressed, although his style was quiet. He had a heavy watch in his pocket, and generally a sovereign or two as well; except you wanted to borrow one, when, of course, he pleaded poverty, as every sensible person would.

Good young man! Bob Sawder's eulogium pleased him vastly. He leant back in a comfortable corner-seat, in a first-class carriage; and having insisted upon the window being closed, to the great annoyance of a hot-headed old gentleman in the opposite seat, who unreasonably wished him to change places, he crossed his hands, and smiling sweetly, thought over the aged retainer's parting words.

"Not much chance of the baronetcy coming to me," thought Mr. Ernest. "Poor old Sir John will pop off some day like the snuff of a candle, quite unprepared—quite unprepared."

He dwelt upon his uncle's pitiable condition, and compared it with his own case with a snug and comfortable kind of piety of a very consolatory character.

"Then there is Maurice! What a horrible life he's leading—killing himself fast! Dissipation and extravagance what do they lead to? If he has been discharged he'll be wanting to borrow some money of me, I suppose. I shan't lend it. It would only be encouraging him. Poor fellow, what a pity it is to see any one so thrown away."

He got out for refreshment at the half-way station, and on returning to the carriage, shut up the window again, which the old gentleman had quietly taken the opportunity of opening. Then he leant back in his corner, and went on castle-building till they reached King's Cross.

He was certainly a good young man, and most anxious to please his relations; for he did not even wait a moment to make any change in his dress, but took a cab direct to Mrs. Falsetto's, and so he thus managed to arrive, looking dusty and weary, and as though he had suffered much in his wish to please her.

"Well, Dimples," said Mr. Ernest to the maid, "and how are *you* getting on?"

He was such a very gentlemanly young man, and so very distant in his conversation with common people, that a little grim condescension on his part went a very long way. I have generally noticed that the best plan for a nob to ensure the respect of a snob, is to be very insulting. Treat him like a serf and he'll

worship you; behave as though he were a fellow creature and he'll soon see you are " no gentleman."

"Very well, sir,—I thank you, sir," responded the maid, who was a pretty little maid, dark skinned, black eyed, and nicely shaped. " Missus has been very bad lately."

"A little fractious, eh, Dimples? Here's a bonnet ribbon, Dimples. What's she been doing?"

"Going on, sir—oh, anyhow !" she shrugged up her little shoulders at the thought of what she had endured.

"Dear me, that's very bad !" said Mr. Ernest, commiseratively. "She suffers a good deal, I suppose."

"She's been going on awful, sir. No one has a moment's peace, with her whims and her tantrums! It's nothing but worry and drive from morning to night. But, oh, my gracious! don't you say I said so?"

"My good girl! The idea !"

"Oh, I know you wouldn't, sir. Ill, you said? She's been no iller than usual. I've no patience with such illnesses." Here the imperious little maid stamped her foot. "The life she leads that Dorcas—Well, before I'd be the pitiful, mean-spirited thing that she is, I'd —goodness me—I'd die first !"

"Does Miss Abbot complain?"

"Not to me—bless you—Miss Abbot is too much the lady, if you please, to talk to so low a person."

"Is Mrs. Falsetto cross to her?"

"Cross! I should think so—when she has her tantrums. Other times, it's 'dear do this,' and 'my love, do that,' as affectionate as you like. But, what pleases me, is Dorcas is so meek with it all—making belief to be a saint, poor thing."

CHAPTER THE THIRTY-FIRST.

THUNDER AND LIGHTNING.

THE old lady was in her bed-room. She sat in an easy chair by the fire. She had a showy cap, with plenty of flowers, and an extra coat of rouge; but her wig was a little on one side, her eyes sunken and bloodshot; and her face, where it was not painted, looked horribly sallow. She had, in all, somewhat the appearance of a sprightly corpse.

"Ah, Ernest, you're a good boy to come to me—I'm very, very ill. I'm sure it's a wonder I'm alive !"

"My dear aunt, you alarm me !"

"I've been alarmed myself."

"What has happened, madam?"

"Happened? Why, where have you been to? Didn't you hear that fearful storm last night? It nearly killed me. Ask Dorcas."

"Yes," said Dorcas, very curtly, without raising her eyes from a book she held before her.

"But I'm glad you've come," continued the old lady. "When did you arrive?"

"An hour ago exactly," he replied, referring to his watch. "I came as quickly as possible, being fearful of keeping you waiting."

"That's a good boy. There's no catching

you tripping. By the way, how is that scape-grace, Maurice?"

"Ah!" sighed Ernest, "not going on very well, I'm afraid."

"Raking, eh?" cried the old lady, with unexpected vivacity. "I like rakes. Give me a man with some of the devil in him. My poor dear first had half a dozen duels at least, and as many seductions and broken hearts—— Before he married me, of course."

Ernest listened in respectful silence while she spoke, laughed when she made a joke, and looked serious when he ought to.

"But I don't want to talk about that prodigal," continued the old lady, after a pause. "Dorcas, give me my cloak, and give Ernest a glass of wine."

Under the pretext of this glass of wine, Dorcas and Ernest got their heads very close together, in a distant corner of the room.

"Dear Ernest, how kind of you to come," she whispered. "Oh! I have suffered so."

He pressed her hand silently to his heart.

"What has happened, dearest?"

The tears were bursting from her eyes as she looked up at him. She could only say,— "That woman!" then smother her sobs upon his shoulder.

The unconscious old lady alluded to was too busily engaged with her writing-desk to take any notice of them. Besides, she was rather deaf. In a minute or two, however, she called out, without turning her head.

"Now Ernest, my dear, I'm ready for you."

He gently disengaged his hand from that of Dorcas, and stooped to kiss her forehead. She looked up at him with that bright and beautiful smile she wore at times, in her rare moments of happiness. Then stood and watched him silently, as he took his place by his aunt.

"Are you ready, Ernest?" said the old lady.

"Yes, aunt."

"Well, then——No, stop a moment——Dorcas!"

The companion came round and stood by her, without speaking.

"Bless me! how you make one jump. Go out and take a walk. I don't want you."

Dorcas left the room. When she was gone, the old lady went on.

"Ernest!" she said, "look outside the door. Is anyone there?"

"No, aunt."

"Very well. Come close to me, and listen to what I've got to say. I've made another will."

It was odd how the fire-light sparkled in the good young man's eyes.

"You know I made my last in favour of that woman, Dorcas."

"I do."

"I've altered it."

"Altered it!"

"Why shouldn't I? I'm mistress of my own property, I suppose." the old lady retorted. "I intended she should have been my heiress. She shall have nothing—not a farthing. I hate her!"

"My dear aunt!" cried Ernest, astonished, "has anything occurred to——"

"That doesn't matter to you, sir, I sup-pose," stormed the old lady. "I've a perfect right to take a dislike to whom I choose without being called to account. Have I not?"

Doubtless the young man agreed with her, for he offered no further remark.

"This will," continued the old lady, when her anger was cooled down a little, "leaves all I have to you."

"Dear aunt," he gasped, half inclined, as it seemed, to fall upon his knees and thank her.

"There—there," the old lady interrupted, tartly, "that will do—that will do. I want you to take the will to my lawyer's; it has been witnessed by the doctor and Dimples. Dorcas knows nothing of it. She'd kill me if she did! Take it directly, and leave me. There, that'll do."

She waved him off with a frown; but not before he had had time to clasp his benefactress's hand, and kiss it fervently. Then he left the room in an unwonted flutter. He had never for a moment dreamed that she could want him in town for such a reason.

One grows so worldly after fifty years or so of this selfish Town life, that it is very hard to analyse the feelings of a good young man under such circumstances. If he had been a bad young man, he would have behaved something after the same fashion that Ernest did, though, of course, actuated by far different motives. He had long been secretly engaged to Dorcas and he knew that Dorcas was to be the heiress of Mrs. Falsetto's property. He had himself witnessed the will. Dorcas was also aware of the circumstance, and it was at Ernest's solicitation that she had consented to live the life of irksome servitude she had endured with the old lady.

"One must make sacrifices, dearest," he had said. "I should never forgive myself were I to cause a rupture between you and Mrs. Falsetto, though nothing in the world would delight me more than to take you away this moment from under her roof."

When Dorcas had suggested that she would prefer to live, however humbly, with him, than to drag on this daily misery, he had silenced her with equally potent arguments.

Now she met him on the stairs.

"Oh! dear Ernest, how I have been counting the moments since I saw you last."

"Why so?" he asked, a little coldly.

She looked up in his face, surprised and hurt. He did not often answer her in such a tone.

"You cannot expect me to be always here. I thought you had more sense than that, Miss Abbot."

"Miss Abbot!" she repeated, faintly. "Ernest, what's the matter? You're vexed with me."

"Vexed! Why should I be? Good-bye: I cannot stay. I have some important business on hand."

"Are you going so—so soon? Without—without——"

"Without what?"

She made no reply, brushed away a tear or two which had sprung up in her eyes, subdued a choking sensation she had felt a moment ago in her throat, then tendered him her hand, cold and formally, as though he were a stranger.

He winced a little at the change; but, making no remark, busied himself with the buttons of his glove as he passed her, then made a bolt of it.

"So far so well!" the good young man muttered to himself, when the door was shut between them. "It must be broken off. I'm glad she takes it so quietly!"

Was he not the pattern of a nephew? The likes and dislikes of an old woman would have had no weight with some young fellows. I'm proud of having such a hero.

Dorcas, left to herself upon the staircase, burst into an uncontrollable flood of tears, and her fair bosom heaved and fell like a tempestuous ocean. It was but momentary—she had been drilled in a stern, hard-hearted school, to act a certain part and hide her real emotions. She went up-stairs slowly to her room, to wash away all traces of her tears—to smooth her braided hair, and pat it down—then she came back as calm and placid, as reserved and silent, as it was her wont to be, only she looked a little sadder, and a few years older; perhaps, a trifle plainer than she had been an hour ago.

The twilight was thickening in Mrs. Falsetto's bed-room. The old woman, propped up in her arm-chair, looked bogy-like, and gaunt, and terrible in the flickering firelight. She called out in a peevish tone,—

"Where have you been all this while? What makes you hide away like this?"

"You told me to go for a walk."

"I did not say you should go out and spend the evening? Do you suppose I keep you here to please yourself?"

"You never led me to suppose so."

"I don't want any of your impertinence. Hold your tongue!"

The other was silent. Then the old lady fretted in her irritability, and poked the fire viciously.

"Am I to sit all night in the dark?" she screamed out in a moment or two.

The companion rang the bell.

"What are you doing that for?"

"For candles."

"How dare you do it? Are you the mistress of the house, or the servant? Are you not my servant?"

"Your slave, Madam, I think."

"You shall be if you eat my bread. I'll have none of your airs here. I'll break your spirit, and your heart too, before I've done with you!"

The servant had not answered the bell, and they were almost in the dark. With a strangely sounding voice, and in deliberate tones, Dorcas Abbot broke the silence.

"I do not care how soon that is," she said. "I've suffered quite enough already. I would not have borne as much—no, nor a half of your mean-spirited tyranny and petty spites, had I not been persuaded so to do."

"You found it to your advantage, I suppose?" the old lady retorted, with a sneer.

"I do not now," said Dorcas, "and I'll leave. Ten years ago, you took me from the parish school. I hardly know what you could have seen in me—a little, sulky, plain-face child. You took me away, as you said, to make a lady of me. A pretty lady! To be your companion, and minister to all your whims and fancies; to be your worse than servant—I've answered at your beck and call like some poor spirited poodle. Enough of it! I should hate myself a hundred times more than I do this moment, were I to live on longer in your service. No, keep your hateful wealth—I'll none of it. Find a fresh favourite, as you have done a dozen times before. Make them your slaves, and leave your money to them. I wish them luck with it!"

She had spoken with such passionate earnestness and energy, although in so subdued a tone, that many of her words were but a hissing whisper, which smote the other's heart with dread.

"You've been listening?" she plucked up spirit to say at last.

"To what?"

"To what I said to Ernest about the will."

"The will!"

The thought that the old lady might have changed her will, and that this might account for the sudden change in Ernest's manner, flashed through Dorcas's mind, and made her for a moment stagger beneath a deadly sickness which crept over her.

"I know nothing about the will," she said, savagely. "If you have changed in favour of some other person, it is only what I would have bidden you do. Had I been benefitted by your death, I might have wished you dead; but, as I'm not, I only wish that you may live, and pray to die. I would not have you lose an hour of your wretched life for all the wealth on earth."

Trembling in every limb with intense passion, standing with curved neck and head erect, and with such a fierce, defiant, scornful look upon her face, this woman, who was at other times sufficiently insignificant and commonplace, grew, under the influence of her evil passions, something grand and awful to look upon. And, as though to heighten the effect, a livid glare of lightning poured through the window full upon her as she left the room, and the noise of the closing door was lost in a deafening crash of thunder, that shook the house to its very foundation.

With a feeble scream for help, the old lady snatched at the bell-rope and rang it violently —so violently that she broke it.

Dimples had gone out for a half-holiday to the play. One of the gentlemen in plush had accompanied her; another was taking the chair at a "sing-song;" and a third—a devil of a "fast" fellow in his way—had gone to spend the evening at the Holborn, and take a little party to supper at Prosser's, where he talked so big, and paid the waiter so liberally that they reckoned him a blood of the first water.

No one was in the house but Mrs. Falsetto, Dorcas, and the cook. The latter was at the top of the house; and so no one heard the lady ringing.

She pulled again and again at the broken wire, in an agony of fright, while the storm seemed to increase in fury every moment.

TWO ARE COMPANY.

CHAPTER THE THIRTY-SECOND.

LIFE AND DEATH.

THE livid glare of the lightning revealed the different objects in the room, the quaintly carved furniture, and the heavy drapery of the bed, giving them grotesque and goblin shapes in the frightened woman's eyes. Most ladies are afraid of a thunderstorm. We have seen how Lady Cheveleigh showed to some disadvantage under such circumstances, but this old lady's plight was pitiable.

A godless old woman, at best; an old scandal-monger, sabbath breaker, and evil doer, from her childhood; brave enough, in all conscience, in the broad daylight; but a dark room and a flash or two of lightning, made a miserable coward of her.

It was an ugly sight to see, and one that did you little good. She lay upon the ground, all creased and tumbled in attire, and every time the thunder broke with deafening din above the house, she shrank, and writhed, and cringed like a lashed hound, in whining, abject terror.

She was too much afraid to get up and draw the blinds down. Her fear was so intense and overwhelming, she had not even power to rise from where she lay, but, trembling in every limb, awaited each succeeding flash with dread anxiety.

While thus she cowered miserably in her

childish terror, Dorcas came back to the room, and, without heeding her in the slightest, began to search upon one of the tables for some object she wished to take away.

"Who is that?" whined the old lady weakly, afraid to turn her head in the direction of the light.

The companion's lip curled in contempt, but she otherwise made no sign of having heard.

"Who's there—who's there?" the old lady cried again. "Why don't you speak?".

The young woman paused in her occupation, and, coming towards the prostrate form of her late mistress, looked down upon her with a sneering smile.

"Who should it be?" she asked. "What do you want?"

"Dorcas!" the old lady cried, clinging to the other's dress, "Dorcas, is it you? Don't leave me! I am so afraid."

"Afraid of what, woman?"

"Of the lightning, Dorcas. Oh, when will it leave off? There—there! Did you see? Pull down the blinds, for God's sake."

The companion looked at her even more contemptuously than before.

"Pull them down yourself," said she, "I'm not your servant."

"Oh, Dorcas, I did not mean to vex you, Dorcas. Do not go away, dear Dorcas. I was too hasty. You know I'm very ill, and say things I don't mean. Dorcas, for the love of heaven, don't go away."

The lightning flared in at the window, the thunder followed instantly upon the flash, and drowned their voices in its vibrating roar. The old woman hid her face again, and clung, with frantic desperation, to the other's skirts, as though there were protection in them against the fury of the storm; but Dorcas shook loose her hold with an angry jerk, and, laughing noiselessly, drew back to look with proud disdain upon the pitiful object at her feet.

"How many times shall we act this farce?" she asked jeeringly. "How many times shall we patch up this endless quarrel? Did you not make me your heiress, a year ago, to spite your relations, and now have cancelled the will to spite me? Let us part. Why should I live with you? I have no interest in your life, or death."

"Oh, don't say that, dear Dorcas: I have always been kind to you, I'm sure. I never meant to leave you penniless—indeed I did not."

"Don't tell lies," the other hissed betwixt her teeth.

"Lies, Dorcas! I tell no lies——Oh, God forgive me!"

A fearful glare of livid light—a loud and sudden crash, which well nigh deafened them, —then screams, and groans, and terror.

The lightning had struck the house.

A fallen stack of chimneys—a gaping hole in the roof — a dead woman in the garret— a hurrying, wondering crowd in the street, and scores of pale, scared faces peeping from the windows of the adjacent houses.

These were the consequences of the blow, and further, a wretched shuddering, babbling, senseless wreck of a woman, rolling her eyes, and frothing at the mouth in all the agonies of epilepsy; and, by her side, upon her knees, another woman tending on her, calling to her, begging and entreating her to hold-up, with a dread anxiety and horror written in her ashy face.

A loud, continuous hammering at the street-door, and the sound of voices, shouting in the street, roused Dorcas from her occupation. Throwing open the window, she looked out.

Policeman, Z 3003, with at his back a mob of tag and rag, and bobtail, was alternately pulling the bell and banging at the knocker like a maniac, while the rest cried fire, and murder, and thieves, nigh loud enough to wake the dead.

"What do you want?" called Dorcas. "What is the matter?"

"Murder's the matter! The lightning has struck the house, and killed the woman at the window!"

She ran down to the street door, and let them in. Then they hurried up-stairs, and found the cook, as the policeman had said, lying dead upon the window-sill.

There was a wild and terrible confusion in the house. The old woman insensible and helpless on the floor of her bed-room—the corpse, black and distorted, in the attic— Dorcas at her wit's-end, scarce knowing what to do, with no one to advise or help her. But she was no namby-pamby Miss: a stern, hard school had taught her firmness and self-reliance. She recovered her senses as rapidly as she had lost them; and, bidding the policeman clear the place of some few prying busy-bodies who had forced an entrance, sent a messenger for the doctor, lifted her mistress into bed, and did what she could for the servant.

That was little enough.

"She's quite dead," said the policeman. "It's no use sending for anyone, in my opinion."

It was sometime before the doctor arrived, for the messenger had fetched Mrs. Falsetto's regular medical attendant, our old friend Bolusout. That gentleman pronounced the servant's case as hopeless, and prescribed some remedies for the mistress. Then some one fetched home the gentleman, who had been taking the chair at a neighbouring public; and the housemaid, who had been out to tea with a lady friend; and when the pretty Dimples returned with a head ache, for the other gentleman had got a little elevated, and behaved rudely to her in the cab coming back, she found the house turned topsy-turvy, everything out of place, and everybody out of temper.

"Oh, dear—oh don't—and oh, 'ow orrible!" the little maid exclaimed, wringing her hands in terror at the description they gave her of the scene. "And Missus too, has had her tantrums, has she?"

"Missus' was very bad, indeed, throughout the night, and little Dimples led a life of it. She had to sit and watch with Dorcas, and so fell asleep, and then fell off her chair and cried, and was very wretched until Miss Abbot bade her go to bed, and sat alone, watching by the old woman's bedside.

"I cannot leave her yet," said Dorcas,

musing, "but when she's well I will. I'll see about it directly. And Ernest——"

Her brow darkened as she mentioned his name.. What could she understand from his conduct? For a year past he had professed the fondest love for her, and she had loved him—loved him so deeply—told it him so often, she blushed with rage and shame at the recollection of her folly.

"He shall give me back my letters and my portrait!"

She had none of his. The good young man had never compromised himself in that respect.

"What can he mean, unless it is her having changed her will? And I to love this man! Oh, what a poor, blind fool I've been! And how I've loved him! Great God! it will break my heart."

It was a trial so sudden, unexpected, and bitterly hard to bear, no wonder if it wrung tears and sobs from this proud woman's breast. She would not for the world that any one had seen her in her misery and weakness, but, panther like, she paced the bedroom floor, and, with set teeth and tightly clenching fingers, griped her throat, as though she would have strangled her sorrow in its birth.

The poor old wreck of sin and folly wriggled in its bed, and moaned, and sighed, and in delirium blabbed its wicked secrets unconsciously. But Dorcas heeded them not. Had she done so, and understood their import, perhaps some of the grief and shame of coming years might have been changed to joy and happiness. Who knows?

CHAPTER THE THIRTY-THIRD.

IN THE HANDS OF THE PHILISTINES.

THIRTY shillings a-week won't buy everything.

I've heard of cases where a person has been put about to live upon so small a sum. But, if that be hard, what must the same person find it when he has to keep two.

In those dear old romances I'm so often talking about, when a man keeps a woman who is not his wife, he does it in a style of lavish extravagance which must quite appal some of you twopenny-halfpenny Giovannis. In real life it's done cheaper. There's no knowing how cheap it may be done until it's tried, a profligate friend of mine told me. I would pump him for particulars were it not encouraging him in his immorality.

Maurice found it rather difficult, because he was extravagant. He thought nothing of salmon at half-a-crown a pound, and asparagus at five shillings a bundle. Then he was astonished how the money went, and uncle Attenborough came into some more of his property.

Foot Court, Holborn, was a fine place for them to live in. It was so handy for shopping—so snug and comfortable; and it was always in difficulties, like they were.

The Court was in a very bad way.

In a very small, mean, shabby way, struggling with overwhelming difficulties, in its desperation it begged and borrowed, slaved, sold, and pawned, striving to procrastinate the dread, inevitable smash. When, hopeless in its endeavours, weary-hearted, callous, and reckless, it gave up the unequal battle, and, adjourning to the kindly shelter of the "Hand and Heart," had a quiet pipe, and drowned its sorrows in the flowing bowl.

Quarter-day had come like a thunder-clap: the landlord's myrmidons held it in their iron grip.

The brokers were in.

At first, the Court was extremely sanguine of immediate settlement. It had lent money to "safe parties," who would pay it for the mere asking; outstanding debts could be easily collected; there was lots of money coming in directly. How provoking that this little accident (the brokers) should have occurred at such a moment! Now, if the Court had had but another week! What was to be done?

There was the hereditary watch, and some little trinkets belonging to the Court's good lady, such as her wedding-ring and guard.

Round the corner there dwell two obliging tradesmen, whose mission in this world of trouble is that of acting the Good Samaritan—with a view, too, of profit to themselves. They are the buoys that the shipwrecked speculator clutches at wildly as he sinks. The hereditary watch, when respectfully submitted to the consideration of one of these gentlemen, was, oddly enough, considerably undervalued by him. The Court having taken a half of what it had expected, and a fourth of what it had asked, departed rejoicing, with the money and ticket. The mockery of taking a ticket had been gone through, though really such a proceeding was almost superfluous, seeing that the pledge would be redeemed in a few hours at furthest. So the Court had the watch put somewheres handy, that it might be taken away directly. Alas! it never was redeemed.

There was once upon a time, within my recollection, a great, straggling, over-grown stuccoed tavern, upon the outskirts of a new unbuilt neighbourhood, which was to be let. There was also an energetic young man, of a singularly sanguine turn of mind, who took it. He furnished it, and decorated it splendidly. The minutest details of its arrangements were not over-looked. A Sunday was fixed upon for its opening; and at early dawn, the energetic landlord, and a still more energetic pot-boy, were seen carrying benches into the back garden, to accommodate the (anticipated) public. Somehow the carts carried the public past the door without stopping. About the middle of the afternoon it came on to rain, so the landlord and the pot-boy brought the benches in-doors again; and the rain poured down, and the carts drove past until nightfall, when, I believe, the energetic young man put up the shutters, and hanged himself in the bar-parlour. They christened the public-house "The Forlorn Hope:" and it is to let. It put me very much in mind of Foot Court.

The Court continued to remain in a very bad way. Quarter-Day had passed over somehow, and the brokers bought out somehow; but a vast amount of personal property had been sunk round the corner. The outstanding debts stood out still, and did not look so promising. The safest of the safe parties had "acted shabby." Credit looked on sternly, with its breeches-pockets tightly buttoned up.

I fear me there is but little moral to be gathered from the sad court history. I have been telling you. From the endlessbread struggles of its inmates; from the famished tailor, with the sickly wife who works day and night, Sunday and week-day, at the garret-window; from the publican, smiling faintly upon the unliquidated chalks behind the bar; from the all-sorts' shop, which is to let, and the ghostly shutters, which are up; rfom any of the poor dull people who can't get over their difficulties, who are always in a bad way, what lesson does it all teach? That "Men must work and women must weep." That life is hard, very hard for some of our poor brothers, "and the sooner 'tis over, the sooner to sleep." God help them!

———

CHAPTER THE THIRTY-FOURTH.

SHYLOCK.

BUT, to go back to the thirty-shilling question.

My publisher, an arbitrary man, who seldom relaxes in his stern demeanour towards me, except at those pleasant little dinners at his cottage in Putney (how is it he has not asked me lately?), says peremptorily,—

"No descriptions."

I own that it is a capital rule to go by, but it makes your story a little unintelligible. I never yet have had a fair chance given me of explaining who's who; for no sooner does my stern employer see a long nice paragraph beginning with "It is now some forty years ago," or, "the sun was slowly sinking," when out goes the paragraph with a dash of his pen, and my humble lodging is beset by desperate boys, who smite their breasts, and call aloud for "copy."

I ought to have told you long ago that Maurice had left the Bad Bargains—had spent his quarter's salary, and run into debt.

"How the deuce am I to live?" he used to say to himself sometimes.

He wrote home to his mother for small sums of money, and borrowed a pound or two of his friends. Uncle Attenborough supplied the rest.

He had a tolerable allowance from home, but this he had spent. There was a faint hope of his getting on again at the Bad Bargains, but that would not be yet awhile. He was heir to Skearcrows, and would be well off some day, but until then how was he to keep the pot boiling?

There was only one way—Shylock. He consulted Mr. Bux about it.

"What am I to do, Charley?"

"Do a bill."

"But I shall have to meet it."

"Don't."

"What shall I do then?"

"Renew it."

"They won't stand that for ever though."

"Time enough to grumble when they refuse."

This was a very jolly, devil-me-care sort of philosophy, which pleased Mr. Maurice immensely. But he had read in novels some very queer accounts of doings with moneylenders.

"I shall have to take a lot of bad wine and rubbishing pictures, shan't I?" said he, after a little hesitation.

"Nonsense! You'll get it in hard cash. All you want is a security."

"But I haven't got one."

"Ah, well," said Mr. Bux, "that's awkward certainly. However, I can help you. I want a little of the ready myself, and, if you like, we'll do it together."

Wasn't that kind of Mr. Bux? Jack Ochre, who, of course, must put the worst construction upon his generous offer, hinted that probably Mr. Bux was not sorry to get a new hand to help him with his little kites; and he advised Maurice to have nothing to do with it.

"But that's all very fine," said Maurice; "what's to be done? I can't go without my dinners, and there's Nelly wants a new dress, and she can't walk in rags to the theatre. A fine bone that would be for those wretched cads to pick, wouldn't it?" The cads were the second-rate people over whose heads Mrs. Nelly had jumped.

While these thoughts were agitating her lover's mind, my yellow-haired heroine took things pretty comfortably. I never knew a woman improve so with her circumstances, though it is much more easy for a woman than a man to get rid of vulgar habits and associations.

She was truly a magnificent creature. You would have taken her for a duchess, had you seen her sailing down the Court in that *moire antique* of hers, and that ermine cloak. The poor, shabby people stared at her. The matrimonial interest of the Court—mothers who had great, gaunt, ugly daughters on their hands, turned up their noses at her, you may be sure, and were sarcastic. If she had been a plain, vulgar person, like themselves, they wouldn't have noticed her; but she was a beauty you couldn't put down or pass over. If the women had ignored her, the men wouldn't. And it was rather fine to see how careful some of the goodwives were of their husbands in her presence, as though she were a kind of spider lying in wait for them; when, all the while, in her magnificent pride and haughtiness, she was utterly unconscious of the wretched creatures' existence, and passed them by like dirt.

When Maurice had made up his mind to do a kite, he called upon his friend Charley Bux, and they talked matters over. First of all, Mr. Bux wrote to a gentleman who discounted, to ask whether he would do business with them; and, a favourable answer having been received, they set out together.

Shylock lived at a pretty little cottage, at Highgate. A sweet, innocent, little, stuccoed house, with a little grass plot, surrounded by big poppies and pansies.

When the young men got there, Shylock was out; and a little innocent maid, who answered them, did not seem to know whether she should ask them in, or slam the door in their faces. So she did neither; but, opened her mouth like a little fish, and gasped at them.

While they were hesitating what to do, a little pony dragged a little gig up to the garden-gate; and, a little chubby man inside, called out,—"Wo!" and jerked the reins. Then the little maiden ran out to help them, and, seizing the little pony by the head, struggled with, and overcame it, eventually bearing it and the little basket-carriage off in triumph.

Which, having been done, the chubby little man, who, when he took his hat off, turned out to have no hair under it, came forward and bowed, and shook hands with Mr. Bux; then ran away to bawl out to the little maid, not to give the pony any corn, as it was already a deal too frisky.

After this, Shylock came back, and ushered the young men into his counting-house.

It was the snuggest little counting-house imaginable—full of neatly bound books, and tastefully labelled boxes. There were, also, a sleepy bullfinch in a cage, two fat, sleepy fish in a bowl, and a concertina and flute upon a side-board.

"Very fine weather for the time of year?" said Shylock, rubbing his hands together. "Beautiful down at Brighton!"

"Is it, sir?" said Cheveleigh, anxious to conciliate him.

"Splendid!" Shylock replied. "I took Mrs. S. and the little ones down there on Saturday. Heavenly!"

Here he raised his leg, and rocked himself to and fro, lost in pleasant recollections of connubial felicity.

"Did you get my letter, sir?" asked Mr. Bux, at the end of five minutes, deeming it wise to open the business.

"Your letter? Oh, yes—I got it. Certainly.

"Can you—ahem—manage the little affair?" stammered Mr. Bux.

Maurice was on tenter hooks.

"Well, yes, I think we can," said Shylock, rubbing his chin, thoughtfully, though he was evidently thinking of his family at Brighton, instead of the little bill. "Three months?" he said, inquiringly, as he began to fill up an oblong piece of paper, with a stamp in the corner.

"Six?" suggested Maurice.

"Six?" repeated Shylock, without changing a muscle. "Fifty pounds for six months. Sign your names there; and, you may as well put your addresses."

They signed their names eagerly. While they were doing so, Shylock unlocked the safe, and counted out the money as unconcernedly as though he were giving them change for sixpence.

With a quickly beating pulse, Maurice picked up the notes and sovereigns which fell to his share, and thrust them into a pocket of his pegtops.

Shylock took no notice of them; but mount-ing on a chair, began whistling and chirruping to his bullfinch. When they had got outside the house, and were shutting-to the garden-gate, a soothing melody smote sweetly on their ears. It was Shylock playing "Home, sweet home," upon his flute.

As they were leaving the garden, a gentleman passing by, turned round to look at them, and stopped to speak. He was a queer-looking man, with long bony hands, and large dog-like teeth. He wore spectacles, and, had a curious habit of twitching his mouth.

"Hallo! Mr. Hadget," said Maurice, rather confused. "I didn't know you were in town."

"Just come," said Hadget. "What are you doing here?"

He glanced towards Shylock's bright door-plate as he spoke. Maurice coloured up.

"A little bit of stiff, eh?" continued Mr. Hadget, smiling. "Pay dear for it here. You should have asked me?"

"I would if I'd known of it!" retorted Maurice,

So they shook hands and parted.

On his way home, Maurice changed the notes, and flung the twenty-five sovereigns into Nelly's lap.

"Oh, my gracious!" cried the lady, "where on earth did you get them from?"

"Never mind, young woman: you can buy your new frock, anyhow," he said, playfully. It happened that Nelly only acted in the first piece that night, and, as it was a very short one, she had finished by eight o'clock. The young couple, therefore, came up to town, and had supper at the "Cafe de l'Europe," where they regaled themselves upon the choicest delicacies, and afterwards had some further refreshment at Mrs. Hamilton's,—thereby making a big hole in two sovereigns.

One of the Bad Bargains' men said, next day, to another,—

"Do you recollect a man called Maurice Cheveleigh?"

"Man in this office, wasn't he?"

"Yes; man who got sacked lately."

"To be sure. What of him?"

"He's going the pace, I think. Saw him at Kate's yesterday, with a woman who must have cost him a million."

"No!"

"'Pon my honour. Splendid creature, with the most beautiful hair!"

Lord Drawley met Charley Bux upon the steps of the "Rag and Famish."

"Know a man called Cheveleigh?" asked his lordship.

"Yaas—I've seen him."

"Devilish fast, isn't he?"

"In the hands of the Jews, I believe."

"Has he got any money?"

"Expects some."

"Hope he'll get it."

Some one else met Mr. Letchery, the editor.

"I saw Maurice Cheveleigh the other day," said this person, "and with such a terrific swell woman. Does he keep her?"

"Keep her!" replied Letchery, with a laugh; "more likely she keeps him. He's her fancy man."

CHAPTER THE THIRTY-FIFTH.

SMILES AND WILES.

THOSE twenty-five pounds did not last for ever.

You might have expected as much when I told you about the "Cafe de l'Europe" and Mrs. Hamilton's. Then there was a splendid black silk dress; and that isn't bought for nothing, young man, as you will find to your cost, if Cleopatra gets you inside the draper's.

Maurice was hard-up again. His boots wanted mending, but he did not send them. One or two people called with their bills, and gave the Bony handmaiden a bit of their mind with regard to Cheveleigh's habits of procrastination.

"Get along, Mr. Imperence!" cried the Bony-one indignantly. "Leave your nasty bills with me, and I'm sure the gentleman will send the dirty money. Do you think he's going to run away?"

Poor creature! she had the strongest possible faith in Mr. Maurice. He was the grandest gentleman she had ever heard of, and Nelly came up to and surpassed the wildest flights of her imagination with regard to what a lady should be.

But Maurice got harder-up. There was not so much as three-and-ninepence for a pair of new gloves for Nelly. Things were getting serious, and Nelly thought matters over seriously till she fell asleep that evening, and dreamt that she was a princess.

"Jack," said she, next night.

This was almost the first time she had spoken to him since that day she sat down among the paint pots.

"Jack, you don't come and see us lately."

"You're never at home."

"Yes, I am, on Sundays—that is to say, nearly always. Besides, Maurice is there other nights."

"He's generally here, I thought."

So he was. When the manager objected to his being behind the scenes, he took to paying for his admission, and went in front, sitting out the performance, night after night, with the stoical indifference of the chairman at a music hall.

"Well, Maurice will be at home next Sunday. Will you come?"

"With pleasure."

"Don't forget, now. I will rely on you."

That Jack always set Nelly down for a selfish hussy: I think he was wrong.

It is we men who are always cringing, truckling, and abasing ourselves before mammon. You women don't. You often enough fly in the face of your own interests for the man you love—often enough, out of spite, quarrel with your own bread and butter; when man—sordid-souled man—would have stifled the affections and smothered the anger which could interfere with his interests. You, Madam, never trot out your daughter with a halter round her neck, bidding her frisk, and prance, and show her paces, then sell her to the highest bidder. You, Miss, never, on your own account, when the snaffle is on, frisk and prance, leer and ogle; you never prattle artlessly and look pretty, and interesting, and unconscious; never flourish your small accomplishments, jingle over your two or three old tunes upon the piano—chirp, in that small voice of yours, quivering like a reed in a gale of wind, all those old songs you used to sing to the one before the last of your admirers. You never do all this to get married, to get well settled, to get out of mamma's rule, to have a palace and slaves of your own. You never act a tiring part, smiling a weary smile, working harder than the hardest-worked actress upon the stage to please my lord with the money-bags. Oh, no: ingenuous, artless creatures, ever to be wronged and maligned by the inferior animal!

When Sunday came, Mr. Ochre put on what he thought to be his most becoming waistcoat (a terrible thing, with sprigs), and walked himself off to Foot Court.

The room was nice and tidy—the tea-things were set, and Mrs. Cheveleigh, in the most bewitching of merino dresses, sat in the window-seat, pretending to read a French novel. I don't believe she knew enough of the language, though she had a lot of little phrases at her tongue's-end, having picked them up, somehow, from a French lodger in her father's house. The sun was setting over the court chimney-pots, bathing Nell's head in ruddy light. She looked very beautiful.

"Ah, Jack! This is very kind of you," she said, rising from her seat, with a bewitching smile, and laying down the "Dame aux Camellias."

She came forward and took his hat, drew an arm-chair for him to the fire-side, and, sitting down at his feet upon a footstool, with the same graceful ease that I have seen Miss Herbert, at the Olympic, sit down, in "Uncle Zachary," began to toast a muffin.

There was another muffin besides the one she toasted, and that was Jack!

"It's very cold," he said.

"Do you think so? Draw closer."

"No, thank you: I'm near enough."

A pause—in which the muffin having been browned on one side, was turned over, and began upon the other.

"You didn't expect me, I see?"

"Why?"

"Because there are only two cups!"

"How many should there be?"

"Well, isn't Maurice coming?"

"No."

"No—why you said——"

"Yes, I know I did. He'll be here presently. Don't be afraid."

He looked so very blank, she thought, at first, he was going to run away.

"How long have you known Maurice, Jack?"

"About ten years."

"As long as that!"

"We went to school together. I don't believe in school friendship as a rule; but Maurice and I have been good friends enough."

"Who could help being good friends with you, Jack? You are so good, and kind, and considerate."

"Shall I fill the teapot?"

"Yes, thank you. That will do nicely! Have you ever had a sweetheart, Jack?"

"Not that I've heard of."

"There you go again. There's no talking seriously with you!"

"But who wants to talk seriously?"

"I do! Answer me. Did you ever have a sweetheart?"

"What do you mean?"

"Were you ever in love?"

"I don't think so."

"But, then, some one must have been in love with you!"

"I don't see that?"

"I'm sure of it. You are just the sort of man I can imagine a woman falling violently in love with. I don't mean such love as you find at the street-corner; but a real passion—a passion which holds such dominion over a woman as to cause her to throw up home and friends, position, good name, everything for the man who is the object of it."

"Do you want some more water for the teapot?"

What do you say to a man who could be thinking of a teapot at such a juncture?

"No," said Nelly, and was silent for awhile.

"When is Maurice coming home?" asked Ochre.

"I don't know—presently, I believe. I seem to be very bad company."

Then came another interval of silence.

"Do you know anything of Maurice's affairs, Mr Ochre?" Nelly began again, when the tea was over, and she had placed the tobacco before her visitor, and handed him a light.

"About his affairs?"

"Yes. Do you know whether he is much in debt?"

"I should have thought you knew best. I believe he is."

"I don't think there is any prospect of his getting another situation. Is there?"

"Not much, I should think."

"What will he do then? Will his father give him a sufficient allowance to live upon?"

"That depends how he lives."

"You mean to say he won't be able to keep me?"

"Not in very fine style."

"It's very lucky I am able to earn my own living, isn't it Jack?"

"Yes."

"If I couldn't, I should be a great burthen to him."

"Suppose you lose your engagement?"

"No chance of that!"

"I don't know."

"Why, what do you mean, Jack? Have you heard—who has said—what is it?"

"It mayn't be true!"

"What mayn't? Speak, Jack?"

"Well, I've heard that Miss Fleshings has made it up with Bullyrag."

"Will he take her back?"

"I should think it very likely."

"But, then, I take better with the audience. Oh, he couldn't do it!"

"He will, though. He told me as much, in confidence."

Nelly was silent—tears of rage, and disappointment, and mortification filled her eyes.

"How is it *that* woman has such influence over him?" she said, at last.

"You know best how you ladies manage: Bullyrag admires the sex."

"The odious wretch! He's often come bowing and scraping up to me. I didn't understand him."

"He's easily won by a pretty face. Such a one as yours would do his business directly."

"It seems it hasn't."

"That's your fault."

She was silent a long while, dried her tears prettily with the corner of her lace-edged handkerchief, and sat musing, with her eyes fixed upon the fire, and her foot patting the fender. She smiled a little now and then, and her lips moved as though she were rehearsing something.

Mr. Ochre watched her slily from behind his book, and seemed to be enjoying himself.

"Bless me!" cried Nelly, starting up at the end of an hour; "it's nine o'clock, I declare. I don't think Maurice will come at all."

"Won't he? Then I'll be off. I have to call somewhere."

"Have you?" cried she, in a hurry. "Good-bye. Here's your hat. Can you find your way out?"

"Yes, thank you. Good night, Nelly."

"Good night, Mr. Ochre."

She just touched his hand with hers. There was no warmth in the pressure, and no smile upon her face. He might have been a perfect stranger.

As for Mr. Ochre, he walked down-stairs, smiling all the way.

"It was rather too bad," said he; "but she deserved it. A shameful hussy. Besides, she can never find out it was my invention. At least, she isn't likely to ask Bullyrag. I wonder what she'll do. Make love to him, I dare say, instead of to his scene-painter. Hallo, Maurice!"

He ran against Mr. Cheveleigh at the corner, by the "Hand and Heart."

"Hallo, Jack! Have you been to my place?"

"Just come away."

"Ah, I told Nelly I shouldn't be home to-night, but I've managed to get back sooner than I expected."

"Oh!" said Ochre.

"Well, you'll come in again, Jack?"

"No, thank you. I'm in a hurry. Good-night!"

Maurice left him, and ran up-stairs. Nelly had her shawl and bonnet on.

"Why, Maurice!" she cried, with a start "Law, how you frightened me! How did you get away? Oh, I'm so glad you've come back."

"Were you going out?"

"No: I've just come in."

"I thought Jack had been here?"

"Jack—yes. Did you meet him?"

"I only just spoke to him. He said he'd been here," Maurice replied, carelessly.

"Did he say anything else?"

"No. Why?"

He looked into her clear blue eyes. She looked into his, then kissed him.

"Oh, Maurice, such an awful misfortune has befallen us."

"Good God! what is it?"

"Oh, Maurice, my engagement—I have lost it. That wretch, Fleshings —— " And she finished the sentence in sobs.

"What is to become of us? I could get nothing out of the old woman——"

"Your aunt?"

"Yes. She's very ill. She saw me for a moment only."

"But something must turn up."

"A good many things have turned me up," said Maurice, ruefully.

"Won't your family do something for you? They know how you are situated——"

"That's just what they don't know; and they can't understand why I don't go there, if I'm hard-up. It's not unnatural, is it?"

"You might say that you couldn't leave town, as you must be on the spot, should you hear of another appointment."

"Oh, woman, always ready at an excuse."

"To screen those we love," suggested Nell.

"And you love me, then, dear Nelly?"

"Love you, Maurice! Would I have done what I have, did I not love you?"

"No—no, my own dear girl!" he cried, in raptures; and further nonsense to that effect.

She had taken off her bonnet and shawl, and now stood by him, playing with his curly hair and patting him upon the head, as though he were a little boy.

She loved to pet and patronise him in this way; but not so much in private, as before company. As for Maurice, nothing pleased him more than to run about after her, and to obey her orders, then take a pat on the head in payment.

Their little love scene was interrupted by a slight cough behind them; and, turning round quickly, Nelly saw a gentleman standing in the doorway. Maurice had left the door open behind him, and the gentleman had come up-stairs so sliding and noiselessly, they had not heard him.

"Ahem!" said he.

There is reason to suppose that the gentleman intended to be smiling; but there was such a funny cast in his eyes, and he had such large teeth, it was very difficult for him to look pleasant if he tried to. And even when he got up a kind of apology for a good-natured grin, a hasty twitch caught the corner of his mouth, and spoilt it.

One of Mr. Hadget's oddities, was to come upon people unawares, in a cat-like fashion, appearing suddenly at their side, like a man in goloshes comes upon you in a fog, without a single creak of warning.

"Aha!" he added. "Excuse me if I interrupt—I know I do. It's very rude of me. I'm certain I'm intruding."

If he was certain of it, it was strange that he should shut the door behind him, place his hat upon a chair, and otherwise make preparations for staying longer.

"Mr. Cheveleigh, I hope I find you well? You see I've found you out!"

"Yes," replied Maurice, not very cordially.

"I thought you would have looked *me* up before this. Lyon's Inn, you know. It's not far off."

"Thank you—thank you," returned Maurice, a little more politely. "I wanted to speak to you. I'm frightfully hard-up."

"You don't mean it, my dear boy! How's that? I beg your pardon, you haven't introduced me to the lady."

"Mr. Hadget—Mrs. Cheveleigh."

Nelly, who had returned to her book, bowed coldly to the gentleman, and went on reading.

"Lovely creature!" said Mr. Hadget, in a stage whisper. "You've got more taste than the governor."

Maurice Cheveleigh took no notice of this little joke; but that didn't hinder Mr. Hadget from laughing at it in his own peculiar fashion.

"By the way, you haven't heard from Sir John?" said Mr. Hadget, carelessly.

"Heard from him? No."

"Oh, haven't you?" said Hadget, looking a little astonished. "Well, I must be off again; I'M GOING TO BRIGHTON IN HALF-AN-HOUR?"

It was very singular that he should now have changed his intention about stopping, for he certainly seemed as though he had made up his mind to stay much longer a minute or two ago. The host, however, did not press him to remain.

He was full of his oddities again to-night. He went down the stairs twitching and mouthing as usual, gesticulating also, and talking to himself.

As he passed the Perks' servant, crouching in a dark corner, where she had gone to sleep, being expelled the genteel society of her sister up-stairs, he was talking loud enough for he to hear.

"With a twist of the wrist," he said. "That's how it's managed. Simple enough, when you know how it's done."

"What the Dickings is he a talking on?" said the Perks' servant to herself. "What a nasty-looking man, and got a twist in his wrist. He's hurt hisself, I suppose. Lor! it give me the horribles to think of him."

She looked so wild and scared when she came up-stairs, that Nelly asked her whether she had seen a ghost.

"I don't know, mum, what I've seen, or what I've heerd. Don't ask me."

"Look here, Maurice," said Nelly, taking up a pen, "here's a picture of Miss Perks, as she appeared after having seen the ghost of her great-grandmother's uncle. Isn't it like her?"

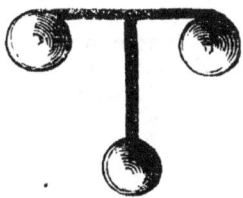

A BACK-HANDER.

CHAPTER THE THIRTY-SIXTH.

AS I told you, Maurice had been to see his aunt. It was a long while since he had paid the old lady a visit. Two, or three of Dorcas's notes remained at that time unanswered, stuck round his looking-glass at No. 7.

the court. The fact was, that the yellow-haired woman engrossed all his attention. Poor simpleton! he fancied that he was her master, when he was nothing but her slave. All through her life men have fallen down and worshipped her, thrust their foolish noddles 'neath her chariot wheels, and worn her livery unrepiningly.

What an awful difference between her life and that of the Perks' simple handmaiden! One was nature's queen, a woman born to be an empress; the other a poor, red-nosed noodle, who'd never had a sweetheart.

I do not believe that any one in the world ever had such a devoted admirer as Nelly had in this simple creature. When she had been one night to the play, and seen Nelly, dressed as a princess, glittering with tinsel and sham jewellery, she came away half stupified. I don't think she understood or heard one single word of the performance, but sat wide-mouthed, and banged her great hands together so long and loudly, that a party behind knocked her on the head with the nozzle of his umbrella to bring her to order, and she narrowly escaped being put out.

But, to go back to Maurice. When he found himself upon Mrs. Falsetto's door-step, with the bell-pull in his hand, he felt more than half inclined to run away again—he was so much ashamed of himself. What excuse could he make? He was a young man with the very best intentions : if he had only done half the good acts he had thought of doing, there would have been some pleasure in writing his history. But he didn't.

Plucking up courage to ring the bell, he rang with a jerk, and disturbed one of the gentlemen in plush, eating some pie in the passage.

"She is dangerously ill, sir," the gentleman made answer, putting on a doleful countenance, and trying to look as though he had got nothing in his mouth.

"I cannot see her, then, I suppose——Ah, Miss Abbot."

As he was turning on his heel, he caught sight of Dorcas coming down-stairs, and stepped forward to meet her. When she first caught sight of him her face flushed, and her heart beat faster, but, calming herself, with a great effort she came forward and placed her hand in his, with the old sweet smile playing on her lips.

"Maurice, I thought you were never coming any more. Have you, too, been ill ?"

"No—that is, yes—a little," Maurice stammered, blushing to his ears, for he was at best but a clumsy deceiver ; "and I have been in the country."

"I thought you had returned some time ago. Your cous——that is, I was told that you had."

"Is my aunt very ill ?" asked Maurice, with a pang of remorse. The old lady had been very kind to him in days gone by. She had often pressed him to come and see her, but he had found no time in the wild and witless life he had led before he met Miss Nelly, and since then he had not been his own master.

When he and Ernest were lads, and Dorcas was a little plain-faced girl, they had often played together. It had been a sort of joke in those times to say that Dorcas was to be Ernest's wife, because they were two such sober-sided old fogies ; but Maurice was not a favoured swain, he was so rough and noisy. When they grew up, Dorcas had come to look upon Maurice as a brother, as she began to consider Ernest her affianced husband ; and Maurice, who was a good-hearted young fellow in spite of his thousand faults, had always treated her with the greatest kindness, though he had never had an idea of making love to her.

Thus was it that the falseness of one cousin made her heart yearn, as it were, towards the other.

"Your aunt has been very ill. She was frightened by that dreadful thunder-storm we had a month ago. She took to her bed, and has not left it since."

"Has Ernest called here lately ?"

"He has called every day. I have not seen him."

"Not seen him, Dorcas : how is that ?"

"We've quarrelled."

"Quarrelled !" repeated Maurice, in astonishment.

Then Dorcas described the interview she had had with Ernest—how his manner had changed after he heard of the alteration in his aunt's will—how she had determined to treat him at their next meeting, as though nothing had occurred between them, hoping that she might have been mistaken—and how s e found that, alas ! her suspicions were but too true, that he, indeed meant to jilt her.

"The scoundrel !" cried Maurice, whose strong point was constancy.

"Oh, dear, Maurice," she cried, "I had never thought to have told you this. It makes me hate and despise myself to know I am so weak. But what am I to do ? I have never known any one so like a brother, as you are to me ; and is it wrong that I should tell my brother my grief. Oh, dear, dear Maurice, how could I be so deceived, so blind, so mad, —to love him so ?"

"Don't speak of him any more," the young man replied. "He's too mean and contemptible to think about."

"Dear Maurice, I have none left but you. You will be always my friend, I'm sure. You have never treated me as a servant, l ke these pe ple here treat me every day. I cannot show you how much I love you, Maurice, for your goodness to me, because I am a stupid, stumbling creature, and never find the words that I would speak when I have found the opportunity. You, like the rest, must have thought me sulky and proud. I never felt a mother's love, nor had a mother's care. Brought up by hard blows and harder words, they turned me out a little churly, unkempt cub. It was my very ugliness and uncouth manner which tickled my mistress's fancy, and she took it into her head to keep me. Oh ! I am a sinful, wicked woman, I know, and sit and nurse my evil thoughts, though every night I pray to God to change my heart. Is it strange that Ernest should tire of me, for what is there in me that he could love ?"

He tried to soothe her troubled spirit with kind words. He forgot his debts and difficulties in the awakening interest and pity he felt for her. He hated himself for his own happiness and selfish love. The same regretful feelings rose up in his heart which the sight of his sick mother in that lonely room in Skearcrows had caused him when he looked in that night, and found her on her knees in tears.

For half a second of time a thought of Nelly's worthlessness, a suspicion of her falseness, the faintest shadow of a weariness and distaste for her society, crept over him, and—was dismissed as quickly.

The twilight thickened in the room ; and, the freshly-lighted lamp without, shone full upon their faces, while all behind them lay in deep shade. The evening was soft and mild, although it was winter time ; and the window stood open. The Sunday street was very still, only the murmur of the distant traffic broke the silence. They stood and watched the lamps spring into life, as the man went on his way, and talked together almost in whispers.

She begged him to tell her how he was getting on; and he described his difficulties briefly, withholding the cause, of course. While they were yet engaged in conversation, the hours flew by, and it was only the violent ringing of the old lady's bell which at last disturbed them, and reminded Maurice how long he had been there.

Hastily bidding her good night, and promising to call again soon, he took his departure.

He had intended to spend the evening at the rooms of Mr. Bux, who was giving a card-party, but a sudden distaste for men's society caused him to turn his steps homewards.

Oh! Nelly, Nelly, your throne trembled—a chance word might have cast your crown into the dust. But it was not to be. She met him with a smile, and patted the young fellow's head. All his scruples, and fine resolves, and moral sentiments were scattered to the winds. There was in the world but one glorious, golden-haired goddess, whose abject slave he was then and for ever.

Next day the Cheveleighs were truly hard-up. Early in the morning Mr. Maurice took the clean sheets round the corner, and brought back a couple of shillings instead of them. "That won't last long," thought he. Indeed, there was not much change out of them, when some tea, sugar, bread, butter, and eggs had been purchased. The salary Nelly had received on Saturday had mostly gone in a new pair of kid boots, and some other little necessaries she required, and there was not much more than enough for her cab fare to the theatre in the evening left out of it.

"It's a beautiful morning. I think I shall go a walk," said she.

"Do, dearest," replied her lover, helping her with her shawl, and buttoning her beautifully-fitting gloves. "You'll excuse me, I know. I must write some letters."

It was very provoking that he always wanted to be doing something else when she asked him to go out with her, the pretty woman said, pouting, and left him in a little pet.

When he was alone, he sat down to think. He saw no way out of his difficulties unless his father or his aunt helped him.

"It must end some day," he said aloud. "What a selfish wretch I am, to expect her to live with me in this shabby misery. She, who could command wealth and position. A beautiful woman! a splendid actress! It's preposterous. What am I to do?"

He thought of his razors, lying snugly in their velvet case, and tried the lock of a pistol, hanging on the wall; then opened the window, and, looking down below upon the flag-stones, wondered whether the fall would be sure to kill him.

Leaning out thus, a horrible sort of feeling crept over him, and he with difficulty managed to tear himself from the window and shut it down, then paced the room in thought.

Something must turn up, or else——

It made him hot and cold to think of his position. He turned out the drawers, and looked out everything that he had remaining pawnable, turned out some of the old duplicates too, and found that one or two referring to articles he had pledged a year ago, when he wanted the money for a lark, had run out, and were lost.

When he had looked up all his traps, and put them together in a little heap, he sat down and contemplated them.

"They won't come to much," he said, mournfully. "I don't think they'll take those dress boots in."

He made the lot into a parcel.

"Nobody would believe it," said he to himself when, after a feint or two, he had managed to get into the pawnbroker's unobserved. "If my swell friends were only to know it. By the Lord, there's no doubt in the matter, I'm going to the bad. Have the kindness to make it as much as you can, Mr. Popham?"

CHAPTER THE THIRTY-SEVENTH.

A BACK-HANDER.

A CORRESPONDENT, who appears to be wise in such matters, writes to inform me that there is no such regiment as the 8th Dragoon Guards, to which I said my Lord Drawler belonged. I'm much obliged to him, but I knew it before. Neither was there ever a lady called Falsetto; or a theatre called the Apollo, that I know of. And Nelly's real name is not Nelly any more than mine is. Bless your dear innocence, don't you see, it's a little joke of mine. I should like, if possible, to avoid an action for libel, supposing you have no objection.

I don't even think that the name of DRAWLER is to be found in the Peerage. If it is—it must be on the same page with Lady CLARA CAVENDISH, Lady ESTHER HOPE, and that branch of the female aristocracy.

Well, what does it matter what I call them, so that I manage to interest you with my characters. Some people have even suggested that the author's name should be affixed to this story; but would it make it any more interesting if BULWER, THACKERAY, PIERCE EGAN, or even Mr. ERRYM's stared at you, in large caps, from my title page? I dare say I shall print my name some day, and, a beautiful portrait, by one of the best artists, not at all like me.

For my part, I contend that author and reader should never be brought face to face. I have not believed half so much in the poet Tomkins since I have known him intimately, and seen him gobbling his knife at dinner with his peas.

At present you, no doubt, picture me with a manly form, a massive brow, and a fine intellectual cast of countenance. Would you be happier, or like my tale a whit the better, did I let you into the dread secrets of my dressing-room?—tell you where I buy these auburn curls? and that these glistening teeth are only my own by right of purchase? Would you have me come before you with a bare pate, shrunken shanks, and toothless gums? No, no! imagine your author what you like; but don't go look at him—it spoils the poetry. He pulls the springs and makes his puppets jump and squeak for your amusement. Don't forget him when he sends round his battered beaver. Put as much as you like into it, but never mind making his acquaintance.

"I say Bux," Lord Drawler said, one day. They were smoking a cigar at his lordship's bow-windowed room in Piccadilly. "How can a fellow get through the evening?"

"Damned if I know," replied the other guardsman. "Can't do it in your chairs."

"I didn't ask you, that's one thing."

"The sofa isn't much account," continued Mr. Bux, musingly. "I had a horrible time of it last night, I can tell you. There's something the matter with its springs."

"There's one broken, I think."

"Yes, I noticed one particularly. It had me between the shoulders. I shan't sleep on it again yet awhile, if I know it."

When they had smoked awhile in silence, Drawler continued,—

"What do you say to looking up some of the second-rate theatres? We might have some fun at them. They are queer places, if what those writing fellows say is true."

"What do you think of the Victoria?"

"Yes, that's the sort. A penny admission, isn't it? Whereabouts is it?—do you know?"

"I havn't the least idea; but we can get into a hansom and be driven there."

"By the way, I saw an account of a place called the Apollo, the other day, in one of the papers, and they seemed to have some choice company. Do you suppose we could get behind the scenes?"

"If we pay for it, I should think. Gold is the latch-key to virtue, eh?"

"I've always found it so. Light another weed, and come along."

"By the way," said Bux, "there's a man I know, called Letchery, who's editor of the *Thirsty Soul.*"

"Licensed victuallers' organ, I suppose?"

"No—a religious paper! He's a queer dog. We'll take him with us."

So they picked up Mr. Letchery, whom they found asleep over some gin-and-water, and his last leader in the editor's sanctum. He was a little startled and much gratified by the introduction to the "toff," as he was pleased to term his lordship, and ever afterwards spoke of him as "my friend, Drawler."

"Have you ever seen this little print, my lord?" said Letchery, improving the opportunity, and submitting that week's *Thirsty Soul* to his lordship's notice.

"No, I can't say I have," Drawler replied, in a tone of voice which would have led one to suppose that he hardly intended to become a subscriber. "High Church is it?"

"Low Church, my lord. Nothing like the Low to pay; can't very well be too Low to please the million. Pitching into the purse-proud priests, brazen images, and all that sort of thing, brings the house down."

They were soon upon their way to the Apollo," and shortly afterwards found themselves, under Mr. Letchery's escort, deep in the mysteries of "behind the scenes."

Now, I dare say, Miss, you think I'm going to be very naughty. It is a shocking place at the back of that green curtain, is it not? And all actresses are shameful women? So the world says. The "Pot-house Pioneer" says just the opposite, and I believe neither of them. You can't talk generally without talking nonsense; any more than you can say all French are monkeys, and all Germans pigs. There is a pretty good sprinkling of angels and devils in all countries.

I don't know whether it is the same with most people, but I was very much disappointed when a fast friend of mine took me "round." He took me round, and left me. I wandered about helplessly, and broke my shins against woodwork, and got wedged tightly into corners. In the course of my wanderings I wandered into a place they call "the green-room." I don't mind owning that I was glad when I got out again. They don't receive a stranger kindly. From thence I meandered I don't know where, but I fell among the carpenters, and paid my footing. It costs a deal of money, that introductory business. Lastly, I had words with the stage manager: and failing to satisfy him that I had business there, I think they turned me out. When next I went "behind," it was in a very humble capacity. I wrote a play, and nobody associated with me except a person who helped to move the scenery, and wasn't proud, and who "went" a two-pence to my two-pence for a pot of beer.

In a short time the three gentlemen began to vote the expedition a mistake. Everything was very dingy and dirty, the actors looked very shabby, and the actresses were anything but enticing.

"This is precious slow," said Mr. Bux.

"It isn't lively," responded Letchery.

"It's a dead sell!" grumbled his lordship.

"Hallo! Look there——"

"What is it?"

"What a splendid woman there, going on to the stage. Do you see?—with the light hair. She's got her back to you now. Wait till she turns round."

Little Bux got quite excited as he pointed to the beauty.

"Keep behind, there, some of you!" bawled the manager from the other side, gesticulating wildly for them to get out of sight. They were all crowding over one another, trying to see what was going on upon the stage.

Of course the lady who had attracted their attention was Mrs. Nelly. She was very splendid in her tinsel coronet and gorgeous robes of cotton velvet. She stalked across the stage majestic, cold, impassive, and stood like some fine chiselled statue, so firm, and still, and grand in her quiescent beauty; then when she spoke her rich voice thrilled through the attentive auditory, and held them spellbound. If there were an H too many or too few, they never noticed it.

Presently, in the course of the scene, she turned her back to the audience, and walking towards our gentlemen, they were able for the first time to get a clear view of her lovely face.

"By Jove!" cried Bux.

"By jingo!" exclaimed the editor.

"It's Cheveleigh's woman," said Bux.

"That yellow-haired party he's always about with," added Letchery.

Meanwhile his lordship was endeavouring to obtain a better view of the actress round the next wing. She came off presently at the place where he was standing, and he made room for her to pass by, catching her eye, and smiling significantly as he did so. She, however, took very little notice of him. Very few swells frequent the behind the scenes of the "Apollo," and she had no suspicion of his lordship's rank.

"What do you think of her, Drawler? Isn't she a beauty?"

"She is, indeed, Charley. That Cheveleigh is a lucky fellow."

"Thrown away upon him though. He's an awful cad."

Nelly did not appear again upon the scene, and had now gone up-stairs to resume her own attire.

At the same time they were clearing the stage, and getting ready for the opening scene of a burlesque which was to follow. A number of threadbare demons with pastboard faces, of which the most prominent features had been a good deal damaged by the wear and tear of a fortnight's business, and a dozen or so sprightly fairies, of every size and shape, from the bony little girl of four to the strongly developed matron of forty, grouped themselves gracefully upon the stage, practised their steps, or shook out their rumpled book-muslins, waiting for the prompter's signal.

"Hallo!" cried Bux, "there's a little woman I know." And he pointed to one of the young ladies. "How do you do, Fanny?"

"How do you do, my noble swell?" responded the playful damsel. "Who's your friend, and what are you going to stand?"

"It's the custom, my lord, to pay your footing," suggested Mr. Letchery, with a laugh.

"Oh! all right—certainly," replied his lordship. "What's it to be?"

"Half-a-dozen of champagne, my lord," cried Fanny, catching at the title, "that's our sort. Here, girls, here's a swell going to stand champagne."

My lord might have liked it quite as well had the treat been a cheaper one, but he pulled out his little silken purse, and sent for the wine by a carpenter who was hovering about them in the hope of picking up a trifle.

As for Mr. Bux, he seldom volunteered when it was a question of payment. On this occasion he contented himself by saying, "You pay, Drawler, and we'll settle afterwards," and never alluded to the subject any further.

The champagne arrived, and these chaste seraphs had each a bumper. In their hearts, they preferred gin; but there is a class of females who think wine is a genteeler thing to call for, and have it though they hate it. My lord was not bashful when sober, and a little drink did not increase his timidity. When another half-dozen had been sent for, and consumed, the party were rather merry; and, had not the bell rung for the curtain, and cut the orgies short, there's no knowing what indiscretion he would have committed. He was a handsome fellow, with a large beard, and pretty moustachios. Perhaps his manners were rather arrogant and insulting; but then he was a lord, and who among us would not have been glad to bow our heads and toady to him. He was the heir apparent to the great Cumbersome estates, and his uncle was the Duke of Doodledum. What matter if the sluggish blood of hereditary idiocy curdled in his lordly veins, there was scarce a mother in all England who would not have sold her child to him, and been but too glad of the chance.

Deserted by his fair companions, his lordship tossed off another glass or two, and rose a little unsteadily, though quite coherent and unchanged as regarded his face. Nelly crossed the stage that moment at the back of the flat, and came towards him. Miss Perks, following in the rear, with her mistress's bonnet and shawl.

"Ah, that's the woman I want!" cried Lord Drawler, meaning of course Nelly, and not her attendant nymph, and he made towards her. "Come here, my dear, I want you."

She turned towards him, and looked him up and down with the expression a tigress might bestow upon a puppy dog that yelped at her.

"Come and have some wine?" he continued, advancing towards her with a smile, whilst a few of the ladies of the ballet, who could see them, nudged each other, and tittered derisively.

She stopped and said,—

"Did you address me, sir?"

"Who else, my darling. Don't look so very naughty."

"What do you want?"

"Dear—dear—how distant we are. I wanted to make your acquaintance, that's all."

"Indeed!"

"Indeed, I did. I never saw so pretty a woman, s'help me."

"Keep your hands to yourself!"

"Pooh—pooh! you're making a mighty fuss. There couldn't be more etiquette in a queen's drawing-room. You don't know who I am?"

"I do."

"Who, then?"

"A blackguard!"

He had approached close to her, and extended his arm as though he would have caught her round the waist; but ere his fingers touched her, she doubled her arm, and, as violently as it was unexpected, dealt him a staggering slap in the face, which made his lordship gasp a moment, stupified, and then clasp his handkerchief to his bleeding nose.

He was too much astonished and hurt to speak; and she passed by with mantling colour and set teeth, unmindful of his half uttered curse, and the loud snigger of the young ladies behind her.

CHAPTER THE THIRTY-EIGHTH.

CHARITY.

YOU know it is not the pleasantest thing that could occur to you to have a slap in the face in public. His lordship had been a little hero five minutes ago. Now, surrounded on every side by grinning faces, he felt as though he would have wished to have gone down a trap, like one of the spirits of evil with the pasteboard heads, and never come up again.

Bux was the first to come to his rescue.

"I hope she didn't hurt you?" said he.

It is not a pleasant thing to be sympathised with under such circumstances.

"Hurt—no. She hasn't killed me. I'll pay her out for it, I'll be sworn."

"Made your nose bleed, hasn't she?" pursued Mr. Bux, in the same consolatory strain.

"Damn my nose!" retorted his lordship, fiercely, trying to make a light matter of it, though he could not stop the blood for all that. "It's come to a pretty pass, when I can't speak to a woman in a hole like this. There isn't an actress on the stage, by God, who wouldn't be proud to be noticed by me."

"I'm sure there isn't, my lord," put in Mr. Letchery.

"A nasty, stuck-up creature!" echoed the ladies. "She's always so high and mighty!"

"What does she call herself? That amuses me."

"A married woman, my dear. Ha! ha! ha! ha! ha! ha!"

Convulsions of laughter at this sally.

Nelly, heeding not what passed, put on her bonnet and shawl in calm and stately majesty as a queen might put on her crown and robes of ermine, and walked away, apparently as utterly unconscious of the small fry she left behind her, as though they had never existed. But, passing out into the street, the doorkeeper, who had been a witness of the little drama, stopped her.

"Do you know who that was?" said he.

"Who who was?"

"The gent. you gave the back-hander."

"Not I."

"It was Lord Drawler—one of the richest young nobs on town."

She might have changed colour the least in all the world, but otherwise showed no sign of surprise or vexation. She always had a wonderful command of countenance.

"So much the worse for him," she said contemptuously. "I hope he liked it."

"That's very fine, I dare say," mused the doorkeeper, gazing upon her retreating form, "but you might have done better. A girl with a face and figure like that, needn't despair of making her fortune. Ah!" he added, with a sigh, as he lit his pipe, "I wish I was such another young woman."

"Who did you say she hit?" asked Bullyrag, who was standing by. "Lord Drawler! God bless me! why didn't some one tell me his lordship was here? The idea of his lordship being insulted in my house. I won't have any one behave rudely to his lordship. I'm surprised at you, Higgins—I really am."

While Mrs. Nelly was creating all this sensation at the theatre, a very different kind of scene was enacting in Mrs. Falsetto's bedroom, in Baker Street.

The old woman lay in bed, propped up by pillows, screened from the light, carefully covered up, and tucked in. She lay motionless, groaning every now and then in a weary, painful way, the result of protracted suffering and exhaustion. Dorcas sat at the side of the bed, reading by a lamp with a green shade. Some broth, in a little saucepan, simmered on the hob. On the mantelpiece stood a row of physic bottles—some half-full, some empty; others stood on the little table on which her book rested; others, again, were crowded upon the dressing-table with some dirty plates, teacups, and saucers, and yet others were to be seen upon the drawers, half covered by Dorcas's bonnet and shawl. A rushlight, burning in a night shade, made demon's eyes upon the ceiling; and the lamp by which the companion read, showed her hands and book in strong relief. All else was dark, save when the red coal flickered for a moment in the grate. No other sound besides the rustling of the leaves of Dorcas's book, and the feeble moaning of the old woman in her bed, broke the dead silence of the sick chamber.

All at once, suddenly, with a piercing scream, the old woman sprang up into a sitting posture, stiff and erect, her eyes starting from their sockets, and her jaw fallen like that of a corpse.

"What's the matter now?" asked Dorcas, rising to her feet, and endeavouring to thrust the old lady back to her place again.

"The lightning's coming!" Mrs. Falsetto screamed. "I feel it in the air. It is the flames of hell come up too soon, before I am ready."

"Pooh, pooh! you must lie back in bed, and go to sleep."

"Dorcas!" the old woman cried, in a changed and awful voice, "Dorcas, I'm going to die. I shall never get off this hateful bed. I—I shouldn't like to be taken unawares, Dorcas. Read the Bible to me."

"I didn't know you had one."

"For God's sake, don't say so, and don't make fun of me. It's too horrible to think of. Read to me, Dorcas, dear. Dorcas, for the love of heaven—for our Lord's sake, read to me."

The companion rose, with something of contempt, something of pity in her glance, and took down a beautifully bound Bible from a shelf, the inside of which looked very clean and new, and as though it had never been opened. The outside was dusty.

Opening the book at random, Dorcas read one of the Psalms, to which the old woman listened eagerly, endeavouring to catch the meaning of the words. After a few minutes she called to her companion to put it down.

"I wonder, Dorcas, if there is such a thing as perpetual torment for the wicked; and, if there is, how is it that God allows us to sin, for if He knows, and arranges according to His will, He could order it to be otherwise?"

The old lady leant back, and mumbled to herself.

"Dorcas—Dorcas! are you there? Hold my hand: I'm afraid of being alone. I have been very wicked to you, my dear. Can you forgive me?"

"I bear you no malice," the other replied, coldly.

"You must be an angel, then, after all I've said and done to you! You, of all others in the world. Oh, what a wretch I am!"

"Why I, of all others?"

"Don't ask me, dear—don't ask me—but go on reading again, and pick an easier part."

There was something horribly ludicrous in this wicked old woman's futile efforts at piety. She had some sort of vague idea, that that there was a better chance for her if she went out of the world with the words of the gospel sounding in her ears.

Trying to concentrate her attention upon it, she presently fell off to sleep, but to wake again with a start and scream as before.

"Dorcas—Dorcas! there's no light. Oh! God, it's all dark. Give me a little air! I dreamt that I was dead, and that they were laying me out, with shillings on my eyes! But I'm not dead. I may live a long while yet—five years—ten years. I might live to a hundred! I've often read of people living to a hundred. Do you think I shall, Dorcas?"

"No."

The old woman rose up with a shriek, and clutched her companion by the arm. In doing so her frilled cap fell off, and a stray lock or two of grey hair fell over her face, giving her a wild and haggard look.

"What makes you say that, Dorcas—dear, dear Dorcas? You don't mean it; you're doing it to frighten me. How long shall I live? I'm not prepared to die—I won't die before I'm prepared. If I get well I'll lead a different life—I'll give a lot of money to charities. Aren't there any I could give some to now? Bring me my purse—there's a fifty pound note in it, isn't there?"

"Yes, madam."

"Well, send it somewhere. Where's it to be? I havn't sent anything to the Conversion of Cannibals to Vegitable Food Society, have I?"

"I think not."

"I don't mean to—I don't care for cannibals——The Lord forgive me, I didn't mean that; only that I'll send it to some one else. It shall be——No. Dorcas!"

"Yes, madam."

"You shall have it."

"I?"

"Yes, yes; put it in your pocket, dear. You ought to have it more than any one else, you whom I have wronged so."

"Nonsense—you'll change your mind again. I'll put it back in your purse."

"You shan't! How dare you? Mayn't I give my money to whom I choose?"

"Why not give it to your nephew, Maurice, who requires it?"

"I won't. He shan't have a penny. He dosen't care to come and see me. Ernest shall have my money—nobody else! I hate you all! Get out of my sight. There—there—I want no more of you. Let me alone!"

Suddenly relapsing into her old fractious, peevish manner, Mrs. Falsetto stormed, and whined, and complained; then tossed to and fro upon her bed, gave orders and retracted them the next moment, until at length she fell asleep, and did not wake again until the morning.

Upon a sofa, in the sick woman's room, her companion also took her rest, or such an apology for it as the discomfort of her couch admitted of.

Next morning, after a hasty breakfast, she dressed herself, and took a cab at the street corner.

"Drive to Foot Court, Holborn, if you please?"

She was going to take Maurice the fifty pounds. Since the Sunday evening they had had that conversation, she had never ceased to think of him. I don't exactly know what she had thought. What a young lady thinks about a gentleman, is more than I can tell, or she either, I'll be bound. But I have told you before that this Dorcas was not the same sort of young lady you've been accustomed to. She must, therefore, have had different notions to these innocent young lambkins.

Suppose that she had been, comparing the two cousins, that at the moment that the veil was torn rudely from her eyes, showing her him whom she had pictured all that was good and loveable, to be a mean, deceitful, hypocrite, her eyes were opened to the merits of the other cousin? Suppose that in these two brief hours they had passed together at the open window, she had found that all her life she had been mistaken in them? That it was this cousin, not the other, who was manly, handsome, bold, and honest-faced? That it was this cousin, and not the other, she should have loved?

Suppose all this, or half of it. Are such things possible? Do women ever marry for whim or spite, and find out, when the chains are tightly rivetted, that it should have been to *the other one?* Suppose some noodle wooed and won a woman's heart by force of perseverance. I mean, suppose no other noodle appeared in the field, and the first had full play, went in and won, and that the day being fixed, in comes Noodle Number Two; in every way a better noodle than the first. Must Number One be married because the promise was made. If you think not, suppose he only came after she had married Number One. What then? We had better drop the subject. It grows difficult!

Would you believe that Dorcas was in love with Maurice? Anyhow Maurice was not in love with Dorcas. The shameful profligate had forgotten her again by now. There was only one idea in his head, and that was much too big for it. Oh! that yellow haired woman, why was she so bewitching and beautiful? why was she made so loveable, when naught but shame, and grief, and ruin, and despair, resulted from a love of her? Ah, me! *those creatures*, madam! Don't you wish we could put them all in the stocks, and have them whipped? What a deal of good it would do them.

On drove the cab, and Dorcas, leaning back in her seat, turned over a dozen pretty phrases in her mind, which she would use when she gave him her little offering.

"I'll say his aunt sent it," she thought at first. "I'll leave it, addressed to him, without a word. No, I'll give it to him, and tell him it is mine." Then she changed her mind again, and was going to do something very different. Suddenly a dreadful thought popped into her head: "Won't it be improper for me to go to a man's chambers? What will people think? Do they admit ladies? I don't suppose the porter will let me pass."

While she was puzzling in this fashion, the cab stopped at the bottom of Foot Court. She alighted, and asked her way to the Chambers. When she arrived there, she found Mr. Cheveleigh's name painted on the door-post, and, following the direction, walked up-stairs to the second floor.

Reaching the door without any interruption, she paused a moment to lay her hand upon her heart, in which there was a strange flutter, and strove to quell a choking sensation in her throat.

At length she summoned up courage to knock.

"Come in," said some one.

She entered, and was face to face with Nelly.

———

CHAPTER THE THIRTY-EIGHTH.

9·30., P.M.

DID you not wonder why that simple remark of Mr. Hadget's, "I'm going to Brighton in half-an-hour," should have been printed in capitals? There seems, at first sight, no reason for it; but I will show you that the funny gentleman took a great deal of trouble to advertise the fact.

When Hadget left the chambers, it was about five or six minutes past nine. You would have thought that he had not much time to lose, if he intended to catch the train at London Bridge in half-an-hour. He, however, thought differently, for he went into the "Hand and Heart" to have a glass of ale.

"Have you got a *Bradshaw?*" he asked.

"Here's last month's, sir."

He took it and turned over the leaves. It is not an easy task to most people to find a place in that mysterious manual; but he seemed to be more expert, or more fortunate than the generality of persons.

"The last train to Brighton is at 9·30., p.m. Shall I be able to catch it?"

"It's all you'll do, if you manage it."

"I've got a cab outside, sir," said a man at the bar, "and a horse as can go agin any in London."

"Then I will try it as soon as you please. I'll give you ten shillings if we're in time."

"All right, governor. I'm ready."

"Take care you're here in time to-morrow morning to take me to the hanging," said a young gentleman standing by.

"You've made up your mind to see the poor fellow swing, then?" put in the landlord, with a laugh.

"Yes. I wish it was eight o'clock now."

"Do you? It's more than he does, I'll be bound."

"Is a man to be hanged to-morrow?" asked Hadget, as he got into the cab.

"Aye, sir, there is. The cove as cut the throats of his wife and children, up Oxford Street way. A beastly murder."

"Do you think so?" said Hadget, smiling; and he leant back comfortably in the corner of the hansom. "Drive on as sharp as you like."

"He's a rum 'un," thought cabby, as he whipped up his Bucephelas.

Ten minutes past nine by a clock in Holborn. It would be all they could do to catch the train. Hadget leant forward over the apron, and now that he was unobserved, threw off his sprightly, pleasant manner for something of the old evil look which the devil's face had worn he nodded to in his chamber-glass that night at Skearcrows. He mouthed and jabbered too, as was his wont. Not much he said, but kept repeating the same phrase, and twisting it into a sort of song, contrived to chaunt it to the rude music of the hansom's wheels.

The noise of passing omnibuses—the buzz of voices in the street chimed in to swell the chorus, "With a twist of the wrist—with a twist of the wrist!"

The hurrying, murmuring crowds swept by A thousand smoothfaces turned towards him, none dreaming that they passed so close to murder.

On—on! Those holiday folk, who crowded the pavement, busy with their little schemes of pleasure-making, heeded not the wicked face which leered at them as they passed by.

And now the aspect of the night has changed —a howling wind has sprung up, which roars and whistles at street-corners with a fury that makes those who lie awake in bed listening to it, think of shipwrecked mariners at sea, clinging to spars, and lashed by boisterous waves; of vessels within sight of shore and home, but out of reach of hope. A wind which, tearing at the window-sash, and rumbling in the chimney, makes the listener dive further down in bed, and drag the clothes more closely round him, with a cosy, comfortable sense of warmth, and shelter, and just sufficient appreciation of the biting blast without to make him thank his stars he isn't in it.

At twenty-nine minutes past nine they reached the station. There wasn't much time to lose, but Hadget oddly enough wasted another minute.

"Here's half-a-sovereign," said he, "and I should like your number. I often want a cab, but I don't often find a civil driver. I'd like to do you a good turn some day, if I could."

"Here it is, sir," cried cabby, tendering his pasteboard. "And much obliged to you."

———

MORE BILLING AND COOING.

CHAPTER THE FORTIETH.

COBWEBS.

HADGET put the ticket in his pocket, and Hadget ran inside. He could not have had much time now, for the bell was ringing, but he still found another minute for gossip.

"First class to Brighton?" said he, going to a window which was disengaged.

"Ten-and-sixpence. Thank you. You're just in time."

"Ha! ha!" laughed Mr. Hadget, "I beg your pardon, but look at my face. You'd know me again, wouldn't you?"

"Yes, I think I should."

No. 8.

"You wouldn't easily mistake me for your own father?"

"Well, not exactly."

"Somebody did, just now. I couldn't hardly persuade them otherwise. It nearly made me lose the train."

"You'll lose it now if you don't look sharp," returned the clerk, after a moment's pause, during which he had stared very hard at his questioner. "That's a queer customer," he added, to a brother-official, as he closed the door of the pay-place.

"He's an ugly one, at any rate: I shouldn't mistake him easily."

"No, nor I either. I'd know him again among a thousand."

"Well, I'm not sorry to knock off. We

shall have to be up betimes to-morrow, if we go to see the execution."

The bell was ringing violently; the inevitable old lady, who is always too late, was making desperate efforts to reach the train before it started. Hadget ran in the same direction. It would indeed have been unlucky had he not caught the train, after all his trouble, supposing he wanted to.

"What class, sir?" asked a guard.

"All right!" cried Hadget, continuing to run on. The train was up at the other end of the platform. It was on the move.

"You're too late, sir!" called out another guard; but Hadget took no notice, and still ran forward.

Not that he took any particular interest in the matter, but merely because he wanted some subject to make a remark upon, one guard said to the other, as they wheeled away an empty luggage barrow,—

"I suppose the gent caught it, after all?"

"Looks as if he did," replied the other, yawning. "The old woman didn't, Next train to Brighton; yes, marm. First thing to-morrow morning.

On flew the train, cleaving the darkness on its fiery way, and taking murder with it.

Unless——Perhaps it was its shadow only, creeping round the carriages, carefully avoiding life and light, and, with a stealthy, watchful apprehension in its glance, stealing along by a circuitous and unfrequented route towards Lyon's Inn.

Hadget had chambers there—three dark, close-smelling, beetle-browed little rooms. An office, with a ricketty desk, a high screen, a broken chair, a stool, a coal-scuttle, last year's almanac, and an iron safe. Two rooms beyond, one choked with lumber, the other containing a wretched bed, and a quantity of old, musty-smelling books and papers. The office and the lumber-room, lighted by small-paned windows, broken and patched, and half obscured by dirt and cobwebs. The bed-room, dark as pitch. A truly miserable abode for any human being to live in.

It seemed as though the spiders liked living there, for their webs choked up every corner, and one or two fat old fellows were doing a little tight-rope business across the ceiling, while in the lumber-room beyond a perfect colony resided. In this wicked town of ours there are many human spiders lurking in such gloomy corners as this, biding their time to dart out and pounce upon the simple gadfly;— so many of them, indeed, that you cannot help wondering about them, as you would have wondered about Mr. Hadget's agile tenants, where the flies came from to feed them.

I suppose there are plenty though, and to spare. Mr. Hadget prepared his web, hid himself round the corner, and waited patiently. He was not usually very long before he caught one. Sometimes a foolish little moth, with scarcely anything to suck in its poor slender body; but often enough a family bluebottle, with a good bit of picking upon him. Now and then a wasp, or a hornet, would get his legs fast, and tear and destroy the net in his efforts to get away again; but spider Hadget would let him kick, and plunge and spend his strength, then wrap him round, and bind him tight, and suck his blood as easily as though he were a moth.

I don't exactly know how Hadget got his living. He did a little in the discount way. Sometimes he helped gentlemen who were "in trouble." He assisted those who would be "whitewashed." He collected rents, and did many other odd jobs to add to his income.

You, who are wise in legal matters, and know that Hadget's name has not been upon the rolls these fifteen years past, may think the circumstance arises from the fact of Hadget's name being an imaginary one. Perhaps you are right; but Hadget's name, or Hadget's real name, had been struck off the rolls before our story began. The names of Craven and Hadget figured on the doorpost in Lyon's Inn. Hadget acted as Craven's clerk; while Craven was, in reality, clerk to Hadget. Nobody saw more of Craven than his name, and that was usually in Hadget's writing, who signed himself, "Your most obedient servant, pro Dudley Craven."

Murder's shadow, creeping back, came noiselessly and unobserved through the outer gate of Lyon's Inn, and let itself into Hadget's office with a latch key. A candle, with a flaring, swollen wick, was burning upon the desk, and such small light as it had the power to give, fell full upon the figure of an old grey-headed man, who slumbered in the broken chair. A handsome old man he would have been, had not the spirit of drink early in life got him by the nose, and pulled it sadly out of shape; and, as if in shame and sorrow for his nasal organ, his eyes had always tears in them. He was very shabby, nay, even dirty, in his attire. Shuffling along the streets, in his unbrushed hat and shoes, nobody would have mistaken him for an English baronet. A French count you might have thought him, because we are accustomed to see the foreign aristocracy at a disadvantage, particularly when our comic authors deal with them: the spurious imitation being about as like the real thing, as one of those foolish creatures I see about the streets in mountebank costume, that they call rifle volunteers, is like a real soldier.

Old Sir John Cheveleigh slept on in his uneasy seat, with his head hanging back so far, that, looking at him hastily, the spectator might at first have taken him for dead.

Did Murder's shadow think him so when first it looked at him through a chink of the door?—for, how it started!

Did old Sir John dream that the hand of death was at his heart? What else could make him spring upon his feet, and shout out,—

"Help! Who's that? Hadget! Who are you?"

"Don't bawl my name so loud, you cursed old fool. Are you gone childish, or only drunk, as usual? What are you staring at?"

"I must be drunk, I think," the old man answered, trembling violently, so that his chattering teeth chopped up his words. "What have you done to yourself?"

If Murder's shadow were Hadget's shadow, it had changed strangely since it left its owner running to catch the train at the London terminus of the Brighton railway.

The shadow which had let itself in so cautiously, wore a large black beard and a wide-awake. Hadget used to wear spectacles, but the shadow had none. Hadget used to wear a long, ill-shaped, baggy paletot, but the shadow had on a pilot-coat, which fitted closely. The shadow had also a great comforter muffling its neck, and carried its body with a swaggering, rollicking gait, more like a seafaring man, than a pettifogging London attorney.

As soon as it was well inside the room, it made the door fast hastily, and double locked it; then, turning to the old man, who sat shivering and wiping his head, eyeing these movements uneasily, said gruffly,—

"What have you done since I left you?"

"I haven't moved."

"You lie."

"I take my Bible oath, so strike me ——"

"Hush! There's some one outside. Hold your tongue."

They listened with baited breath. It was nothing but the flutter of some dead leaves the wind had brought, heaven knows whence, and thrown against the outer door.

"It's nothing!" said the shadow, with a sigh of great relief, "only the infernal wind. You haven't been out, then, you say? And no one's been here either, I suppose?"

"Not a soul."

"That's well!"

"What's well, Hadget? I don't understand you. Why are you dressed up like that?" the old man asked in a quivering voice.

"Why? There are strange things happen every day in London, nobody wots of. Strange meetings, strange disclosures—robberies, forgeries, murders even never found out, and nobody the wiser. I've just seen a ghost."

"A ghost!" the old man cried, starting back. "What do you mean, Hadget? What ails you?"

The shadow by this time had put off its hat and beard, undone its neckerchief, thrown back its coat, and Hadget stood there in the flesh.

"Do you remember Lyons?" he said.

"Yes—yes. What makes you ask?"

"You recollect the fair-time, then—the dancing-girl—the clown of the ring?"

"You know I do. I thought we had agreed to drop the subject?"

"It's sometimes necessary to cancel old agreements when you draw up fresh ones. I must remind you of the circumstances. You and I were travelling together then; I, a young fool just fresh from college, you, a wary man of the world, some ten years my senior; I, an impressionable, hot-headed simpleton, ready to love or hate at a moment's notice; you, a *blaze*, used-up swell, with scarcely a pleasureable sensation left in you."

"Yes, I brought you out."

"I'm much obliged to you. You weren't a baronet in those days, neither were you very rich. You did a little elbow-shaking now and then, and picked up flats—myself among the number."

"You hadn't much to pick," interrupted old Sir John.

"Such little as I had you took—and more. In those days I fell in love. It seems to you, no doubt, a most absurd expression, and odd enough in the mouth of one who has been a blackguard these twenty years. In such society as you and I frequent, one naturally feels ashamed of confessing to such weaknesses. In those days I thought differently. I said before I was a fool, and so I fell in love with a dancing-girl at a show. The way any sensible man of the world would have acted in such a case, would have been to have seduced the woman, lived with her as long as there was any charm in her society, and then thrown her off like an old shoe—left her to rot and die upon the nearest dung-heap. The world would not be too severe upon you for so doing. It is within the limits of possibility that you might have married, and died happy afterwards, while she would have been forgotten—very properly. But I was a fool, you see; I fell in love, intending to act honourably. I had the misfortune to point her out to you. You fell in love with her as well, intending not to do so."

"Well."

"In those days, such a course surprised and shocked me. I had been brought up with old-fashioned, foolish notions of right and wrong. I thought it wicked—I daresay I felt vexed besides,—and mortified to think that you had cut me out. To tell the truth, she never smiled on me. Mine was a gloomy, silent love, which made me look ridiculous; while you had had experience, and knew what sort of manner pleases women. You bagged the bird, while I was beating round the bush. You know I followed and challenged you, and that we fought?"

"I haven't forgotten it!"

"I recollect it well. The long, gloomy, half-furnished room, at the Auberge. One candle, flickering upon the mantel-shelf, we found, was hardly light enough, and so drew back the window-curtain, and fought by the light of the moon. You always prided yourself, that you were a swordsman, Sir John. I, too, was no bad hand, you know. I pinked the French captain at Bruges; but still I know very well you would have beaten me had you not slipped your foot and snapped your sword. You recollect I had you down, and had my hand upon your throat: there was no help for you had I not chosen. I shan't forget the look of horror in your face; or how, as I stood holding you, the moonlight shining full upon your head, I watched the drop of sweat roll, glistening, down your cheek."

"Well, you spared my life."

"I did: and made you promise that you would marry the woman you had wronged. And so I left you. When we met years afterwards, in London, and found you'd stepped into your dead brother's shoes, and wore the title, I was glad to find that Lady Cheveleigh was none other than the dancing girl we two had fallen in love with."

When Hadget had got thus far, the manner of the old man, which had up to now had something of anxiety and dread in it, gave way to an easier one, and he leant back in his chair, and crossed his legs.

"You never thought of renewing the little love passage?" he said carelessly.

"No," returned Hadget; "the romance was over—I was ten years older and uglier. The lady had not improved l'amour se passe. I haven't often thought of it, and had almost forgotten your villany till to-night, when a ghost reminded me."

"What do you mean?"

"I met the ghost of that circus fellow in the street."

"Good God! I thought him dead years ago," gasped the old man.

"So did I," returned the other. "But he isn't."

"That is a further reason for my getting out of the country," continued Sir John, after a long pause.

"It was my coming upon him accidently unobserved, waiting outside this inn, that made me change my dress in the way you see."

"But where did you get the things?"

"I borrowed them from a friend in the neighbourhood."

"Do you think he will know me?"

"You have changed more than I have, Sir John," returned the other with a coarse laugh. "There's precious little of the fine gentleman left about you. I think you'd pass him without much difficulty."

"You had no other reason for disguise, I suppose?"

"Yes, I had. When I went out and left you here, I told the people at the gate that I was going to Brighton. Don't you see?—I want to put Craven off the scent. I don't exactly wish him to follow after us, and ask for his share!"

"But, then, you meant to come back again! Why could you not tell them that when we go out together?"

"Why didn't I? Because the last train to Brighton was at 9·30. Do you see? Damn it! what are you driving at now?"

"Nothing—nothing—Hadget. I beg your pardon. Only you are so mysterious."

"Mysterious! Curse me! would you have me act like a fool?"

"No, no! I know you do it for the best—I'm sure of that. You've acted right all through the business; and helped me to get together a large sum of money——"

"To ring the very last farthing out of your estate. Assisted at a forgery or two——"

"Yes—yes. You could not have done more, only—only I thought from your bringing up that matter again about Louise. At least——But I beg your pardon."

"I suppose seeing that man in the street was not sufficient reason——"

"Of course—certainly—I'm quite satisfied," the old man interrupted, hastily.

"Are you ready, then?"

"Quite ready, Hadget."

"Have you got the money safe?"

"All safe in my pocket-book."

"That's right. I take an interest in it, you know, as a third is to be mine when we reach Boulogne. And now, we'd better be off. The boat starts from London Bridge at one.

We'll get on board, and get to bed at twelve. You're not afraid of being left in the dark a moment?"

The old man *was* afraid; but, at the same time, was afraid to tell him so, so Hadget took the light and went into his bed-room, shutting the door behind him.

When he was inside a fiendish smile crossed Hadget's features. As he busied himself feeling in a drawer, he muttered, below his breath,—"Should I do it here? They did not recognise me, I'm certain. They'll think that he's been robbed; or, I could make it look like suicide. Besides, no one knows he has been to see me. He told no one he was coming to town. I thought his son might have known; but he didn't. Why not do it here, and take away the body in pieces? No! that will make too much mess. It's better as I thought at first."

The old man, waiting outside, grew impatient in the dark, and, coming cautiously to the door, peeped through a tiny chink, and saw the lawyer feeling the edge of a razor with his thumb. Almost the next moment he slipped it into his pocket, and came towards him. Sir John had hardly time to get back into his seat before the door opened.

"What a time you've been," said the old man: "what have you been doing?"

"Putting one or two things I wanted into my pockets. I don't take much luggage when I travel. Are you ready, my venerable friend?"

He had quite a sprightly manner now, this humourous lawyer, and laughed as he resumed his beard and wide-a-wake.

"As you go out," he said, "you must ask the porter what time it is; and be particular to inquire whether their clock is fast. Then ask them what time I went out, and whether I said where I was going to."

"But why should I——"

"Do my bidding, and never mind why. I have my reasons, and shall tell you afterwards."

"Well, you know best, Hadget. I'll do what you say."

"Come on, then, if you're ready."

He was quite ready; and, Hadget putting on his rollicking, swaggering gait, began to whistle a tune.

"You would not know me, would you?"

"Indeed, I shouldn't; but if that man is waiting, he may know *me*."

"No fear of that. Turn up your coat collar and you're safe enough. And now let's bid good-bye to this dingy hole for ever. I'll leave the spiders in possession. Rum old chaps, some of 'em," continued Mr. Hadget, quite jocularly. "Take a deal of trouble spinning webs, to catch nothing—don't they? Here's one been hours making this. I'll be sworn, and see how easily I break it up. Ha! ha! what fools they are!"

So spider Hadget destroyed the web one of his fat tenants had been spinning. Oh! blind, blind wretch! as easily might his web be destroyed, for all the care and cunning spent upon its manufacture.

In company with Sir John does Murder's shadow go forth from the gloomy inn, and the black night swallows them up. Then the howling wind, with gathering fury, shakes the doors and windows of the empty chambers, and the dead leaves in the yard rustle and shiver in a corner, as though they knew what crime was going to happen.

CHAPTER THE FORTY-FIRST.

FACE TO FACE.

WHEN Dorcas turned the handle of the door, and entered Mr. Cheveleigh's chambers, she found the yellow-haired beauty seated at the table practising at her drawing. She had a taste that way, as you can see by that little *fac similie* sketch in No. 6. The female Perks was polishing the stove, and coming round behind her mistress every now and then to watch the progress of the picture.

"Beautiful!" the aged maiden cried. "And where's his other leg?"

"It isn't drawn yet."

"Oh! isn't it, mum? but I suppose it's going to be? Well! however you can do it all surprises me."

"There's nothing wonderful about it," said Nelly, modestly, though in her heart she thought herself only inferior to JOHN LEECH in caricature.

While they were thus engaged in conversation, Dorcas entered. Nelly looked at her in some surprise, and with a certain, cold, fixed stare, with which it was her habit to regard an unwelcome stranger; and Dorcas, astonished beyond utterance at finding her there, stood silently upon the threshold with the handle of the door in her hand; while the female Perks rubbed her nose in an abstracted, thoughtful fashion with the black lead brush, and stared at both of them.

"I beg your pardon," said Dorcas, when she could find her words; "I see, I have mistaken the room. I thought Mr. Maurice Cheveleigh lived here——"

"Mr. Maurice Chevelegh does live here!"

"Oh," said Dorcas, and seemed embarrassed.

"I'll take any message you wish to leave for him," continued Nelly, a trifle colder and more haughty in her demeanour, as though she instinctively scented the presence of a rival. "What do you want with him?"

"My business was of a private nature," said Dorcas. "I can deliver the message only to Mr. Cheveleigh himself."

"Mr. Cheveleigh has no secrets from me," returned Nelly, more haughtily still. "You can say what you have to say."

"Might I venture to inquire whom I have the pleasure of addressing?" Dorcas asked, with something of a sneer crossing her face.

"My name is Cheveleigh," the actress answered, studiously uncommunicative.

"I did not know that Mr. Cheveleigh was married," continued Dorcas, with rather more contempt.

"Did you not?" the other answered, with a frown and a toss of her head, whilst she continued her sketch, joining on the man's leg all in the wrong place, in her agitation.

Dorcas's eyes wandered to Nelly's left hand, and saw the wedding-ring there. Then she felt doubtful. There are many thousands of simple, guileless creatures who place implicit faith in that little piece of metal. But I have seen very nice ones in the shop windows for 4s. 6d., and I dare say they may be had cheaper. Besides, there's no law against "those creatures" wearing one on every finger if they choose.

"Mr. Cheveleigh did not inform me of the circumstance when I last saw him," Dorcas said presently.

"What circumstance?" asked Nelly, looking up.

"His marriage!"

"That's a great pity, I'm sure. Pray who are you, to be his confidant?"

"I can see what you are," retorted Dorcas.

"It's more than I can do by you, then," said Nelly, rising from her seat, and speaking through her clenched teeth, pale as death, but very calm. "You're not his wife, I know. Perhaps you're his woman."

"How dare you?" the other cried, blushing crimson, while her eyes flashed fire.

"Or, perhaps," pursued the actress, with withering contempt, "you're what they call a modest girl. Poor thing! did he promise to marry you, and were you very much in love with him? I'm truly sorry for you,—on my word, I am."

She laughed insultingly as she said this, and, pulling open the door, held it for the other to pass out.

Dorcas, drawn up to her full height, confronted her with a look of such scorn and hate, that any one less audacious than the woman she addressed must have quaked beneath the glance. But it took a good deal to frighten Nelly. She stood there in an easy, graceful attitude—a saucy, mocking smile playing upon her pretty face, her small foot tapping the floor, to all appearance as much at her ease as though she were having a cosy, familiar chat with some old friend.

The other woman, with her eyes fixed unflinchingly upon the actress, stood motionless before her, not offering to move an inch. Thus were the representatives of the two great antagonistic classes of society confronted with each other. Virtue and Vice were brought face to face, and Virtue found itself in the minority. The situation was one which should never occur in any novel. I don't know how it has crept into this, but I have no imagination, and am always copying from life. Virtue ought to be triumphant, and Vice grovel in the dust. It is what always occurs in transpontine melodrama, and though our every-day experience teaches us the reverse, we should take no notice of it.

"You may leave my apartment, *Miss*, as soon as it is convenient. I am not anxious to prolong the interview."

The other found no words to say, but still moved not an inch, for fear that the creature whom she despised and hated so should think herself victorious.

"Unless," continued the actress, it affords you any pleasure to study my manners and appearance. You virtuous women dearly love to do so. You would ignore our very existence if you could, but then your brothers and husbands would not. Sometimes they prefer our company to yours. They like our free-and-easy fashions. We are not *lady-like*, it's true, but our society is more entertaining. They leave your side to come to us, and tell us how you've bored them. Often enough, the nearer you approach in your imitation of us, the more they like you. To win their favour, you play at being shop-girls at your fancy fairs. Before now, you've taken our pleasure gardens from us, and played at being "gay." I should not wonder if next you took the Haymarket for an evening promenade, and issued vouchers to have it all proper and select."

When she had concluded this little address, which she delivered with considerable irony and bitterness, Nelly curtsied low to the other, and prepared to shut the door.

For one moment longer did Dorcas tarry on the threshold, looking her antagonist up and down with the same mixture of hatred and contempt; then said, in low and measured tones, without any change in the expression of her face,—

"Poor creature! how I pity you!"

"Ha! ha!" laughed Nelly, still commanding her features by an almost superhuman effort, "How very kind of you! *Bon voyage!*"

Then Dorcas swept out of the room, and strode away, the heels of her boots grinding the floor.

"What do you think of that!" the actress asked of her companion, when the door was closed. But poor Miss Perks, not knowing what to think, still stood polishing her nose, until it acquired a dazzling brilliancy of black-lead.

The good old soul had no great reasoning powers. She was very much astonished by all she had heard, and had not understood a half of it.

"What does she pity Mrs. Cheveleigh for?" thought the Bony maiden. "It's like her imperence!"

As for Nelly, she paced the chamber to and fro, repeating all that she had said, and smiling to herself. While thus engaged, her foot kicked against a paper lying on the floor. It was an envelope, addressed to "Maurice Cheveleigh, Esq., Cleveland Chambers, Foot Court, Holborn."

"What's this?" said she.

She broke the seal and looked inside. It contained a fifty pound note.

She stood and looked at it a moment in blank astonishment.

"I suppose that woman dropped it. What did she bring it here for, I wonder? Who is she? Perhaps she has come from his aunt. I wonder whether it's a good one?"

She twisted the note over and over in her fingers. Her face wore a thoughtful, absent look.

"Give me my bonnet and shawl," she said, presently.

Then paused again, and twittered the bonnet-strings between her fingers.

"No," she said, half aloud; "it would be scandalous! I couldn't have the heart to do it."

What could she not have the heart to do, that yellow-haired syren? In after years, poor writhing wretches, beneath her chariot wheels, cried out in anguish that she had no heart at all, or she could not have made them suffer so.

It seems to me, the heart is a very useless organ, and but a trouble to its owner. Every day are the designing practising upon us tender-hearted ones. My brother Tom gets me to lend him twenty-pounds, then goes away and says I robbed him. Conjointly with my friend Sloper, I have promised to meet I don't know how many little bills, of which I never had a halfpenny; but which I have always had to pay. The very beggars know at a glance that I am a soft-hearted fool. They sidle up to me, and whine, and shiver, and offer to show me their ugly sores. I feel convinced that I am being done; but, still have not the presence of mind to refuse them my penny. It's a great advantage to be born without a heart. You men of the world can pack the rascals off, talk to them of the stocks, and recommend them to look in upon the beadle. You're quite right, the parish is the proper place for them; and I don't believe that "skillogolee" is half so bad as it is represented.

While Nelly had the note in her hand the door opened, and Maurice entered. She thrust it hastily into her pocket, and turned to greet him.

CHAPTER THE FORTY-SECOND.

WHICH WAY DOES THE WIND BLOW?

MAURICE came in, moody and silent. He looked tired and dusty, and his face and hands were not of the cleanest. He sat down wearily upon a chair, and, crossing his legs, cocked up one boot, and contemplated a hole in it, with a gloomy earnestness which was sad to look upon.

"Dear love, what is the matter?" Nelly asked, coming to his side, and seating herself on a low stool at his feet.

"Heigho!" said Maurice, with a woful sigh. "Things don't look up, Nelly."

He had been on a borrowing expedition, and returned with empty pockets.

A good many of Maurice's aristocratic acquaintance had given him up, and were out when he called. I think that his popularity with his swell friends began about this period of his life to be upon the wane. When first he obtained his appointment at the Bad Bargains he was very kindly received. His cousin, who was pretty generally a favourite with the genteel young men of his department, as well as with the senior clerks, introduced Maurice to their society, and he maintained for some time a position of honour amongst them, which circumstance was attributable to the social qualities and pleasing manners he possessed. He had a tolerable voice, and sang a good song; he could also tell a story pretty well; he was besides such a careless, random, open-handed fellow, ready for any lark, stopping at nothing, and speaking of the wildest extravagances as matters of every-day occurrence, that the novelty of his character and eccentricity of his domestic life excited a mixture of curiosity and admiration in those whose conduct was more regulated by a regard for the opinion of society.

Those acquainted with the kind of home which Maurice had had, and the neglect and want of discipline which had characterised his youth, wondered little at the playful vagabondism of his words and deeds, but were only surprised to find him so much of a gentleman, and so little of a blackguard. As for his moral character, the young men with whom he associated saw nothing very uncommon in it. It's all very well moralising, you know, but we all of us like these racketty young dogs who sow their wild oats. It is only when the extravagance happens to affect our own private purses, that we don't see the point in it.

When Maurice was at the height of his popularity, he affected to be a heavy swell. He wore clothes of the newest cut, and collars of the latest fashion. He spoke with pardonable exaggeration of the home of his ancestors, and the number of his desirable connections. His allowance from his father was very liberal‘ but he must have exceeded it considerably by his expenditure. The genteel mania usually attacks a man at some portion of his life. A desire to be looked up to, and a regard for appearances are as innate to the British character as are lion-like courage and piggish obstinacy.

"Heigho!" said Maurice again, "if things don't take a turn, I don't know what we shall do, or how it's all to end."

"All what's to end, dear Maurice?"

"My love," said Maurice, "if I do not get something to do, or find some way of making money, we shall have to break up our little home. I can never be sufficiently thankful that you have found a way of supporting yourself. You know, dearest, the little money that I have got lately has been barely sufficient to keep us in meat and drink, and buy you such trifling necessaries as you require. I feel that I am nothing but a drag upon you: without me, you would make your fortune. You are so clever—so beautiful! A thousand others, better off than I can ever be, would be at your feet. Bux told me, this morning, that Lord Drawler saw you at the theatre last night, and was raving about you."

I have heard Nelly's enemies assert that she was the most deceitful slut on earth; but, then, I have also heard the same authorities say that all women are hypocrites. I don't believe them.

"Dear Maurice," cried the pretty woman, "I don't care twopence for his lordship's ravings. While we can struggle on we will, and what's enough for one we'll have to make do for both of us. You are the only man I ever loved, and, if you knew more of women, you would know those whom we love in wealth we don't desert in poverty."

He pressed her to his heart, and kissed her beautiful yellow hair, which brushed, in soft and silky masses, against his cheek. She looked up after a few moments, and asked,—

"Have you had an answer from your father?"

"No; and I have been round to Hadget's chambers. He has not yet returned from Brighton."

"Well, we must hope for the best. You know to-morrow is what Bullyrag calls my benefit. I suppose I may make an extra pound by it, if I am very fortunate; though he takes care not to let me have too much. By the way, dear, this clock has stopped, would you mind running down to the "Hand and Heart," or "The Plumes," to see what time it is?"

The moment his back was turned she took the Bank-note from her pocket, and hastily lighting a taper, re-sealed the envelope, placed it on the mantel-piece, and, blowing out the taper, again sat down to read by the side of the fire.

"Maurice, dear" she said to him, when he returned, rising from her seat, and gently taking his hand in hers, "how could you ever think so badly of me as to imagine I should leave you?"

"I know you would not, my dear, generous girl," he cried, again kissing and hugging her.

"Oh! what a horrible creature I am," Nelly suddenly exclaimed. "I had quite forgotten. There is a letter waiting for you. A person brought it from your aunt, I think."

Maurice opened it; then with a tremendous expletive, shouted out,—

"It's a fifty pound note, Nelly! Hurrah! It's from the old lady. Our fortune's made! This won't be the last by many a one. What a good old thing it is; and I to neglect her so! I'll go and thank her this very night. What an ungrateful wretch I am! What shall we have for dinner?"

A hundred ridiculous exclamations of sorrow and delight the young man shouted as he capered about the room.

"I don't know whether they'd change it at the "Hand and Heart," said he. "I'd better have a cab and go to the Bank."

They had not money enough to pay for one; so, eventually, he walked, got the money, and returned home smoking a regalia,

"I've a very good mind to lay in another pair of boots," said he, regarding the shabby pair he wore with a mournful smile.

"I wish you would, Maurice; and I wish you would take more care of yourself. I never saw anybody changed like you. You used to be something like a swell when first I knew you, and one, one need not be have been ashamed of being seen out with. Let me tie your neckerchief for you. How can you go about such a guy?"

She had never gone about a guy during all their difficulties, and, by her appearance, you would never have imagined how hard-up they were.

While Nelly was engaged tying a bow in Maurice's neckerchief, old Mrs. Perks looked into the room.

This worthy woman seldom intruded herself upon the Cheveleighs' domestic economy. She did not approve of Mrs. Nelly, and spoke of her connection with Maurice as "goings on." If it had not been that the young man submitted without a murmur to all her shameful extortions and petty larcenies, she would long ago have complained about him to the landlord.

"It's sickening,' she used to say to Mrs. Mobbles at the coal and potatoe warehouse, round the corner, with which opinion that lady agreed. They both led rather unhappy domestic lives. Mr. Perks had a weakness for three-ha'p'orths of gin, and Mr. Mobbles was in the habit of returning home under the influence of malt liquor. It was the cat and dog life both ladies lived with their liege lords, which made them particularly bitter against the Cheveleighs' billing and cooing.

That red-nose simpleton, the Perks' servant, on the contrary, was trumpetting the young people's good qualities all over the neighbourhood to everybody who would listen to her. After she had been to the theatre two or three times, she became quite an authority upon the subject, and spoke of the different performers with abbreviations of their surnames, as she had heard Nelly do. So that when she was talking about Tomkins the tragedian, she said,—"The other day, Tom says to Missus, he says——" and, somebody naturally asking,—" Pray who's Tom?" it was her custom to retort,—" Who's Tom? why who do you suppose? Tom, of the Apollo, to be sure; who else do you think I am talking of?". She always called Nelly her mistress when she mentioned her; and Nelly had made some sort of vague promise of taking this ancient virgin to live with them when they moved away from the chambers, which they intended to do in the summer time.

"Dear, dear Maurice, I will never leave you," Nelly cried, as she looked up into his face, during the operation of tyeing the bow.

"They've been having a row, I suppose," said old Mrs. Perks to herself, with a chuckle. "I knew it wouldn't last for ever!"

She had been out marketiug, and, meeting the postman on the stairs, brought up some letters with her, which she now delivered to them.

"One for you, sir, and for the young woman," said she.

"What young woman?" asked Maurice, rather indignantly. But Mrs. Perks having delivered the letters, retired without another word. It was a great triumph of hers, this was, and she chuckled over it for an hour afterwards.

The letters were from Mr. Ochre and one or two other gentlemen, concerning the benefit. Jack had sold several tickets for them.

"Well," said Maurice, "you see now, one bit of good luck brings another. Things *are* looking up, after all!"

"And to whom do I owe it all, dear Maurice?" cried blue-eyed Nell. "Had you not rescued me from the streets what would have become of me?"

After which more kissing and hugging, of course.

"I don't know that there's any particular merit in what I've done," Mr. Cheveleigh

thought to himself. "I've acted very much like a scoundrel. I am a scoundrel, there's no doubt about it. A miserable, selfish hound! why should I not have married her? She is the most beautiful and the most agreeable woman I ever met. Pray what would my dignity suffer from the alliance? I see nothing. I shall never leave her: then why not marry her? And I will too, by Heavens, if she'll have me?"

"Nelly, my dear——" said he.

But at that moment Miss Perks came in to ask whether she should get anything for their dinner, and so he put off the proposal until a more fitting opportunity.

It was agreed that upon the strength of the thirty-five shillings' worth of tickets they had sold, and the unexpected arrival of the 50*l.* note, that they should give a little supper next night, after the play was over.

To a person who took a delight in studying human nature, it would have afforded no slight amount of gratification to have watched the progress of this little entertainment.

"What shall we have to eat, do you think?" Maurice said.

Then followed a consultation.

If they were to prepare a grand supper—game pie, cold fowls, lobster salad, and such like—it would be only throwing money away.

"You must have champagne then, and see what that will come to. Besides, I don't believe men care a button about the victuals as long as there is plenty of drink."

With which Nelly agreed. However, it is a very great delusion, which most ladies labour under; for I believe a great many greedy fellows only go out for what they can get.

"Well, what are we to have?"

"I don't think sandwiches will do."

"What do you say to cold beef?"

"No—oysters."

So they agreed it should be oysters.

"Then, what should they have to drink?"

"Nothing but beer and spirits," Maurice said decisively.

And so it was settled. Only, about an hour afterwards, Nelly observed,—

"I don't think oysters would look well by themselves."

"Certainly not," said Maurice. "I never thought of that."

Then came the question, what would look well with them.

Cold boiled beef was decided upon.

I wont wear out the reader's patience with any more of this nonsense. When the evening of the next day arrived, it had been decided that a first-rate hot supper should be ordered at "The Plumes," and everything done in first-rate style, with a first-rate waiter, in a spotless tie, to wait upon them.

It was a very full night at "The Apollo." Bullyrag was fond of benefits. That is to say, every now and then, when business was slack, he posted London with large bills announcing the benefit of one of his stars, drew a large house, and allowed the actor about three pounds' worth of tickets to sell, if he could.

WANTED.

CHAPTER THE FORTY-THIRD.

WHEELS WITHIN WHEELS.

ON the occasion of the benefit a host of talent was announced, and unprecedented attraction. The people stood outside the doors an hour before they opened, and Bullyrag, looking through an eye-hole in the curtain, gazed upon the crowded benches with immense satisfaction.

Nelly went on when her turn came, and met with her usual hearty welcome. She had become something of a ranter now, and nothing pleases the British public so much as the leather-lunged style. When she exclaimed to

No. 9.

the wicked lord who would have tempted her to desert her happy cottage-home with the practicable window and her aged sire with the thin legs, for his companionship and a more eligible residence, "Take back the dross, my lord, for virtue is a priceless gem the wealth of India could not purchase!" you should have seen how it brought down the gallery. The ladies and gentlemen in that elevated region seemed to be quite of the same way of thinking, and had probably found it to be true by their own personal experience.

"Well, sir, how did you think I went off to-night?" asked Nelly of the manager.

"Capital, my dear young lady, capital. You'll make your fortune some day."

"Not on thirty shillings a-week, I think.

Pray. sir, when are you going to raise my salary?"

"I can't afford it. The house won't pay for any more."

"Well, I can't act for such a little; so I must beg to tender my resignation."

"Well, I shan't give any more."

"Oh! yes, you must. Don't you think I'm worth it? Why, you never had such a pretty woman in your company before. Mr. Bullyrag, I ask for your candid opinion, do you think I'm pretty?"

"Well," said the manager, rubbing his chin, and grinning like an ogre, "I don't suppose anybody could think much different."

"Don't you, dear Mr. Bullyrag? Now, I know you're only joking."

They were in the manager's private room,—a quiet snuggery, where no one intruded unsummoned, under fear of fearful consequences. "I'm sure you're only joking, because you don't think me half as pretty as —— as Miss Fleshings, for instance."

"She's no beauty then," said Bullyrag, with a horse-laugh.

The traitor had often called the lady in question a Venus and an Angel. He used to spell it "angle" in his letters.

"Well, Miss Fleshings had twice the salary I have," pouted Nelly. "Had she twice the talent, or did you like her twice as well? Oh, you men, you men! if we only find out the soft side, what a lot we women can get out of the sharpest of you."

"They wouldn't get much out of me," said Bullyrag, with a grin.

"No—not out of you. I believe your heart is stone." Here she sighed. "I'm sure it is."

"You mean my pocket is," said Bullyrag.

"What an ill-natured remark! We've dropped the subject of the salary, Mr. Bullyrag. I would not ask for another halfpenny to save my life. No! I shall go. I'm very sorry, Mr. Bullyrag, because —— because I have been very happy here; but it's better that it should be so——"

"Why?" said he. He was obtuse enough.

"Never mind, sir. Nothing—nothing."

And she took out her pretty lace-edged pocket-handkerchief.

What did the designing minx intend to do, I wonder? Was she going to follow that rascal Ochre's advice, and make love to the manager?

I have heard it asserted that Nelly was one of those women who don't know what is meant by love. I really believe that there are some women as passionless as a fish, particularly those fair-haired beauties like my heroine. But I don't know whether the fair or the dark are the greatest hypocrites.

"What's the matter now?" asked Bullyrag, watching the pocket-handkerchief business with a blank expression of countenance. "What are you crying about?"

Nelly made no reply, but sobbed the louder. Her enemies affirm that she had always a wonderful supply of tears ready at a moment's notice. Perhaps her feelings were easily worked upon, for we have found her similarly affected upon several occasions already.

As she made no answer, and as the manager was not the quickest man in the world in decyphering the mysteries of a woman's heart (ah, me! who is there can?), he looked on stupidly for a while; then lit a cigar, and looked on again, but volunteered no other observation.

After he had smoked about an inch, very slowly, and deliberately an idea occurred to him. Nelly did not leave off crying, and probably would never do so unless he took some steps in the matter, so he determined to take them. What were they to be? Suppose you are alone with a woman, and who will keep on crying, and you don't know the reason, and what's the matter with her, and she won't tell you, what would you do? Bullyrag took the only course that anybody could under such circumstances. He put his arm round the beauty's waist in the most persuasive, coaxing manner he could assume (he was—and is—a repulsive person to look at, with the manners of a pig), and softly whispered,—

"What is it, my dear, tell me all about it?"

"Oh! oh! oh!"

That would not do, so he drew her a little closer to him, and turning her head towards his, would probably have kissed her, only she, instead, leant her face upon his shoulder, and was entirely overcome by her emotions.

"I never will tell you. I daren't tell you. You might have seen—that is, if you're not blind. Oh! dear, oh dear, oh dear! I wish that I was dead."

It's very lucky wishes are of so small avail in such a case, or pretty Nelly would have been dead a dozen chapters ago. She so frequently expressed a desire for mortality.

Now Bullyrag was not a very bashful man—few theatrical managers are. He was tolerably vain of his accomplishments; and, by the way, he adorned that fat and vulgar person of his with huge masses of gold and vast expanses of gaudy velvet. So, I suppose, he thought he was a well-made creature, and pleasing to the female eye.

"How was I to know her game? I thought she was no good she, always seemed so precious uppish. There's no reading these women. However, as she throws herself at one's head, I'd be a fool if I didn't."

Such thoughts as these passed through the Bullyrag brain, as he smoothed Nelly's golden hair with his hand, and played with the lillies in her bonnet. He was, perhaps, one of the most selfish, worldly, meanspirited, petty schemers alive, and perhaps that was the reason why a woman could so easily get the best of him. When you worldly ones only get caught there's no folly, in my opinion that you would not commit, supposing a pair of bright eyes are the object of it.

This poor booby had long admired the actress in secret; but Mrs. Nelly's manner was, in general, so cold and repellant, that it would have had to have been a very hardy person, indeed, who would have attempted to take a liberty with her. You see what my Lord Drawler got for his impudence. Now that the ice was broken, Bullyrag was as bold as a lion.

The audience had all left the theatre, and

most of the actors, carpenters, and other persons employed upon the stage, had taken their departure, when Nelly left the manager's room. He had re-lit his cigar, which had probably gone out in the heat of argument, and he offered her his arm as they left the theatre.

Who should be waiting for them at the stage-door, but that everlasting Jack Ochre?

"Hallo, Nelly!" said he, "I have been looking for you everywhere. Wherever have you been?"

"I suppose I can go where I choose, Mr. Ochre?"

"Certainly—when and where you choose; only I was waiting to see you home."

"Thank you, sir," replied the lady, coldly; "I am very much obliged to you, but I will not trespass on your kindness. Mr. Bullyrag has offered me a seat in his brougham."

"Oh, very well! Then I'll trudge off on foot. I shall see you at the chambers?" Ochre added, turning round.

She looked at him a moment fixedly and full in the face; then, without answering, stepped into Bullyrag's brougham.

"What chambers does he mean?" asked the manager, as they drove away.

"He means the chambers where I live," replied the lady. "He's coming to supper."

"Oh, is he? We might as well have given him a lift."

"I don't see why."

"There's plenty of room."

"I would rather his room than his company."

"Well, if that's the case, he could have gone outside with the driver."

"He can ride behind on the spikes if he likes, can't he?" said the lady, with a laugh.

Then, as they drove on, she added, in a different tone,—

"Pray is he of much service to you? You give him a very high salary, and he is a most wretched painter. Everybody says so."

"I thought everybody said the reverse."

"Did you? You're mistaken."

Then they rode on in silence.

"Those dazzling dells of delicious delight are rather poor," thought Bullyrag, pondering over the transformation-scene for his next pantomime, on which Mr. Ochre was at that time busily engaged. "Smudger, at the 'Royal British,' would turn out a better thing than that, I know."

The deluded Jack meanwhile went paddling through the rain, never dreaming that he was the subject of the manager's thoughts. He was far from comfortable, though, I can tell you.

"Good heavens!" said he to himself, "what ever will Maurice do? He'll go distracted. To desert him in that sort of way! It's horrible. It will break his heart, I'm sure of it. He is so infatuated about her too. I'm sure he thinks her an angel. Oh, dear, how can any one be so blind!"

It is a singular fact that there is seldom any middle course in these matters: a man either loves or hates the mistress of another man. It is generally the latter.

"How so-and-so can be such a fool!" one says.

"A Gorgon like that, too, with neither looks nor manners!"

Then they imitate the lady's peculiarities, if she has any, and make great fun of her.

The wretched youth who is the protector of the party in question would doubtless be very indignant did he know that the friends who came and smoked his pipes, and ate his bread-and-butter, could thus ridicule the beloved one; but such sensitiveness would be very foolish, after all; for surely she is not kept to suit their whims and fancies.

Ochre went paddling through the rain, which was coming down like it does in winter in some other countries, or in summer in this. By the time that he reached Foot Court he was almost wet to the skin. However, he rang the bell, too much occupied with his unpleasant thoughts to heed his dripping garments.

"How I am to tell him I don't know," said he, as he walked up-stairs.

He entered the room with a wofully long face, turning a sentence over in his mind with which he meant to break the dreadful news to Maurice.

Right in front of him, at the supper-table, which was beautifully laid out in "The Plumes'" best style, sat Mrs. Nelly, with a wine-glass in her hand, hob-nobbing with the manager and Cheveleigh.

She looked at Ochre with something of a smile in her half-closed eyes, and Mr. Ochre felt very foolish indeed, as most wiseacres do when they make a grand mistake.

Almost at the same moment a knock came at the door behind him, and, on its being opened, Charley Bux walked in, followed by a stranger.

"I've taken the liberty of bringing a friend, Maurice," said he. "I am sure you will excuse me, Mrs. Cheveleigh. He's a jolly fellow, when you know him. Allow me, Mrs. Cheveleigh, to present my friend, Lord Drawler."

Nelly's face turned all sorts of colours for an instant; then she recovered herself. She was one of the cleverest women in the world, if not the greatest actress.

"I think I've had the pleasure already," said she, with a smile.

Then his lordship got very red, and bowed, and tried to laugh, and said, "The pleasure was mutual."

CHAPTER THE FORTY-FOURTH.

A LITTLE OF THE LUDICROUS, AND A LITTLE OF THE HORRIBLE.

IT is an extraordinary thing what a difficulty it is to write a novel without putting a lord in it—particularly a novel in penny numbers. I can scarcely recollect a penny serial that is not literally bursting with the aristocracy. And, when you come to think of it, it is very mortifying that these writing persons can't make up a story about us common people. Perhaps they think that our lives are not sufficiently interesting. But I've never noticed that fault about mine: have you?

You may say, perhaps, you remember several stories where the hero or heroine has been chosen from very low society, and turned out very interesting. That's true enough; but the worst of it is, they, alas! turn out to be heirs to some immense property, or come into some impossible title. So it is very evident they are a cut above us, after all.

However, it's a great shame that the lords and ladies should have got hold of my story as well, like all the rest; for I have been told that this novel is altogether unlike any other novel in our language, which I cannot account for, unless it is that I have endeavoured to write of life as I see it at the end of my nose, instead of drawing on imagination. Between you and I, I must put in a lord or two, because this book has been advertised as a ROMANCE OF GOOD AND BAD SOCIETY. People are calling out for the "Good." Could you have better than a lord? Come, you shall have it.

And now for the supper. It was a very extensive one. Soup, to begin with, roast turkey, and other trifles of that sort. Hock and Madeira on the table, and a dozen bottles with lead over their corks, cooling in an ice-tub, lay in the bed-room. Then everybody was as polite, and genteel, and uncomfortable as you please. One or two of the most presentable of the young ladies from the Apollo, and a lady-friend of Mr. Letchery's. There was some chaff with Jack Ochre about his bringing some fabulous inamorata, supposed to sell water-cresses in Whitechapel, but it fell through at the last. As for gentlemen, there was a queer mixture: one or two very genteel creatures from the Bad Bargains, who came in evening dress, and were troubled in their minds about their white ties, which they touched up on the quiet every now and then when they had an opportunity. There were, also, the low comedian from the Apollo, and a comic singer from the Great Orpheus Music Hall, who came almost in evening dress because they had no other dress, but varied it a little by wearing blue and purple satin waistcoats

But decidedly the feature of the entertainment was the first-class waiter from the "Plumes." He was a nice, fat man, who wore a nice fat curl upon his forehead, patted down flat. He was a great, big, comfortable-looking person, who ought to have been a beef-eater, instead of a carver of plates and dishes, and an attendant sprite in an eating-house, at the beck and call of any young jack-anapes who took into his head to go there for his dinner. But he was just the sort of waiter I should have liked to have kept if I had had a cook-shop, for to see him set you wondering what the meats must be like that could produce so fine an animal.

"I'm very happy to see you, my lord," said Maurice, who was not much embarrassed by the unexpected arrival of his distinguished guest. "I believe I had once the honour of meeting you at Charley Bux's rooms. Can you find a seat? Allow me."

He would have offered Lord Drawler a chair at his end of the table, but his lordship helped himself to one by Nelly's side. Thus she sat between Drawler and Bullyrag.

Then the supper began, and the guests removed their eyes from his lordship and fixed them on their soup plates.

"May I have the pleasure of a glass of wine with you, Miss Raymond?" said his lordship, addressing the actress by the name with which the public knew her. "You cannot imagine how long I have been pining to see you."

"You could have seen me any night for a shilling," replied Nelly, with a laugh. "That's the price of our boxes."

"I mean in private life," said Drawler. "My first attempt was not very successful."

"I wonder you tried another."

"You went the very way to make me."

"Indeed! I wonder what kind of treatment would have had a contrary effect."

"I can't say, I'm sure; but you know that more obstacles a man meets with the more——"

"A glass of wine, Mrs. Cheveleigh?" said Bullyrag, from the other side; then in a lower voice,—"Dash it all, if you're going to talk to that swell all night I shall cut my lucky."

"My dear Mr. Bullyrag, how unreasonable you are. I must be polite to the creature at my own house. You can fancy how much I esteem him by the way I served him the other night."

"I know you're too sensible a woman to care for a puppy like that; and I wanted to talk to you. If you must have an increase of salary, you must. You puss, you'd get blood out of a stone, you would!"

"I wonder you waste your talents in such a poor theatre as the Apollo," said his lordship. "If you would only allow me, I would speak to Webster, or Buckstone about you?"

"You are very kind, my lord, but I am sure I am not clever enough."

"Not clever enough! I swear by heaven, I never——"

"A glass of wine, my lord," interrupted Maurice.

All this time the supper was disappearing, slowly but surely, before the voracious professionals. A good deal of wine went the way of the supper, and everybody was getting a little more at home.

"I recollect, when I was in the West Riding——" the low comedian began, several times during the course of the meal, serving up a course of old Joe Millers as fragments of personal experience.

Then some of the ladies grew talkative, and entered into lengthy details of nothing in particular; until, upon the arrival of the dessert, somebody called upon the host for a song, and he obliged them with a description of the happy domestic life of Mr. and Mrs. Johnson, putting his hat on the back of his head, and lurching his coat a little off one shoulder, after the manner of the great W. G. Ross, *vide* portrait.

It is rather a mistake when harmony sets in at private parties, for, if you are not a singer, you never get another chance of a hearing. However, the wine kept circulating, and some spirits-and-water somehow got upon the table. One or two of the songs were of a startling character, but nobody found fault with them. One or two of the stories were not strictly correct. Somebody began telling a tale before somebody else had finished, and nobody in particular was listening to either. At length, one of the gentlemen from the Bad Bargains went and leant his head out of window to get a breath of air, and came back looking very ghastly, and one of the ladies was troubled with a hiccup.

"Pleasher—glash o' winsh," said some one, very seriously.

"Veshy happy," replied another, as solemn as a judge.

They then began to enjoy themselves.

"I beg your pardon, sir," said the first-class waiter, coming in from the passage a little flushed in the face, as though from recent violent bodily exertion, "there's one of the gents is very bad outside, and I can't do nothing with him."

It was that Bad Bargains' man again, who was lying full-length among the dirty plates and dishes, with his feet in ice. He said he was "all right," when they asked how he found himself, and bade them mind their own "bishnesh."

After almost inconceivable trouble, this unfortunate gentleman was induced to lie down upon the bed in the back room, from which he fell off once or twice with a great thump, and was lifted on again by the big waiter, who undertook to watch over him until such time as a friend could take him home in a cab.

It is wonderful what a difference there is, in these sort of parties, at the beginning and at the end. At first, everybody is so freezingly polite, so cold, and so distant. You would imagine Arabella Fitzmountmorency a dragon of virtue, and Baby Jordan an awfully unapproachable young virgin; but, Lord! how they alter when the drink sets in. Baby is the most affable of women, and Fitzmountmorency no prouder than she used to be when she was plain Sally Hodges, and lived in Church Street, Soho, on second floor back, and "bilked" her landlady.

Thus was it that the party became very lively indeed, and the other lodgers began to hammer on the walls in the same sort of indignant chorus that they did on the night when I first introduced Maurice to the reader. Indeed, the same irascible old gentleman underneath having gone to bed in the same way, with the same sort of sick head-ache, was aroused in the same manner, and was vowing vengeance on the landing, in the identical tasselled nightcap which he wore that evening we last heard of him.

Somebody had suggested asking him up to join the party, and a deputation of ladies waited upon the old gentleman with this object, but were somewhat uncourteously received.

I should mention, by the way, that the disagreeable tenant had moved his rooms from the first to the second floor, and Cheveleigh having moved his from the second to the third, they had consequently retained their relative positions.

"Let's have a dance," said Charley Bux; "that'll amuse him."

Now, Maurice's apartments were scarcely qualified for Terpsychorean exercises. It was a pretty tight fit with the supper-table in the middle of the room; but the company were not to be daunted by trifles. The table was taken to pieces and pushed on to the landing, the chairs thrown in a heap, Mr. Ochre struck up a polka on the piano, and Mr. Bux would have resorted to that celebrated post-horn—only it was in pledge (Maurice said he had given it away)—and so he danced, instead, stamping with all his might upon the floor.

Bullyrag took the opportunity, while the rest were thus engaged in boisterous mirth, to speak to Nelly.

"Tell him there's a morning rehearsal to-morrow, and come and see me. I'll have my brougham waiting for you at twelve in Theobald's Road, opposite 'The Raglan.' Do you hear?"

She squeezed his hand in reply.

"Oh, Mrs. Cheveleigh—Nelly—you will let me call you Nelly, for I feel as though we were old friends."

This time it was Lord Drawler who had got an opportunity to talk to her unobserved.

"You may call an actress what you please, my lord. Their names are public property."

"Would that I might call you by one name!"

"What is that, pray?—Lady Drawler?"

"Alas! that is impossible. I've been married these six months."

"How jealous I should be, if I were her ladyship."

"Had I met you, you angel, she would never have been her ladyship."

"Gracious, what nonsense! As if you meant it?"

"On my soul, I do—I swear to you! I know I'm acting like a villain to say so under this roof, but, by heavens, I have loved you from the first moment I saw you."

"But, then, you're married."

"What does that matter? If everything that wealth can buy, or love suggest——Nelly, dear Nelly, listen to me——"

"Who says a gallop?" cried Jack Ochre.

"Will your lordship show the example?"

"To-morrow, at twelve," whispered Bullyrag. "I must be off now."

"Will you dance with me, Nell?" said Maurice. "This is quite like old times, is it not? By Jove, Nelly, how beautiful you look! Lord, how proud I am of you!"

Just then they heard heavy footsteps coming up-stairs.

"It's the police again," suggested Charley Bux.

"It's that old fool down-stairs."

"Shy some oyster shells at him."

"No—no—bring him in, and let's make him drunk!"

"How can we, though?"

"Pour some gin down his throat with a funnel."

"No; let me shave him with an oyster shell."

"Stop, perhaps it's old Perks. Wait a moment?"

They waited. It was neither, but a bleareyed, grey-headed, disreputable-looking old man, in a battered hat, very shabby, and rather drunk, who wanted to see Mr. Maurice.

"Hallo, Bob Sawder!" cried Cheveleigh,

coming forward. "What on earth has brought you here?"

"I'd like to speak to you, sir."

"Speak away, then? Will you have anything?"

Then nodding to the company he added,— "The drollest old fellow you ever saw! we'll make him dance a hornpipe. Here's a glass of gin, Mr. Sawder, and now what's the row?"

"Thank you, sir. Ladies and gentlemen, your good health! I'd like to speak to you alone, sir."

"What nonsense. You can speak up."

"I think I'd rather not, sir."

"Well, well, come this way; never mind us, ladies and gentlemen. Mr. Sawder will give us his hornpipe presently."

The ancient servitor followed Mr. Cheveleigh down to the other end of the passage towards a window, at which they paused.

The cold, reproachful, sober day light was breaking over the housetops, and showed the old man's face, pallid and agitated; the young one's, sodden and flushed.

"What is it, Bob?" asked Cheveleigh, anxiously.

But the old man, dragging out a wretched rag of handkerchief, smeared his eyes and whimpered.

"What is it, Bob? Are you drunk?"

"Oh! hush, Mr. Maurice—sir. Hush, sir, not so loud. Oh! sir, so horrible — so horrible!"

"What is it?"

"Oh, sir, my poor, dear master!"

"Great God! what has happened? Is he ill?"

"Ill, sir? Oh, worse than that!"

"Dead!"

"Dead—dead! — worse than dead. Oh, God have mercy on me, I've been a graceless wretch, I have—I have! We live in the midst of graves and yawning sepulchres——"

"Speak plainer!" gasped Maurice, seizing him by the throat. "Is he dead or not?"

"Yes, yes, he's dead enough. I've run all the way to tell you, sir. *I've just come from seeing it.* It's at a public-house. Oh, dear— oh, dear! how horrible it was. I feel as though I should die myself. I'd like to have another drop of something if you have it handy, my poor knees tremble so."

"Hallo, Maurice!" called Charley Bux; "when's this hornpipe coming off?"

But Maurice did not hear them. He had fallen on his knees, his head clasped in his hands, and he was sobbing like a child.

CHAPTER THE FORTY-FIFTH.

A LITTLE MORE OF THE HORRIBLE.

"THERE'S fuss enough about Mr. Hadget when he goes to Brighton," said the party to whom Sir John had spoken on his way out.

"There's rather a run on the time, too," said another party, who had been spending the evening in the lodge. "We shall know what o'clock it is when we've done."

It was twenty minutes past eleven, and a stormy night.

There was, besides the wind, a drenching rain, which drifted in the faces of those unfortunates who were compelled to walk the London streets at such an unseasonable time.

Between the hours of eleven and twelve, the leading streets of the metropolis are usually well filled with holiday folk; but the unexpected setting in of wet weather—it had been beautifully fine during the fore-part of the day —had driven the wayfarers pell-mell into cabs, and omnibusses, archways, and doorways—in fact, anywhere for shelter.

Thus were the principal thoroughfares unusually lonely and deserted, while the back streets, slums, and blind alleys were silent as the grave. Here and there you might have seen a stray pedestrian endeavouring to seek shelter under the side of a house, or some miserable, houseless wretch creeping into a dark corner out of the rain, and shivering as though with the ague. A very damp policeman now and then came clomping round a corner. A baked-potato can here and there suggested a little warmth and comfort; or a gleam of gaslight through the half-closed door of a coffee-house relieved the air of general dreariness and desolation.

At twenty-three minutes past eleven exactly, two men passed round at the back of St. Mary's in the Strand, and stood still at the edge of the pavement directly in front of Sams' Coffee House. One looked like an old country gentleman, the other like a seafaring man, with three sheets in the wind.

"I wish we had made it a little earlier," said the country gentleman, "then we could have got some brandy before the public-houses shut up."

"I never thought of that," replied the seafaring man. "However, you can get plenty on board, of better quality, and quite as cheap. We'll get something to eat, though. Are you hungry?"

"Not particularly."

"Well, we'll walk on a little, first."

"I expect we shan't get a cab this wet night," said the country gentleman, presently; "though there seems to be very few people about."

"A great deal too many—curse them!"

"Why, how do they hurt you?"

"I don't want to be recognised, that's all."

"What nonsense! Anybody would think you had just committed a murder."

"Or was going to commit one, eh?"

There was such a queer expression on the seafaring man's face, as the light from a street lamp they were passing fell full upon it, that it gave the country gentleman, who caught a glimpse of it, quite a turn.

"By God!" said he, "if I didn't know you, old fellow, I should be quite afraid of you. You look so very odd at times."

"But you do know me, though," said the seafaring man. "And so you're not, eh?—so you're not?"

"Certainly not! Don't be so fierce about it. How queer you are to-night."

They walked on in silence through Temple Bar, and past St. Dunstan's Church. Presently they came to a coffee-house on the left-hand side of Fleet Street, going towards Farringdon Street, before which the seafaring man stopped.

"What do you say to a cup of tea and something to eat?" he asked.

"I don't care much about it, but we'll go in, if you like."

So they went in, and the seafaring man selecting the most retired corner he could find, they sat down in it, and ordered some refreshment.

There were very few other customers. A man fast asleep in one of the boxes, with his head on the table; and another one asleep, propped up uncomfortably in a corner, something like the little hunchback in the story, who swallowed the fishbone, and was found reared up in the fireplace by the merchant, when he took him for a robber, and cudgelled him.

In the next compartment but one to that where our two friends were sitting, three young men, apparently the worse for liquor, and employed in that dreary British pastime called "making a night of it." At present they were only discussing such mild beverages as tea and coffee, but one was smoking a rank Cuba, which the attendant Hebe had several times requested him to put out.

"All right, Mary, my dear,' said this gentleman, in reply to her earnest solicitation. "If it's disagreeable to these gents, out it goes. Only say the word."

"I have said it, sir."

"Put it out, Bill; we shall have smoking enough before eight o'clock to-morrow, I'll be bound."

"You don't mean to sit up all night, do you?"

"What else do you propose?"

"We might as well go and have a snooze somewhere, and be called at six."

"Oh, ah! It's very fine talking over-night. You wouldn't see the pull of it to-morrow, I can tell you. That's why I didn't see the last scragging-match."

"There's precious small joke in sitting up all night, in my opinion. I never knew of anything that made it worth one's while to do it."

"That's just like you, that is. When ever you come out for a lark, you want to go home again directly."

"I tell you what, Bill," said the third gentleman, joining in the conversation, "I dare say that poor cove we're going to see worked off at eight o'clock would be precious glad to change places with you."

The seafaring man, who had been listening to this conversation, suddenly grew impatient. "Come on," said he, "there's quite enough of that. There's an infernal fate about it."

"A fate about what, man? Whatever is the matter with you?"

"Didn't you hear them talking?"

"I don't know what it's about. What are they going to see?"

"Going to an execution. There's a man to be hanged to-morrow."

"Serve him right!" said the country gentleman. "Here's the coffee."

The seafaring man drank his cupfull in silence. Then said with a laugh,—

"You're right. He was a clumsy lubber. He couldn't have expected much different."

"Ah!" said the country gentleman, sententiously, "murder will out, you know. However artfully the murderer lays his plans, however carefully he hides the deed, there's always some corner left sticking out."

"Pooh! there are murders enough that are never discovered at all, and lots more that never would be, did not the craven-hearted wretch 'peach on himself."

"Because the horrible crime has preyed so on his mind, that life becomes a curse to him."

"Then such a fool as that had better lose it. Come on, I'm ready."

"What a desperate hurry you're in all at once. Wait till I've done my bread-and-butter."

"Be quick then. Don't be all night about it."

While the country gentleman hastily despatched his meal, the other sat patting his foot upon the floor, and fumbling at the corner of the table with his hand. It was lank and long-fingered, with something very horrible about it. Not at all the sort of hand you would have expected to find belonging to a seafaring man. They say that they can read your character by your hand, as by your hand-writing, or as gipsies read your fortune by your palm. If ever there was a hand which spoke of cruelty, rapacity, and griping avarice, that was the one. If ever there was a hand which you would have disliked to feel near your throat with a razor in it, that was the hand. It would have ruined any barber.

The country gentleman was too intent upon his bread and butter perhaps, to notice his comrade's ugly fist, or perhaps he had seen it often before, and got used to it. However it might have been, he took no notice of the man's restless fingers, which were busy clutching and clawing at the wood-work, as though they would have torn it piecemeal.

Would to God he had, and seen a warning in their ugly twistings.

When he had finished his meal he rose, and the two went out together into the stormy night. The rain was pouring down in torrents; the street seemed totally deserted.

An empty cab was passing at the moment: they hailed it.

"Drive to St. Katharine's Docks. Which way will you go?"

"By Cheapside."

"No—by Thames Street."

They got into the cab, which drove along rapidly in the direction indicated, turned down towards Blackfriars' Bridge, and then to the left into Upper Thames Street.

"Nothing could be better," said the seafaring man, looking right and left out of the cab windows, and shutting them both up. "It's the very time for it."

"The time for what?" the country gentleman asked. "What the devil is the matter with you?"

The other paused for full a minute, looking his companion full in the face, then suddenly made a tiger-like spring upon him, twisted his neckerchief tightly, and still more tightly, round his throat, until his face grew black with suffocation, then held him down, and hissed at him between his clenched teeth—

"I'll tell you what's the matter!"

The other, in his sudden terror and surprise, had not a word to say, had he had the power; but, with eyes starting from their sockets, widely-opened mouth, and lolling tongue, regarded his antagonist, speechless and inert.

"I'll tell you what is the matter, Sir John Cheveleigh. The matter is, that you're a worthless, graceless, God-forsaken dog, I mean to rid the world of. The matter is, that the accumulated hate of twenty years has steeled my hand to a deed to-night that I might swing for, like the blundering hound they're going to hang to-morrow at the Debtors' door. Your murder they'll never find out—be sure of that. You're going to death, as certain as this cab is going up Thames Street. There's no hope for you."

The old man struggled feebly in the other's gripe, but could not give utterance to a sound.

"You're going to die, Sir John," the other continued, with a sort of subdued ferocity which was much more terrible than any noisy demonstration of wrath. "I'm going to cut your throat. That's why I brought you here!"

Seemingly fearful lest the old man should die of strangulation before the proper time, the murderer loosened his hold upon his victim's throat, holding the neckerchief in such a way that he could tighten it again instantly.

"Do you recollect my leaving you early this evening, when I told you that I had yet a little business to transact? Nod, if you unstand."

Perhaps the old man was too frightened to do what he was bid, or perhaps the tight hold which the other maintained of his neckerchief, prevented him from moving his head, for he only rolled his eyes, and glared at his antagonist.

"The reason I went out was, first of all, to see your son, Maurice, and ascertain whether he knew you were in town. I thought that if you had had a spark of affection—a single atom of a father's love to redeem your swinish nature, you might have called upon him before you left the country for ever, to say good-bye. You hadn't, though. Secondly, I went out to prove an *alibi*."

At this word, the old man commenced struggling afresh, but a twist of the other's wrist silenced him. When he was quiet the seafaring man continued with even more ferocity in his look and tone, "To prove an *alibi!* I have taken every precaution to let people know that I have gone to Brighton, even to taking a railway ticket, which I have this moment in my pocket. Everything has been well arranged and thought over. I took a cottage at Brighton, where I have lately been down to sleep two or three times a week. An old woman comes about noon, and rings the bell to know if I want anything, and if I'm there I let her in. *I shall let her in to-morrow.*"

Again the old man struggled desperately.

"I shall let her in to-morrow, having settled accounts with you to-night. You see, now, that there is very little chance of my being connected with your murder. You yourself have helped to prove my *alibi*. You and a sailor-like man left Lyon's Inn together. Got into a cab together, and asked to be driven to St. Katharine's Docks. The sailor got out by the way, and you were driven on. When the cab got there, you were discovered to have had your throat cut. Supposed to have been done by the sailor, who is nowhere to be found. There is no connecting link between Mr. Hadget and this sailor fellow, who in no way resembles him. I like to tell you this, to show you how utterly powerless you are in my hands, and how, after having cut your throat, I shall walk away without the slightest breath of suspicion attaching to me. Do you see?"

Like a madman tearing at his fetters, so the old man fought and battled in his murderer's grasp—then fell back, weak and panting.

The noise of the wheels upon the stones covered every other sound. The windows were all closed; the street deserted. There was not the slightest, faintest hope of rescue. The cold sweat of agony rolled slowly down the old man's face. The other, with the strength of a giant, held him down upon the seat; and, as his struggling ceased, continued in the same low tone,—

"You know—or ought to know—before this, how much I hate you. You know very well the scoundrel's part you acted with regard to her whom I was fool enough to love. When I found out your villany, I swore to have your blood, and only put it off to have a better opportunity. I've thought of this time for many a month, and seen it coming. You have in your pockets twenty-seven thousand pounds in notes and otherwise; I mean to take it all, and stop at home to spend it comfortably, after I have cut your throat!"

Here he paused, and then gave the neckerchief another twist. The old man, half suffocated, lay motionless before him; then he took the razor from his pocket with one hand, retaining his hold with the other.

Although he could not move or speak, the wretched victim, seemed yet to retain sufficient sense to know what the other was doing, and watch him with his eyes. The murderer forced down the neckerchief to give his razor full play, planted his knee upon the old man's breast, then, with a scrunching, grinding twist he severed flesh and muscle, cutting the victim's throat from ear to ear, and leaving a fearful, yawning gap, from which the hot blood gushed out upon his hands.

Upon his hands, upon his wrists, upon his breast, upon his face! Blood everywhere—all round—all over him him, it seemed at first. Still he cut on, until he had near severed the grizzly head from its trunk. Then throwing the body back, he wiped his hands upon the dead man's clothes, and then began to rifle his pockets, deliberately.

While thus engaged the cab stopped.

———

DREAMING AND SCHEMING.

CHAPTER THE FORTY-SIXTH.

THE BLOOD AMONGST THE STRAW.

WITH a sensation of intense, unutterable horror the murderer looked around towards the driver's seat. He had turned round, and was tapping at the window. Had he heard a noise within?

"What is it?"

Something the matter with the harness; he was going to get down and mend it.

"Very well."

While thus engaged the assassin kept the window, to guard against surprise. At any moment might the cabman have opened the

No. 10.

door, and discovered all. However, he had no such thought; and when, with a piece of string, he had made such repairs as he deemed necessary, he clambered back and whipped up the horse again.

They were by this time underneath London Bridge. In a few minutes they would have reached their destination—not a moment was to be lost. Emptying the murdered man's pockets of everything they contained, and, taking care to see that the bank notes were among the contents, the sailor thrust them into the breast pocket of an under-coat he wore, and letting down the window, opened the door and called to the cabman,—

"Hi! Stop! Hold hard," he cried," "I want to get out here."

The cabman stopped, and was jumping down to help him, when the other interposed,—

"No—no! Stop where you are. I want you to drive on my friend as fast as you can, or he'll not be in time for his boat. I'll come after him."

While speaking, he had alighted, and was now struggling to fasten the door. A horrible door it was to fasten, and one which, somehow, most perversely refused to catch.

"I'll do it for you," said the obliging cabman, again descending from the box.

"No—no," the sailor man replied, almost fiercely. "Stop where you are—can't you? Damnation seize it! I beg your pardon, gov'nor, only you've no time to lose. Drive on as fast as you can. Good night, old fellow."

He feigned shaking hands with the murdered man inside; then, as the cab set off, he ran across the road, and turned the corner of a narrow alley sharply. No sooner had he passed it than he tore off his beard, and threw it away from him. Then darted down another narrow passage; and, pausing in a dark corner, where there was a grating leading to a sewer, threw the razor down, and taking off his pilot coat and wide-a-wake, rolled them up and left them on a doorstep. When this was done, he loosened an opera-hat, which was suspended in front of him by a piece of string and over which his coat had been buttoned, shook it out, and put it on. After which he walked more deliberately round the next corner, and was just beginning to whistle a tune, when he felt a heavy hand laid on his shoulder.

He started back in mortal fright, and, shivering in every limb, looked towards the person who had touched him, and who had as quickly withdrawn his hand again.

He was a wretched, not to say repulsive-looking person, a swarthy-faced, grey-headed, scowling vagabond, with a true cut-throat cast of countenance.

Miserably thin and dirty, ragged and forlorn, bearing in such poor scraps of raiment as he still possessed something of the appearance of a foreign sailor who had been shipwrecked and was out of wardrobe.

It could not have been that the murderer was afraid that his crime had been discovered. Such an idea had at the first moment flashed across his brain, but a glance at the dilapidated habiliments of the stranger reassured him—he did not look much like a policeman. And then he reflected, that except in the rather suspicious circumstances of having thrown off his beard, and left his coat and hat upon a doorstep, what else could be proved against him? Most certainly the man had not followed him from Thames Street, for he had looked around twice to see if he were pursued. Besides, he felt confident that this ragged fellow had been hidden away in a corner into which he had probably crept for shelter from the wind and rain, and from which he had reached out his hand to touch the sailor as he passed.

What made him, then, at the second glance he took at the stranger's face, utter a wild cry of alarm, surprise, and recognition, and staggering backwards into the road, but to save himself from falling full length upon the ground by clutching at the wall, against which, leaning and panting, he surveyed the apparition with horror and dismay?

The beggar, for such he seemed to be, had just began to mutter some half-indistinct prayer for alms, in such broken English as he was master of, when the sailor's surprising conduct made him pause and stare at him in his turn.

"What is it?" he growled, with a long string of "sacre dieu's!" and "sacre bleu's!" "Keep off—keep off!" the other screamed, wildly. Begone! man or devil? What do you want here to-night?"

"I want to eat," the Frenchman answered, catching a stray word of the sailor's speech. "I have hungry."

It seemed a monstrous relief to this murderous seafaring man to think that he wanted no more. He took some half-pence from his pocket, and handing them to the beggar, said, with a grim smile, in French,—

"I took you for a ghost."

"A ghost, sir!" the beggar answered, laughing, "I'm thin enough to be a ghost's shadow. I'm only a poor Frenchman, sir, from Lyons."

What made that seafaring man start back, and, leaving go of the half-pence before the beggar had got well hold of them, send them flying into the gutter, then take to his heels and run as though the devil was after him, splashing through mud and mire, recklessly tearing round corners and across streets, heedless of whose way he ran in, and whom or what he overthrew in his wild career?

What makes him still run on and on, without pausing or feeling any fatigue, till he finds himself again in Fleet Street, where he summons up courage to walk more quietly, and even to look in again at that coffee house where he and the country gentleman had partaken of some food together? There are still the three young men, and they are yet talking about the execution which they are going to see to-morrow. Will they never exhaust the topic? There still is the man asleep with his head upon the table, or else he has gone away, and another man, the very counterpart of him, is slumbering in his place. Even the other sleeper has not changed his position very much—perhaps it is a trifle more uncomfortable, but still very much the same.

It is very light in this coffee-house, and when the sailor man had come in, and taken his seat at the table where he sat a little while ago, the reflection of a lamp falls full upon his face, and you can see that he has changed so much in the short interval that had elapsed since he was here last—it cannot be much more than an hour at most—that it is hard to believe he is the same. He has lost his beard, his wide-a-wake, and pilot coat, which makes an immense difference in him. Indeed it would take an eye a great deal sharper than that of a London detective—wonderful men though we all think them—to discover any resemblance between the close-shaven, cunning-looking gentleman who sits there reading the paper, and the half-smuggler, half brigand who had occupied the same seat a little while ago.

"So far, so good," said Mr. Hadget. "Nobody's likely to meet me in town to-night. I don't feel much inclined for bed, and so I'll knock out the time the best way I can. It'll amuse me. I couldn't go to sleep very comfortably."

He ate and drank heartily of what was placed before him; then leant back comfortably in his seat.

"Whatever made that man turn up to night?" said he to himself. "It was devilish odd—devilish odd! He didn't know me, though."

He sat and clawed the table edge, as was his wont.

"To think that I should have made up the lie, and that it should have come true. It's most extraordinary!"

More clawing, and twitching of his ugly mouth.

"It couldn't have been managed nicer. It was beautiful. There's not a trace left!"

As he spoke his eyes fell on those restless fingers of his working at the table edge. They were red with blood. A spot or two were upon his wrists, and on his legs and shoes. There was also blood beneath his nails.

Busily employed scratching away the traces of his crime, we leave him for a while, and return to look after the body of his victim in the cab.

. . . .

Happy driver! how blithely he whistled on his box. He might have had a wedding party for his fare instead of the mangled corpse, which jogging too and fro with the motion of the vehicle, fell into hideous shapes, the head rolling on one side and the tongue lolling out in a gastly fashion.

On they went, the driver whistling still, until another coach, forcing its way out from a gateway, somehow got its wheels entangled with those of the cab containing the body, and after an infinity of plunging and backing on the part of the horses, and shouting and swearing on the part of the drivers, came to a sudden halt.

"Now then—now then!" cried a policeman, who was standing by. "Where are you going to, both of you? The only way is to lift up the wheel. Here, let me try?"

He stopped to do so, and pulled at the spokes. In raising himself again to get a better hold, he looked at his hands.

"What the deuce is this?" said he; "I'm all over blood. See, here's blood coming out underneath the cab door! What have you got in it?"

They flung it open, and uttered an exclamation of surprise and horror at the sickening spectacle within. Next moment the officer had the cabman by the collar.

"What are you doing?" said he. "Where are you going to with that?"

"I haven't done it!" roared the man, in terrible alarm. "It was a sailor fellow. Take your hands off, will you?"

———

CHAPTER THE FORTY-SEVENTH.

IN WHICH NELLY PLAYS WITH HER FINGERS.

YOUNG ladies, before proceeding any further, I must beg of you to refrain from reading this history; it is not a fit book for you. Your dear papas, I am sure, would agree with me in forbidding you to continue its perusal. It is a nasty worldly story, all about naughty people, who do naughty things. There's nothing about beautiful young ladies getting married to handsome young gentlemen, and living happy ever afterwards. There is not, upon my word, a marriage in all the book. So, you see, it can't be interesting, and you ought to feel obliged to me for warning you in time. Now, put it down, like good little girls, and get on with your needlework, or your *Family Herald*, or some of your other little fal-di-dals.

You and I, Madam, have lived longer in the world, and know more of its evil doings, its trials, and its hardships; we know that there is oftentimes much quiet heroism in bearing with, hiding, and stifling that long heart-sickness succeeding the honeymoon, when the mask has fallen off, and they have found each other out *too late*. We know that it does not always follow because people are married, that they love one another. We know, too (for do not the newspapers tell us so every day?), that all love-making does not lead church-wards. We have heard, in our time, horrible stories of temptation, ruin, desertion, and shame, the heroines of which, beautifully dressed and tastefully painted, may be seen flaunting in the Park, the Haymarket, or elsewhere. In fact, to cut it short, we know a thing or two, and are not surprised to find that there are such horrible hussies as Nelly Raymond alive and flourishing, or that young men of family should keep such low company, and have such vicious tastes. We'd like to have the naughty creatures whipped, but only there are so many of them, I hardly know whether there are enough of us good people to do it.

I left Maurice upon his knees in the passage, and Mr. Bob Sawder looking down at him stupidly, and wiping his own eyes with the rag of handkerchief he carried.

"Don't take on so, sir, there's a good young gentleman. You always was a real gentleman, and had a good heart, as I have always said."

"Come on, Maurice! What the devil are you talking about?" some one called from the room.

They would, I dare say, have come out in a body to see after him, had not pretty Nell taken it into her head to strike up a roaring bacchanalian ditty, the first verse of which she sang in a rich melodious voice, that rang through the house, and at its conclusion, the rest of the guests taking up the chorus with rather more noise than harmony, made a din that seemed to shake the very window frames.

Staggering on his feet, the young man mastered his emotions in the best way that he could, and going to the door of the room where the company were thus entertaining themselves, beckoned to Nelly to come to him.

"What is it, dear?"

"I have heard something which obliges me to leave you for a few hours. Don't send them away. Get me my hat quietly, there's a dear?"

She fetched it to him, then put her arm round his neck.

"What is the matter, Maurice? Have I done anything?"

At first she was afraid he might have overheard a whisper from one of her admirers, and was jealous

"Have I done anything to offend you, dear?"

"You, Nelly?" he answered. "No, no. It is nothing. A misfortune has happened to me."

"Do tell me what it is."

She drew him closer towards her, and he might have done as she desired, had not their guests at that moment burst out again with another chorus. A kind of indescribable but intense hatred for everybody and everything possessed him at the moment, and he disengaged himself from her embrace rather impatiently.

"No, no; it's nothing about you. Curse their noise!" he said, then ran down stairs.

She stood and looked after him wistfully. He was always so gentle, kind, and considerate, his altered manner surprised and angered her. Of course, she had not the least idea what caused it. As for him, as he reached the last step of the staircase, or even before he had reached it, he had repented, and was reproaching himself with his harshness. He had more than half a mind to run up-stairs again, to say good-bye, and kiss her, and ask her not to be uneasy at his departure, and assure her that he would quickly return. He did not do so, because——because he never did half what he intended to do, or what he knew he ought to have done, any more than you or I do, or will do, to the end of the chapter.

Nelly went back to the good company after she had heard the street door slam to. You know the outer door of Cleveland Chambers is usually kept closed, like the doors of those houses let out in a similar manner in Buckingham Street, Strand, and the adjacent streets of the Adelphi.

Another quadrille, or polka, or some wild kind of dance, without any particular step or figure, was going on. The large waiter had knocked up and gone home an hour before (your large men have not generally great powers of endurance), and somebody else, taking his place, was endeavouring to boil some water in a bachelor's kettle, using, on an average, three wheels and a half to one pint. The company were having another allowance of hot grog, though, to judge by their flushed faces and disordered attire, they did not stand much in need of it. In fact, everybody was more or less intoxicated.

There are two ways in which I might describe the scene this graceless revel presented at six o'clock in the morning. One would be voluptuous and sensual; the other a la GOUGH, with a great moral lesson in it about the bottle; then, if Mr. GEORGE CRUIKSHANK were to draw a lot of coarse, vulgar wretches boosing, or lying stupidly drunk about the floor, after his well-known style, the picture would be as unlike life as any teetotaller could wish it to be.

I have no power of language to describe, nor do I possess a draughtsman's skill to sketch the scene before me. Photography might do it perhaps, for otherwise a hundred details which give it its force and character would be missed. The candles, guttering in their sockets; the wreck of supper, lying about the floor and on the side-tables; the empty bottles, rolled in corners; the sleeping sot, stretched on the bed in the adjoining room, whose face some wag has decorated with burnt cork. Lou, flushed and boisterous in her mirth, Jenny dreamy and sentimental, Nelly's golden hair all wet with wine, a cigar 'twixt Fanny's lips, and Sally snoring. Bright eyes, still brighter with drink, white necks and snowy bosoms glancing in the candle-light, silks and satins crumpled and stained. Noise, and riot, and disorder!

That cold-blooded monster, the new-born day, gazed unsympathisingly at the drinking-party, when some one was rash enough to draw aside the window-curtain. And thus the revelries broke up.

Not quite. They had yet to seek their hats and bonnets, yet to go singing down stairs and whooping out into the street, to chaff such members of the police force as they might find upon their way, and amuse themselves with such cumbersome pleasantries as the British mind, when it is in its cups, delighteth in.

And it was thus that Maurice wasted his money! In such witless orgies as these his guineas were squandered. He thought this pleasure, and pinned his faith, poor deluded one! on that enormous, awful sham—"Jolly-good-fellowship."

Now they had all gone, at last. The last faint echo of their voices died out of the court, and Nelly was alone. A horrible scene of dirt and disorder the apartment presented, littered with the fragments of the repast. It was very late, and time that all good folks, who had gone to bed in proper time, should have been thinking of getting up again. The early worm had been up a good hour, I dare say, all ready to be caught. Sagacious animal!

But Nelly, it would seem, was not inclined for sleep. She threw up the window, let some air in and some tobacco smoke out, and sat down close to the casement to think. She had a great deal to think about, and she sat down comfortably to do it. She held up three fingers of her pretty hand, and, nobody being by to overhear her, talked to them like little girls talk to their dolls.

"My lord, stand forth," she said to one finger, the tallest of the three, "what has your lordship got to say? 'If all that wealth can procure and love dictate——' That's what you say, sir, is it? I don't think you could hardly promise more. Love might probably dictate the purchase of many pretty little articles a lady requires, and wealth could procure them, without mortgaging his blucher boots, like poor old Maurice does. You are a handsome fellow, my lord, and one I could feel proud of. I wonder whether you would feel proud of me. You ought to do. I am as beautiful as anybody I ever saw, and more so, besides being what's called a superior sort of woman for my station. I wonder whether my station is always to be what it is now? or shall I some day be equal with it? Heigho!"

She sighed, and letting his lordship fall in her lap, sat silently looking out of window. After a while, she addressed the second finger.

"Mr. Bullyrag, pray what do *you* say? 'I say that I am the manager of a great East-end theatre, and worth a mint of money. You are an attractive actress, and a very pretty woman, and I love you to distraction.' That's what everybody says, Mr. B.; and, pray, what do you propose? Will you marry me, for instance? 'No, my dear, I can't do that, because I have a wife already—an ugly, faded bit of goods, who is bedridden, and all sorts of horrible things besides. But she won't die; and, and so I can only offer a brougham, a cottage at Putney, an increased salary, and a few other little inducements.' Well, my lord, will you marry me? 'No, madam, I too have a wife, whom I married six months ago, and registered a vow to love and cherish—— which I'm doing!' A pretty prospect for wife number two, my lord, supposing such a thing could happen."

She sat and mused again. What fun it would have been if her adorers could have heard her opinions of them through the key-hole. How it would have astonished their weak minds!

"And who is this little gentleman?" she asked of the third finger—a pretty little fellow it was—decorated with a beautiful little ring of pearls. "'My name is Maurice Cheveleigh, and I am a kind-hearted young man, without more brains than are absolutely necessary. I am a young man of property—or more properly, I shall have some property when my father dies; but when that's going to happen goodness only knows!' Well, sir, and what do you say? 'I love you more than all the world — more than my life— —more than my soul!' And would you marry me, sir? 'With a little persuasion I have no doubt I would.' And when you had? 'Then you would be Lady Cheveleigh.' Well, that's better than nothing. Heigho! I'm very sleepy."

The window began to be rather cold, and pretty Nelly began to feel rather sleepy, and thought that she would go to bed.

So to bed she went, and lay coiled up like a little mouse; her pretty head nestling upon the pillow, her soft yellow hair floating round her like so much floss silk. Oh! how beautiful she looked. Oh, what a pity it was that she was such a naughty girl!

If this were only an imaginative novel, I would have a very different sort of person, I can assure you. I am a sober-sided, solemn, old fellow. It would astonish you to see me after reading this terrible history. We writing people are shocking hypocrites.

There is the author of those athletic novels, for instance, full of strapping six foot heroes, who ride on horseback like wild Tartars, or circus men, and who think no more of taking a six-bar gate than I should of stepping over a fire plug-hole; and big, bouncing, healthy wenches, who literally knock the breath out of you at the end of every chapter with their bold tom-boy frolics. The author of these outrageous books, is a poor cripple, who could not take a "five-bar" any more than I could, who is no nearer six foot than I am—and that's a long way off—who, were he obliged to pass an evening with two or three of those playful kittens of heroines of his, to slap him on the back, and pull his ears, and knock him and his crutches all in lump, I expect he'd take a fancy to some gentler maidens for the future, with little less animal spirit in them.

Oh, Nelly—Nelly! I hope you will grow a better girl. There's room for improvement. Is there not?

CHAPTER THE FORTY-EIGHTH.

STREET WALKING.

HAVE you ever wandered about the streets all night? Not likely by choice—not by force, I trust. It is a dreary occupation. While the shops, or the public-houses are open; while people are about in the streets, and cabs and carriages are rattling home with late revellers, it is well enough; but between three and four begins the weary time. Seeing day-break is all very well once in a way (I have heard of maniacs who have got up on purpose), but when you have waited for it, and seen it rise, and have to wait till it gets warm, that's where the fun flags.

I expect there are many of our poor brothers and sisters whose bed is stone all the year round, who skulk away in doorsteps, nurse their knees and shiver, who sit and listen to the clocks strike, and are stirred up by the policeman on his beat every hour through the live long night. When we turn over in bed, and hear that it is only four, and there are hours of happy slumber left to us, it is just about the time that poor Jack Rag is being moved on by an active member of the A Division; or Jane Shore, faint and weary, has wandered down to the river's brink, and thinks how cold and quiet the water is looking.

When Hadget had had his meal, he left the coffee-house, and strolled along towards the Haymarket. The rain had somewhat abated in its violence, and the wind gone down; but his clothes and boots were wet, and he was very cold.

He turned up Wych Street, and came by Drury Lane and Brydges Street to Covent Garden Market, where nobody particular being about, he sat down upon a basket and lit his pipe.

Sitting here he fell a thinking—how IT was going on in the cab? and whether they had found it yet? The illuminated clock upon St. Paul's Church told him the hour—half-past one. It was found, of course, hours ago; almost directly he had left it. Then he began wondering how it looked, and whether it had moved after he had left it? Suddenly a horrible thought seized him—was he quite dead? It was but a momentary idea, and passed away as quickly as it was conceived; but the notion of his coming to life again for even an hour — for five minutes—for long enough to say who did it—made his hair stand on end.

"Pooh!" said he, passing his damp hand across his pale face. "He's dead enough. Why, damn it, I'm growing a coward, after all. It's contemptible—it's contemptible," he repeated.

He tried to laugh. It was a forced, unnatural sort of laugh, with very little mirth in it. He got up from the basket and shook himself something after the fashion of a Newfoundland dog when it comes out of the water. He had quite made up his mind to forget the ugly body he had left cooling and stiffening in its gore, and so took up the tune where he had dropped it when he fell across the ragged foreigner, and walked along whistling it with all his wind.

Just by St. Martin's Court stood something tawdry and brazen, which hailed him as "my dear," and asked where he was going to; and, wanting company, he answered, with a smile, that he was going nowhere in particular, and inquired whether she knew where they could get something to drink.

"They sell coffee round the corner. Come and give me a cup," she said.

"Dash coffee! I've had it two or three times already. What o'clock do the publics open?"

"Oh! not for hours yet? You won't stop up till then, will you?"

"Yes. I'm going to walk the streets all night."

"Well, that's rum taste. You wouldn't, if you had as much of 'em as I do. What do you do it for? I suppose you're one of those midnight-meeting people. Have you got a ticket for tea and toast in your pocket?" said she.

"No, he hadn't.

"Well, then, what's your game? Oh! I know."

"What is it, then?"

"I didn't think of it before. You're going to see the man hanged, that's what it is, I know."

"Curse the man!" The mention of him made Mr. Hadget jump. It was very queer that nobody could talk of anything else but that infernal execution. "What a sensation it creates!" he thought to himself, with something of a chuckle. "And this man was only a low carpenter, or something of that sort. Supposing he had been a gentleman?" mused he.

It was a strange thought, you'll say. Many stranger ones were running through the murderer's brain — every thought but remorse. He did not for a moment wish his victim alive. Had he still his life, Hadget would have been ready to cut his throat, and would have done it with the same ferocity, and in exactly the same fashion. He would have said more to him perhaps, for he remembered several bitter and galling speeches he had forgotten at the time.

Hadget was not one of your stage villains who see fearful visions, scream out, and fight with phantoms of the air. The mere throat-cutting business troubled him no more than the same sort of thing did GEORGE CASS, whom they hanged the other day at Carlisle. His only fear was detection. He would have liked the inquest over, and the body under ground; and then, as for remorse of conscience, and that sort of thing, he did not believe in them. I don't believe that murderers do. It is quite a vulgar error.

"Well, come and stand us something," the young lady said. "What are you thinking of? They aint going to hang you to-day, are they?"

"No—not yet: not before we've had the coffee."

They went to a disreputable shop in the immediate neighbourhood, and without much trouble got some gin, instead of the milder refection they had spoken of. The place was crowded with low, dirty-looking men and common, tawdrily-dressed women, whose senseless jokes and loud, unmeaning laughter seemed to say that they too had managed to gain access to the gin-bottle, or that they had laid in a good supply "before the houses shut."

"I wonder whether the old bloak 'll kick the bucket easy?"

"He'll have to kick it somehow. The easier he makes it, the better for him," said one.

"It's a gallows shame the scraggings comes off at sich a time. It don't give a cove a chance at getting a doss, nor nothink," rejoined another.

"It's a gallows shame there is any at all, in my opinion."

"Is it, old Psalm Singers? You needn't go to see it, then. It's as pretty a pictur as there is a showing for nothing anywheres."

It was the old subject—the execution that morning at eight. Had et did not stay long to listen to them, but wandered out again into the streets, and turned his steps towards the Haymarket. There might be something doing there that would amuse him; surely, something else to talk about, anyhow.

The Haymarket was very dreary and desolate. A couple of policemen stood at the top, and looked at him very hard as he passed by, as though he were an old offender. A wet and draggle-tailed female stood in a doorway, with her eyes shut, half asleep. As he walked down the fashionable side, a clock struck three.

"Five hours more!" muttered Hadget, and then, indignant with himself at finding that he was still thinking of the condemned cell, went on with that tune of his, louder than ever.

"I'll go and see what they are doing in the Park," thought he. And walked down the Duke of York's Steps.

They weren't doing very much there, it would seem. Two or three hideous phantoms passed him, with a leer and croak, and faded into darkness, and were again replaced by other phantoms more ragged, shivering, and woe-begone, who leered, and croaked, and vanished in their turn. Gaunt, half-famished spectres, screwed up in uncouth shapes, lay on the benches here and there—poor wretched outcasts, glad of even this miserable resting-place!

It wasn't the place to cheer him up, and Hadget soon quitted it; and wandering on among the trees, climbed over the railings at Birdcage Walk, and came back again towards the Haymarket, by Charing Cross.

What a great yawning sepulchre of a place was that Trafalgar Square, with its dark statues, its silent fountains, and its bare pavement. He walked about, and read what he could see of the inscriptions, and sat down upon some steps, and heard the clock strike four.

Then on again, more like the forced pilgrimage of the Wandering Jew than like a man who merely walked for his amusement.

If he were tired, then, why did he not go to bed? the reader asks. He could scarcely tell himself. He was fatigued and weary. At first he fancied he could not sleep, and now he felt as though he'd sleep for hours. Yes, he would find a place. Where? Where he had been for the coffee? No! He might be robbed of all the money he had about him. He would go to that coffee-house in Fleet Street. Having an object in view, he walked on briskly, and was soon there.

The shop was shut. He rang the bell again and again, but received no answer; then hammered at the knocker. Somebody next door opened the window and asked if he was the sweep.

"There are other places in the world," said Hadget to himself. "Besides, I might be seen to morrow, coming out, and that would not do, I reckon."

He walked on past St. Paul's, and into Cheapside, looking on one side and the other for some likely house; and so in time he reached the Poultry.

There was a policeman standing at the pavement edge, just at the corner of the Bank, and Mr. Hadget asked him whether he could recommend some quiet and respectable place.

"Well, let me see," said the policeman, turning round to look at the Bank, and then carefully studying the Mansion House and Royal Exchange, as though he were not quite sure which to fix upon. Then turning his eyes towards Mr. Hadget, and scanning that gentleman's attire, said,—"Cheapness no disadvantage, I suppose?"

"None to speak of," said the lawyer. He was not very elegantly attired at any season, and the soaking his old clothes had had some hours ago did not improve them, so that the officer would hardly have been led to believe by his appearance that he had over twenty thousand pounds in his pocket.

"There's one I know of," said the policeman. "Go down that passage, and keep straight on till you come to it on the left hand side."

He pointed as he spoke to a passage at the side of the Mansion House, and Hadget went in the direction indicated. He walked along for some time, and turned to the right and to the left, without being able to see any sign of a likely place. At last when he was almost giving up the search he came upon a little dingy coffee-house, through the dirty brown blind of which there gleamed a faint light.

The first glimpse of the interior was so uninviting that he felt half inclined to close the door, and run away again; but he was so cold and weary, he determined to go in.

Four or five rough-looking men slumbered in the different boxes, one or two of whom looked up and scowled at him. It was a villanous-looking place, gloomy, and close smelling.

While he was debating in his mind whether or not he should beat a hasty retreat, a voice called to him to know what he wanted.

"I want a bed. Have you got one?" asked Hadget.

"A shilling. Pay me, please."

It was a decrepit old woman who answered, and a slatternly girl, very dirty and sleepy, raised her head to stare at him, and would have gone off to sleep again with it on her knees, had not the old woman bawled to her to show the gentleman up-stairs.

She showed him to a little dungeon of a room, and, leaving the candle on the table, shut the door. It was truly a condemned cell of a bed-room, with the scanty bed, the bare floor, and dark papered walls. So Hadget thought, as he looked round at it as well as the flickering light would allow. He looked under the bed first, then saw that there was a bolt to the door; and, before fastening it, peeped out into the passage stealthily. Then he sat down upon the bed, and taking out the pocket book, counted the money he had taken from the murdered man, and looked over the papers. Some of these he burnt at the candle, and would have burnt the pocket-book too, only he thought it would make too much smell, so he put it away in his pocket until he could do so more conveniently at Brighton. Then he looked over his clothes very carefully to see if there were any spots of blood upon them, and, finding one, he lit a "Vesuvian" he had in his waistcoat pocket, and placing it upon the spot, burnt it out.

While thus engaged a clock struck five. It was nearly time he went to bed, if he was going to sleep at all before the first train in the morning. As he lay down, he thought this, and also thought that the condemned man had just three hours more to live. He muttered a curse at his own folly. What made that thing keep running in his head? He must go to sleep at once, if he meant to sleep. Two hours would be enough for him. Two hours——Good heavens! he had forgotten to look what time the train started. What was to be done? Should he get up, and go and look. The station would perhaps be open. No! What folly. He was sure that it started about seven, and he could go to sleep for an hour, anyhow.

Sleep! The worst of it was, he did not feel sleepy. How was that? He wondered whether that other fellow was asleep who had only three hours to live. Suppose he had only three hours left him, would he be asleep? He was wide-awake at the very thought.

He would count a hundred: that would send him off. One, two, three, four——No, that was tiresome. He began to doze. He was almost off now. No, he wasn't: he had got up again, and determined upon going by the second train, and going first to see the man hanged, but on the way down stairs, he met them bringing up the body, and they laid it on the bed. No: that was a dream. He was all right, and he was going to sleep. He must make haste, because they were going to hang Sir John Cheveleigh in three hours. Nonsense! How could that be? for there the corpse sat, bolt-upright, on the chair beside the bed, with his throat cut horribly, and his tongue lolling out, as though he were showing it to a doctor?

Great God! he could lie there no longer. He started up, and put on his clothes again. Walking about all night was better than this, a hundred thousand times.

He paused for a moment, and a feeling of shame crept over him. What would the people of the house think? He looked round more calmly. The room was dark and miserable enough, but there was nothing very terrible about it, and so he threw himself once more upon the bed. Once more he shut his eyes and tried to sleep, but again the horrible dreams returning, he started up, as he had done before; this time determined to walk the streets until the hour the train started.

He took the candle, and went down stairs. Telling the woman he had forgotten something, and must go back to fetch it, he mumbled and stumbled so over the sentence, that the old woman was frightened, and whispered to her sleepy companion to go up stairs, and see if it was all right. Finding that it was all right, and that Mr. Hadget had not pocketed any of the valuables, they let him go, and he wandered forth into the streets again.

Out into the streets again.

They looked wet, and cold, and dreary. He shivered as he stept out into the damp air, and felt something of the curse of Cain had fallen on him.

Going on without any object, and walking at random, he found himself presently *on the very spot!* Yes, that was where he had descended from the cab—that the court he had run up. At the first glance, he felt inclined to retrace his steps, and put a dozen miles between him and the scene of his crime, but an unconquerable impulse thrust him forward, and he bent his steps towards the Docks. He could hear there what had happened, and what had been done with the body.

He walked about vaguely, and, where he saw a group of men talking together, went up and listened to their conversation, but nobody was speaking of the subject which engrossed all his thoughts. Could they have found the body? Yes, of course they had; but at the time none of these people were about, and so they had not heard of it. *He* would hear of it before long, and he must wait patiently.

He noticed no signs of anything unusual having taken place. Everything seemed quiet. There were a few sailors and porters loafing about, and a few such stragglers s there are always to be ound about the Docks, staring at nothing in particular, with their hands in their pockets.

He did not know how to put the question, and so waited till something should occur that might lead to an inquiry. Nothing turning up, when he had waited a long while, he went into a public-house which had just opened, and, sitting down in the tap-room, rang for the waiter.

The barman came, after some delay, and asked what he wanted.

"There's so much going on up-stairs, I hadn't time to come before," said he.

"What's going on? You've early customers."

"There's been a murder going on, for one thing."

"Murder!"

He turned deadly pale, in spite of all his strength of mind.

"Ah! A man murdered in a cab. His body's up there."

Hadget turned round with a start, as though he expected to see it dangling from the ceiling.

"Where?" said he.

"It's lying up-stairs, waiting the crowner's 'quest."

"Oh! Bring me six of hot brandy."

The man went to fetch it. While he was gone, the other stirred the fire, and drew nearer to it. It must have been the cold that made him shiver so. When the man returned, he said, "Have they caught the murderer?"

"Yes."

"Yes!" echoed Hadget, his hand jerking so he upset half his grog. "Who is he?"

"I don't see anything to be surprised at," said the barman. "They always are nabbed, sooner or later. It was the cabman."

He hurried off to attend a host of customers who were flocking in, and Hadget was left by himself. He drank his grog at a gulp, and sat silent and motionless. Presently a smile stole over his face, and he broke into a low, fiendish chuckle.

"He'll have some trouble to clear himself," said he, talking in a low tone, and giving utterance to his thoughts aloud, as was his wont. "He'll have some trouble to get out of it, if some one else found the body there. I suppose they did, or else they wouldn't suspect him. Gad, I'd like to have his case to manage myself. That would be very neat. Ha! ha! I'll come up from Brighton on purpose. This is really very interesting." He sat and babbled thus, then pondered silently awhile, then chuckled over the unhappy cabman's fate. "Poor fellow! if he doesn't clear himself, I'll see him off. I never have seen a man hanged. By God! I've half a mind to see the one to-day."

He was about to rise, perhaps with the intention of following out his resolution, when a heavy hand was laid upon his shoulder. He had been sitting with his back to the door, and had not noticed any person come in. He raised his eyes with a start, and the cold sweat broke out upon his face as HE SAW A POLICEMAN LOOKING DOWN UPON HIM!

MERMAIDS.

CHAPTER THE FORTY-NINTH.

THE HOUSE WITH THE MUFFLED KNOCKER.

TURNED out of Mr. Maurice's room in the unceremonious fashion I have described (for put it which way you like, that audacious hussy, Mrs. Nell, had the best of it), Dorcas walked away, boiling over with rage, and, without for one single moment turning to the right or to the left; but, biting her lips and stamping her heels with suppressed passion, pursued her course down Holborn. It is more than probable that she passed by young Cheveleigh, who was lounging along with his hands in his pockets, and that remarkably woe-

No. 11.

begone aspect the young man's face always wore during moments of great financial difficulty. Such, for instance, as when Nelly and he had set their hearts upon a lobster salad for supper, and they found that the money would not run to it. Though a negociation with the pawnbroker dispelled the gloom, and he was again as happy as a sand-boy, supposing that a sand-boy enjoys the amount of felicity usually attributed to him.

Most likely Dorcas passed him; but neither noticed the other. She walked all the way home, far too much engaged with her own thoughts to think of riding. Those thoughts of hers were far from pleasant, if one might have judged from her face; for it wore an angry frown, which, passers-by observing, made them turn round, and look after her astonished.

"The vile woman! The horrible, filthy hussy! The degraded, shameless wretch!" A hundred other such expressions of hatred, loathing, and contempt did Dorcas heap upon her late antagonist. "Oh! I could like to have torn her bold face with my finger nails," she thought; and, thinking so, clutched and tore at her mantle, as though it were Nelly's rosy cheeks.

It was not until she reached her own room, and had lain aside her walking-dress, that she thought of the bank note.

She put her hand in her pocket, expecting to find it there, then finding it not, searched hastily in her muff, and on the table, and on the ground.

What had become of it? Had she lost it on the way there in the cab? No. She remembered to have had it in her hand when she reached Cleveland Chambers. What had become of it, then? Had she dropped it in Cheveleigh's room? In that case would he ever get it? Most likely not.

That woman was bad enough for anything, she was sure of that. I do not myself see anything very unreasonable in the opinion, ladies. All of you think the same—don't you? If a woman is not virtuous she is quite as likely to commit a murder or highway robbery as to leave them alone.

Dorcas was distracted. What should she do? Write and ask Maurice whether he had found the note? No! He had left the Bad Bargains, and she knew no other address than the one at Cleveland Chambers, where more likely than not the letter would fall into the hands of *that wretch*. In such a case, of course, it would share the fate of the bank note.

She went down stairs to attend upon the old lady, who still lay a-bed, no better, and no worse; only that she was a little more gentle and patient—a little kinder in her manner towards the dependant.

"Is that you, my dear? I have been waiting for you. Where ever have you been?"

Thus she spoke to Dorcas, as the latter entered the sick room, and, softly taking the companion's hand in hers, patted it, and held it, almost lovingly, between her thin claws. Strange it may seem, but the younger woman did not respond to this act of affection, but, disengaging herself rudely, walked away to the other end of the apartment; at which rebuff the old lady rolled her head from one side to the other, in a fretful way, and whimpered like a whipped baby.

"You haven't got any heart, Dorcas! How can you go on so, Dorcas? You'll be old and sick, like I am, some day. You will—you will, you wicked woman! You, of all others in the world, to treat me so!"

"What makes you use that phrase so frequently?" asked the companion, coming forward, and with her arms folded behind her, looking down scowlingly upon the invalid. "What do you mean by it?"

"Oh, dear! oh, dear! oh, dear! she'll kill me! she'll kill me!"

One rolling her head and whimpering, the other frowning down upon her, as before.

"Haven't I done everything I could to please you? What makes you hate me so? I've torn up my last will and made one in your favour. You wouldn't have me die before my time, Dorcas, would you? I haven't much pleasure in my life, God knows! but let me drag on just a little bit—only a little bit longer, Dorcas."

"I can't delay, or accelerate, your death, can I?"

"Oh, dear! oh, dear! I don't suppose you can. But, oh! how is it I don't mend? The doctor says it's strange I do not mend. I ought to mend, Dorcas, ought I not? Do you think I shall when spring comes round?"

Dorcas deigned not to answer her, but walked away again slowly, and absorbed in thought. Then she carefully drew the curtains at the bottom of the bed, and began to mix the old lady's medicine, and, having done so, brought it to her.

At sight of the physic the invalid whined, and rocked her head again.

"I can't take it," she said. "It makes me so sick. I won't have any more of it. Why does the doctor send such nasty stuff?"

"What nonsense you talk!" the other exclaimed harshly. "Come, sit up, and take the draught. You *shall* have it!"

With many moans and groans, the old lady sat up in bed, and gulped down the nauseous physic, but had scarcely done so before a violent fit of vomiting seized her.

"How's the old woman to-day?" said one of the fine gentlemen in plush to Miss Dimples, whom he met upon the stairs.

"About the same as usual, I believe, Mr. Charles."

"What do you call the complaint now, Miss Dimples?"

"I'm sure I don't know, Mr. Charles; but she's very peevish over it."

"There's some parties as is peevish, and some as is patient, Miss Dimples. There's some as comes out angels in hadversity."

"Go on, with your nonsense! Calling me such names."

"Not half so good as what I would call you, if you'd allow me."

"And what would that be, if you please?"

"Simpkinson. And we'll put it up next Sunday."

"You may put it up where you like, Mr. Charles, and yourself along with it. It's like your impidence."

And she flounced away, leaving plush confounded.

"No, thank you," said Miss Dimples, laughing ironically, as she recounted the particulars of the late interview to cook. "None of your footmen for me, I'm obliged to you. Marry a thing like that! Goodness me, I'd as leave marry a clerk!"

While the old woman lay ill in bed, the house was not in mourning. There was straw down in front of the door, and some round the corner of the next street; the knocker was muffled, and people approaching the sick chamber talked in whispers, and walked on tiptoe; but below stairs the fatted calf was slaughtered. There were during that illness such tea-drinkings, such company-keeping such jauntings and junketings as you ne'er saw the like of.

Charles Simpkinson, Esquire, with legs a-straddle and cigar in mouth, taking the evening air upon the door-step of the Baker Street mansion, was a sight to see and wonder at, and small boys, of feeble understanding, would eye the splendid fellow respectfully from a distance, and watch his movements, like the people watch the hippopotamus wagging its tale, at the Alhambra, wonderingly, and a little frightened.

However painful the old woman's illness might have been, I do not believe that any member of the household would have been violently delighted to have seen her down stairs again. When she was well, to use cook's own expression, they " led a life of it." She was very peevish still, as Miss Dimples has just told us; but then, very few but Dimples and Dorcas came in her way. To the latter she had changed in a most extraordinary manner. Dimples had noticed it, and reported it in the kitchen, where it was duly weighed and considered.

" She's feathering her nest, you may depend upon it," Dimples said.

" Nasty stuck-up thing !" the housemaid joined in. " I'd like to see her sent to the right-abouts."

" She's a queer temper," Mr. Simpkinson observed; " but a devilish fine woman."

" Fine woman !" screamed all the ladies, hysterically. " I wonder where your eyes is !"

While the good people below stairs were thus passing judgment upon the proud-spirited woman, whom they all alike feared and hated, the subject of their remarks was racking her brains to think what she could do about the bank-note. The day passed by without her having come to any conclusion: the next day, the same. She had been hoping that Maurice would call, whether he had received it or not. He had promised that he would do so; but, alas! Mr. Cheveleigh's promises and good intentions were all of the pie-crust order. While she was thus fretting herself about her loss, that fearful young profligate and his mistress were holding high-jinks at Cleveland Chambers, as we have seen. Dorcas awoke on the third day in the same perplexity. She was now quite certain that he had never received it, or surely he must have called or written before this. Then, what could she do? It was impossible to broach the subject to him. How could she allude to that vile, disgraceful woman? The bare thought was pollution.

The vile and disgraceful Mrs. Nelly lay in bed that morning, smiling, dreaming, and scheming, caring little what the rest of the world thought or said about her. I do not believe that for one single instant she ever fancied herself an object of pity, much less contempt. I have reason to think that she imagined a great portion of the virtuous community envied her, and would have liked to have worn her shoes.

When she chanced to think of the dialogue she had had with Dorcas, she smiled to herself, to think how she had routed her enemy.

" Who was she, I should like to know ? It must have been that Abbot I have heard Maurice talk about. A kind of upper servant. The old lady's waiting-woman, I suppose. A poor menial, who has nothing but her virtue to look forward to, who'll live and die in harness, running here and there, bobbing curtsies at her mistress's pleasure. Pretty person to turn up her nose at me ! Chaste creature, how I pity her !"

Then Nelly smiled again, when she had concluded her little soliloquy, and began to muse upon a pleasanter subject.

" What will she say when I am Lady Cheveleigh ? Yes, that is the best course, after all. Maurice will be heir to a large property when his father dies; and with money and a title, I think I can dispense with the good opinion of such persons as Miss Abbot !"

She was very beautiful lying there, and would have made a splendid duchess—as far as looks went. She asked Miss Perks's opinion on the subject.

" A hempress, mum, or the Lord Mayor's lady. And I wish you was—with all my heart, I do."

And I really believe the simple creature did.

CHAPTER THE FIFTIETH.

A TITLED RUFFIAN.

SUCH a man as the heir to the Cumbersome Estates, nephew of the great Duke of Doodledum, brother-in-law of the Marquis of Barebones, and bearer of the illustrious name of Drawler (at the very mention of which I hope all British hearts beat quicker), have a right to be rakes and spendthrifts. Stop a moment: I mean, they have a better right than such small fry as you and I, my brother sprat.

When you and I go wrong, and do not pay our bakers' bills, we come to grief, and serve us right; but with my lord it's different. There is no fawning, smooth-faced trader alive, who would not go down on his marrow-bones and pray for his lordship's custom. Nobody wants his money, bless you! and, to do him credit, I don't believe they often get it. The spoon they found in my lord's baby-mouth was none of your NIKEL silver, but the real genuine article. When he opened his infant eyes and looked around, the world lay smooth and smiling at his feet. He had but to cry and have.

Ah, me ! ye threadbare ones, think of the glorious prospect—THE BOUNDLESS REALMS OF EVERLASTING CREDIT ! What a transformation scene for one of the coming pantomimes !

Lord Drawler was an awful profligate, and sowed his wild oats like another Sardanapalus. Oh, Sprat ! thou canst not imitate him, with thy scanty purse: thou art too small and mean an animal. Happy, over-dressed clerkling ! Thou knowest whom I mean, and I think I see thee quail beneath my scornful glance. Ha ! ha ! flutter, oh ! flutter, my small-sized friend, round the enticing flame of dissipation !

Long may thy vacant laugh and witless jest resound! Long may thy whiskerless and careworn face shine at the day-break revels! Go, while there is yet time, and anoint thy simple pate with the midnight oil, don thy unpaid-for finery, and spend thy shillings freely. Here, Phillis, Chloe, Flora, and Cora, come and help him! Who knows how near may be the steady, matrimonial monotony of Brixton, high shoes, cotton gloves, a pew at church, and other adjuncts of heavy respectability! Have thy playful fling, my little man, for in a while, mark me, thou wilt tire of it, and affect (perchance, without much previous experience,) the languor of the used-up roue. Then wilt thou cast aside thy larking friends and faithful latch-key, and talk of settling; and then, maybe, thou wilt take unto thyself a wife, pay taxes, and have babies; and then, behind thy glass of Port, wilt thou wink thine eye, and talk bigly of thy "gay days," leading poor little Mrs. Sprat to think that thou wast once a very devil among the petticoats!

When his lordship left Foot Court, he chartered a hansom, and bade the driver take him to "the 'Market." The Market had gone to bed an hour ago, and so my lord drove home to his rooms in Piccadilly. He was as handsome a young man, when sober, as you could have wished to meet with, but late hours and strong drinks do not improve any of us. With his hat a little smashed on one side (one of the young ladies had sat down upon it), his shirt-front crumpled and soiled, his hair rough, and his face flushed, he looked about as big a blackguard as it is possible for a member of the British aristocracy to look.

Undoing his door with a sudden bang, after a desperate struggle, accompanied by a few choice oaths and imprecations, he went staggering headlong into the passage, and, falling over a bench, brought himself and a candlestick with a thundering crash to the ground. The other inmates of the house, probably accustomed to noisy entrances at all hours of the night, lay quietly in their beds, and did not offer to interfere. So, after he had rested where he was for a minute or two, he scrambled somehow to his feet, and, slamming to the door, began to strike a light.

"What the devil's come to the matches!" he grumbled. "There doesn't seem to be any phosphorus on them. Oh! all right—that's the wrong end. What's become of that scoundrel of a man of mine? I suppose he's gone to bed. What an infernal headache I've got with that tumble! What a beautiful woman that Nelly is, to be sure! Divine creshur!"

He spoke a little inarticulately, and, leaning there against the wall, with his hat altogether smashed in by the fall, and a maudlin sentimental smile upon his face, his lordship cut a very ridiculous figure.

It was broad daylight out of doors, as I have said before; but in Lord Drawler's rooms the blinds were drawn down, the curtains closed, and all was dark and quiet. He staggered in, and, placing the candlestick in front of a looking-glass, contemplated himself with much drunken gravity, as tipsy folks are fond of doing.

"You look precious seedy!" said he to himself. "Anybody who didn't know what you'd been having, would say you were drunk."

He looked at his reflection sternly, and shook his head at it. Then, relenting a little, continued, with a sickly smile, "And they'd be right. You are drunk, Drawler, old fellow, I regret to say, ash drunk ash——a lord."

Quite overcome with the intense comicality of this idea, he sat down in an arm-chair to laugh at it, but shutting his eyes to enjoy the joke more thoroughly, he forgot all about it, and nearly fell asleep.

He might have nodded thus for five minutes, when he opened his eyes again, and, rising from his seat, went, in a staggering, pitching sort of walk, to look for the water-bottle. It stood upon a distant table, and he was crossing the room to fetch it, when some objects on a chair attracted his attention.

"Why, damme, what's that?"

A bonnet and shawl, both of costly fabric and the latest fashion, lay there before him. He took them up, and, turning them over and over, examined them minutely.

"I've seen that shawl before, somewhere or other," he muttered. "I think I bought it for some one, but who the deuce it was I can't remember. I wonder how it came here!"

While he was wondering thus, his foot kicked against something on the floor. It was a little kid boot: a tiny thing, of exquisite shape and workmanship; a Balmoral boot, with little brass eyelet-holes, silk laces, and heels high, and pointed to about the size of a shilling. His lordship looked at it awhile, and whistled.

"Whoever it is," said he, "she cannot be far off."

He tried to stand as upright as possible, and looked round the room; but, in so doing, a shade passed over his face. Who could the visitor be who made so free with his rooms? He thought of several of his cast-off mistresses, but could not decide upon any one of them who was likely to have given him a call.

I told that infernal scoundrel, Parsons, not to let any woman in while I was out. He shall pack up his portmanteau to-morrow, I can promise him. Who the devil can it be? I don't think Kate would come here. By Jove! she shall take herself off again, if she has, in double-quick time. No, it can't be Kate! That tailor's wife can't have found out my name and address. It will be infernally awkward if she has, by Jove!"

A great idea struck him. Suppose it were Nelly? But he dismissed the thought almost as quickly as it had been conceived. How was it possible, when he had left her in Foot Court barely an hour ago? Ah! but, then, if she had taken a cab, and come by a direct road, without stopping, she might have got there before him. But, then, who would have let her in?—and how did she know where he lived? Well, Bux might have told her? But, then, again, she had refused to make any appointment with him when he left her. No, it could not be Nelly.

"Then who the——"

Surely the better plan was to go and look. Who ever it was, they must, probably, be in the adjoining bed-room. The folding-doors, communicating with the sleeping apartment, stood partly open. He took the candle in his hand, and strode towards them.

Perhaps the noise he had made blundering about the room had awakened his uninvited guest—or, perhaps, she had not been to sleep at all; but had been listening to him. As he approached the folding-doors, he saw a figure in white standing motionless within them, which, coming on him thus so suddenly, made him start back in alarm; and, though a second look at it assured him that there was nothing supernatural about the apparition, seemed to arouse other unpleasant feelings in his breast, and, to judge from the gloomy scowl upon his face, he would have been nearly as glad to have seen a ghost. IT WAS HIS WIFE!

They stood silently gazing at each other for several seconds—the woman with an anxious, appealing kind of look, as though her heart yearned towards him, but she was uncertain what reception she would meet with; the man with a sodden, sullen determination to thwart, and cross her in all that she might say, and to refuse any favour she might ask of him.

"George," she said, softly, moving towards him, and endeavouring to take his hand in hers; "I have not done wrong in coming to see you, have I?"

"Done wrong? Damnation! you've acted like a fool; but that's nothing new."

She drew back from him a little frightened, and great tears welled up in her gentle eyes. She was a slender, graceful creature, scarcely more than a girl, with thick, dark brown hair, which hung down loosely on her shoulders. I cannot say that she was beautiful,—in truth, all women are not so out of books,—but she had a beautifully mild, patient expression, like I have seen upon the faces of angels in old pictures.

"Oh! George, I did not think it would have vexed you so."

"Or else," said he, with a sneer, "you'd have stopped away, wouldn't you? You're so considerate. Damn you! what are you whining about now?"

He turned round with such a brutal oath, and such a menacing gesture, that the woman shrank back terrified, against the wall, as though he had struck her; then burst out sobbing violently.

"Oh, George—dear George!—what makes you treat me so? What have I done? What shall I do to please you?"

"Do?" said he, fiercely "Die! That's the best job for you. Do it as soon as you like."

Turning away from her, he walked across the room unsteadily, and getting the water-bottle, a tumbler, and a small decanter of brandy, mixed himself a glass, lighted a cigar, and sat down in an easy chair. So he sat and smoked; his young wife, crouching on the ground, sobbed silently—scarcely above her breath. The clicking of the glass upon the table, when he put it down after a draught, and the faint tapping of his fingers upon the arm of his chair, alone broke the heavy silence, which was so oppressive to the senses, one could almost touch it.

My lord had made up his mind he would not speak first, only this sort of thing grew tiresome. When he had finished his cigar and brandy-and-water, he began to feel as though he would have liked to have gone to bed. Some effort must be made.

He turned his eyes towards her very slowly indeed, and with the greatest caution, so that he might jerk them back again, should he find her looking at him.

She was not looking, however, and he had time to consider her attentively. The attitude in which she sat, or rather lay, upon the ground, was very graceful; and her scanty drapery revealed the almost faultless symmetry of her form; her face, pale with weeping, was half shaded by her hair, which hung in beautiful disorder on her neck. One white and rounded shoulder, and one little naked foot, were visible.

Many men might have loved such a woman; most men would have admired her; but his lordship thought differently. He regarded her with a feeling of intense dislike, and in his prejudiced eyes she seemed ugly and common-place. Besides, he had very little sentiment in his nature, and thought her tears were artificial, and her grief sham.

Something must be done, and Drawler felt as though he would give the world to go to bed, but did not exactly know how to get rid of his companion. Having thought over one or two very sarcastic speeches which were likely to drive her away, and upon second thoughts rejected them, he began deliberately to divest himself of his coat and waistcoat without taking any notice of her.

Unfortunately she lay in such a position that he must either step over or move her on one side to get into the bedroom.

"Now, then," said he, thrusting her roughly with his foot. "What are you lying there for? Get up and dress yourself."

She rose with a shiver, and stood watching him.

"Are you—are you going to send me away?" she asked.

"You came of your own accord, and you can go again the same way," he replied.

"But, George, — dear George, I was so lonely and wretched in the country by myself. You never came, as you promised."

"When did I promise?"

"Oh! dear George, you promised to love me little more than six months ago. You promised to——"

"Curse the promises! If you put any faith in them you'll be disappointed. I'm sure I was disappointed with you."

"But, dear George, it was not my fault that I brought you no money. I thought you could have loved me for myself."

"Love be d——" growled Drawler. "Do you suppose a man ties his leg to a log for nothing? Just for the sake of the company, I should imagine."

"Nonsense, George," she said, with a very faint smile; "you do love me—a little bit, now, don't you?"

"No," he answered, surlily, "I don't, and the sooner you take yourself off the better."

"But, George," she cried bursting into tears, "How can I go? Where can I go to—at this hour—alone?"

"Go how and where you choose, I don't care. Come, look sharp and dress yourself."

He thrust his hands into his pockets, and leaning against the mantle-piece, waited for her to go. She began very slowly to get ready, sobbing all the time.

"Now, then," he cried, irritated by the tardiness of her movements. "The sooner the better. I'm waiting for you."

She hurried on her clothes any how, scarcely waiting to fasten anything. By the time that she was ready, he had gone into the other room, and stood by the dressing table, with his back turned towards her. She was a moment undecided whether she should speak to him before she went, or leave thus without another word. After a minute or two's hesitation, she plucked up courage to approach him. Stealing up gently behind him, she took his hand, and would have raised it to her lips had he not turned round fiercely at the moment, and struck her down.

Perhaps he did not intend to hit her as he did; or perhaps he was irritated beyond endurance. Everybody agrees that it is a coward's act to strike a woman; and my friend Tittlebat, I have heard quite eloquent upon the subject, though in his case, poor little man, I believe that great woman, his better three-quarters, would be more than a match for half-a-dozen such champions, at a fair stand-up fight.

My lord was not a coward, certainly; for had he not proved himself to be a lion in the trenches, before Sebastopol? The newspapers tell us so. There is an innate love for bullying born with every Briton. We all like to bully something. I have known young ladies, gentle, soft-hearted creatures, who shed tears at the death of a fly, who were tartars to their younger sisters, and bullied their poor old mamma unmercifully.

That it was a brutal deed, I can't deny. His wife rose slowly to her feet. Her mouth was sadly cut by his violence, but she made no complaint—never uttered the slightest sound; but, walking as firmly as she could—though that was rather unsteadily—she left the room, went down-stairs, and out into the street.

There was nobody about to notice her. Had there been, I doubt much whether she would have seen them. She walked on something like one in a trance—looking neither to the right nor to the left, and seeing nothing, though her eyes were wide open and staring.

She did not go far. Her strength failing her, she staggered, and fell upon the pavement. A gentleman passing at the same time ran forward and took her in his arms, raised her up, and carried her to a door-step, where he endeavoured, with the assistance of a woman who came up at the moment, to bring her to her senses.

"Poor thing, she's fainted. See how she's cut her lip! Did she do it in falling, sir?"

"I don't think so. She came out of one of those houses. She must have been ill-used."

"She's not half-dressed. I wonder who she is?"

"She can't lie here, in any case. What shall we do with her?"

"Here's a cab."

"Ah! that will do. Here, cabman, help me with this lady, will you?"

"What's up with her? Is she drunk?" And the cabman descended from his box to render such assistance as lay in his power.

"I'll look in her pocket," said the gentleman; "perhaps there's something there to show where she lives."

He was such a very sober, solemn-looking gentleman, although not more than twenty-seven, or thirty, and looked so very steady and respectable, that the idea of him robbing the fainting woman never occurred to any one. So he rummaged about in her pocket, and presently found a card-case.

There were several cards in it, on all of which he found the name of Lady Drawler, but no address.

What should he do? Where should he take her? In spite of all their efforts, she yet remained insensible. After some consideration, he told the cabman to drive to the Burlington Hotel, and there leaving her ladyship in the care of half-a-dozen sympathising females, and a doctor hastily summoned from his warm bed to attend upon her, our considerate young gentleman took his departure.

"Show this card to her ladyship when she is sufficiently recovered, and say that I will do myself the honour to call upon her," said he.

The person he addressed promised to do so, and looking at the piece of pasteboard, after the gentleman's departure, read thereon the name of MR. ERNEST CHEVELEIGH.

CHAPTER THE FIFTY-FIRST.

SEEING A MAN HANGED.

WHO shall say what Hadget's feelings were, as he looked up and saw the policeman scowling down at him? An ill-favoured, surly member of the force, who looked as though he'd rather die than take a bribe, or see a joke."

"You're wanted, sir," said he.

"Wa-anted?" gasped the lawyer. "Who by? what for? on what charge?"

"No charge, as I knows on," the other answered, glumly. "You're to come up stairs. You're the doctor, aint you?"

Oh! what a weight was taken off his heart! Mr. Hadget breathed again—smiled—laughed.

"No—no," said he, "I'm not the doctor. It's a mistake. Ha! ha! How very odd. I didn't know you took me for the doctor. No —no, I haven't seen him. What a queer coincidence."

He smirked, and chuckled, and rubbed one bony hand over the other in a very uncomfortable fashion, and the policeman, after staring stupidly at him for a minute or two, walked out of the room, to make inquiries for the medical man, at the bar.

Left to himself, Mr. Hadget munched his nails and meditated.

"I must be more cautious," he muttered. "I mustn't think so loud. It's a miracle I did not say something, just now, that that fool could have taken hold of. And," he continued, after a pause, "I must be braver, and more certain of myself in a moment of danger. I must not be taken by surprise at the sight of a policeman, and blab out the secret before I'm asked. I must become accustomed to hear about it and keep my countenance, for I shall have to do so before long."

He walked into the bar, and, seeing by the clock that it was near seven, left the house, and bent his steps towards the railway station. He had not gone very far, however, before he changed his mind.

Why should he not go and see the execution? There was a fine opportunity to learn courage and self-command. Besides, he had never seen a man hanged, and felt curious to know whether they died easy. Going into a booking-office which he found open, he purchased a time-table of the Brighton Railway: and finding that it would be possible to get to his house before the old woman called to give him his breakfast, after he had been to the execution, he turned his face towards Newgate.

He went round by the Post Office, and, following the direction in which the crowd was tending, soon found himself before the prison walls. The crowd was not large, or closely packed, but the first thought that struck him was, that he had never seen so many blackguards before in his life. On they came, pouring down all the narrow streets towards the great centre of attraction. Every court and alley vomiting forth its repulsive inmates, helped to swell the assemblage of vagabonds.

As he looked around, he saw almost every phase of vice and profligacy represented. At the window yonder, some over-dressed young noodle, who had on lavender kid gloves, and smoked a cigar, was throwing down hot halfpence for the rabble below to scramble for, after the fashion of the young bloods in the days of the Regent, when such senseless absurdities were taken for wit. The fashion has exploded now; our knockers and bell-pulls are unmolested; spring-heeled Jack has jumped clean out of our recollection; the noble marquis, who was the king of practical jokers, and in whose jokes there existed a certain germ of humour which atoned for their attendant blackguardism, is dead; and his poor imitators, whose name is legion, and who had all the blackguardism without any of the fun, have passed away and are forgotten, and we young men are now much wiser, and happier, and enjoy ourselves much more reasonably, if we are not in our hearts more virtuous than our fathers were.

In another window lolled a couple of gaudily apparelled ladies from the Haymarket, who had come out for the lark, and made up their minds to enjoy themselves, although they did not half like it, for all that. With these exceptions the windows contained nobody very noticeable, their occupants all resembling each other in a uniformity of unwashed dinginess. Indeed, on every side, Mr. Hadget noticed the spectators wore an appearance of having been up all night, or got up much too early, so very seedy, sallow, and haggard, everyone appeared.

The crowd below, which gradually increased in size as the hour approached, was, for the most part, composed of the very scum and sweepings of humanity. From the scowling, skulking, low-browed blackguard, sodden and bloated, with forty years' career of crime and profligacy, to the evil-eyed, ill-looking young, sucking prig, who had not yet been in difficulty, and knew naught but by hearsay of Her Majesty's jails; from the squalid, draggle-tailed old procuress of sixty, to the bold-faced young prostitute of ten years old. Everywhere there were a great number of boys and girls romping, and larking, and chasing one another in and out of the crowd.

Hadget looked round in vain to see some serious faces. Every moment he heard some brutal jest, either obscene or blasphemous, at the expense of the wretched culprit, whose dying hour was fast approaching, hearty bursts of laughter, and, occasionally some humourous sally at the expense of the swells at the windows, which excited the risibilities of the mob below.

It was, indeed, a very cheerful, good-humoured, and facetious mob, and one that had come out to enjoy itself; but altogether the scene was as unlike what Hadget had heard it described, or expected to find it, as it well could be. But what struck him more than anything else, was the insignificant appearance of the gallows itself. Although he knew exactly where to look for it, and had looked in that direction the first moment he turned the corner of the Old Bailey, yet, owing to his being a little near-sighted (he had not his spectacles with him, having left them at Lyons Inn, overnight), and owing to the scaffold being much lower, and smaller than he expected, he did not see it at all for some little time, a circumstance which occurred to several other strangers, one of whom, after standing by his side for more than ten minutes, and staring in the same direction, asked when they were "going to put it up?"

When he did discover the object of his search, Hadget squeezed his way through the crowd, and keeping his hand tightly clasped upon the money he carried in his trousers'-pocket, struggled on until he was within fifteen yards of the instrument of death. Just as he reached this spot, the crowd were silent and attentive, for the show had begun. A nice, comfortable, stoutish person, in a cut-away coat, who they said was CALCRAFT, had come out to fasten the rope to the cross beam, which having performed with great dispatch, he retreated again, and left the crowd to stare at it.

"He looks hearty this morning," observed a gentleman in fustian to another in corduroy.

"I don't agree with you," says Corduroy. "He looks reyther pukey. I thought he would."

"Why so?" asks Fustian.

"Because," says Corduroy, oracularly, "he's cause to be."

Relapsing into silence, and puffing at his pipe, he for some time obstinately refused to give any explanation of this mysterious remark, after the manner of your wiseacres making a muckle out of a mickle.

However, after many inquiries, he thought fit to inform his hearers, that there was a rumour current to the effect that the hangman had received a threatening letter that morning, intimating that some one in the crowd would shoot him when he came upon the scaffold. This story, as it turned out had some truth in it, may in some measure have accounted for what followed.

"It's time the chap was hung," said some one, looking round at the clock, which wanted two minutes of the hour. "What's keeping 'em ?"

"Big wigs aint had their breakfast yet," said one.

"Go on with you. They'll be here directly," added another.

"They's trussing him," rejoined a third, jocularly.

"He aint eat much, I guess."

"Why not? They al'ays gives up a reglar blow out the last morning. It makes 'em die game, and not disgrace themselves."

"This bloke wont die game, then, I'll be sworn. Mr. Jemmys, the under turnkey, is a friend of mine, and uses "The Last Drop" public-house, over the way, and I see him this morning as he was a havin' a drain. How's the dewoted one? says I. 'Who's that?' says he. The tight-rope performer, says I. 'You mean the man we're goin' to work off,' says he. 'You're al'ays at your jokin', you are.' Well, says I, how's he behavin' hisself? Will he want any proppin' up behind. 'Don't you make no mistake, says he, 'he's the pittifullest beggar I ever clapt my eyes on. Fust he's faintin', then he swoundin', then he's unconscious; and when he come to, he's insensible. I never see a human creeter make sich a object of hisself.' You don't mean that, says I. 'Who says I don't?' says he. 'I wish you'd had the sitting up with him as I have. Last night he throwed hisself into the fire, and was burnt, and scarred his face—a sight to look at. It's something horrible——' "

But here the narrator's story was cut short by a great movement in the crowd, a sort of surging and heaving, and striving on everybody's part to get their head above their neighbour's shoulders.

"Hats off ! Down in front !" roared those in front.

"Where are you shoving to? Keep back some of you !" roared those in front, elbowing their assailants unmercifully.

"Hats off ! — Lie down ! — Shut up !— Silence !"

The terrible procession was coming out slowly by the Debtors' Gate. Hadget held his breath, and strained his eyes to see what was going on, sucking in with fearful avidity all the minutest details of the horrible scene before him, though at the same time feeling that had he a hundred eyes, and all employed at once, he would not be able to see *everything*.

What he managed to see, seemed like a ghastly nightmare, more than a reality. He saw the chaplain, praying, and the hangman, busy with the rope: he saw a crowd of persons, looking up from the steps. Then he saw them carrying something up upon a chair—a human form, certainly, but so pale and distorted in face, so shapeless and helpless, that he thought, at first, the man was dead.

It was, as it seemed, with the greatest difficulty that they got the poor wretch upon his legs, underneath the drop. Hadget noticed a convulsive twitch in the doomed man's face, and his jaw dropped, as he stared round at the crowd with a wild, shuddering horror in his eyes, and the murderer watching him, feeling that those eyes were fixed on him, so intensely excited did he become, that in another moment he would have shrieked aloud, or fallen backwards in a swoon, had not the hangman drawn down the white cap upon the quivering face, and shut it from his view.

A moment or so he stood, as it seemed, half supported by the rope, and half, as Hadget fancied, by the chair behind him, while a death-like silence reigned around, in which the clergyman's voice sounded plain and distinct full fifty yards from the scaffold. Then of a sudden, with a loud *cluck*, which made the listeners' hearts spring up into their mouths, the body fell, and hung quite motionless.

For a moment only, and then the white cap before the hanging man's mouth was violently agitated by his breath as it came and went in gasps, and then his limbs were all twisted and convulsed, and his arms, free from the elbow downwards, worked backwards and forwards at his side, his fingers clutching and tearing at his throat, and then to the spectators' terror and surprise, his legs got loose, and the rope swinging wildly to and fro, he managed to get his feet upon the edge of the trap, and in a manner at once fantastic and horrible, danced round the side, struggling to gain an upright posture, with his head cocked on one side, and the white night-cap bobbing over his shoulder.

Giddy, sick, and half-fainting with the sight, the murderer gazed upon the fearful spectacle before him. Three times he saw the dying man's legs rise from the trap, and struggle round the side, and then the hangman, managing to get hold of them underneath, swung to them, and held them down. And thus the culprit died, amid the deafening yells and execrations of the mob !

Hadget staggered from the scene, and half-unconscious of what passed around him, was carried along in the rush, and at length found himself on the outskirts of the crowd. A great many remained to see the body cut down, but he had had enough already, and made his way into a tavern to get a glass of brandy.

"Great God !" he muttered to himself, as he gulped down the raw spirits and replenished his glass. "How horrible ! And they call that dying easy !"

———

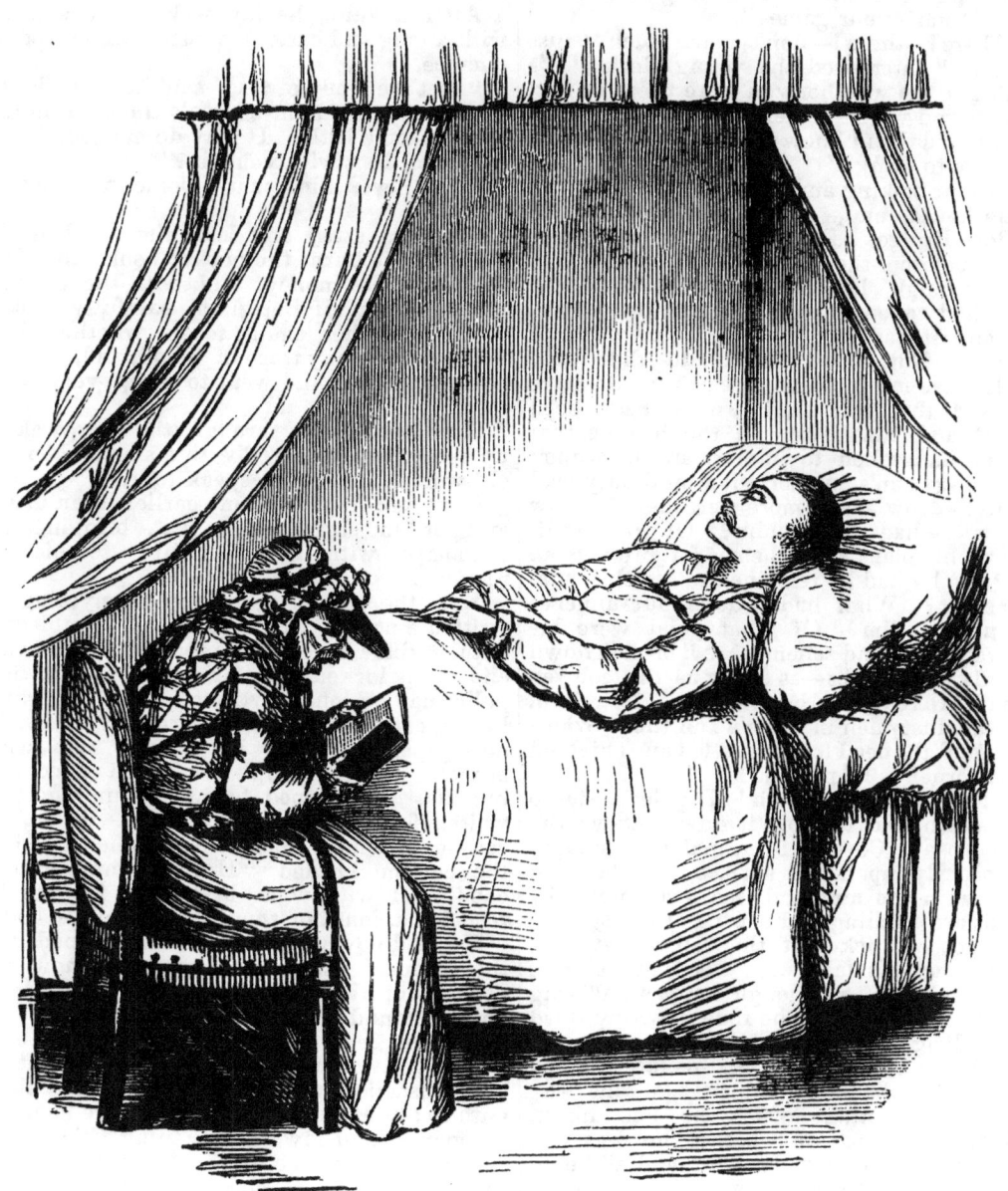

MISS PERKS—A GUARDIAN ANGEL.

CHAPTER THE FIFTY-SECOND.

OVER-DOING IT.

"NOBODY calls it dying easy," said a young man who had overheard Mr. Hadget's remark, and who stood beside him at the bar. "I've seen a dozen hangings, and never saw so bad a one. This is your first, I suppose——"

The speaker had turned round to address him, and having got thus far, stopped short, and stared in blank astonishment at Hadget's face.

"What are you looking at?" asked the latter, uneasily. "Is there anything wrong about me?"

No. 12.

"Nothing that I know of," replied the man, still staring; "only I've seen your face before, somewhere, and can't recollect the circumstance."

"Likely enough," said Hadget, fidgetting more and more. "Any one can do so, who likes to look at it."

"Ah! I have it."

"Have what?"

"You came for a ticket, last night, at London Bridge station."

"Me?" said Hadget, deadly pale. "What do you mean?"

"You asked me whether I should know you again. Don't you remember? You were going to—let me see—you were going to Brighton."

"It's a lie, I tell you! What do you mean?

I never was at London Bridge in my life. What the devil are you driving at? curse you! What's your game?"

"There!—there!—don't make such a fuss about it!" interposed the young clerk, "it's nothing to me whether you were there or not. Only, if you weren't, there's more ugly chaps in the world than I knew of—that's all. What'll you have to drink?"

Without making any reply, Hadget left the public-house, and, calling a cab, drove to London Bridge. He would get there probably before the ticket-clerk could arrive; though he had no doubt that the latter had taken a holiday to see the execution, and it was thus that they had chanced to meet. But, how unfortunate that they should have met! Who on earth would have supposed that this clerk would have been present, and that, after all the trouble that Hadget had taken to impress his face upon the young man's memory, it would only lead to this? How many more were here? How many more had noticed him? Of what avail were all his plans and schemes for proving an *alibi?* Why had he remained to see this horrible sight? What had it done but unnerve and unman him? Of what good were his elaborate plots and schemes? All broken down as easily as cobwebs—as easily as the cobweb he had broken when he took out old Sir John from the dusty den in Lyon's Inn the previous night, and the dead leaves rustled and shivered in the corner as he passed.

Oh! blind, blind wretch! Dig deep, stamp in the earth, and trample it down, above the gory corpse! Cover it over, make all smooth and orderly upon the surface, the taint of blood is in the air; and, see, even now the hounds are smelling and tearing at the spot!

He got his ticket at the railway station, covering up his face with his handkerchief while he did so, as though he was suffering from face-ache. Then he rode down by third class to Brighton.

Alighting, and still keeping his face muffled up carefully, he made the best of his way to the little cottage which he had hired. Looking round to see whether he was observed, and seeing nobody about, and all being very quiet, he let himself in at the back door with a key he carried, made his way up stairs, and, taking off his clothes, jumped into bed.

He had not been long there, when the old woman who attended him rang the bell. He went to the window, and, wrapping up the door-key in his handkerchief, threw it out to her.

"Well, Mrs. Slops," said he, "I shall be glad of a cup of tea, for I feel very seedy."

"Do you, sir? How's that?"

"I don't know how it is, unless I overexerted myself last night running to catch the train. I had a close shave for it."

"Did you come last night from London, sir?"

"Yes."

"You got wet, sir, didn't you?"

"A little. Why?"

"Because your boots is wet still."

He sat up in bed and eyed her suspiciously, but there was nothing in the old lady's face to show that she meant anything more than she said by the observation.

After a while, he lay back again, satisfied with a long and careful scrutiny of her countenance.

"Get me a cup of tea," said he; "and look in, in about an hour or two's time. I think I could sleep a little. It may do me good."

"Shall I sit with you, sir?"

"No, never mind that. Come in again presently."

She went away and left him. When she was gone he burnt the pocket-book which had contained the money, and, with the aid of a powerful magnifying-glass, carefully looked over his clothes again, to see whether there yet remained any trace of blood, and, finding none, lay back, and went to sleep very comfortably.

Thus he slept on through the day, waking up every now and then with a start, when the old woman came in to speak to him.

Next morning she came earlier than usual, and got him something to eat, bringing the newspaper with her, according to his directions.

Has the reader ever done anything?—written a poem? won a prize at Wimbledon, with a rifle? had a little too much to drink, and been locked up for knocking down a policeman?—done anything, in short, which he expected to find a description of in the newspaper? If so, he knows with what anxiety he picked up the broad sheet, at breakfast, and turned to the column where it waited for him in large capitals. If so, he can imagine how Hadget felt as he turned to the column headed "Horrible murder in a cab," and with what breathless interest he read the account of the discovery of the body.

He read how the cab had been stopped, and the cabman taken into custody; how the pockets of the corpse had been rifled, and nothing found upon the dead man which could in any way lead to his indentity; how the cabman had given some cock-and-bull account of the transaction, which the police placed little faith in; how the murdered man bore no name nor marks; and how the only thing which could in any way be a clue to the mystery was, A PAIR OF SPECTACLES picked up at the bottom of the cab!

Could it be possible that the spectacles alluded to were those which he supposed he had left safely locked up in his drawer at Lyon's Inn? If so, must not discovery ensue, as a matter of course? Well, not as a matter of course. Suppose suspicion fell upon Mr. Hadget, and it somehow came out that Sir John was known to have visited him in London, which might not transpire even if the body were recognised. What then? Would the spectacles connect him with the murder? Supposing they should be his spectacles, had anybody had them in her hands, or seen them elsewhere but on Hadget's nose? Never—except—he did recollect one day that old Bob Sawder picked them up in the garden of Skearcrows, and was trying their sight, when the owner chanced to come up and claim them. But, then, he was a poor, muddle-headed, beer-swiping sot, always half hazy with strong drink, and he had swilled away his wits a quarter of a century ago. Then was it likely that he would come to town and see them. Besides, after all, the spectacles might belong to Sir John, for he sometimes carried a pair, though he seldom used them.

There was no description of the glasses in the newspaper. Should they turn out to belong to himself, Hadget determined to purchase another pair directly. They were a common sort, and easily matched. But had he not better go to town immediately, and ascertain the truth. He felt it was impossible to rest—he was in a fever. However, force of circumstances compelled him to wait a little, for there was no train to London for full three hours. Taking the newspaper in his hand, he walked down to the Chain Pier ; and sitting down near the bathing machines, lighted his cigar, and re-read the account of the finding of the body.

Young ladies strolling pass scanned his appearance, and tossed their pretty heads contemptuously, as they do, dear creatures, at many other things they do not understand. Little children frolicked and gambolled round him innocently, little dreaming who and what he was. He seemed a commonplace, ordinary-looking man, shabby and vulgar. Just such another sits before me now as I am writing these lines upon the beach at Shingleshore. Perhaps that party is a murderer too. He is an excursionist, I perceive, and is enjoying the sea after the true excursionist style ; that is to say, he is blowing his tobacco-smoke at it with all his might, and keeping off the breeze as though it were a fever. There is a grey-headed old gentleman yonder, romping with some little children, and gravely assisting at the manufacture of a huge sand-pie. Here is a pretty creature, in a matadore hat with a white feather, who—goodness me ! but yet it is—she's reading "The Woman with the Yellow Hair," quotes some passage to the young lady beside her, and they toss their heads and say, "Oh ! how ridiculous !" or words to that effect. I do not catch them, but I hide my head, and tremble. If they knew who it was——They will next week, when I am gone from here, and laugh at this little anecdote. There, I can see two ladies bathing. What are they about ? They seem to be quarreling. Where's my opera glass ? Ah ! I see now who they are. The fair one is Mrs. Ingots, the banker's wife, who lives at No. 2 upon the terrace ; and the dark one is a nobody-knows-who, who's no better than she ought to be, and lives at No. 3. Mrs. Ingots leads the fashion down here, and has the biggest pew in church. Nobody-knows-who defies the fashion, and don't go to church at all. There have been more than one quarrel about her, I can tell you ; and she has caused much unhappiness in some of our little turtle-doveries. There was a dreadful row between the Ingots : for instance, because Ingots would smoke his cigar on his balcony of an evening, when Nobody-knows-who had her drawing-room windows open. Just now Mrs. Ingots has mistaken her bathing-machine, and by some ill-luck attempted to enter that belonging to this objectionable person.

"This isn't your machine, mam."

"Thank you. I have no wish to go into it."

How they stare and frown at one another. How Nobody-knows-who hates the respectable woman, and how the respectable woman hates her rival. I think I hear Mrs. Ingots saying to some one in her select circle.

"The society here, my dear, is very mixed. I shall never bathe any more ; for really one can't say who they may meet in the water."

And very proper too. I think the matter should be looked into—the ocean kept more select.

Even here you see at this slow and sleepy little town, we have a sprinkling of the bad with the good. All round me there are holiday folks, enjoying themselves after their various fashions. Who knows but the Road murderer may be among them ? Murderers, unfortunately, are not labelled, or our wonderful detective officers would catch them more easily.

Thus Hadget sat and read the account of his bloody deed, and noticed, here and there, some little inaccuracies in the liner's narrative. When he became a little more familiarised with the appearance of the print, which at first sight seemed much larger and more distinct than any other type in the paper, he even began to criticise the writer's style, and thought to himself that it would have read much better had there not been some unnecessary repetition.

After he had almost got the paragraph by heart, he turned to another part of the paper, where he found an account of the execution in front of Newgate, and saw how, owing to the apparently exhausted and feeble state of the condemned man, some of the usual precautions against his struggling were omitted, and thus arose the horrible scene I have described.

"But that does not prove," thought Hadget, "that it is not a painful death. If they are so secured that they cannot struggle, it does not follow that they should not be suffering intense and prolonged agony."

He saw an advertisement of a lecture upon the subject of executions, and determined to go and hear it when he returned to town.

In the meantime what should he do ? How long should he remain there inactive ? Would he not be better in London—on the spot ? Suppose he proposed to defend the cabman ; he would then be upon the scene of action, and able to watch the case. To stop where he was in uncertainty was more than he could bear. No, he would face the danger at all hazards.

And what was the danger he was about to face ?

One he never expected ; for it was old Bob Sawder, *who had had the spectacles in his hand.*

CHAPTER THE FIFTY-THIRD.

A STAB IN THE DARK.

ONE of the young ladies who had been at the Cheveleighs' supper party, Miss Fanny De Courcy, in fact, the well-known and talented danseuse at that time engaged at the Apollo, happened to be slightly acquainted with Miss Fleshings, whose nose, as you may recollect, Mrs. Nelly had put out of joint.

As it was a nice morning, and she had nothing else to do, Miss De Courcy made herself as smart as circumstances would allow of (they were all of them seedily attired persons in the nasty, unbecoming day-light, these ladies of the Apollo), and walked round to Stanhope Street, Clare Market, where her friend resided over a shaving-shop.

"Clarinda, my love, how are you?"

"Fanny, my dear, how kind of you to come and see me."

"How are you getting on?"

"Very well, dear, thank you. How are you?"

The dear creatures embraced each other rapturously, and then sat down affectionately upon the sofa, where, as they talked, they could take stock of one another's clothes: Miss Fleshings picking out the shabbiest parts of Fanny's mantle, and Fanny scrutinising the old faded furniture in Clarinda's apartment.

"Everything's in a dreadful muddle," said the latter, noticing the direction of Miss De Courcy's glances. And, indeed, there was no occasion to say that, it being sufficiently apparent, as was also the fact of Clarinda having had a red-herring for breakfast.

"Oh! never mind the muddle; one can't always be in apple-pie order," replied Fanny. "How are you doing now—professionally? Have you got an engagement? I don't see your name anywhere."

"No—I've not been trying," replied poor Miss Fleshings, who had worn a pair of boots out walking after situations. "I'm thinking of leaving it."

"Oh, dear! I am glad to hear that. It's a dreadful life, is it not, when one is only second rate?"

"Thank you, my dear; but I was not always second rate, I believe. I have done leading business at several theatres——"

"In the provinces——"

"Certainly, it was in the country."

"That's the pity, dear; for one never hears of it."

I like to see the admirable tact with which two women who hate each other continue to keep up an amicable conversation. What wretched blunderers we men are in like circumstances. When we are enraged with our neighbours, we straightway resort to law or fisticuffs: while a woman bolts her anger like a pill, and meets her foe with perhaps a vengeful heart, but with so sweet and smiling a face, that you would never dream that underneath those pouting lips lie hidden teeth that water for a bite.

"You have heard of Miss Raymond, I suppose," continued Fanny; "the lady who superseded you?"

"I have only heard of—I have not seen her."

"Oh! you ought to. She's very good."

"Is she? Accounts vary."

"Some people are so jealous of her, dear, they won't speak the truth. She's in a different line to me, you know; so I have no cause to be. I think her a very clever person. I often go to her house [she had been once], and have spent some very pleasant evenings there. There are some jolly fellows visit her; Charley Bux, of the Guards—you know him, and Lord Drawler. Drawler's a very nice man, only an awful character, and I won't have anything to say to him, though he pesters me out of my life."

"Very grand company, Fanny. I did not know you were so fashionable," said Fleshings, bitterly.

"Oh, nonsense, Clarinda. There's nothing so very wonderful about it. I'm sure his lordship's very much like any other gentleman when you know him intimately."

How small poor Fleshings felt.

"But I have not come to talk to you about Lord Drawler, Clarinda. Indeed, what I came to say I hardly know whether I shall tell you. The fact is, I thought you were out of work, and wanted an engagement."

"Well—I—that is—if it is something good, of course," stammered poor Clarinda, who could not afford to keep up her dignity. "What is it?"

"Well, what do you say to the Apollo?"

"The Apollo?"

"You were always a favourite with Bullyrag—at least, so they say."

"I don't know that I was particularly a favourite," said Clarinda, blushing.

"Oh, dear, no. How innocent we are!"

Here Miss Fanny tittered.

"They did say, you know, Clarinda,—there are some people whose only business is telling lies about other people,—they did say that Mr. Bullyrag admired you as something more than an actress. Indeed, I have often thought it very extraordinary that he could prefer a person like Miss Raymond to one who is so lady-like and accomplished as you are."

"What do you say?" cried Clarinda, in a flutter, knocking about the breakfast things she had begun to put away, and abstractedly pouring some tea into the sugar-basin. "Is the odious wretch making love to Bullyrag?"

"Either she is, or he's making love to her."

"I wish her joy of him. She's welcome to my leavings."

"No, but Clarinda—between friends, you know—why should you let her cut you out?"

"Miss De Courcy!"

"Rubbish, Clarinda! Don't try on that nonsense with me. Let us act together. I have reasons for disliking this woman, and wish to get her out of the theatre. You have reasons for disliking her, and wish to get yourself into it. We'll do it."

"Agreed. But how?"

"Leave it to me," said Miss De Courcy, assuming a tragic tone, and holding her parasol like a poniard,—"'We must be bloody, bold, and resolute, nor fear to strike when comes the time!'"

"But how shall we do it?"

"Hush!" cried De Courcy, with an air and gesture worthy of Ristori, "by a stab in the dark."

"Lawk-a-mercy! Fanny, you wouldn't kill her, would you?"

But Miss De Courcy, perhaps thinking it derogatory to a dark conspirator to be intelligible—they seldom are upon the stage; or perhaps not having made up her mind what she was going to do, refused to explain; but, nodding her head thrice in a mysterious and impressive fashion, departed majestically, and was heard to tumble over a dust pan, left inadvertently upon the stairs.

Maurice did not return all day, but he wrote Nelly a short note, explaining the cause of his prolonged absence. The letter was full of feeling, and, moreover, was badly spelt, and had a grammatical error or two in its composition; for the young fellow was half-stupified with his grief, and hardly knew what he was about. But you don't expect, surely, that the lady was to be equally sensitive. I should not go into mourning if Jones's father were to die, though Jones and I are sworn friends: we have borrowed money of one another frequently. I have known men who have not broken their hearts at the death of their mother-in-law. So why should Nelly be downcast? You sentimental folks would like her to tear her hair, I dare say. Don't you think now, seriously, that she had cause to rejoice instead? Don't you see that the old gentleman's death made her lover SIR Maurice Cheveleigh and——You see the *sequitur.*

All day long she amused herself by picturing her life as it would be when she was the mistress of Skearcrows. She was quite determined about one thing, and that was that she would not waste all her existence down in some poking old place in the country. No: they would sell off the country-house, and live in London—in Park Lane maybe, or in Belgrave Square. Then, upon second consideration, perhaps it would be best to keep on Skearcrows as well: live in town during the season, and go down there to spend the winter. Dear heart! what a happy time it would be, what a splendid lady she would make, and how envious those paltry people at the "Apollo" would be of her good fortune!

She told the news to Miss Perks; but that old noodle did not understand her for a long time, the news seemed so extraordinary. When she did catch a glimmering of Nelly's meaning, she gasped again, and opened those old goggle eyes of hers until it was painful to look at them.

You may be sure everybody in the Court heard about it before the day was out.

"Oh! bless you, yes," she said to Mrs. Mobbles, at the coal and potato warehouse; "harristoscratchit, I believe you! You see, as missus's mother's dead, it makes her Lord Cheveleigh; and then, you see——No, he's Lord Cheveleigh, and she's Lady Raymond,—no——Well, I don't know how it is, but it's all right, I can tell you, and missus is going to leave here and take me along with her, and we're to cut this old dirty place altogether, and live in a manshing, and ride in a carridge-and-four."

"Them will be times, Miss Perks, and I wish you joy of 'em," replied Mrs. Mobbles, with just the smallest dash of irony, for one don't like other people's good fortune thrust down one's throat. "Only don't forget the proverb."

"We don't want nothing to do with proverbs, Mrs. Mobbles."

"But it's worth remembering, Miss Perks."

"What is it, mum?"

"'Don't count your chickens before they're hatched,'" said Mrs. Mobbles, and burst out laughing in Miss Perks' face, much to that ancient maiden's discomfiture.

In the evening Nelly went to the theatre. She had half a mind not to do so; for what would be the good of keeping on the profession any longer. That must be cut at the same time as the Court. As she rode to the "Apollo" she remembered one thing she had forgotten all day—that is to say, she had just given it half a thought; but immediately dismissed it for more agreeable topics. It was her appointment with Mr. Bullyrag.

Mr. B's brougham had no doubt been waiting all day in front of the "Raglan," and he had been stamping and fuming at her want of punctuality.

"He doesn't like to be crossed, I know," said Nelly; "but it does not very much matter to me what he likes or dislikes. I am not going to put myself out of the way to please him."

Acting with this determination, Mrs. Nelly took not the slightest notice of the black looks of the manager, who scowled at her like an ogre as she passed him on the stage, and was in like fashion very haughty and distant to the other members of the company.

"How's your good gentleman to-day?" said the low comedian, sidling up, wanting to be familiar on the strength of having been to the chambers the previous evening.

"SIR MAURICE CHEVELEIGH," replied my lady, in the largest capitals, "is quite well, I thank you, Mr. Gag." And she swept by him with the contempt that a duchess might bestow upon a presumptuous crossing sweeper who had winked at her.

Poor Gag! he sunk into his shoes at the rebuke, and never addressed her again all the evening.

"But what does she mean by 'Sir Maurice,'" thought he. "I never knew he'd got a title. After all, if he has, it don't make her a lady, unless she's married to him. By Jove, perhaps she is. I must mind my p's and q's."

"Perhaps she misunderstood me!" said Bullyrag, to himself. "She might have thought I meant her to meet me to-morrow, and not to-day. Perhaps she was prevented from doing so by some unavoidable circumstance. I'd better speak to her, anyhow."

While he was ruminating upon what course he should pursue, some one tapped him on the shoulder, and turning hastily, the manager saw Lord Drawler standing before him.

"Hallo! Bullyrag," said his lordship, "you told me to look you up. You see, I have done so. What's going on to-night? How's our pretty friend, Miss Raymond?"

Lord Drawler never for a moment imagined that Bullyrag was a successful rival, and *vice versa.*

"Oh! she's very well, my lord, I believe. I have not seen her yet."

"She's a charming woman, eh?"

"Splendid! my lord. With proper training she'd make any one's fortune."

"She's a deuced deal too good for that fellow, Cheveleigh."

"There are not two opinions about that."

"I wonder she has such a little taste."

"I suppose he's well off, if we may judge by the feed last night."

Mrs. Nelly appeared at that moment upon the stage, and Bullyrag left Drawler's side to speak to her.

"Good evening, Mrs. Cheveleigh."

"Good evening, Mr. Bullyrag."

"You didn't keep your appointment."

"What appointment?"

"Do you not remember?"

"I'm sure I don't, Mr. Bullyrag. Pray enlighten me."

1　"I thought you understood," said the manager, with a slight frown. "You promised you would come. I was in front of the 'Raglan,' this morning, at twelve."

"And how long did you wait?"

"Two hours."

"Ha! ha! ha!"

Nelly responded, with one of those clear, musical laughs which were so popular with the "Apollo" audiences. It went through him like a knife.

"Lord! Mr. Bullyrag, how ever could you be so foolish?"

And she walked away, singing as blithely as a bird, and leaving the astonished manager with his mouth and eyes wide open.

"Damn you!" said he, betwixt his teeth, "you shall smart for this." And he began to blow up the carpenters indiscriminately.

"My dear Miss Raymond," said his lordship, "how beautiful you look this evening."

"Do you think so?" she asked, with a slight yawn.

"You know I do. You know I think you are an angel."

"There are lots of other angels besides me, my lord."

"No other I care for, though——"

"Poor fellow! I'm very sorry. But, you see, I am already engaged."

"Engaged, Nelly? Break the engagement, then. If you leave him for me, you shall never repent it."

"Leave Maurice for you! Pray what does your lordship propose to do with me?"

"My dear Nelly, you shall want for nothing. You shall have a carriage—a box at the Opera—a cottage *ornee* at Brompton or St· John's Wood: everything that you can wish for. Your slightest fancy shall be law to me——"

"But, bless my soul, Lord Drawler," said Nelly, with affected surprise, "I thought you told me you were married. Has your wife died during the night?"

"Well, curse her impudence," thought Drawler. Then said aloud,—"No—no—you know marriage is impossible; but why should we care for such hollow mockery?"

"Oh, yes, I dare say," retorted the lady. "We have heard all that before—it's in all the story books. But you see, I do care; and

I do not see that I shall better myself by going under your protection."

"Damn me!" cried Drawler, in an altered tone, considerably surprised and annoyed, "you would gain considerably. I should think it is better to be kept by a lord than a cad."

"I don't know what you mean by a cad; but if you mean that it would be a more enviable position to be Lord Drawler's kept woman than Sir Maurice Cheveleigh's lawful wife, I differ with you. No, my lord, bestow your favours where they will be more valued; and should you have anything further to say to me, be kind enough to say it through my husband. I have no secrets from him. I wish your lordship a very good evening."

While my heroine was thus sending her admirers to the right about, those two dark conspirators, Misses Fleshings and De Courcy, had concocted a little scheme by which they were to get round the manager.

"I could only have an interview with him, without appearing to seek it," Miss Fleshings had said; and Mamma Fleshings, who had been leading tragedy herself once upon a time until she got too fat and lost her voice, and who now lived upon her daughter, approved of the notion, and said she was quite certain "her Rinder" would carry all before her, if she could only come face to face "with feller."

But how was it to be done? At last they hit upon a plan. Fleshings, at the beginning of her professional career, had been a dancer. Even now, upon her benefit, she did a sailor's hornpipe, or a Highland fling with considerable success. Miss De Courcy proposed that she (De Courcy) should pretend to be ill, and that Miss Fleshings should take her place that evening in a little pas-de-something or other, which took place between the pieces. When Bullyrag saw her in a short skirt, and a pretty boddice bound with silver, he would be quite overcome, they were all certain of it. It would be much better than sending her in her old shabby bonnet and little "skimpetty" silk mantle. Certainly, there was some little danger of Fleshings playing her friend false, and endeavouring to supersede her, but this she had promised on her honour not to do; and then, the triumph it would be, to get that horrible woman turned out of the company, made it worth while to run a little risk. De Courcy hated Nell like poison. Indeed, so did every one of the ladies at the "Apollo." Some of the men liked, and all admired her. The call-boy was in love with her, and talked about her in his sleep; but she did not smile upon his passion, poor little lad!

Thus, you see, while Nelly was snubbing my lord, Miss Fleshings, already dressed for the ballet, was waiting with her mamma in the dressing-room, ready for her turn to come.

"How do I look, mamma?"

"Beautiful!" replied the doting mother; "you needn't be afraid of half-a-dozen stuck-up, carrotty-headed creatures like her."

Every hen is proud of its own chick.

Presently the prompter's bell rang, and the call-boy summoned Miss Fleshings to th wing.

Her heart beat so she could hardly breathe, and her face was deadly pale beneath "the smack."

It so happened, on this particular night, that Miss Nelly did not go quite so well with the audience as she usually did, which was perhaps owing to her acting very carelessly, and with rather more disregard for the opinion of the spectators than she was in the habit of showing, and so they took it into their heads to hiss her. Now, in this enlightened city of ours, to hiss anything stupid or objectionable at a place of public amusement, is a very good way to get put outside the doors. The audience are almost certain to take the part of the stupid or objectionable person, and it is quite as likely as not, that he will insult you, in his turn, from the stage, if you take the liberty of disapproving of what you have paid your money to be allowed to come and see.

Nelly was very bad this evening, and the audience were very silent, and, when somebody hissed, nobody took her part, so that she left the stage with anything but flying colours.

"She don't take now," said Mr. Bullyrag. "I'll teach her to play the fool with me. She shall have the sack."

As Nelly passed by him, he called her.

"May I have the honour of a moment's conversation?"

"Certainly, sir."

"You asked me, yesterday, to raise your salary. I have been considering the question, and I regret to say that the present state of the exchequer will not allow of it; but, as I am confident you would make your fortune anywhere else, I won't stand in your way, and so consider our engagement ends with this week."

"That'll bring her to her senses," he thought to himself.

"I've gone too far," thought she. Then said aloud, "I'm very glad you mentioned it first, Mr. Bullyrag; for the fact is, I was going to tell you myself that I must leave your company. Circumstances have occurred which render it necessary that I should quit the profession. *My husband* has come in to his title and property by the death of his father; and, as *Lady* Cheveleigh, I am inclined to think that even the 'Apollo' boards would be rather out of place."

Having delivered herself of this speech, she tossed her head and retired, leaving Bullyrag blue with passion, and it was at this very moment that Miss Fleshings came towards him.

She might have chosen a more propitious moment—he was in an awful temper.

"Ahem — ahem!" said Miss Fleshings, trembling, and coughing behind her hand.

But he took no notice.

"Mr. Bullyrag—ahem!—I--I — beg your pardon."

"What is it? Hallo! what are you doing here?"

"I—I hope you'll pardon the intrusion, sir, but my friend, Miss De Courcy, having been taken—I may say, not being able by indisposition—severe indisposition—to appear, I

ventured to take her place—for—for this night only."

"Indisposited! Damn her indisposition, she was well enough last night. What does she mean? You needn't trouble yourself, I'll cut out the ballet."

"But, Mr. Bullyrag—sir—I am all ready. There is no occasion."

"Here, you up there!" cried the manager, shouting to the men in the flies, "pull up the garden again, and let down the rocky pass for 'The Maniac Mother;' we'll cut out the dancing."

"But, Mr. Bullyrag—Thomas!—you would not be so unkind."

It seemed as if he would, though, for he continued to bawl to the carpenters.

Poor Fleshings, in tears and misery, stood shivering at the wings!

"Am I then to take off my dress again?" she said to him, when she got another opportunity.

"You can do what the devil you like," replied the ruffian. "If you're a friend of De Courcy's, tell her she need not trouble herself to come here any more. I'll do without her. Curse me, if I can't get on without putting up with the whims and fancies of a lot of women, I'll close the house altogether!"

And he retired to his own room, and was heard swearing fearfully for an hour afterwards.

"Here's a pretty kettle of fish," said Mamma Fleshings, to Clarinda.

"What ever am I to say to Fanny?"

"Goodness knows!"

As Nelly rode back in her cab to Cleveland Chambers, she said to herself,—

"I hope I haven't gone too far. I'm almost sorry I said what I did. Supposing Maurice won't marry me—good heavens! But oh, he's sure to do it. Can't I twist him round my little finger?"

"I've made a fine night of it," thought Bullyrag. "How the deuce I'm to keep open the theatre, I don't know. And two new plays in rehearsal, too, with that hussy in the principal part. I wish I hadn't been so hasty."

"What the dickens made me in such a hurry?" thought Lord Drawler. "I don't believe she's married, though she says so. I've spoilt it all by coming to the point so soon; but she seemed all right last night. There are some women you never know how to manage."

"I hope you haven't been saying anything in the Court about what I told you," said Nelly to Miss Perks.

"Me! mam——"

"I suppose you have, but don't say any more. It's best not to boast of these things before they happen. One never knows what may occur."

"But, mam, the old gentleman can't come to life again, can he?"

"No, I suppose not. Only, hold your tongue about it, do you hear?"

"I'd rather die than breathe a syllable, mam."

CHAPTER THE FIFTY-FOURTH.

UPON THE SCENT OF BLOOD.

THERE is great excitement in and about Lower Thames Street. Heavy-looking men hang, in a heavy fashion, over their pots of heavy-wet, expounding cumbersome opinions in clumsy phraseology. All the public-houses are doing a roaring trade, and all the customers before all the bars are talking of the same subject—the murder in the cab.

At the sign of the "Frisky Drayman" (that's where the body lies), they are doing a miraculous stroke of business. The bar is full, the taproom is full, the parlour is full, the little room behind the bar is not unoccupied, and the "good, dry skittle-ground" is overflowing. Up-stairs, in the clubroom, the coroner is sitting, and in a little room behind, lying on the bagatelle-board, covered over with a sheet—very bloody, stiff, and horrible—lies the subject of inquiry.

Stopgap, the beadle, in all the majesty of cocked hat and gold lace, has served the summonses, but the jurors display the same unwillingness that we may observe in the public which assembles outside a circus at a fair " to step furrads," so matters are at a stand-still for the present.

In and out among the crowd, up and down stairs, now at the bar, now in the clubroom, wanders a seedy gentleman, in very old kid gloves, the third finger of the right hand of which has got the end torn off, and shows a blot of ink upon the nail. He is understood to be on the press, and at that time officially engaged, and wears an important and preoccupied air, which makes the people outside at first mistake him for the coroner.

Outside the house there is a goodly crowd, who watch all there is to be seen outside—which is not much—with breathless eagerness, and parties of a morbid turn go round to the back of the house and feast their eyes upon the windows of the room where it is supposed the body is lying. One young man chips a piece off a door-post at the back of the house with his pen-knife, and taking it home carefully in a paper, adds it to a little museum of similar curiosities which he is collecting.

By this time three of the jurymen already arrived having been strengthened by the arrival of two more, who looked in casually to say they could not stop, and were informed that it would go hard with them if they didn't, the coroner asks the beadle, sternly, what it means.

The beadle asking what *what* means, is told to take care what he is about, or he'll get himself into trouble, at which rebuke that functionary, hitherto rather arrogant and bouncible in his behaviour, sinks into insignificance, and becomes as nobody.

Here the coroner, calling for pen and ink, proceeds to put down the missing jurors' names, with the determination of fining them; which operation is interrupted by the arrival of the delinquents, who are straightway threatened and sworn in, among some whispered remonstrances and objections.

"Gentlemen," says the coroner, " you are here impanelled to inquire into the circumstances connected with the death of a certain man. You will hear evidence respecting those circumstances, and you will give your verdict according to that evidence, and not according to anything else. We will now proceed to view the body."

Attended by the beadle, the jurymen go into the next room, where the body is lying out, ready to receive them; and they peep over one another's shoulders at it, and get as far as possible away from it, and look rather pale and frightened, and one juror, rushing out upon the stairs, is taken very ill, and unable to proceed with the inquiry.

By this time a cab has arrived, containing two policemen and the prisoner, who looks very wretched and dejected, and who, everybody agrees at first sight, looks every inch a murderer.

Then comes another cab, bearing a very stiff, clean-shaven gentleman, who is said to be Inspector Bucket, the celebrated detective officer. And the crowd says.—

"He knows all about it, bless you."

"There's no secrets from them chaps."

The celebrated Inspector Bucket says nothing; but thinks a great deal instead.

Maurice Cheveleigh is up-stairs, and old Bob Sawder waiting to be examined; and the crowd, for whom there is no accommodation in the clubroom, hang about upon the staircase, and in the passages, and think themselves lucky if they can catch a glimpse of these or any other persons connected with the case.

When the jurors had returned from viewing the body, all looking very much as though they had come from a bad sea voyage, and the particular juryman who has been particularly ill among the spittoons on the landing, has been revived by the judicious administration of hot brandy-and-water, the business is resumed.

"Bless me, Mr. Cheveleigh—I mean Sir Maurice—this is an awful business. I called in at your chambers, and heard of the distressing circumstance. In the prime of life, too. My dear old friend! How all of us will miss him."

It is Mr. Hadget who has just arrived, and who wrung the young man's hand as he spoke.

"How did you hear of it?" he continued. " How did it happen?"

"Bob will tell you all about it," says Maurice, turning away. "He found it out."

"Oh! you found it out, did you?" cries Mr. Hadget. "It was you, Mr. Sawder, was it? And pray what have you discovered? What'll you have to drink?"

"Thank'ee, sir," says Bob, who looks very red about the nose, and watery about the eyes, and is troubled with a hiccup, " I've had enough. I've got to give my evidinch."

"Nonsense, old fellow; you want something to put some life in you. Come and have some hot grog—just a teaspoonful, and tell me all about it."

"If I do," says Bob, " I shan't be able to swear to anything."

"All the better," says Mr. Hadget to himself; " I'll take care you don't."

PREPARING FOR CONQUEST.

CHAPTER THE FIFTY-FIFTH.

STILL UPON THE SCENT.

OUTSIDE the house in Lower Thames Street the excitement is intense, for it is rumoured that the examination of the witnesses has begun.

Those at the bar ask those upon the stairs what is going on, and they inquire of those nearest the clubroom door, who, in their turn, jump up, and struggle to see over one another's heads, and ask questions of their lucky neighbours, until silenced by the beadle.

Not being able to see or hear anything whatever, or come to any conclusion as to what is

No. 13

going on, the public outside shows signs of flagging interest, and to give way at the knees, and groups retire dead-beaten to adjacent bars, and go "Tommy Dod" for malt liquor.

A tendency to chaff springs up among the rabble, particularly among the boys, and the appearance of the beadle in Lower Thames Street is the signal for much unseasonable pleasantry.

All this while they are examining the prisoners in the clubroom.

The substance of the evidence is as follows :—

John Taylor, the prisoner, called in.—Is a cabman, and lives in Plum-tree Court, Clerkenwell. Don't know the number—believes there is none. Has been a cabman the last five years. Was several other trades before that. A dozen, perhaps. Doesn't recollect what he was last.

By a Juror.—Knows he is upon his oath. Don't know what he was doing before he got his present birth; but rather thinks he must have been out of work, for he remembers he was starving.

By another Juror.—Means to take care what he is about, and wants to be getting along a little quicker, if they will give him the office.

Examination resumed.

Was, on the night of the murder, plying for hire in Fleet Street, and was hailed by two gents (the party deceased and his murderers), who wished to be driven to Saint Katharine's Docks. One looked like a country gentleman; the other had a large black beard, and looked like a foreign sailor. The sailor asked which way he was going to drive them. Suggested Cheapside, as it would make a longer fare of it. To this the sailor objected, and told him to go by Thames Street. He drove as directed. When he was passing underneath the arch of London Bridge which crosses Thames Street, he noticed that the harness of his horse wanted repairing, and got down to do it.

A Juror.—Is the harness in court?

Prisoner. — No, nor the horse neither. (Laughter and confusion.)

The prisoner having been cautioned that "this is neither the time nor place for joking," proceeds with his story.

While engaged mending a broken strap with a piece of string, the sailor put his head out of the window, and asked what he was doing. He said he was mending the harness; to which the sailor replied, "Very well," and remained looking out of window at him while he did it. He then got on to his seat again, and drove on; but he had not got very far before the sailor called to him to stop, and, getting out, bade the other gentleman inside good night, and ran across the road. He then drove on until he reached the Docks, and was going through a doorway, when the wheels of his cab got entangled with the wheels of another cab coming out, and a policeman who came up to help him noticed some blood trickling out underneath the cab door, looked into the cab, and, discovering the body, took him (the prisoner) into custody.

Cross-examined by the foreman.—When the sailor stopped the cab, and wanted to get out, had attempted to get down to open the door, the handle of which moved very stiffly, but the sailor would not allow him. When the sailor had alighted, and was trying to shut the door again, he descended from his box, and offered to assist, but the sailor, in a great passion, said, "You've no time to lose. Stop where you are, damn you!" or words to that effect. Could not see into the cab very well through the windows, as they were dirty, and, besides, the cab was standing at the time in a dark place, away from any lamp. Did not hear the man inside reply to the other when he said good night, but did not take much notice of the circumstance. When he was taken into custody, told the same story to the policeman, and knows no more about it.

"You can stand down," says the coroner; and cabby stands down, and is taken away to a room above by a couple of policemen, leaving a strong smell of tobacco, and the very worst impression, behind him.

The policeman who found the body is now examined.

Was on Sunday night on duty before St. Katharine's Docks. Observed the collision between two cabs, as described. Came forward to render assistance. Had his attention drawn to the contents of the cab by some blood which trickled out from underneath the door upon his hands. Opened the door, and discovered the corpse. Took the prisoner into custody, who, after being cautioned, told the story which he has just been telling.

Then the policeman describes the appearance of the body, and how the pockets had all been emptied.

"Did you find nothing in the cab that might lead to the identification of the deceased?" says the coroner.

"I found these spectacles," says the policeman, and hands up a pair with gold frames.

"Pass them round to the gentlemen," says the coroner to the beadle.

"Ugh!" says the foreman, with a jump, "there's blood upon the glasses."

"There was a good deal of blood on everything inside the cab; the floor was swimming in it," says the policeman, with a relish.

Then the spectacles travel, per beadle, round the room, most of the jurors eyeing them timidly and askant, as though they were some dangerous instrument in the explosive line, and might go off at any moment without notice. And the juror who was ill on the landing has a relapse, and again suspends the business.

Examination resumed.

Searched the prisoner, and found in his pockets five shillings, a latch key, a turnpike ticket, and a knife.

Objects produced.

Cross-examined.—There was blood upon his clothes and on his hands. Might have come upon them in helping to move the cab, in the same way that blood had come upon the policeman. There was no blood upon the knife.

"Are there any more witnesses who have anything to say?"

Yes, there are two or three who have a good deal to say about one thing or the other, waxing fluent upon topics extraneous to the matter in hand.

To these witnesses have the jurors many and weighty queries to propound, some of which are over-ruled by the coroner.

After these, the surgeon, who describes the state of the body as he found it, and enters at great length into the appearance of the wound in the murderd man's throat.

Relapse of juror, who says he can't stand it.

"Is there any one here who can speak to the deceased's identity?" asks the coroner, after the juror has somewhat recovered, and the doctor has bowed himself out.

Somebody says that there is somebody else down stairs who was there the day before, and recognised the body as belonging to his master.

"Summon this person," says the coroner.

But just at this identical moment a seedy person in black, very polite and affable, though wearing withal a somewhat sinister and cunning look, worms himself through the crowded room until he reaches the coroner's side, where he stands bowing and smirking.

"My name is Hadget, sir," he says, in a confidential kind of whisper behind a shabby kid glove. "Hadget, of Lyon's Inn; in the law, sir. I was the deceased's legal adviser, a most excellent gentleman, Sir John Cheveleigh, of Skearcrows, Yorkshire."

"Indeed," says the coroner.

"The person below, sir, is a drunken servant of the deceased, who is at present in a—I may say——Though really it is too disgusting at such a time, too."

"What's the matter with him?" asks the coroner.

"He is, in point of fact—I may say——"

"Well, sir?" (a little impatiently.)

"If you will have it, he's too drunk to stand."

"What's he mean by it? How did he become so?"

"To tell the truth, sir," says Mr. Hadget, still bowing and smiling with the affability, if not the grace of a dancing master, "he generally is so. He's drunk half his wits away."

"But he must come forward."

"Do you think it is necessary?"

"Certainly."

"But there is the deceased's son, also, the heir to the estate and title, Sir Maurice Cheveleigh. He is waiting outside."

"Oh! that alters the case. I suppose this servant had nothing else to say but prove the identity."

"Not a word, sir. Indeed, in his present state, I doubt whether he could do that by his own father."

Sir Maurice Cheveleigh, here called forward, states that the deceased is his father, and that he did not know his father was in town, until he heard that the body had been found.

Having given his evidence, Maurice retires, and the coroner asks if there is anybody else who has anything to say.

There is a drunken old wretch, who can't stand upright, who is alternately whining, raving, and whimpering, in a maudlin state, and is a highly unedifying spectacle to look upon, who says he knows all about it, and knows why his master came to London, and whom he came to London to see, but nobody listens to or understands him.

He would be turned out into the streets by the potboy, did not Mr. Hadget kindly take charge of him.

The celebrated Detective, Mr. Bucket, has, however, something to say which everybody is eager to listen to. Indeed, so many people are desirous of hearing him, besides those whom the room, already packed to suffocation, will contain, that the squeezing on the stairs is perfectly terrific.

Inspector Bucket deposes that he has been specially employed upon the case for a couple of days, and that he has picked up a thing or two in the way of evidence.

"From information" Mr. Bucket "received," he went straight to the prisoner's house, and made important discoveries, which, at that early period of the day, he would prefer not to disclose.

Sensation, not unmixed with disappointment, experienced by the bystanders.

Inspector Bucket knows something of the cabman's early history. He begs to inform the coroner and jurymen that John Taylor is a ticket-of-leave man.

Extraordinary sensation and astonishment at the awful, unfathomable, and unlimited extent and depth of Inspector Bucket's knowledge and power. Small trader, on the eve of bankruptcy, who is serving on jury, trembles in his highlows at the thought that perhaps it is all known to Bucket, together with the details of his last insolvency, a quarter of a century ago in Great Tiddlewinkinton, that year when they rose the water rates, and there was such a panic among the milkmen.

The fact of John Taylor being a ticket-of-leave man is no great secret by the way, and in Plum-tree Court it is as well known as the fact of Her Gracious Majesty being Queen of England—perhaps better. But the coroner does not know that, and the foreman does not know it, and the jurors do not know it, nor do the spectators, nor those upon the stairs, nor those outside; so there is very great wondering, "Oh! lor'"-ing, head-shaking, and mouth-opening, and everybody agrees that the knowledge of Inspector Bucket is something awful in its profundity.

Having given what information he thinks it is safe and necessary to give at this time, which, summed up, comes to nothing very particular, imparted with considerable circumlocutive pomposity, he waits, with a smirk of tremendous import, for any question anybody may have the hardihood to put to him.

"So you think this cabman did commit the murder?" asks a juror. But the question is withdrawn, as an improper one.

"However," says the juror, who is a churchwarden, and does not like being shut up, "Mr. Bucket, I suppose, if he is the guilty party, you'll soon bring it home to him?"

"I dare say I shall, sir," says Mr. Bucket, with a compassionate smile for the churchwarden.

And the bare idea of Mr. Bucket not bringing anything home to anybody when he wanted, is so absurdly preposterous, that the whole room is moved to mirth, and the churchwarden retires advisedly, thinking he may get the worst of it if he goes any further.

The coroner then recalls John Taylor, and reads over the whole of the evidence in his hearing. He asks no questions; but when the ticket-of-leave is mentioned, looks a little foolish, and says in reply to the coroner, who inquires why he did not mention the circumstance, that he was not in the habit more than any of the other gents present of crying "stinking fish," unless there was a positive necessity for so doing.

He is then removed, while the coroner proceeds to sum up the evidence.

The room is cleared, and after a lapse of a few minutes, the coroner is recalled, and the foreman announces that the jury are unanimously of opinion that the deceased has been wilfully murdered by John Taylor, the cabman.

The coroner immediately makes out a warrant of committal, and John Taylor is given back into the custody of the police.

Then the meeting breaks up.

The coroner goes home to dinner as hungry as a hunter, for he is at least an hour and a half behind time owing to the long delays.

Some of the jurors go home, and some stay and partake of spirituous refreshment. The foreman challenges one of them at skittles, and they stop and make a night of it. The sickly juryman, on whom the sight of the corpse took such an effect, goes home and sends for the doctor, takes physic, and retires early, jumping and screaming out in the night to the dire alarm and consternation of his better half.

The crowd outside spend all they have about them at the adjacent bars, talking the matter over, and then go home not much the wiser.

Up-stairs upon the bagatelle board, still covered by the sheet, the corpse lies cold and stiff, a streak of moonlight playing on the head, while all the rest is profoundly dark and silent.

Upon the scent of blood departs the celebrated Bucket, closely followed by his myrmidons. Upon the scent of blood the ever busy hounds go, sniffing round, and round, and up and down, while Murder, smiling grimly to itself, takes home the only living evidence of its crime, and locks it up in Lyon's Inn. In other words, our artful legal friend has taken away that drunken old wretch, Bob Sawder, and still plying him with more and more brandy, bids fair to drive him to delirium tremens, and so make an end of him.

CHAPTER THE FIFTY-SIXTH.

SOMETHING LIKE A HERO.

DO you like reading about Mr. Ernest Cheveleigh? I should not be at all surprised if you said that you didn't. It is a very melancholy fact, but one does not like being improved and instructed. Who reads the useful information part of the penny miscellanies? Scarcely anybody, I should think, besides the sub-editor, who looks through it in search of typographical errors.

Now you can't believe—you wicked ones—how delighted I am that I have got such a young man for a hero—a young man every body admired and looked up to. He was in his conduct as scrupulously irreproachable and correct as he was faultless in his attire. He always wore a frock coat, and carried a walking-stick or umbrella, and had his boots as brightly polished as those of a mechanic on a Sunday.

Since he had left his cousin Maurice, he lived in that ambiguous, neutral piece of ground, lying in that part of London the post office people decreed should be known as the S district, which has no right to be called Belgravia, but is yet much above owning to a relationship with plebeian Pimlico.

He belonged to the Wind Bags Club, in St James's Street, which, though only second rate, is highly select, and won't admit any body but Government clerks and half-pay captains.

Mr. Ernest Cheveleigh was highly esteemed in the Bad Bargains, and was as great a favourite with Mr. Parchingby, the chief clerk, as his cousin Maurice had been an object of dislike.

Parchingby and Ernest both obtained their situations under the Sansculotte administration, and they were friends from the first. Parchingby was a Scotchman, and Ernest, too, had some of the Scotch blood in him. I, myself, know nothing, but by hearsay, of public offices; but they tell me that the Caledonian Clutch family is strongly represented in the Civil Service.

Ernest Cheveleigh was a tremendous worker. When Her Majesty had made more bad bargains than usual, and entered upon a more than ordinary number of disastrous arrangements for being supplied with preposterous quantities of useless articles at exorbitantly high prices, the assistance of Mr. Ernest was called in to get through the business.

"Look here, Cheveleigh. What's to be done?"

"How much is there to do?"

"This, and that, and the other. Half-a-dozen clerks' work for a fortnight."

"Give me half the number, and I'll do it in a week."

And so he did—somehow.

There is very little doubt but that this talented gentleman would, in course of time, have reached the summit of clerkly ambition, and become the Bad Bargainers' General, had not circumstances arisen which completely changed the aspect of official affairs.

One day, Mr. Ernest sat in his room at the office, knocking off bundles of work with the ease and rapidity that people's heads are knocked off in those countries where they decapitate criminals by the baker's dozen, when he was interrupted by a tap at the door.

"Come in," said he.

And in walked Mr. Hadget.

"Good morning, Mr. Cheveleigh. I hope you are quite well, sir? I sincerely trust you are quite well?"

"Quite well, thank you," replied Ernest, coldly, for the jocular attorney was no favourite of his.

"That's right," said Mr. Hadget, as though a great weight was taken off his mind. "I'm very glad to hear it."

Here there was a pause, in which Mr. Hadget, absorbed in thought, took a chair, and sat down upon it.

"Yes," he repeated, "I'm very glad to hear it indeed. For how little does one know, when in robust health how soon the time may come. It's my turn to-day, and yours to-morrow. King Death is always sharpening the scythe——You've heard of that sad case, of course?''

"Of course I have heard of my uncle's death. An account of the inquest appeared in all the papers.''

"Did it? To be sure—yes—of course. A sad bereavement, sir, for all of us. He was a most worthy man.''

"Doubtless. I could have wished that he had led a better life though, and that his son did not promise to walk so closely in his footprints.''

"He's rather wild, sir, isn't he?''

"He lives a life of disgraceful profligacy, according to accounts. I called there the other day, and found that that person was still living there.''

"Ah,'' sighed Mr. Hadget, "I think she is. I noticed somebody myself. It's odd how our young friend does it. That sort of thing costs money, you know.''

"I *don't* know; but I suppose it does.

"To be sure—certainly, Mr. Ernest. You were never partial to these wild excesses.''

"Anything but partial.''

"Anything but partial. Certainly; and quite right too. You think that the son will waste the property like his father did?''

"I should fear so.''

"I feared so too. And there is only one way of preventing it.''

"What is that?''

"Don't let him have it.''

"What do you mean?''

"Only what I say. If he would waste it, why should he enjoy it? If he has no claim to it, why should he possess it? If there i another legal claimant, why should he not come forward?''

"But there is none that I know of.''

"But I know of one.''

"Who, pray? Did Sir John make a will?''

"No: if he had, Maurice would have been the heir, I have no doubt. But he *didn't*; and that's where the point lies.''

"What on earth are you driving at?''

"Sir Ernest Cheveleigh, allow me to congratulate you.''

As he spoke, Hadget bowed low to the gentleman addressed, who stared at him in blank astonishment.

——

CHAPTER THE FIFTY-SEVENTH.

A WHISPERED SECRET.

"DID I not know, from my own personal observation, Mr. Hadget, that you could drink any other half-dozen men under the mahogany, and still maintain a cool head and steady hand, I should think, decidedly, that you had been drinking now, and were suffering from the effects of it.''

"I never was more sober, Sir Ernest Cheveleigh,'' said the lawyer; "never more sober, and never better acquainted with the meaning of the words I make use of. I seldom talk at random. In liquor I do not talk at all. Ha! ha! When you have drunk enough to lose your senses, don't stop, but keep on drinking

till your speech goes after them. It's safer, if you've secrets worth the telling.''

But Ernest was not listening to this bit of wisdom. Certainly, his eyes were bent on Hadget's ugly face; but, by their vacant and unmeaning stare, you might have seen his mind was busy with some other subject. Perhaps he was studying the pattern of the wallpaper directly behind the lawyer's head, for he seemed to be looking right through him.

"Sir Ernest Cheveleigh, allow me to congratulate you.''

"What do you mean by 'Sir Ernest?''' asked the other. "I have no right to the title that I know of.''

"Haven't you?'' said Hadget, with a chuckle. "Not only a right to that, but a right to all the property.''

"You're mad, man—you must be mad.''

"It sounds uncommon like it, don't it? But I'm sane enough.''

"What do you mean, then, in Heaven's name—for I don't understand you?''

"The recovery of property—re-instatement of the lawful heir, and ousting of the unlawful ditto, is lawyer's work. I'll be your lawyer, if you like. Will you employ me?''

"I don't know yet that there is any occasion. Unless you are more explicit——I don't understand you, I say.''

"Will you employ me to get you the Skearcrows' property? That's what I want to know.''

"I will, if you can. But how is it to be done?''

"Look here,'' said Hadget, glancing round. "I'll whisper a word to you. Your cousin, Maurice, is——''

If a serpent had stung him, Ernest could not have started more than he did. "Good God!'' cried he, "who told you so?''

He was not a young man who used bad language, and, as a general rule, was very careful of his expletives. What could the secret have been which could have called forth such an exclamation?

For a few moments he stood pale and half-stupified, like one who has been walking in his sleep suddenly awakened. Then he turned to his companion, and, clutching him eagerly by the arm, asked him if he was certain what he said was true.

"Aye, I'm certain enough, you may be sure, or else I should not have said so.''

"What do you propose, then?''

"Put yourself under my entire guidance, and you shall have your title and your property before a month is over. Can you leave here?''

"Yes—yes, when you like.''

And Ernest jumped up, and took his hat.

"Not now,'' said Mr. Hadget, smiling slightly. "To-morrow will you apply for leave of absence? You may have to go down to the country. Come and see me to-night at Lyon's Inn—at eight, and we will talk it over. Or, stay—shall I come and see *you?*''

"No. I would prefer coming to Lyon's Inn.''

"Well—yes, if you like.''

He had remembered something, it seemed, and half repented of the invitation; but, recovering himself after a moment's struggle, shook hands with Ernest, and took himself off.

When he was safe outside the building, he chuckled, and rubbed his hands together, in a way that caused no small astonishment to the passers by.

"Hallo! old gig-lamps, have you found a farden?" some facetious youth in the newspaper trade asked of him, noticing his radiant face.

"Aint he pleased about it, Bill? Don't you wish you was agoin' to have roast pork for dinner?"

"Many happy returns of the day, sir," cried a crossing-sweeper, touching the part of his cap where the peak ought to be. "Wish you joy, sir." And then splashed the mud over him, when he found the lawyer was not good for a copper.

"Ha, ha!" laughed Hadget, to himself; "so much for you, Mr. Maurice. I'll teach you to turn up your nose at me. You always were a proud-stomached cur; but humble pie will be your only prog in future. As for the other, I hate him, too; but if I hated him twice as much as I do, I could not punish him more than I shall do befriending him."

When left to himself, Ernest Cheveleigh fell back in his chair, and cogitated profoundly. An energetic junior clerk came running in to ask his opinion upon some difficult point.

"Do so and so," said he, without looking at it, and at the same time suggesting some gross absurdity, which sent away the young official sniggering and crowing for an hour afterwards.

"Do you know what he said?" cries little Nibbs.

"No!" says old Quill and big Bonum, in a breath. "What was it?"

Then little Nibbs narrates, and Quill and Bonum smile; and then all three agree that Ernest, like all other geniuses, is over-rated. Poor old Quill is growing grey, and nobody has yet found out his merits. Big Bonum is an ass, as everybody knows. In secret, they must think very little of each other, though they raise their voices together against the common enemy. Little Nibbs does not think much of either of them, and is not surprised that they should be at the bottom of the ladder, while Ernest is climbing to the topmost staves. He hopes to pass them, too, upon his upward course.

Ernest little thought, or little cared what his envious juniors were saying about him. He sat and cogitated. He bit his nails, and pondered, pondered again, and hacked at the table with his pen-knife.

Could what he had heard be true? It must be: for Hadget could never have dared to hint at such a thing, unless he had some proof of it. And what would be the consequences? What course should he pursue? If he were to be rich, and a baronet, could he remain any longer a clerk in a Government office? The thing was impossible. No—he would bid farewell to quill-driving for ever. There would be a chance when he was gone for little Nibbs.

CHAPTER THE FIFTY-EIGHTH.

OLD LOVE RENEWED.

AFTER his dinner at the Wind-Bags,—he could not eat anything, but drank instead a little more than his usual quantum of sherry,—Ernest strolled down Saint James's Street, munching his tooth-pick, and ruminating.

He turned round by Sams's, and retraced his steps, apparently changing his mind with regard to the direction in which he should bend his steps.

"I had forgotten," he thought to himself, "I must call at the Burlington."

"How is Lady Drawler?" he asked of the porter.

"Her ladyship is much better to-day, I believe, sir."

He was turning away when a natty little maid stepped forward.

"My lady said, sir, if you please, that if you would be so kind, she'd like to speak to you."

"It is too late now, is it not?"

"Oh! no, sir, whenever you came, her ladyship said. Will you come up now, sir?"

Ernest turned and followed her up the spacious staircase. She bade him wait a moment in an ante-room, whilst she announced his arrival to her mistress, and then returning, conducted him to her ladyship's presence.

A young and elegant woman sat by the window, which was a little open; for the weather, although winter time, was very mild.

"Madam," said he, advancing timidly, "I trust that you have recovered from your illness?"

She had looked up as he entered the room, but the window was not facing the door, and so the light did not fall upon his face. The candles had not yet been lit, and where he stood his form was half hidden in the dim obscurity.

At the sound of his voice, however, she had risen from her seat, and, with one hand pressed upon her heart, said,—

"Ernest!"

"Margaret!"

In another moment, he was at her feet, and kissing her fair hand, which lay helplessly on her lap, where it had fallen as she sank back into her seat.

"Ernest—don't! For God's sake, get up! Should anybody come, what would they think?"

"No one will come, dear Margaret. Oh! how happy I am to meet you again."

"I knew—at least, I thought—that is, I felt that it was you, Ernest. Before I saw the name upon the card, I felt it could be no other; but yet I could not imagine how your name should be associated with my illness, and my mysterious arrival here in this hotel. Pray did you find me in the streets?"

"You had fallen upon the pavement, in a fainting fit, when fate sent me to your rescue. I had risen at an early hour, intending to go into the country by the first train, and, not finding a cab, had walked on down Piccadilly.

You came out of a house, and, staggering about a dozen yards, fell down."

"Did you see where I came from?"

"No."

"It was from my husband's rooms."

"Lord Drawler's."

"Yes, he drove me out, striking me in the face, and cut my lip—as you can see. He bade me leave him; and I went out, without caring which way I turned. Oh! Ernest, I have been so unhappy."

There was a pause of a few moments, and then Ernest asked,—

"Does he, then, treat you ill?"

"Lord Drawler has never treated me otherwise."

They were silent again for a long while, and busy with their thoughts. What were they, think you?

Two years ago, they first had met, and loved each other. The story is old enough. Ernest had nothing but his heart to offer. The old romance of "bread and cheese and kisses." Margaret's mother had thought the match a foolish one, as everybody in their senses would. Miss's boxes were packed, and mamma and she went travelling. The doctor recommended change of scene, as, I believe, is usual in such cases. As for Ernest I do not exactly know what he did. He prayed for the heavens to fall down and bury him. He was the most miserable wretch upon earth. Life was a blank. The only wonder is, how he ever got over it,—though he did, you know; and, after a period of intense mental agony, he resumed his customary diurnal consumption of animal food, thus temporarily interrupted.

Bah! how I am disgusting you young ladies. But, believe me, it is not intentional. I sympathise with the Blighted Being, but I am clumsy at these descriptions. Do you think I am laughing at you? Was I not myself crossed in love? When I was a very little boy, in a very big collar, did not I fall in love with the mother of the cock of the school—a middle-aged married woman, at that time nursing her eighth? I was then not quite as old as her eldest boy. It is—I should not like to say how many years—and I have quite forgotten what her name was, though I have taken tea at her house a score of times—so, you see, people do get over these sort of things. I have no doubt she, too, has recovered, and is dead and buried years ago. God rest her!

And was it possible, you ask, that Ernest—a straight-laced, cold-blooded, matter-of-fact young man like he seems to be—should fall in love, and disport himself thus ridiculously? Besides, how about Dorcas? Had he loved both together? No. You see, at the time that he proposed for Margaret, he was not paying his addresses to the poor companion. It was only afterwards, when, with a bruised and throbbing heart he came to her for that sympathy and consolation which all dear women have so large a store of, and healing of the wound, he fell in love with the doctor: or did he perceive that she loved him, and, though not loving her, determine to make her happy? At that time, he thought she was to be Mrs. Falsetto's heiress. As he could not marry the woman he truly loved, perhaps he thought, and not unwisely, that he could be pretty comfortable with Dorcas and his old aunt's money. But, then, there was the old aunt's consent to be obtained: no easy task, with such a fanciful lady. Ernest soon found that it would never be given. Must he wait for her death, or forget the money? Wait, of course. And while waiting, Mrs Falsetto alters her will; upon which Ernest acts, as I have already told you.

Let that all be as it may, here he was upon his knees at the feet of Lord Drawler's wife, kissing the soft hand which lay so lovingly and unresistingly in his. Oh! Margaret, it is true that you were coaxed and threatened into a marriage with my lord, and that the old love had never died out. But, then, you *are* married, you know. You have, before Heaven, registered a vow, upon your knees, that you will be faithful to the ruffianly cur whose hand has marked your face; and this young fellow on his knees before you, who whispers his love with such impassioned eloquence, is nothing to you, and must never be.

Why do not the stupid servants bring the lights? Do they suppose ladies receive visitors in the dark? Ah! they have come at last, and tap at the door.

"Shall I light the gas, my lady?"

"Yes—directly. Why ever did you not come before?"

"I must take my leave," said Ernest.

"You will come to-morrow?"

"At what time?"

"As soon as you can?"

He went away then, giving the natty housemaid something for her trouble in showing him out.

"I am at home to nobody to-morrow," said her ladyship to the maid, "except my legal adviser—the gentleman who has just gone."

How servants talk about us, their masters, and mistresses. "No one is a hero to his valet," they say. Is any lady an angel to her lady's-maid, think you?

"Who was that?" a fellow servant asked the young person just mentioned.

"Who do you think?"

"Lor! how am I to tell?"

"Her ladyship's legal adviser."

And then they both laughed, as if there was some joke in it. I do not see the point myself.

CHAPTER THE FIFTY-NINTH.

A LULL BEFORE A STORM.

ABOUT ten o'clock upon the same evening Miss Perks sat in an arm-chair by the side of Maurice Cheveleigh's bed, doing her best to read the young gentleman to sleep.

He had returned to the Court about an hour previous to this interesting operation dreadfully wearied, excited, and feverish. He had been occupied throughout the day in attending his father's funeral, and in consulting with Inspector Bucket with a view to catching the murderer.

When he came home to the Chambers, he

found that Nelly was still at the theatre; and as she had the day before requested him not to come and fetch her (she did not want Mr. Bullyrag to repeat what she had said about her marriage), he sat down to wait for her.

Maurice had written to his mother two days ago, acquainting her with Sir John's death; and telling her that he would come down to Skearcrows directly the funeral was performed. There was no train that night or he would have set out at once.

He walked about the room, and tried to smoke; his pipe went out without his noticing it, and he drew and puffed at imaginary vapour gravely and silently. As he paced the floor from side to side, he passed in review before him the various events of the last few months. How he had met Nelly that morning walking from the Haymarket; and how they had talked about the relative merits of *Lockhart's Life of Scott*, and the *Family Herald*. Then, again, how he had found her sitting on the door step in the rain, and taken her in for the night. Then, of all, his awful schemes and plans for her seduction! What an infernal villain he had been; and after all, for what? What, indeed! He had imagined that the attachment might be like most of its kind, ephemeral and easily forgotten; or in any case, that it would be lowering the dignity of the great House of Cheveleigh were he to marry that vulgar little brush-drawer. But did he think her vulgar now? Had she ever been vulgar?—or had she improved with such astonishing rapidity, that in six months she was not like the same person? Or, again, had he sunk so low, and changed so much in the disreputable life he was leading, that the woman had risen above him, and he had lost all delicacy of perception, and was unable to see her faults?

Well, one fact was indisputable—she was a most beautiful woman—the most beautiful, and the cleverest he had ever met with, and he loved her with all his heart and soul. To think of rising in the social scale himself, and leaving this woman whom he had wronged, but who still, in all his struggling, shabby-genteel poverty, had remained with, and been faithful to him, it was monstrous. Why should he not marry her? Would he ever meet with any woman whom he loved so much? What would society say to it? A fig for society—he would have money and position, and could snap his fingers at society's upturned nose.

Long ago he had determined in his own mind that he would propose it to her. A dozen times had he had the words upon his lips. Had it not been for the horrible events of the last two or three days, before now he would have asked her to marry him.

What prevented him, then, the next opportunity.

I'll tell you. He was ashamed to do it. He was a very singular young man, as you must have thought before this. He had the strangest notions about virtue, and honour, and so on. The idea of a profligate like he was, living with an outcast like she was, having ideas about virtue and honour! Is it not absurd?

Well, he was ashamed after his conduct to this woman to propose to marry her. He never for a moment dreamt that the subject had occupied her mind. I believe he thought that she would laugh at the proposal.

But would not this attempt at reparation be a tacit acknowledgment of the wrong he had done her? If it did, what then? He had made up his mind that it should be done; and the best way out of the difficulty was, to propose to her in writing.

He took up a pen, and, without another moment's hesitation, wrote his letter:—

"My own dear love,—Through all these days of anxiety, poverty, and misery that we have passed together, I believe that you have always loved me the same; and as I am sure that you never have addressed a word of reproach to me, who am the author of all our troubles, so do I believe that your affection for me is unaltered. If you think that you could content yourself with such an ordinary sort of fellow as I know I am—when you, rising in your profession, have the world before you where to choose—I would ask you, dearest Nelly, to forget the wrong that I have done you, and be my wife. I have now, you know, riches and a title to offer you; and add to that a heart which is and always will be yours.   MAURICE."

When he had written this, he folded it up without reading it, and put it in an envelope. Then he reflected for a moment. Should he give it to her? No, she would then answer without consideration. He would prefer that she received it in his absence. The best plan would be, then, to post it to her after he reached Skearcrows; or, better still, he would place it somewhere in the room where she would be sure to find it next morning. Where should that be? On the table there lay open one of the younger Dumas' lively novels. He placed it at the spot where she had last been reading, and closed the book.

When he had done this, he yawned and stretched, for he was very tired, and had scarcely had an hour's sleep during the last two days and nights. Miss Perks looked in at the moment, and asked what she could do for him.

"Nothing, thank you, I'm going to lie down a little while." And as he spoke, he took off his coat and waistcoat, and threw himself upon the bed.

"Aint you well, sir?" asked the old woman. "You look very pale. Mayn't I make you some tea, or fetch you nothink?"

"I don't want nothink fetched, thank you."

"Then let me cover you over with the counterpane. Can I sit here, and keep the fire in?"

"If you like," said he, for he knew that otherwise she would have had to sit upon the cold stair-case, her usual resting-place. "And if you like you can read to me."

He had once heard her spelling through a penny novel—a wonderful performance it was, but one you might go to sleep listening to very comfortably. So he lay back in bed, and she began to read. The droning of her voice, and the ticking of the clock alone broke the silence. IT WAS A LULL BEFORE A STORM.

OLD LOVE RENEWED.

CHAPTER THE SIXTIETH.

IN WHICH THE STORM BURSTS FORTH.

"WHAT are you going to read?" asked Maurice, with a yawn.

"This, with the picturs, sir."

"What's the title, Miss Perks?"

"What's the what, sir?"

"The name of it. Look at the first page."

"'Claudy Val, the Dashin 'Ighwayman; or, Hooroor for the Road, and Down with the Perlice.'"

"Good gracious!" said Maurice, with a smile, "whoever does that belong to?"

No. 14

"The circ'latin' lib'ry, sir. Mrs. Cheveleigh got it for me to read."

"She doesn't read it herself, then?"

"Oh! no, sir. She says it's rubbish. She reads others."

"What others?"

"Something about a fair, was the last one, sir."

"Greenwich Fair?"

"No—not that, but something like it. Wexation—no, Wanity—Wariety Fair, sir."

"Who's the author of that?" asked Maurice.

"The author?"

"The person who wrote it?"

"Oh! I don't know, I'm sure. Missus says he's very clever."

" Does she ?"

" Yes. She says he describes his women beautiful, but his men is fools."

" And what do you think ?"

" I aint no scholard, sir ; and I don't quite understand it."

" No, I should think you didn't," said Maurice, with a laugh. " Let's have a little of ' Claude Du Val.' "

" Well, I aint no reader to speak of," said Miss Perks, with an apologetic cough.

And, as she read, he lay back in bed, and recalled the particulars of a similar conversation he had had that morning with pretty Nell, on her way to work. How her opinions must have altered since then ; and still it was not so very long ago, for all that. He smiled as he remembered how she had said, in speaking of Sir Walter Scott, " him as wrote the story in the ' Journal.' " She made no mistakes in grammar now, unless, indeed, she was in a passion, when her language was not choice. At such times she talked as great nonsense as the generality of ladies, under similar circumstances.

" ' 'Old !' cried Claudy Val, thrustin' his spurs into the already l-a-s—las-c-e-r—lascerated flanks of 'is nobil charger. ' Avaunt ! mis-c-r-e—miscrent,' shrieked the bu-chus maiding, her raving tresses stremin' in the wind.' "

The old lady read on, assaulting, and carrying by main force, the longest of the hard words, slurring over others, and skipping some altogether. As she never, by any chance, made a pause at a full stop as printed, but took her breath anywhere, in the middle of words, a listener would have been put about to follow her. However, Maurice, did not try to do so, and, lulled gently by the monotonous droning of her voice, soon fell fast asleep.

Thus she read, and he slept, for a time, very comfortably. Meanwhile, down stairs, in the court, a curious scene was enacting. A man and woman, hurrying towards the same house, but from different directions, met upon the doorstep, and, recognising each other, uttered an exclamation of surprise. One was a cunning-looking, seedily attired man, who might have been a begging-letter writer, an author, or a dissenting minister, but was in reality a lawyer: the other was a dowdily attired French woman, with swarthy features, travel stained, and dusty.

" What brings you here ?" the man asked, harshly and imperiously. " How long have you been in London ?"

" What right have you to question me ? What business is it of yours ?" she replied, in French.

" Just this much," he growled, still in his own language ; " I shall speak first."

" Speak first ? What will you say ?"

" I'm going to tell him all——"

" No, no, Hadget, you wouldn't be so wicked. Hadget, I implore you, on my knees. For God's sake, Hadget——"

" Pooh ! Get up, you fool; some one will see you."

" I don't care who sees me, and who hears me. If you tell my secret to him, what matter if all the rest of the world despise me ?"

" Hold your tongue, woman. There's no particular occasion for anybody to despise you, that I know of. Besides, the case would have been different if you had preferred me to the other. It was very well while he lived. For some reason that I don't know, he kept up the farce ; but now he's dead, and the game played out. You didn't expect that it would last for ever, did you ?"

" Until I died, I thought it would," she said.

" Ha ! ha ! you were wrong. Did you think it would not come out at Sir John's death ?"

" Why should it, Hadget ? There would be be no question unless you raised it."

" Wouldn't there ? Do you suppose it is nobody else's interest to raise it ? The property's worth having, I suppose."

" Has anybody put forward a claim ?"

" Yes, they have—and I'm going to help them."

" Oh ! dear, oh ! dear, oh ! my poor boy." And the woman wept convulsively.

" Hush !" Hadget said again, grasping her arm. " Hold your noise, can't you ? I'll go first, and tell him. You'd rather I broke the truth than you, I suppose ? Wait in the court till I call you. That's his window, up there, with a light in it. Watch it."

He jerked her arm painfully, as he spoke, to silence her tears, and pointed to the window of Maurice's room ; then turned to leave her. Retracing his steps, however, before he had gone a dozen yards, he came close to her, and said,—

" You see a man standing at the end of the court ?"

She looked in the direction he indicated.

" Yes."

" That's the claimant—Ernest Cheveleigh, He's watching the window too. When I open it, you must come together. You'll both be wanted."

Saying this, he left her, and rang the bell. After a short pause, Miss Perks opened the door, and admitted him.

" Is Mr. Cheveleigh in ?" Hadget asked.

" Ye-es, sir," responded the old lady, shivering, she hardly knew why.

" Well !" cried the lawyer, fiercely, " what are you staring at, stupid ? Show the way."

" You know the way, sir," objected Miss Perks. " I'd rather you went first."

As he passed by her and ran up-stairs, she trembled, without any particular reason.

" It's the cold," she said to herself, in answer, as it seemed, to a second shiver which shook all her old bones like a fit of the ague. " I've took a chill, I suppose. I think I'll have a little drop of something." She felt, as she spoke, in her pocket for a penny. " I wonder what old ' twisted his wrist' is arter ? No good, I'll be bound."

And she toddled into the " Hand and Heart" for a glass of gin.

The French woman left to herself, continued to moan and ring her hands. The court was very quiet, for a wonder. The shower of rain had driven the troop of noisy children, who usually played in it, in-doors, and scarcely a soul was to be seen.

When Miss Perks had had her "drop" of gin, she took a nap, as was her custom, upon a bench in a corner of the public-house bar, and was presently saluted and treated to another drop by little Perks, who, as usual, after earning a few shillings by "over-time," was, as he termed it, "on the swipe." And so they spent an hour together very cosily in definace of old Mrs. Perks, and the door-bell.

The French woman stood for about ten minutes wistfully watching the window, and then a sudden thought seemed to strike her. The figure Hadget had pointed out, still stood at the end of the court, leaning against the wall. She looked at it fixedly for a moment, as if debating with herself whether she should approach and address it. Should she implore the young man to have pity on her poor boy; and if he would not consent to share the property, at least, not to leave her Maurice destitute.

With a great effort she overcame her fear and shame, and drew nearer to the unconscious Ernest.

"Mr. Cheveleigh," she said in a low tone.

He turned quickly on hearing his name, and his face flushed as he recognised the speaker.

"What do you want?" he cried hastily, and waving her off with his hand. "I don't know you. My good woman, I've nothing for you."

CHAPTER THE SIXTY-FIRST.

ONE OF HADGET'S SECRETS.

THE lawyer mounted the stairs, tapped at the outer door, and, receiving no answer, passed through the sitting-room with his usual cat-like tread, and looked into Maurice's sleeping-chamber.

The young man lay upon the bed, as last we left him, fast asleep. On a chair at his side lay "Claude Duval," with the page turned down at the place where Miss Perks had left off reading. The lamp was a-light, and standing on a table near the bed, on which were strewed a mass of papers, Maurice had commenced sorting and left unfinished.

Having coughed loudly, to ascertain whether the young man was really asleep, and assumed, by his motionless face and regular breathing that he was, Mr. Hadget sat down by the table, and began, coolly and deliberately to look through the letters. "There's time enough to tell him yet," said he. "Nobody will come in, I suppose, and Mr. Ernest can wait. It'll do the upstart good to kick his heels a bit."

He turned over the letters, only glancing at the superscription of some, and reading others.

"His affairs seem to be in a nice condition," muttered Hadget to himself. "Plenty of bills. What's this? 'Beg to acquaint you I hold a bill of yours, which becomes due——' Ha! ha! That's rather amusing. Poor Boddle! He did it on the strength of the property, I suppose. Oh! Lord, won't he be savage?

These money-lenders are much to be pitied. Some one's always letting them in."

Presently he came to another letter. It was much worn and creased, as though it had been carried about in the owner's pocket. He opened it, and read:—

"'My own dear, neglectful, cruel child, am I never to see you again? Has your poor mother, living here alone and so sad, these many months, no place in your heart? Can you not spare me a little moment? Will you not rob your dear friends of a few brief hours to spend with a poor sick woman who so loves you? I have been very, very ill, and am still so unwell as to be unable to leave my room. I am left quite to myself, though the house is full of company. There is Mr. Hadget, the London attorney, money-lender, thief-catcher, or whatever he may please to call himself.'

"Oh!" said Hadget, "that's what you call me, is it?"

"'There is also a choice collection of rustic seducers and beer-drinking louts always at your father's table. It is with such people that he now spends his whole time. I spend mine in my room on my side of the house, little troubled by this agreeable society, save when the chorus of their horrible songs, or the roaring of their coarse voices as they sing or quarrel, come up the stairs in the middle of the night, and wake me trembling.

"'I would not write thus, my own dear Maurice, did I not feel so sad and lonely. Oh! for some dear one to whom your poor mother could confide her griefs, and sorrows, and secrets. Maurice, my son, I have a *great—a dreadful secret to tell you:* one which I dare not trust myself to write—one which my heart tells me I dare scarcely confide to you in words. It can be told only when holding your hands in mine, my dear boy—leaning my head upon your breast—lying at your feet.

"'My God! I am talking too fast; I am feverish and excited!

"'I love you, Maurice, my dear child. Your mother kisses you! I send you a little money. Come to me without delay.—LOUISE.'"

When he had finished reading this letter (which, perhaps, the reader may remember, in the eighth chapter of this history), he folded it up carefully, smiled to himself, and tapped his chin with it.

"If she had mentioned it," thought Hadget, "there's no knowing but what everything might have been managed. Sir John was an old fool, and had always a maudlin regard for her. 'Egad! perhaps that's why he never let it out."

As he spoke, he walked up to the bedside, and gazed upon the quiet, sleeping face, rather thin and careworn with the anxiety of the last few days, but yet very open and honest-looking. You could not have looked upon him sleeping, and thought that he was a knave. He was, indeed, a generous, open-handed, kind-hearted young fellow—his own enemy, and everybody else's friend. He was, it is true, a profligate and a spendthrift. I wish that no worse could be said of many other of your honest-looking persons. I know myself at least a dozen fair-faced, hearty fellows, who are no better than they ought to be, and any day could lay my finger on one of them, who is as thorough-paced a scoundrel as there is unhanged.

The lawyer studied his handsome features as the light fell full upon them. "He's a good-looking chap," thought he, " and very like his mother—like what she used to be, as I remember her. She's altered now: one could never believe it was the same woman. By Jove! all things considered, it's lucky the affair ended where it did; though, if it had happened otherwise, I might have been a gentleman now, and an honest man—anyhow, not a——"

"I'll find him—I'll track him! I'll never rest until I have the murderer by the throat."

It was Maurice, who sprang up shrieking thus, struggling with the horrors of nightmare, and, grasping Hadget by the shoulder, stared him wildly in the face.

"What now?" gasped the lawyer, when he could get his breath, and wiping the cold sweat from his ashy face. "What the devil are you dreaming about?"

"Is it you, Hadget? I thought I had got hold of my poor father's murderer."

"Did you? Curse, me! I thought so, too. Do you often dream like that? You've pretty near frightened me out of my life!"

Seating himself at the table, he wiped his face again and again with his pocket handkerchief; and, Maurice, rising from the bed, poured him out a glass of cognac from a long-necked bottle standing on the mantel-piece, under the exhilarating influence of which his courage and colour gradually returned, and with them, the recollection of the business that brought him there.

"It's rather a late hour to make a call," said he; "but what I've got to say is of such vital importance to you, I know you'll excuse the intrusion."

"Certainly—certainly. What is it?"

"The business I would speak to you about, is respecting the property which your father left behind him."

"Unless there is really an immediate necessity or discussing the business, Hadget," said the young man, "I would prefer that we talk it over in a day or two. The horrible cirumstances connected with my poor father's death have so unnerved me, that I feel totally incapable of listening calmly to anything concerning him."

"You seem to grieve for his loss," observed Hadget, "more than I should have expected."

The young man turned round hastily, with a warning scowl upon his face; but, thinking that he could not hear aright, he asked Hadget to repeat his words.

"I never thought he was a very good father to you," said Hadget.

"What do you mean?"

"I hardly think he took the trouble about your education and bringing up, that I should have done with a son of mine."

Maurice was silent.

"He was fonder of his drink than any thing else," pursued Mr. Hadget, helping himself to another glass; "and drink's the very devil."

"Your remarks are very offensive," said Maurice, betwixt his teeth. "Say what you have to say, and do it quickly."

"I am saying it," replied Hadget. "At least, I'm getting round to it. Did it ever occur to you, now, let me ask you, that you had nothing to thank Sir John for; and, on the contrary, that you had cause to curse him?"

Pale as death, Maurice regarded his questioner, but said no word.

"I'll tell you how if you will condescend to pay attention without any offensive interruption. If not, you can remain in ignorance, for I have no interest in enlightening you. Your mother sent me here to do it, or I shouldn't have come."

"My mother! Speak man. What have you got to say? What is this mystery?"

"No very particular mystery, that I know of," said Hadget, doggedly. "It's not a mystery of my making, any how."

"What have you got to tell me?"

"I suppose you wish to enjoy your father's property?"

"I suppose I do; and I suppose I shall."

"I don't think so."

"What do you mean, Hadget?"

"There is another claimant."

"Another claimant? Bah! what claim have they got? Am I not my father's son?"

"Yes, you're your father's son, no doubt," said the lawyer, with a slight smile. "But still, not the heir to the property."

Maurice stared at him in astonishment.

"Who is, then?" he said presently, with a gasp. "Did my father will it otherwise?"

"He made no will, worse luck. At least, it seems he didn't, and that's the worst of it."

"What do you mean by the worst? I can't understand you. Who is the heir, then, if I am not?"

Maurice fixed his eyes upon the lawyer with a thoughtful, searching look, as though he would read his soul. But he read nothing.

"Have you ever heard your mother mention any secret which she was anxious to tell you?"

"A secret—yes. In a letter that she wrote me, asking me to go home (it was before I went last time—when I met you there), she alluded to some secret which she was anxious to tell me. She spoke of it with such earnestness that it made a great impression upon me. When I was at home she several times was on the point of telling me, but something occurred to prevent her, and she never did so. After I came back to town, I wrote to her and asked her to tell me by letter. She said, in reply, that she would prefer telling me verbally; and urged me to return home. I was always prevented by—by—one thing and another—and so the time was slipped by somehow, and I never yet have heard it."

"Procastination has been your ruin, Mr. Cheveleigh," said Hadget with a sneer. "Had you gone home you might have been in time to have remedied all. Had you known the secret, you might have taken some steps to secure the property; as it is, you are a beggar."

"A beggar!" cried Maurice, aghast.

"That's what I said," replied the other.

"You never heard your mother's early history, I dare say."

"No."

"Well, I shan't repeat it. Indeed, you can guess it, when you hear what I've to say. In four words, then, YOU ARE A BASTARD! Your father was never married, and your mother was his——"

He finished the sentence with a gurgle, for the young man had seized him by the throat, and, in his fury, held him back, half strangled, in his chair.

"You lie, you scoundrel—you lie! Retract your words, or, by the God above us! I'll have your life."

"Help! help! Hands off! Curse you!" roared Hadget, wrestling furiously with his antagonist. "Are you mad, you fool? I didn't make her what she is, did I?"

The young man loosened his hold, and, stepping back a pace, glared at his informant.

"How do you know it?" said he.

"The way I came to know it," replied Mr. Hadget, considerably relieved by the removal of the other's hands from his cravat, for the situation so strongly reminded him of a similar assault made not long ago, under different circumstances, that, putting on one side the choking sensation, the recollection was a most unpleasant one; "the way I came to know it was curious enough, though I had suspected it a long while."

"How came you to suspect it?"

"Well, I'll tell you. You've spent so much of your time away from home, I hardly think that you knew your father so well as I knew him. Of late years I have had many opportunities of studying his character under a variety of circumstances. When sober,—but particularly when in drink,—the worthy gentleman was frequently a little overtaken, you may remember. Was he not?"

"Go on."

There was something so insufferably, unbearably insulting in Hadget's manner, that it required an almost superhuman effort on the part of the young man to restrain his passion and listen calmly.

"During his drunken fits," continued Hadget, "I used to watch him, pump him, and listen to his wanderings. I had a reason for it."

"Indeed."

"I've known your father for many years. When quite a lad, I first met him. He did me an awful, irreparable injury with the woman I loved, which——which I forgave him. The woman was your mother. She was an actress. At least, that is to say, a dancing-girl, tight-rope walker, and such like. I fell in love with, and wished to marry her. Your father intercepted me, and carried off the prize. I followed. We fought; and when I had him on the ground, and might have taken his life as easily as I could kill a fly, I stayed my hand, and made him promise he would make an honest woman of her he had so wronged. He promised on his oath he would. Of course he broke it: and, now he's dead, she's a beggar, and you're a bastard. Do you understand?"

Maurice listened with a choking sensation in his throat, nodded his assent, and Hadget continued.

"For a long time I never suspected that he had acted falsely. I did not see him for many years; and when we met again, he was the owner of Skearcrows, and your mother was, to all appearances, his wife. The people called her Lady Cheveleigh; and, when everybody else was satisfied, I thought I might safely be satisfied myself. To tell the truth, I never troubled my head about the matter, and would never have found it out, had not Sir John, in his cups, let slip a word which put me on the scent."

He looked towards the young man to see if he was listening, for at other times he kept his cunning eyes fixed upon the ground, and finding that Maurice's face wore an attentive and anxious expression, proceeded.

"When I once suspected it, I set about finding out the truth. I questioned your father and mother. They both persisted in the same legend about some marriage supposed to have taken place in France, but I caught them out in several prevarications. At last, said I to myself, 'If there is a marriage, won't there be a certificate?' I looked for it. I turned everything inside out in your mother's room——"

"How dare you?" exclaimed Maurice. "By whose authority did you commit this outrage?"

"Well, I can't say that I had any special authority for doing so," returned the other, with a quiet, sneering laugh, "but I took the liberty. I searched everywhere, I tell you, and could not find it. 'If it is in existence,' thought I, 'it's somewhere about her.' When I was rummaging for it, I should tell you, your mother had gone to sleep. It was on the night of a thunder-storm. Dreadfully afraid of the lightning, like most weak women are, I believe, she had wrapped herself up in a heap of old silk dresses, got into a corner of the room as far as possible from the window and the fire, and fallen asleep, waiting for the storm to subside."

"Well!"

"When I was bending over her, just about to feel in her pockets, she began to talk in her dreams—a lot of nonsense, of one sort or other, but, among other things, she gave me all the information I was in search of. There was no marriage certificate, and she had never been married."

As Hadget ceased here, and, looking at the other with a grim smile, put on his hat again, and began to fidget with the button of one of his old kid gloves, Maurice concluded that he had finished his story.

"And so," said he, "you told this to Ernest, and, in the hopes of getting a picking out of him, have espoused his cause?"

"Exactly so. We lawyers live by these sort of things. Rightful heirs, and wrongful heirs, are our trump cards, like they are to story-book writers. It's what we make our money by."

"And do you want my opinion of your story?"

"Yes," said Mr. Hadget, blandly. "I'd rather like to hear it."

" Then I consider it," cried Maurice, banging his fist indignantly upon the table, " to be a lie, sir. A damnable and wicked lie !"

" Ha ! ha !" laughed his companion ; " I'm glad you're of that way of thinking. We shall have some proceedings, after all. To tell the truth, I was afraid the evidence I had would be too strong for you, and that you would not attempt to defend. In that case, down go the profits."

" What evidence have you ?"

" Oh ! it's a wonder you condescend to ask me. Your mother and Sir Ernest Cheveleigh are waiting down below in the court. Shall I call them up."

As he spoke he moved towards the window, but Maurice caught him by the collar.

" You low-lived, dirty, pettifogging scamp," cried the young man, pale with passion. " I've a good mind to wring your neck, and throw you down stairs."

" Two can play at that game, Mr. Maurice," said the lawyer, fiercely, shaking off his grip. " Keep a civil tongue in your head, if you can. It's for your own good that I have come to tell you, and to spare your mother the shame and humiliation of making the confession herself. If you don't believe me, ask her. I'll call her up."

" Stop !" cried Maurice, " I'll go down myself. Where is she ?"

" In the court—just by the door—I left her."

" Stop where you are, then," said the young man. " And if I find, as I expect, that what you have said is all a lie, by heavens I'll make you smart for it."

" Pooh ! pooh !" ejaculated the lawyer ; and taking off his hat again, he sat down in an easy-chair and crossed his legs, with a smile of the utmost unconcern and contempt. " I'll wait for you."

Maurice stood confounded. It was impossible to disbelieve the truth of the man's statement, though to disbelieve in the marriage of his parents was to disbelieve everything he honoured and loved on earth. To believe that the man for whom he these three last days had been shedding bitter tears of regret, was a perjured scoundrel, that his mother was a beggar and outcast, and that he himself, instead of being heir to a proud title and large property, was but a child of shame—an impostor and penniless spendthrift, without even a right to the name he bore and disgraced. The thoughts were madness. What could be done ? Was there any escape from the infamy and ignominy with which he found himself surrounded ?

" Hadget," he said, " before to-night, I have never done anything to cause you to hate me, that I am aware of."

" You've never done anything to cause me to love you," replied the other, curtly.

" Well, perhaps not. My conduct, even a moment ago, was extremely blameable. I am sorry for my loss of temper and violence ; but, man, you can make allowances for it. I should have been a white-livered cur had I not acted as I did when you used such language with reference to my poor mother. By God ! it makes my blood boil now to think of it ; and if she were a thousand times as bad as ever woman was, I still would love her as I have, and always shall, more than anything else on earth. Hadget, I beg your pardon if I have judged you harshly. Here's my hand."

The lawyer rose and took it ; and, as he did so, something like a pang of remorse shot through his heart, while, at the same time the likeness between Maurice and his murdered father struck him more forcibly than it had ever done, blanched his cheek, in spite of all his efforts to be calm, made his lips quiver, and his eyes quail before the honest face of his companion.

Maurice was, himself, too much excited to observe minutely the other's demeanour. He hurried from the room, and ran hastily down stairs into the court.

He looked to the right, and to the left, went down to one end, and then to the other ; but could see nothing of his mother. However, leaning against the wall, he found his cousin.

" Ernest," said he, " you came with Hadget, I believe. Where is Lady Cheveleigh ?"

" Who ?" said Ernest, coldly.

He did not offer to shake hands, and held himself aloof from the other, as though he were a crossing-sweeper.

" I have seen the woman who calls herself Lady Cheveleigh," continued the young baronet. " She spoke to me just now. I did not listen to what she said."

" What do you mean ?" said Maurice, between his teeth. " Do you, then, believe this story about my illegitimacy ?"

" Believe it ! Of course I do."

" And you mean to put forward your claim ?"

" I should hope so," said Ernest, with a sneer. " It is not likely that I should leave the title and property in the hands of Sir John's mistresses and bastards."

" You coward—take that !" Maurice cried, and struck the other a sudden blow in the face, which sent him reeling against the wall.

" Help ! help !" shouted Ernest. " Police —police !" And the next moment, Maurice, turning, saw a constable by his side.

" Take that man in charge," cried Ernest, in a state of great excitement, keeping the policeman well between himself and his assailant. " Take him into custody. You saw the assault."

You know the disinclination that the police force always exhibit to mix up in street rows.

" What's it all about ?" asked the constable, warily.

" You saw the assault," repeated Ernest ; " that is sufficient for you. Do your duty."

" Well, if you give him in charge, of course, it's my duty to take him," began the constable.

" Do it, then, without further parley. My name is Sir Ernest Cheveleigh. I will accompany you, and prefer the charge."

" Come on, will you ?" cried the policeman, becoming suddenly energetic. " None of your tricks, you know, they won't do here."

" I will walk quietly enough," said Maurice ; " you need not tear my coat. I'm a gentleman, if I don't look it."

And without more ado the party started for the police-station.

As they walked along, the constable could not restrain his curiosity, and addressed the prisoner in a low tone,—

"Sir Ernest Cheveleigh," said he. "Is that the son of the Cheveleigh as was found murdered in the cab?"

"No—I am."

"Oh! you are, are you? Well, that's rum, too. He's an eccentric chap that you struck just now, aint he?"

"Why!"

"He wanted to give a French woman in charge, before you came up."

"A French woman?"

"Ah, if she hadn't gone off pretty sharp, she'd have been locked up. Begging, or something, I think, she was up to. She seemed to have some claim on him, about her son, I think she said. The old story, I suppose. Rather too old a woman for him, I thought. Though, p'raps, she's been a fine 'un in her time."

CHAPTER THE SIXTY-SECOND.

NELLY IS BROUGHT TO HER SENSES, AND MISS PERKS GETS A GOOD SHAKING.

HADGET sat waiting for Maurice's return, and chuckling softly to himself, as he imagined what a meeting there would be between mother and son.

He was interrupted in this pleasant amusement by a rustling sound in the adjoining apartment.

He sat and listened to it.

It moved across and across the room slowly. All the rest of the house was silent as the tomb. Not a sound was to be heard in the court without. Was it the wind playing with the window curtains? No, that was not the sort of noise. Perhaps it was a cat. He daren't tell himself what he thought it was. The bravest of us believe in ghosts when we are alone in the dark. In a room full of company it is different. As he listened and waited in terror, the sound approached the door, and a pale face looked in upon him.

"Wha—at do you want?"

"Hush," said a woman's voice, and Nelly entered the room, glancing behind her, cautiously. "Was all that you have been saying to Maurice true?"

"Aye, it was true enough. What makes you ask? Were you listening?"

"Yes," she answered, fiercely, "I was. I am the woman he lives with. He,—ha! ha!—he was going to marry me!"

"Was he?" said the lawyer, eyeing the angry beauty, half astonished and half amused. "Not much of a catch, I think."

"A catch, indeed!" she said, more to herself than to him. "And to think that I should have been such a fool!—such a wretched fool!"

As she spoke, she was engaged re-adjusting her shawl, which she had taken off, and tugging furiously at the strings of her bonnet.

"And he's a bastard, is he?" she said presently, turning round to Hadget, who at the time was looking out of the window; "and has no more claim to the title and property than I have. Oh! I could cut my tongue out!"

"You take his misfortune to heart, madam."

"His misfortune! I take my own to heart. To be the laughing-stock of all those grinning, low-bred wretches! No, I would rather die first. Is Maurice coming back?"

"I believe he is. I don't know what can make him so long."

"Look here, sir——Mr. Hadget is your name, I believe?"

Hadget smiled and bowed.

"I like this woman," he thought to himself. "She's a perfect devil."

"Do you think Maurice had any idea of what you have just told him?"

"I should think not."

"And you can prove its truth?"

"I am going to."

"What will you get by the business?"

"Nothing."

"Why did you do it, then?"

"That's my affair."

She said no more, but took a seat, and, tapping her pretty hand upon the table, seemed to be thinking deeply. The lawyer eyed her stealthily, and thought he never had seen so beautiful a woman.

"And infernally clever, too," he thought to himself. "No mawkish sentiment about her, no damned whimpering and puling. A regular plotting, scheming woman, I should say. She'd be worth a fortune to any man."

Half-an-hour passed like this. Then Hadget said,—

"He doesn't seem to come. I suppose he has met with his mother, and they are gone away together. There is no occasion for me to stay any longer. My client is waiting for me, I imagine, at the corner."

As she made no remark, he added, after a pause, at the same time taking a card from his pocket, "Should you be undecided in your plans for the future, madam, and desire my advice—and—and assistance, a note addressed to my chambers will meet with immediate attention."

As she did not take the card, he laid it on the table beside her, and bowed himself out, muttering as he went, "A magnificent creature—quite Mephistophelean."

She sat there a minute or two, considering what course she should pursue. Miss Perks came in while she was thus engaged, bringing a scrap of paper, which the gentleman who had just gone out had directed her to deliver to Mrs. Cheveleigh.

It said:

"Our mutual friend, Maurice, has been taken to the station-house for assaulting my client. Do not be alarmed on his account. I suppose he will get bail. Do not forget my address."

"You're home very early this evening, aint you, mum?"

Nelly made no answer. Miss Perks began to fuss about the room.

Presently she found out that Maurice was gone. Among other trifling drawbacks the old lady was nearly blind. In general she wore a green shade over her eyes, under which she peered up at you in a bird-like fashion, ridiculous to see.

"Lawks! if Mr. Cheveleigh isn't got up again. He went to bed an hour ago."

No answer.

"He was unwell, mum. I asked if I could get him anythink, but he wouldn't have it."

Still no reply.

"I hope you're not ill, mum. Worrited, and weared out, I suppose. Shan't I get you nothink?"

"No."

"I was a-reading to Mr. Maurice, mum, to-night," continued Miss Perks, for the little drops had mounted in her old noddle, and she felt "chatty like." "I was telling him about you, mum."

"What about me?"

"About your reading books, mum, and what you said; and he did laugh so."

"You're a stupid old fool," cried Nelly, and suddenly springing up she fell upon the old lady, and shook her till her cap fell off, and her head shook about like a plaster of Paris rolly-polly. "You stupid, old, prattling, mischief-making busy-body, tattling about the court when you're told not to say a word. Drat you, I've a good mind to shake your head off."

She did not shake it off, I suppose, because it would not come off easily. As it was, when she was tired she let go, and poor old Miss Perks tumbled in a heap something after the same fashion that a doll doubles up when it has an insufficient supply of sawdust in its interior arrangement.

"Oh, deary me! oh, deary me!" sobbed the old lady, an hour afterwards upon the landing, "to think as I should ever have lived to be shook up this way—and that SHE should a done it. The world is turning upside down, and all along of Twisted-his-wrist a writing letters. That's how it is, I know. Oh, dear! oh, dear! why aint I in the cimitry?"

* * * * *

About three days after the occurrences I have just related, there was in all the London, and most of the provincial, newspapers, a small paragraph, descriptive of a suicide under rather unusual circumstances. It was such a very small paragraph, and in most cases, occupied so insignificant a corner in the journal where it appeared, that it attracted very little public attention. The *Penny Newsman* was not in existence in those days, or it might have given it the honour of large type. I hardly know whether the *Daily Telegraph* was going on then. If so, perhaps they had a leader on it.

The interest it caused was very trifling; and, though most certainly the three-half-pence-a-liner who described it in the first instance, said that the neighbourhood in which the unfortunate circumstance occurred was thrown into a state of the most intense excitement, is more than probable that they never even heard of it in the next street.

As, however, it relates particularly to my story, I will give you the details.

Very early in the morning of the day which succeeded the events I have been chronicling, a foreign woman, indifferently attired, knocked at a door of one of the gloomiest houses in Stamford Street, Waterloo Road, and, pointing to a card displayed in the window, asked to look at the apartment to which it referred.

A close-smelling, stuffy little room it was, with a cracked window, looking out upon a wilderness of chimney pots.

"How much is this?" she inquired.

"Ten shillings a-week," replied the landlady, putting on an extra five shillings, as she saw that the other woman was a foreigner.

"I will take it."

"Certainly, ma'am. I've usually had a reference with my lodgers. You see, in this neighbourhood there are so many queer characters,—not that for a moment——but, of course, you understand."

"I understand. Here are the ten shillings."

"Thank you—that's quite satisfactory. Do you want anything?"

"Nothing."

Upon this the lodging-housekeeper departed, and the lodger closed the door. In about five minutes some one tapped at it.

"What do you want?"

"Oh! I beg your pardon, but, I should have said——Of course, you have no visitors calling?"

"I have no visitors."

"Thank you. Will you require attendance? Because that is generally charged——"

"I do not require anything. Please do not disturb me."

"Oh! certainly. Bless us and save us!" said the good lady to herself as she went down stairs, "one can't ask a civil question now without one's nose being took off."

The new lodger required no assistance, spoke to nobody, troubled nobody, was not heard to move for hours. In the afternoon she went out and purchased a few articles in the neighbourhood. As it afterwards appeared, these were some cold ham and beef, a pound of flour, a box of matches, and some charcoal.

Nothing more was heard of her after this; but, from what transpired at the inquest, her course of conduct must have been as near as possible as follows:—Having eaten a slight portion of the ham and beef, she made some paste in the washhand-basin, and with a quantity of old newspapers, which had lain at the bottom of the drawers standing in the room, plastered up all the cracks round the door and window. Then, with the hearthrug and a piece of carpet rolled into a bundle, she stopped up the chimney, so that no air could possibly come into the room that way, and having thus made her arrangements, lighted some charcoal in the coal-skuttle, lay down upon the bed, and waited patiently for death.

It came. How soon, or how late who shall tell? When the door was broken open, and the smoke partially expelled, the body was found lying upon the bed, the features calm and placid, as those of one who sleeps. She had began to write a letter in pencil,—"My own dear child, forgive me," were the words in French traced upon the paper; but it had not been finished.

ON THE WAY TO PARIS.

CHAPTER THE SIXTY-THIRD.

WHAT COMES OF LOVING A WORTHLESS WOMAN.

SAID the inspector who took the charge, "We'll take bail, if you can find it."

Said Maurice, indignantly, "Of course I can."

Said the policeman who had brought him there, "If you don't, you'll find the boxes precious uncomfortable."

They were rather busy at the station that evening, and before Maurice's case was disposed of, two others were waiting for their turn.

"Who are you going to send to?" asked the policeman, who was inclined to be friendly.

No. 15

"Well," said Maurice, beginning to consider, "let me see——"

"Lock him up, and he'll think it over," broke in the inspector, whom a press of business had rendered irritable. "He can't stop there."

And Maurice was locked up accordingly.

"I'm waiting for your orders, you know," were the policeman's last words as the door closed.

Ever so many years ago, in the writer's hot youth, when he was much higher up in the world in the way of lodgment, and much lower down in the way of funds (there is a little balance at the "NATIONAL," of which no more at present), in the days when the writer sowed his larky oats, he used sometimes to want to borrow a pound or two, and used to find it difficult. You other young bucks must have likewise discovered the difficulty before now, I expect. What consideration it requires, does not it? And does it not always happen that the person you ask the last, and hesitate so much about asking, is the most willing to advance the little sum required?

I suppose it is as bad to find a bail as a money lender. Anyhow, Maurice found it so.

He sat and thought of all his friends, counting them twice over, and checking them off upon his fingers. First of all, who were his friends, and which of them were householders? Well, upon mature consideration, there was Jack Ochre; but he was not a householder.

"After Jack Ochre, let me see." He thought a long while without any other name appearing to him, "There's Jack Ochre," he repeated. In fact, Jack Ochre was his Alpha and Omega; and, as I said, he counted him twice over, and told him off upon his fingers.

"Well, sir, I'm a-waiting," said the policeman outside.

"All right. Stop a moment."

It is horrible work, thinking against time. I know I have found it so, when the boy has been waiting down below for the copy of this very book, and while I have been struggling with my ideas and a headache, I have heard the young rascal teasing my estimable landlady's cat, or engaged in noisy altercation with the maid about the origin of a Crusoe-like footprint in the hall. In vain did Maurice rack his brains for somebody to whom he could appeal in the present emergency. He could think of nobody. Once upon a time he had known a score of fellows to whom he could have applied, but since he had "gone to the bad" (that's how his connection with Nelly was spoken of by his genteel acquaintance), he had gradually and by degrees slipped out of society, and was now barely on nodding terms with the generality of his former boon companions. Who did he know who was respectable? Lord Drawler they would take, no doubt, but he had only so lately made his acquaintance. Charley Bux he did not know where to find. Ah! a great thought—Bully-rag! But no, on second consideration, to be disturbed so late at night would annoy anybody. It might vex him, and so injure Nelly.

"Come, I say," cried the policeman outside, "have you gone to sleep?"

"No," said Maurice. "But, never mind. I shan't send for bail; so you need not wait any longer."

"Well, hang me!" muttered the constable to himself, "if I didn't think he was no gentleman from the first. Curse my stupidity, why didn't I go by first impressions? If I hadn't been wasting my time with that fool, I might have got the swell to stand a drain for my trouble."

And away he went, in the very worst of tempers, as the first beggar-boy he chanced to come across discovered to his cost.

There could not be two opinions upon one subject. The "boxes" *were* precious uncomfortable. Besides being small, and evil smelling, and cold, and damp, they were this evening crowded and noisy. A drunken woman, on one side, was alternately screaming and laughing; and on the other an individual, also in beer, was indulging a select audience of a pickpocket and a Lascar, with a song to a woeful tune, something between "Sam Hall" and "Limerick Races," but which was meant for "Good-bye, sweetheart," and supposed to be addressed to the object of his affections, from whom, owing to the misappropriation of half-a-yard of gas-pipe, he had been untimely severed. I only wish that my friend, FOURNESS ROLFE, the most pleasing of our English tenors, who sings that song so tenderly and feelingly, had been there to hear his upper notes.

"After all," said Maurice to himself, as he tucked up his legs upon the bench, and, leaning back in the easiest corner he could find, prepared to go to sleep, "after all, it won't kill me, I suppose. I wish I had got a pipe to smoke, and then I should really be enjoying myself."

He was dozing off, when the thought struck him that Nelly would be anxious about his absence. He had thought of it before, but was undecided whether or not he should break it to her. If he wrote to say that he was in the station-house, would not she be still more alarmed than if he did not write at all, for then she would probably go to bed, and not wake again until the morning, when he could pay his fine—if a fine were necessary—and go round to see her. He felt in his pocket when he had come to the conclusion that he would not write, and found that he had no money with him. Then he must send to her. He knocked at the door, and, when a policeman answered the summons, inquired whether anybody would take a letter for him. Somebody would for a small consideration.

"Pay the bearer half-a-crown," he wrote upon the envelope. He had not more than fourpence in silver, an Isle of Man halfpenny, and a "duffing" sixpence

After despatching the message, he waited most anxiously for nearly a couple of hours, at the end of which time the policeman returned.

According to his account, for a whole hour at least had the zealous officer been tugging at the door bell of Cleveland Chambers, without any other effect than that of bringing the heads of half the court population in their nightcaps to the bedroom windows, and eliciting a few of those flowers of rhetoric which the court wits kept at their tongues' ends for like occasions.

At last, just as he was about to give it up for a bad job, the door gave way with a jerk, and the person who had opened it fell out on the top of him. This he described to be an ancient lady of delapidated aspect, dirty in face, and tumbled in attire, whose nose was red, and whose eyes were watery, like those of one who had been indulging too freely in alcoholic stimulants; added to which, she smelt of gin, and talked "husky." On inquiring whether Mrs. Cheveleigh was at home, the inebriated individual had been moved to tears, and in a roundabout fashion, at once inarticulate and incoherent, had informed him that to the best of her knowledge there never had been no Mrs. Cheveleigh, and that it was all along of Twisted-his-wrist, as had been a-shaking of everybody's life-time out, and everybody else was locked up in the station-house, and was going to be murdered in a cab. At which melancholy state of affairs the narrator had become quite hysterical, and falling again on the top of the policeman, much to that gentleman's inconvenience and disgust, had been propped up in a corner of the stairs to come to of her own accord, where she was heard faintly to request that some one would get her a little drop of something, being particular about its being warm, and laying extra stress upon the necessity of its being accompanied by a small piece of sugar about the size of a nutmeg.

Without paying any particular attention to the old lady's wants, the officer had walked up-stairs, and, by dint of hammering at all the doors he found on his way, at last ascertained from a little man, who appeared to be in charge of the establishment, and who was himself considerably the worse or the better for liquor, that Mrs. Cheveleigh had been at home, but had gone out again.

"Which I ask your pardon, sir," said the policeman, in conclusion, "but I've had a good deal of trouble, one way and the other, and if you can make it a trifle more, shall feel obliged to you."

"Well, to tell you the truth," replied Maurice, fumbling nervously in his pocket, and rattling up the fourpenny bit and the half-penny, "I supposed you would find some one there, and they would have sent me some money. However, they won't be long before they come, I imagine, and then I will give you double the amount I promised."

The policeman departing, though not quite so blithely as he might have done, perhaps, if he had had the money in his pocket, Maurice was left to himself and his reflections. No pleasant company, I can assure you.

He racked his brain for a thousand reasons to acount for Nelly's absence. She had no doubt heard of his incarceration; but, why on earth had she not come to inquire after him? He was locked up in the nearest police-station to Foot Court. In all probability she had gone to some other one in search of him. Well, he would not bother his head any more about it. All in due time, she would come, and he would be liberated.

He leant back again in the easiest corner (which, after all, was not over easy, for the seats in a cell are not of the softest material), and tried to go to sleep.

In vain. The church clocks struck hour after hour. As he lay awake, he counted the strokes, and sprang up to listen to every noise he heard without, expecting that each new arrival must be she whom he was waiting for so anxiously.

Thus wore away the night, and day-light broke, but still she had not come.

Ah! Maurice, well may you wait—the happy days were never to return. Of no avail your prayers, and hopes, and expectations. The dream is over, and the castle you built yourself, poor fool! lies trampled in the dust!

CHAPTER THE SIXTY-FOURTH.

A BOLD STROKE FOR A LOVER.

PRAY how shall I account for pretty Nelly's behaviour? What has become of that capricious damsel? Where has she got to?

I have told you before that when she was roused, Mrs. Cheveleigh could use as bad language as a costermonger. I believe I am not maligning that excellent class of persons when I say that their expressions are, at times, unnecessarily emphatic. I have spent some time in studying their language, and habits, commercial and social, and find them, as a rule, given to excessive beer and blasphemy; though I have no doubt that there are many scores who are strictly correct in their conduct and talk—to use a common saying—like a book.

You would think that I was exaggerating if I described the way that the passionate beauty clenched her little fists, and stamped the heels of her pretty kid boots. Then how she stormed and raved. Indeed, she was in a towering passion; and I think it was very lucky for her that that old stupid Miss Perks had taken refuge on the staircase, and was well out of the reach of her fair mistress's fingers, or she might have had another good shaking.

It is a very common thing for high and mighty people when out of temper to fall upon and buffet their poor dependants. Do not we read in history how young princes have had "whipping boys," unfortunate young wretches of lowly degree, who were kept on purpose to be flogged when his royal highness was stupider than usual over his A B ab's! I can fancy I see the worthy pedagogue, near flaying the young plebeian alive, when he had got more than ordinarily exasperated with his prince's blockheadism. And do we not see the same thing in a pantomime? When the King cuffs the Chamberlain, does he not turn round and box a Stick-in-Waiting? And, gracious me! does not the Stick assault a Man-at-Arms, and let him have it? I believe you.

She sat down when the first paroxysm of senseless passion was over, and reviewed her chances carefully and patiently.

Could she stop with Maurice any longer? Impossible. After all she had said, to be nothing more than his mistress! And as for marrying him, the thought was absurd. What means would he have of supporting her? At best, could he hope for anything better than to be a clerk? Would they not have to struggle and fight their way in life? What would she become if she was not successful in obtaining another engagement? A mere drudge—a scourer of pots and pans—"a twaddling married woman," as she derisively termed a domestic matron. Again, did she obtain another situation, and did Cheveleigh even join the profession, could they live upon what they earned? Would it not be, at best, a miserable, squalid existence? Besides, it is much easier for a woman to get on in the theatrical way than a man. Most likely he would never rise above mediocrity. She pictured him to herself, careworn, sallow, and seedy, and very blue about the gills. She had no very high opinion of Maurice's talents, by the way, and thought it next to impossible that he would ever achieve the success she had done.

Yes—decidedly, for both their sakes, it would be better that the connection should cease at once. She abhorred all sorts of messing and muddling, and, in fact, had very few vulgar tastes and sympathies, considering her "bringings-up." I have heard her myself descant quite learnedly upon delicate matters connectd with music and high art. To hear her upon the relative merits of MILLAIS, HUNT, EGG, and SOLOMON, would have staggered Mr. RUSKIN himself. She could appreciate a choice dinner, too, which is more than can be said of most English ladies; and, saving a vulgar partiality for roast pork and raw onions—a taste which, by the way, is shared by almost every living woman (including your ethereal Jemima, young man)—I have not much to say against her upon that score.

"What shall I do?" she thought, to herself. "Shall I make it up with Bullyrag?"

It was a peculiarity of this audacious young lady that it never entered into her calculation that the other party might have a say in the matter.

"Perhaps, all things considered," she continued, "it would be best to drop that man altogether. If I thought that I could secure his lordship; but after what has passed that would be impossible. However could I have been so hasty?"

I suppose that what I am going to relate will be called improbable. I do not deny it; but, at the same time, you cannot deny that it is possible, also. Do we not every day meet with the strangest coincidences?

Nelly, while thinking, had approached the window, and was looking out into the court—a favourite pastime of hers—when somebody below caught sight of her, and stopped.

"Good morning," a voice called to her from the court.

Good heavens! it was Lord Drawler.

"Good evening, Lady Cheveleigh," repeated his lordship, standing respectfully uncovered, in the gas-light. "If it were not so very late, I should have asked to be allowed to come up, and pay my respects to Sir Maurice."

"Not at all too late," she replied. "I will come down, and let you in."

"Thank you; but I am afraid I am disturbing you?"

"On the contrary, I am very happy you have come."

She went down stairs hastily to open the door to him.

"What the deuce is her game now?" thought Drawler. "I should not have believed that she would have spoken to me. Whatever it is, I can't lose much by going up-stairs, unless, indeed, she's going to set that infernal cad on me. I wonder whether he can fight?"

He had just got thus far in his meditations, when Nelly opened the door and stood before him, candle in hand, looking, as he thought, far more beautiful than ever.

"She's worth a thousand lickings," thought his lordship; "so, here goes."

He raised his hat to her in the most respectful manner, and she preceded him up-stairs.

"I am very much afraid that this is an intrusion," he said. But again she assured him to the contrary.

When they reached the sitting-room, Lord Drawler glanced round hastily.

"Maurice is not here?" he said.

"No."

"I thought you said he was?"

"No. I don't expect him."

"Nelly——"

He had stepped forward, with a bright smile, to take her hand, when he checked himself.

"Perhaps he's hiding in the other room, and he'll pounce out upon me," he thought. "It is just the sort of trick she would play, I should fancy. I'll try her."

"After what occurred between us," he said, aloud, "I hardly expected to be allowed the honour of another interview; but since you have granted me one, I take this opportunity of expressing my sincerest regret that I should have said anything to hurt your feelings. From your conduct, I never imagined you were Cheveleigh's wife, or I would have spared you any insult. That will touch him up if he's listening," thought Drawler.

"What shall I say?" thought Nelly.

The situation was embarrassing. Very few people like owning to a lie however small it is; and when a person has made such a statement, as Mrs. Nelly had been making, to acknowledge that there was not a word of truth in it, was dreadful, indeed, and required more than ordinary strength of mind to face it out.

However, Nelly had plenty strength of mind, and to spare. When it came to a matter of daring, I don't know what she would not have dared. He *must* find out some time or other that she had told an untruth. She would then be the first to tell him of it. And why should she not? She had now no reason for wishing to make him believe that she was married to Cheveleigh. Stay! a plan suggested itself to her ingenious mind—she would act on it.

"Take a seat, my lord," said she, pointing to a place upon the sofa, where she herself sat down. "You have acted very unfairly towards me."

"Madam!"

"You had no right to persecute me as you have done. From our first meeting your attentions have been always so marked and unmistakable, that people have begun—begun to talk about it."

"I—I?" stammered his lordship. He really did not know what to say, so did not attempt it. He did not feel particularly sorry that his gallantries had been talked about.

"Ah! you men are so very inconsiderate—so rash—so bold in your love making. What does your reputation suffer if the honour of a dozen victims is tarnished by your smile? We women have to plot and scheme to hide our hearts, and wait until you are pleased to speak, my lord, before we dare to raise our demure faces, and sigh our gratitude."

There was, generally, something so bitterly ironical in Nelly's tone and manner when expressing her opinions upon the observances of civilised life, that it quite frightened the poor weaklings who hearkened to her. I believe that you Bohemians hold, mostly, similar opinions. The grapes are horribly sour; are they not? You look at Paradise through the bars of the closed gates, aud swear it is not half so bright as we others think it.

Lord Drawler was not very wise. His bosom friends never gave him credit for more sense than was absolutely necessary; so on this occasion, not exactly understanding Nelly's drift, he sat and listened to her silently.

"We women, my lord, must wait, I say, till we are spoken to; and, if we have no kind mamma to do the arithmetic for us, must make our own little calculations. We poor creatures are not like you lords of the creation. It is quite possible that when you are tired of us, you will desert us; but when our beauty is gone, we still must eat and drink, and it is that fear of some day starving—of shifting our quarters from your palace to the union—which makes us a little careful."

"If you mean, my dear Nelly," cried Drawler, at last beginning to understand her, "if you think it possible that I shall ever desert you, I swear by everything in heaven and on earth that it shall never happen."

He was so earnest and so energetic in taking this oath, that what simple maiden could help believing him? That yellow-haired calculating machine, who sat with her soft blue eyes, all innocence and love, looking into his, although she squeezed his hand, and was to all appearances convinced, no more believed him than I do.

"You fair-spoken liar," she thought to herself, "have not I heard of your goings on? — your treachery and your villany? You'd throw me up, like all the rest, when you were tired of me."

Then came another thought—what woman is there who would not have had it? Was there not a chance that she might fare differently to the rest? A set of namby-pamby, spoony creatures—ignorant and ill-bred—what could *they* expect? She did not pity them the least bit in the world.

While thus she thought, she squeezed his hand, silent with emotion, as he fancied.

My lord was not very sentimental, and though he was silent, it was only because his vocabulary was somewhat limited.

"I believe you," she said at last, in tremulous tones; "I believe that *you*, of your own free will, would never leave me; but circumstances might arise that would compel you to do so."

"By heaven!" cried he, "if you will only come and live with me, I'll settle three hundred a year on you—I will, by all that's holy. You shall have nothing to wish for. Only say the word. I tell you, I never did love a woman as much as you. I've told you so a hundred times before. If I can't marry you, it's not my fault. You wouln't have me kill the other

woman, would you? I swear I'll always be true to you. I do, by——, and——, *et cetera.*"

He wound up his speech with the most tremendous oaths, to make it more impressive. Indeed, as far as his capacities for loving went, he loved the woman, as he said, more than any other he had ever met with. To be sure, he had never had half the trouble with any other, and that goes a long way with some of your rakes.

"I do love you," he kept repeating, with trifling variations, finding, when once he had said it, that it was easier to say than anything else.

She looked magnificently beautiful to-night, her rich silk dress fitting tightly to her splendid form—her yellow hair, loose from the comb, hanging in disorder on her plump white shoulders, for her gown was low in the neck. A corner of her skirt, caught on a nail upon the sofa, left her small foot and daintily-fitting boot exposed, and an inch or two of her silk stocking, round which the fire-light played hide and seek among the soft depths of elaborate embroidery.

My lord had, as usual, been drinking freely, and the wine was in his foolish head. He drew her gently towards him, muttering all the endearing little tendernesses that he could think of. Her head rested on his breast, and he smelt the faint scent upon her hair.

"And if I leave my husband for your sake, you will never desert me?"

That was the crowning stroke. She was, then, married to him. The idea of its being an intrigue with a married woman, made the affair a hundred times more piquant.

"Never!" he cried vehemently.

"Oh! George," she sighed, "if I could believe you, how I could love you."

For him to swear to his unalterable attachment by everything imaginable, for her to speak her love by the eloquence of her bright eyes and pouting lips, is what in such a case we might expect that they would do. I do not feel at home in describing these soft love passages, and am apprehensive lest I may make them too improper.

"I am going to Paris to night, or rather this morning," said Drawler. "I had been up to the Apollo, on the chance of seeing you, and thought I would come round this way, and see if there was a light in the window, though I never expected to be asked in. The train starts at some impossible hour in the morning, and so I was not going to bed. What do you say? Will you come with me?"

To go to the most beautiful city in the world—the place, of all others, she had so longed to visit—such an entire change of life. To say good-bye for ever to the Apollo, and its mean associations; the dirty court, with its sneering, prying, busy-bodies; the paltry tricks and dodges of her daily life with Maurice; their alternate magnificence and squalor, and all that horrible pawn-shop business. To wipe away all this, who could resist the temptation?

She said she would take a few things with her, and be ready in an instant.

"Be quick, then," said Drawler, " or Cheveleigh may look in and prevent us."

"I do not expect him to-night," replied Nelly. "He has gone to the country."

She did not expect him in the least, or you may be sure she would not have asked his lordship in. She knew Maurice's circumstances as well as he did ; and doubted whether he would be able to find bail. Anyhow, he would send to her, in all probability, to get it, so she thought——Of the landlord of the "Hand and Heart," perhaps.

"I say, don't take more than you want for the journey," Drawler remarked. "We can get some new things in Paris."

She had soon made up her parcel, including a book to read in the train, and they left the house together.

She turned a moment to glance round the old room as she passed out ; it looked shabby and smoky enough to excuse her for feeling very little regret at leaving it.

Old Miss Perks, hanging over the banisters, the worse for "drops," saw her mistress depart. With her went all the poor creature's dreams of coming grandeur. The tipsy old thing shook her head in a maudling fashion, and shed tears. She did not understand that the Goddess was going for ever, and henceforth the dreary old tenement would fall back into its original gloomy state, and be, until it tumbled down, or was taken away, an abode of melancholy and despair.

Nelly never gave the stupid old woman a thought; but, handing her parcel to my lord to carry for her, drew her silk skirts carefully round her to keep them out of the dust, and picked her way down the dirty stairs, and out into the court.

There was so much to see, and think, and talk about, that they had reached Folkestone, crossed the Channel, and were rattling along as fast as the train could carry them towards Paris, before Nelly could altogether realise her altered fortunes.

My lord, wrapped up in his Inverness, was having a quiet little nap; and she, much too excited and flurried by the events of the last few hours to feel inclined for slumber, opened M. Dumas' *fils's* amusing volume, and thought she would read a little.

She turned the pages over carelessly to find the place. Ah! there was a marker in. What was it?

MAURICE'S LETTER.

"My dear, what is the matter? Nelly—Nelly, my love, speak to me. You are ill."

It was Lord Drawler, who, waking up, had found her leaning back, deadly pale and motionless, with her eyes closed.

"No—no!" she replied abruptly, almost savagely, "it's nothing—only a faintness. Does this train stop anywhere?"

"Nowhere now, until we get to Paris."

"I must go back," she cried. "I am a wretch to have acted as I have done. Oh! my lord, let me go back. The fault is all mine. I may, if I return directly, be able to explain my absence. What a fool I have been to treat him as I have—so good and generous a heart, and one who loved me so."

She pushed his lordship from her when he would have pulled her hands from her face, and, leaning her head upon the window-sill, trembled and sobbed with her new emotion.

"Damn this sort of thing!" said Drawler to himself. "A little of it goes a deuced long way. It's lucky we've got the carriage to ourselves."

Then he tried his best to soothe and comfort her, and said all the pretty things he could think of.

Did she return?

Of course she did not. The hardest-hearted of us all have our little weaknesses. When they pass over, then "Richard is himself again."

Was it likely that she should remember the old shabby love affair in the midst of the gaieties of that glorious French capital? By the side of it, did not the finest streets of the smoky town she had left behind her sink into miserable insignificance? What was Regent Street to this city full of Regent Streets? And to think of those dingy old parks she had always thought were unequalled, by the side of the beautiful Bois de Boulogne? She was a heartless, unpatriotic young person, who valued very little the country she had had the misfortune to be born in. She always spoke disparagingly of its institutions, and I really believe would have held the most ferocious volunteer, in the most imposing regimentals, in the most unmitigated contempt.

Oh! why was she such a scandalous hussy? Why am I her historian? Could I not have chosen a much better subject? If you come to that, why are you reading it?

I hope it amuses you.

———

CHAPTER THE SIXTY-FIFTH.

MORE COUNTING OF CHICKENS.

TO get on well in clerkly life, you must, I should imagine, be necessarily something of a sneak. To undervalue your associates, ferret out and snigger over your superiors' faults, seems to me to be a sure way of acquiring credit as a zealous servant. Add to that a preposterous affectation of interest in everything connected with the work, and you may depend upon getting a rise when your turn comes.

Though you and I (I mean by *you* the right-minded reader) are inclined to admire that very exemplary young man, Ernest Cheveleigh, I do believe that there were many of his companions in the Bad Bargains who detested him!

His line was what is called the "nagging."

He was for ever worrying and stirring up those beneath him, and when he was in a bustling humour they hated him more than usual.

But it was extraordinary what a change took place in Ernest's demeanour about this time.

The morning after the day on which Mr. Hadget had communicated the important secret concerning Maurice's illegitimacy, he was at least a couple of hours behind time at the office.

There was of course a fixed hour for coming to business, and to be fifteen minutes too late was pretty nearly a hanging matter.

"Hallo! Cheveleigh's not come yet," said one.

"What's o'clock?" asked another.

"By Jove!"

"What is it?"

"Half-an-hour after time."

"You don't mean that? He must be ill."

Then they began to wonder whether it was anything serious and to calculate who would be benefitted by his demise.

There is nothing makes men more selfish than office life.

He came, however, at last, and what was most curious in one of such regular habits, scarcely alluded to the lateness of the hour. But what surprised everybody the most, that he went away again after stopping about an hour and doing nothing whatever.

Next day was the same, and the day after that, when there was a tremendous press of business in arrear, he never came at all.

"He's going the way of his cousin," some said.

"Did not you notice that he had been drinking?" said others. "He's half drunk now. Look at this sum he has been doing. Seven and five are fourteen."

"No!"

"Let me see!"

"Well, I never!" And so on.

At last his behaviour really became so unaccountable that Mr. Parchingby, the head clerk, felt it was his duty to call him to account.

"Between ourselves, you know, Cheveleigh, this sort of thing can't last," said Mr. Parchingby. "I can, of course, make every allowance for your feelings after so very unpleasant a circumstance as that connected with the death of your uncle; but with the work in the present state I really cannot put up with any more irregularities."

"My dear sir," replied Ernest, "we will avoid any future irregularities by removing the cause of them. I am going to tender my resignation."

"Your resignation!" cried Parchingby, astounded. "Oh, indeed! I always heard that you were independent of the office. I am very happy to find you are."

"Thank you," replied Ernest, freezingly polite. "I am. By the demise of my uncle, I succeed to the property and title."

"I am happy to hear it," continued Parchingby, who would, at the moment, much rather have heard of his burial. "Though, by the way, I always thought your cousin would have had the title?"

"The person who was known here as my cousin had not even a right to the name of Cheveleigh. He was illegitimate."

Parchingby looked astonished, and Ernest continued.

"But, though I leave this office, I trust that our friendship may not cease. I shall feel very much delighted and honoured if you will give me the pleasure of your company to dinner to-morrow at Long's."

Mr. Parchingby smirked, and smiled, and bowed his acknowledgments.

After all, one does not mind having a baronet or two among our acquaintance; and a dinner at Long's is not to be despised.

Sir Ernest Cheveleigh included several of his fellow-clerks in the invitation, and very mysterious and self-important did those gentlemen become. Indeed, this dinner formed quite an epoch in their lives, and excited no small commotion in their suburban homes that evening, when they took thither the astounding intelligence.

The dinner was a very grand one.

You and I, who have dined at Long's fifty times at least, know how a dinner can be served in that aristocratic tavern. It never cost a penny less than thirty shillings a head, I am certain, and perhaps a little more.

Those poor clerklings! how their gentle bosoms were agitated with alarms about the condition of their dress waistcoats, and the propriety of going in white kid gloves. Old Parchingby bought a new pair of boots for the occasion, which pinched him horribly, and I am not sorry to say (I met the man once, and dislike him exceedingly) that he did not enjoy himself at all in consequence.

But although grand, the repast was prodigiously dull, and between the fish and the dessert scarce fifty words were spoken. One of the younger men asked another, across the table, some question about the work, to which the other replied, and they talked a little "shop." Otherwise, no topic was started in which anybody felt any particular interest, and everybody being upon their best behaviour, felt very weary and weak in the back. However, Sir Ernest Cheveleigh cared very little whether they enjoyed themselves or not, as long as they were sufficiently impressed with a sense of his magnificence. Mr. Hadget was of the party, and Mr. Bucket, the celebrated detective, with whom the lawyer had contracted a strong friendship, and whom he had, after some trouble, induced the baronet to invite.

Mr. Hadget drank pretty freely, and Mr. Bucket, after attempting one or two professional anecdotes of a facetious character, which were a dead failure, subsided into silence, and followed his example. One of the gentlemen went to sleep, and Mr. Parchingby would have done the same, had not that infernal boot prevented him. As it was, he sat with it half off, to relieve the pain, unable to think of anything else, and did not speak to anybody.

"I say, Bucket," Mr. Hadget observed, as this dreary feast broke up, "we'll go and have half-an-hour somewhere, if you're agreeable. By the bye, I should like to see that chap, Taylor, to-morrow. How's the evidence getting on?"

"Swimmingly," replied Mr. Bucket; "and dead against him."

"Is it? Poor devil!"

During this colloquy Sir Ernest was paying the bill in majestic silence.

"Come heavy?" asked Mr. Hadget.

"Rather," returned the other, and coldly, handed it to him.

"Dash it—yes," cried the lawyer, with a laugh. "I don't think it will run to this sort of thing."

"What do you mean?"

"Why, between ourselves, the Skearcrows property isn't worth ten pounds a-year. It's almost all sold away or mortgaged."

Ernest turned ghastly pale, and grasped the banisters for support.

CHAPTER THE SIXTY-SIXTH.

DOGGED TO DEATH.

MOST extraordinary, mysterious, marvellous, inexplicable, unfathomable was the sagacity displayed by the celebrated Bucket in collecting evidence in the cab murder case.

Paragraphs touching upon the celebrated Bucket's early career, and the details of his private life, were handed about among the weekly papers; and every day the placards outside the newspaper-offices told of "Fresh discoveries," "Astonishing disclosures," or "Apprehension of a supposed participator!"

I think it must have been the rapid succession of apprehensions which kept up the public curiosity; for though upon examination, it turned out that the supposed culprits had no more to do with it than the worthy magistrate who heard the case, every body expected that it would be proved against them; and it showed that the celebrated Bucket was giving every one a turn, and would, undoubtedly, get hold of the right one at last.

But, although himself little short of a Vidocq, there is no denying that the celebrated Bucket received very valuable assistance from Mr. Hadget in bringing the murder home to John Taylor; and had it not been for the skill and perseverance of that gentleman in raking out little prejudicial scraps of Taylor's family history, many important details which led to his conviction would have been omitted.

He *was* convicted. A most intelligent jury of twelve enlightened Britons adjudged him guilty, and he was sentenced to be hanged.

He was a sullen, savage-looking fellow, this John Taylor, and the court was prejudiced against him from the first. When asked for his defence, he told a long and rambling story, contradicting himself several times, and, as his counsel said, quite spoilt the case.

When taken back to prison, he grew more taciturn, and savage, and morose, refusing to see the chaplain, or make any confession. He kept himself aloof from everybody, and squatted in a corner of his cell, glaring at his captors like a bloodhound at bay.

Four days before the day fixed for his execution Hadget called on him. He asked if he might speak to the prisoner alone. It was against the rules, the jailer said, but for a golden something slipped into his hand, he left them by themselves.

Mr. Hadget was not exactly employed as the prisoner's solicitor, as that unfortunate person had refused his services; but he had somehow mixed himself up in the business, one way and another, and was a kind of factotum.

Left alone with the prisoner, Hadget took a seat beside him on the bed.

"Well," said he.

"Well."

"There's not a chance left for you."

"Who says so?" screamed the prisoner suddenly, starting up, and sinking back again exhausted. "Has my petition gone on?"

"Refused. The law's to take its course."

"God have mercy on me. I am innocent."

"What's the odds? You'll be hanged the same for all that."

"But is there no escape?"

"Not with life."

"How then?"

"By poison. I have some with me. Be a man, and take it. You'll so escape the pollution of the hangman's touch."

"But if I do," said Taylor, after a gloomy pause, "it will be thought to be another proof of my guilt."

"Whatever you do's a proof of guilt, now that everybody thinks you guilty."

The prisoner was silent for a while.

"What makes you so anxious about it?" he asked, at last.

"What makes me?" said Hadget, with an uneasy laugh; for the other's eyes were fixed upon him, piercingly. "Nothing. What should? What are yous taring at?"

"At you," the other said, in a subdued tone, half of fear and half of ferocity, as, with his eyes still fixed upon his questioner, he crept closer to him upon the bed, preparing like a tiger for a spring. "Go on talking. I want to hear your voice. I see it all. I know you. I've thought as much before. I say *I know you.*"

But Hadget made no reply, nor changed a muscle of his face, only his colour went, and his lip twitched. He kept his eyes fixed on his antagonist, and, in his turn, prepared himself for a struggle.

Another moment, and they were clasped in each other's arms. Desperately, fiercely, but noiselessly, they battled for the mastery.

If the jailor had been close outside the door, he could hardly have heard them; as it was, he was some distance away down the passage.

Thus, then, they rolled and fought, with set teeth and straining muscles. And so, at last, Hadget, getting the upper hand, held down his foe; and, twisting and wrenching at his neckerchief, half stangled him.

He had a lion's strength, and, in his hands, the other was like a child.

"If you know me," hissed Hadget, between his teeth, "you know my reason for wishing for your death. Your safety is my danger; and I shall rest only when you're dead."

As he spoke, he dragged the panting wretch's jaws apart, and, forcing back his head, emptied the contents of a phial down the victim's throat.

Even as he did it, the shadow of death stole over the prisoner's face, and his hold upon his murderer's clothes relaxed, and tightened again on air.

"Help!—help!" screamed Hadget. "The prisoner has poisoned himself. Help!"

THE ONLY WOMAN ERNEST EVER LOVED.

CHAPTER THE SIXTY-SIXTH.

" GOING—GONE."

THERE was no mistake about it. Hadget had not in the least exaggerated the woful state of affairs when he said that the Skearcrows' property was not worth ten pounds a-year.

As it turned out, it was not worth five.

I don't suppose the readers would thank me, were I to give them a page or two of law. I have struggled through a thousand folios, trying to get a glimmering af the case into my head; and though I understand no more about it than when I began, if I thought it would

afford you any gratification, I would go at it again, and give you a couple of numbers of legal business directly.

Suffice it to say that it was at length satisfactorily proved that Maurice was a bastard, and Ernest the heir to the title and property.

He came into it without any great flourish of trumpets. After the grand dinner I have told you of, he made no more attempts to celebrate his accession to riches; indeed, the expense of that repast drained his pocket of all his spare cash, and left him almost penniless.

Maurice defended his claim; but, the cause being decided against him, he had no money to pay the costs, and, as is not unfrequent in such cases, the lawyers looked to the other side for their money.

As the other side hadn't got it, much unpleasantness ensued, and I believe that both plaintiff and defendant were for many weeks playing at hide and seek in that exciting pastime commonly known as " dodging a judgment."

This was a pretty state of affairs, was it not?

You can imagine how those trumpery clerks at the Bad Bargains did chuckle and crow when they heard of it.

Old Quill and little Nibs used to go into convulsions whenever the subject was mentioned. That stupid fool, big Bonum, was inclined to sympathise with Ernest, and said that, after all, he wasn't such a bad sort. But, then big Bonum was an idiot, as everybody knows, and you may be sure that nobody agreed with him.

Down at Skearcrows there was a good deal of excitement.

When the astonishing news of Sir John's murder, and Maurice's illegitimacy, reached the dwellers in those parts, they received the intelligence open-mouthed, and were a long while before they recovered the power of speech. When they did, they said they had expected it all along, and that anybody with half an eye could see what sort of a lady " that woman" was. But as, instead of having only half an eye, unfortunately, the parson, doctor, and neighbouring small gentry, had two whole ones a-piece, nobody had hitherto penetrated the mystery, and, had it not thus come to light, most probably never would have been any the wiser.

It is true that a few ladies had, at different times, tossed up their noses at the mention of the late Lady Cheveleigh's name : but they had done so without having any particular cause for so doing, — merely because it is natural to the female mind to be spiteful to those of their own sex who are inclined to be " bounceable;" and which of the dear creatures is there who will not make wholesale accusations, without a word of truth in them, upon the like occasion?

" Well, I hope, as there is to be a change, it will be a change for the better," said the doctor's wife.

" Plenty of room for it too, my dear," said the parson's lady.

" Whatever will become of that young man, Maurice, brought up like he has been?"

" Dear me, it's more than I can tell, my dear. It's awful to think of."

" A ne'er-do-well he always was."

" Ah! yes, Mrs. Squills, ' train up a child in the way it should go——' "

" Heigho !"

" Heigho !"

And the good ladies sighed over the probable fate of this black sheep.

" And that——that baggage, what's to become of her?"

" She's feathered her nest, I'll be bound. Poor, simple old man !"

" Haven't you heard the news?" somebody broke in.

" What news?"

" About her committing suicide.

" No. Tell us all about it."

Here imagine a full and particular account of the same, with all the revolting details repeated twice, by desire.

" Well," said everybody, " it's just what I expected. It's the only thing she could have done."

As soon as Sir Ernest Cheveleigh came into full possession of his worthless property, he determined upon selling everything that it lay in his power to dispose of; and, calling in the assistance of Mr. Rattletrap, the well-known auctioneer, who chanced to be in the neighbourhood, put forth advertisements to the effect that, on such and such a day, all the choice collection of ancient and modern furniture, glass, plate, books, &c., lately belonging to Sir John Cheveleigh, Bart., would be sold by public auction, at a great sacrifice, owing to the present proprietor being about to take up his abode on the continent.

On the day of the sale, I can tell you, there was a strong gathering of the small gentry— at least, of the female portion. There had been such awful tales about the goings-on at Skearcrows, that the gentle ladies naturally felt anxious to see what the interior was like. And again, do not they always take every opportunity of learning all they can about a certain class?

The house and land, it was discovered, were already sold to a Jewish gentleman. That disreputable old scamp, Sir John, had sold everything he possibly could sell without its becoming public. It was a wonder he had not given bills of sale upon the furniture, as a way of raising money ; for he had not scrupled, as it turned out, to mortgage land and other property which were no longer his, and a terrible amount of litigation ensued.

Perhaps the reason he had left the furniture sacred was because he thought it worth nothing. It fetched very little under the hammer. There was not a bid for the celebrated " ancestors," although Mr. Rattletrap extolled the merits of that gloomy family of fogies of all ages in the most glowing language.

" One advantage of them," said he, pointing to a remarkably obscure specimen, which looked something like a cracked poor man's plaister ; " one peculiar advantage is, that they look equally well whichever way they're hung. They're like the sunset scenes of the late Mr. Turner; upside down makes no difference to them. Who says eighteen pence for Sir Hilderbrand Cheveleigh, a knight of the time of King Richard the First? Going at eighteen-pence !"

So, to cut the story short, such of the things as would sell, were sold ; and Ernest came back to town, with very little money in his pockets.

Quite an awful change these few last weeks had effected in him. He looked so haggard and worn. His hair, too, had grown a little grey. It was difficult to imagine him to be the smart dapper gentlemen we used to know him.

" Fool !—cursed fool that I have been," was his constant thought. " Why did I throw up my situation before I was sure I could live on the property? But, then, how was I to imagine that affairs were in this awful state? I wish that vagabond Hadget had kept his secrets to himself. Why should not the bastard have had his title, and come into nothing a year to live on? He always was a blackguard, with blackguard tastes and associates. I suppose he knows the art of pawning thoroughly, and is up to most of the dodges for getting credit. I'm not. I've always been respectable, and now it has come to this. If I beg to be taken back into the Bad Bargains? Even if they allow it, what a dreadful degradation! My only chance is a rich marriage. My title may tempt some one. What a fool I was to break with Dorcas. Again the old woman has made a will in her favour. I must have known she would, had I not been an ass. And Margaret—what of her? The only woman I ever felt any love for. But that must go now. I must work hard to get a position. I must begin the world afresh."

———

CHAPTER THE SI - SEVENTH.

NO MORE OCCASION FOR MR. BUCKET.

ROUSED by Hadget's cries for assistance, the jailers came running into the cell, and, seeing the position in which the prisoner was lying, endeavoured to raise him up, while the lawyer, at their suggestion, went in quest of somebody who could fetch the doctor.

The doctor came; but was no good to Taylor.

He was as dead as lead.

"He's cheated Jack Ketch," said one of the men. "Never any one deserved a sounder hanging. How did he do it?"

"How did he get the poison?" asked the doctor.

"He must have had it about him," answered Mr. Hadget. "I came to tell him, you know, that the petition to Her Majesty had been refused, and that the law would take its course. He became awfully excited; and taking something from his breast, that phial, I presume, gulped down the contents. But, as you say, sir, it's extraordinary how he got it. Stay. Who has visited him?"

"His wife came yesterday."

"That's it, then. She brought it, no doubt. She had better be questioned. She can be punished, can't she?"

"There'll be an inquest, of course," said the doctor, "and all here must be present at it."

"A really tragical affair," said Mr. Hadget, as he walked away with the medical man. "The murdered gentleman was a dear friend of mine. But I had always had a kind of sympathy for this felon; for I never until his own act revealed it to-day, believed him to be guilty."

"Did you not?" said the doctor. "And still," he pursued, musingly, as he shook Mr. Hadget by the hand and stared him full in the face, "we physiognomists can almost always tell a scoundrel at the first glance.

"Ha! ha! To be sure—to be sure it's a disagreeable knowledge, though, too, is it not?"

"Sometimes."

"Sometimes to be sure. Pretty generally so, I should think. There are so many of them about."

"They don't always hang the worst."

"To be sure not. Ha—ha!—that's very good. I must remember that. 'They don't always hang the worst.' That's very true, that is. I really must not forget that. My friend, Mr. Bucket, the detective officer, will be very much amused by it, I'm certain. Good morning, sir—good morning."

"An agreable fellow, that," thought the doctor, as he walked away. "Shrewd observer of human nature, I should say, if I am a judge of faces; though, from the glance I took at him, I should fancy rather deficient in caution and secretiveness. I think he calls himself a lawyer. A lawyer ought to have those qualities, though."

"Infernal old fool!" said Hadget. "I couldn't tell at first what the devil he was driving at."

Then he walked on whistling "the sailor's hornpipe." He had not gone far before he met Mr. Bucket, to whom he recounted the particulars of the scene he had just witnessed, or, at least, such a version of it as he chose to adopt.

"There's an end to the inquiry now, I suppose."

"I suppose there is," said Mr. Bucket.

"You won't continue your search for his accomplice now, I suppose?"

"Who said he had one?" asked Mr. Bucket.

"You don't think he had, then?"

"I haven't found him," replied Mr. Bucket, significantly.

"To be sure," said Hadget. "That didn't strike me before. To be sure. If there had been one, you would have found him."

"I should reyther think so, Mr. Hadget."

"Ha! ha! they have to get up precious early to do you, old fellow. Mr. DICKENS didn't choose you for a hero before he found out there was something in you. I'm devilish glad of one thing——"

"What's that?"

"That I didn't do it myself, or you'd have had me before this."

"Well, there's a chance of it."

"Now, if I had murdered Sir John, do you know what I should have done?"

"Hooked it, I suppose."

"No: I should have made your acquaintance somehow, and helped you to look for myself."

"Ha! ha!" laughed Mr. Bucket, though not best pleased. No professional person can brook a suggestion from an "outsider."

"That's a precious stale dodge."

"But it's a good'un."

"I shouldn't advise any one to try it."

"Well, not with you, old fellow. But with any one else I would. You're such a downy one, you are. Let's go in somewhere and wet our whistle."

———

CHAPTER THE SIXTY-EIGHTH.

WHO TOUCHES THE PHYSIC BOTTLES?

YET was the knocker muffled at the house in Baker Street, where that wicked old woman lay a dying.

Yet did the straw lie in the road before the black and frowning portal, while broken pieces drifted round the corner, and down side-streets, littering tidily-kept door-steps, to the discomfiture of tidy maids.

Yet, in the quiet eventide might have been seen the graceful symmetry of the majestic Simpkinson, quiescent in the twilight-gloom, and, grandly silent, puffing at his weed. Yet, as of yore, small gatherings of street boys watched him admiringly, and wondered, perhaps, if that was all he did, and what he got for doing it.

Yet was everything going on the same within and without the house of sickness, and the old lady lay a bed, no better and no worse.

One afternoon, "between the lights," a seedy figure came up the darkening street, and walking up the steps, stood face to face with Mr. Simpkinson.

If Mr. Simpkinson was, as the saying is, a little "took a-back," please to attribute it more to the suddenness of the other's approach, than to any bashfulness on Mr. Simpkinson's part at being found in such an attitude, and so employed.

"Hallo!" said the visitor.

"Hallo!" said Mr. Simpkinson.

Then they stared at one another.

"Oh! it's you, is it?" continued the fine gentleman, regarding the seedy person contemptuously.

"You can see that plain enough, I suppose," retorted the seedy one.

"You're demned impidint!" said Mr. Simpkinson.

"I meant to be," retorted Seedy.

"I've a demned good mind to pull your nose," said Plush, indignantly. "I wonder who you call yourself, you six-and-eightpenny fella."

He was so confident of the strength of his position, and the servility of the shabby person (for is it not the nature of the shabby to be servile?), that he scarcely deigned to glance at his antagonist, but puffed the cigar-smoke in his direction.

"I want to pass," the seedy man said presently.

"Wait till I move, then, fella," replied Charles Simpkinson, Esquire, going on with his cigar.

A pause of half a minute.

He could not have been more surprised had an earthquake happened, and the yawning earth swallowed up at one huge mouthful the other side of Baker Street,—I say, he could not have been more surprised, though the result might have caused him further inconvenience; for, as true as I am alive, that shabby man fell bodily upon him, and, catching him by the nape of the neck, with a jerk which was terrific in its power, sent Charles Simpkin-

son the magnificent, the imperturbable and grand, head over heels down the steps, and on his handsome nose, in the dirty, vulgar mud.

"Fella," said Mr. Simpkinson, rising to his feet, and rubbing himself behind, "I think you touched me with your toe."

"You ought to know I did," replied the shabby man, with a laugh at once ironical and savage. "I'll do it harder next time."

Though Mr. Simpkinson came up the steps looking quite appalling in his ire, and turning up his coat cuffs the while, he did not resort to any violence. He only looked at the other, very white and rather shaky, trembling, no doubt, with suppressed passion.

"I should like very much to know what you call yourself," said he, at last.

"My name is Hadget," replied the other. "I am a lawyer by profession, and a boxer by pleasure. If you haven't had enough already, I can let you have it to any extent. It's all of the same pattern."

"I wouldn't demean myself by touching you," replied Mr. Simpkinson.

"It would be safest for you not to do so," said Hadget. "I hit hard when I'm out of temper; and, at such a time, might wring a puppy's head off. Do you hear?"

"Ah! I hear," cried Mr. Simpkinson, backing up against the wall. "There's no occasion to bawl so."

The lawyer eyed him over, then laughed, and walked up-stairs.

"WELL, Mr. Simpkinson," exclaimed little Dimples, who, unobserved, had been a spectator of this disagreeable scene, "before I'd be kicked, and say nothing about it, I'd—goodness me—I'd cut my nose off!"

It was a very pretty little nose that this fascinating damsel turned up as she spoke.

"You call yourself a man," she continued, derisively. "I wish he'd killed you, I do. Oh! you pitiful thing. Won't I tell them all down stairs!"

Poor Simpkinson, no longer grand, majestic, or imposing, left to himself and his conscience, leans despondingly against the wall, and is moved to tears. While thus he weeps, a loud and maddening peal of laughter shakes the house. They are talking it over down stairs, and he is henceforward a degraded man. Putting on his hat, he wildly flies the house, and Baker Street never sees his like again.

That night, in company with the nine o'clock beer, a small boy brings a crumpled note, in which Charles Simpkinson says that he is dangerously ill, and wants the balance of his wages, and his "things."

Then are the "things" packed up and sent. The broken comb, the mangy brush, the pot of bear's grease, and the bottle of dye, the ragged shirt, the pair of stockings, and the two smart dickies, in company with the suit of private clothes he wore at night; a few ends of cigars, and some odd numbers of the "Mysteries of the Court of London." The little boy departs, bearing with him, besides, Mr. Simpkinson's effects, a mocking message touching Mr. Simpkinson's indisposition, and thus does Simpkinson merge into one of the things that were a recollection of pretentions, humbug, a laughing stock, and nothing more.

After this little exhibition of hasty temper, the male kind below stairs were more respectful in their demeanor towards the gentleman whom Mr. Simpkinson had somewhat slightingly termed " six-and-eight-pence." They might, in some measure, have been influenced by the fate of Simpkinson, or they might have had other reasons for being more civil. No matter which—they were so.

This was by no means the first visit that Hadget had made to Mrs. Falsetto's, though; for the purposes of my story, I have not as yet found occasion to describe his doings there.

He was not exactly her legal adviser, though he was generally employed to do such little pettifogging jobs as she required. When well, the old woman was very energetic and business-like. She conducted her own affairs, and in the matter of wills, which of late seemed to occupy a great deal of her attention, she was quite an adept.

Mr. Hadget collected her rents—a disagreeable, worrying, bullying sort of work, which required a bold, hard heart, a scowling face, and a loud voice, to manage nicely. Mr. Hadget had struck her as being a very likely person for the job, and she employed him. She did not think him a very respectable or creditable person to represent her; but as far as she could learn, he acted fairly by her, and as since he collected it she had drawn nearly twice as much as she drew before, she was not dissatisfied. Her tenants were almost without exception blackguard people, and it wanted some one who was a little of a blackguard to deal with them.

She was, indeed, quite satisfied with him. He had been recommended to her for his bad qualities, and, upon the strength of that recommendation alone, she had engaged him, though he had other claims to her consideration.

" Come in," a voice answered to his modest tap at the door of the sick chamber. It was Dorcas who spoke.

" It's only me," said Mr. Hadget, apologetically, and with a fawning, smirking sort of manner that he occasionally put on, under some delusive notion that it was pleasing to the person addressed. " It's only me, that's brought my little rents. I hope I don't intrude."

Dorcas made no answer, but Mrs. Falsetto called out, in weak treble, from the bed, " Come·in, sir,—come in. I've been waiting for you."

" I hope you're better to-day, mam. You look much better. I'm very happy to see you looking so well."

" I don't feel well, if I look so," retorted the old lady, a little snappishly.

" Don't you, mam? I'm very sorry to hear it," pursued Mr. Hadget, taking a seat, and feigning to arrange some papers in his hat, while he eyed Dorcas and the old woman cautiously.

" You said you had been waiting for me, mam," he observed presently. " It isn't everybody is waited for by the ladies."

" How have you got on to-day?" asked Mrs. Falsetto.

" About the same as usual, mam. A little unwillingness in some quarters. Put the brokers in at two houses, and going to put 'em into two more to-morrow, if they don't shell up."

" Confound the wretches!" cried the old lady, between two violent fits of coughing, which shook her like a leaf; " what do they expect?"

" That's how I put it to them myself. ' Here you have a beautiful house in one of the most crowded and convenient blind alleys in London, close to all the principal places of amusement, retired, and almost private—although, as for that, company only makes it more cheerful, snug, and shady (there's never any sun there, in any weather)—open and healthy.' By the way, there's always something wrong with the drains. Two of the tenants have got the typhus, and I expect the parish will be down upon us if we put them to much expense in funerals."

" Lord bless the man! don't talk to me of funerals. Have the drains looked to. We mustn't have the wretches poisoned."

" No. No good in that, that I see."

" What have you collected, then, Mr. Hadget?"

" Here it is," said the lawyer, going over the accounts.

" Oh! thank you. Will you pay it into the Bank?"

" Certainly, mam."

He rose as he spoke, but hesitated, and fumbled with his hat.

" Have you anything more to say, Mr. Hadget?"

" I have—a-hem!—that is——" And he glanced towards Dorcas.

" Dorcas, dear, leave us," said the old lady, and Dorcas quitted the apartment.

When she was gone, Mr. Hadget took a seat again, and put down his hat again.

" You will be surprised at what I'm going to say," he remarked.

" Indeed !" said the lady, fixing her eyes earnestly upon his face.

" Yes, madam. I am going to resign my post."

" Why?"

" You'll be inclined to laugh, I'm sure, when I tell you; but the fact is, I have had something left me, and am thinking of setting up as a gentleman."

" I am surprised indeed."

" I thought you would be. It will come a little difficult at first, I dare say, having been so long hard up and seedy, to make oneself at home in respectable society; but it's to be learnt, I suppose."

" I suppose so."

" I should not wonder, now," pursued Mr. Hadget, " but that you would not be ashamed of owning our relationship one of these days."

" Had you not disgraced yourself, I should never have been ashamed."

" To be sure. It runs in our family—this weakness for breaking the law—doesn t it, eh?"

" Excepting you, I know no other——"

"Except yourself, eh? You haven't quite forgotten that, I hope."

The old woman rose up in bed with a frightened gesture, and motioned him to be silent.

"What bosh!" said he impatiently; "there's no one listening. And if there were, what odds? Both men are dead, and there is no one left to prosecute."

"You talk like a fool. Do you suppose that I could show my face again in society if it were known? The very shame would kill me."

"For the matter of that, I expect old age will kill you before the end of another hundred years. Why, woman, you're old enough to——"

"Silence! how dare you talk so, you wretch?—and I ill as I am." And the old lady rocked herself and sobbed.

"Hold your noise!" said Hadget. "I'm not going to tell anybody. 'Gad! I'd like to know where you could find such another relation as I am. Do I go about bragging that I'm connected with you? Ever since you were pleased to cut your family, upon your marriage with Sam Cheveleigh, I have never thrust myself forward. When Sam died, and Jack skipped over his head, and slipped into his father's shoes, so that you just missed being "my lady,"—when you were hard-up, and cut by everybody, didn't I come forward generously, and lend you——half-a-sovereign I think it was?"

"Is it to talk this folly that you wanted to be alone with me?"

"No—not exactly; but I must take this opportunity to show you what a relation you have got. You know you never have treated me well; and, though I might have blabbed to every living soul who I was, I never did so. Because I got into trouble about those cursed title-deeds, and was struck off the rolls, you thought you had got a good excuse for continuing your unnatural conduct, and when you picked up with that jockey chap——"

"Hush! hush! for God's sake, man; the very walls have ears."

"That jockey chap," continued Hadget, apparently not noticing the interruption, "when he ill-used you, and deserted you, you never appealed to me as you might have done. Why didn't you, I wonder? You were quite right, in my opinion, to marry the old banker, although the jockey chap hadn't kicked the bucket. He kicked it afterwards, and made things square. I didn't forget you, you recollect; but kept him out of sight, and persuaded him to be quiet."

"For which I had to bribe you pretty heavily."

"Had to bribe him, you mean."

"I don't know who got the money!"

"What do you mean?" He started up in virtuous indignation. "By heavens! if ever you say as much again, I'll blow upon the whole affair next minute. Haven't I served you these two years well and honestly, as honestly as though I were no relation to you? What d'ye mean? Do you call this gratitude?"

"No—no—Hadget. I beg your pardon. I did not mean to say so; but why will you rake up these old grievances?"

"I've only raked them up to show you that you owe me something. It's a capital plan to freshen a person's memory now and then when they are in your debt. One naturally so soon forgets an obligation."

"There—there—Hadget, don't go on so; I own that I was in the wrong."

"Well, I'm glad of that, anyhow. But when I'm accused of acting dishonestly, curse me if I can stand it. Now even about those children of yours——"

"Hadget—Hadget! Silence!"

"Well, while I'm on the subject, I'd like to speak my mind. About those children——I never did clearly understand what became of them. I saw the doctor's certificate, it's true, but I hope it was all right."

He looked her earnestly in the face as he spoke; she, violently agitated, sat up in bed and, glaring at him wildly, panted for breath.

"Wh—at do you mean?" she gasped.

"Nothing," said he. "You wanted to be rid of the brats, and a dose too much one way or the other, could make no difference."

"You monster!" she screamed. "Do you think I murdered my own children?"

"Didn't you?" he retorted, coolly.

"No, no, as Heaven is my witness, I did not. Oh! God," she cried, as she sank back in bed, "that ever I should have sunk so low as to be thought capable of such a crime."

"Well, well, don't take on so. A baby's not so bad as a grown-up person."

After a pause of a few moments, she, making no reply, he continued,—

"What I want you to do, and what I'm driving at is this. I want to come and live with you. You can own me if you like, or leave it alone. I am not particular about that. Only here I must live, and you must introduce me to society."

"It is impossible."

"That's likely enough; only impossibilities are got over every day. You must get over this. Come, without any more fuss. I say it must be done, or else—or else—we'll quarrel. Is that enough for you?"

"Quite enough."

"I'm glad you're reasonable. You must tell that friend, or companion, or whatever she is, that you are going to ask me——By the way, she seems to be a surly sort of woman. Why do you keep her?"

"Because it pleases me."

"Oh! all right. Keep her still, then, for what I care. I suppose you'll leave her your money when you die."

"I've made a will to that effect."

"Oh!" exclaimed Hadget, with a slight start, "have you?" After a pause, he added,—

"Who gives you your medicine?"

"She does."

"Always?"

"Almost always."

"And she is the only person who would benefit by your death?"

"What do you mean by that?"

"Nothing whatever. Only it dosen't do you much good. Don't forget to speak to her about my visit. Good bye to you."

So saying he walked away, and muttered to himself, as he walked down stairs,—

"That was a happy thought. I don't like that woman Abbot. She must go. So the old woman didn't kill her whelps. I hardly think she did, or she'd have shown her guilt when I put it to her so plainly. If there was any mystery about it, I'll find it out. Patience—patience! A little more scheming and contriving, and then—a glorious future, or the gallows!"

Left by herself, the old woman lay trembling in her bed, her old toothless jaws chattering with fright.

"He cannot mean he thinks she poisons me," the old woman thought. "Then why should I get no better? I'll watch her closely. She shan't touch my physic. But no, it is impossible. She, of all other women! Oh, it's too monstrous!—too horrible! And he thinks that I killed my children! Let him think so. If he knew all, I should be more in his power than I am. Oh, *if he knew they were alive!*"

She shuddered at the thought, and hid her head under the bed clothes.

Dorcas came in, and found her thus.

"It's time to take your draught," she said, looking at a watch over the mantelpiece. "Come, sit up, and have it."

CHAPTER THE SIXTY-NINTH.

ANOTHER VICTIM OF PERFIDIOUS WOMAN.

FANCY pictures to me your pretty faces, fair maids and matrons, as you read the heading to this chapter. The very idea of your sex being false and heartless! Is it not absurdly unjust and ridiculous? I daresay now you think me mighty hard upon the ladies; but I'm not, you know. I like to speak my mind. It is the novelty of the thing which I suppose makes this book sell as it does. We are not accustomed in our literature to hear an appropriator of other folk's goods called a thief, a teller of untruths a liar, and a decidedly improper person of the softer sex a—— (The printer thinks it best not to put it even here—in this outrageous history.) I should, upon my honour, be just as hard upon the men, only really they are not worth it. When I look round there is not a male character in my story I care a fig for—they are all such dreadful rascals, or such thorough fools. "The ladies are not much better," you retort. Just you wait a bit, you don't know what I'm going to do with Miss Nelly. You have had a taste of all her bad qualities, but I have plenty of time to show the good ones, haven't I?

Well, Maurice, then, was the victim of perfidious woman, to whom I alluded; and I will, if you please, go on with his adventures.

I left him in the lock-up. Next morning, when the cases were called nobody appearing against him, he was discharged.

"I hope you won't forget me, guv'nor," said the policeman whom he had overnight sent to Nelly with a letter; "I had a deal of trouble along of that job."

"Certainly not. Call any time this evening, when you are off duty, at my chambers, and I will reward you."

"Thank you, sir, I'll do so. Though," added the policeman to himself, "I've got my doubts about getting anything. I don't like the looks of it by any means."

Without very particularly caring what the worthy man thought of him, Maurice went upon his way, whistling as gaily as an empty-headed clod at the end of a plough. That was the way with him. No sooner was one misfortune over, than his head was up again, waiting for another, as bold as brass.

This time there was plenty of unpleasantness waiting for him.

As he walked along, poor booby, he offered himself a number of premature consolations. As usual, he was reckoning without his host.

Nothing particular, thought he, had come of his incarceration, except a slight cold caught in the cell, and the loss of a night's rest. Then, as for that story about his illegitimacy, there was not a doubt about it, it had all been trumped-up by that rascally lawyer. When his mother came that day to call upon him, he could triumphantly refute all Hadget's false statements, marry Nelly, and live happy ever afterwards. His mother, he felt certain, would not throw any obstacles in the way of a union which would afford her son so much happiness.

Thus busy, castle-building, he neared the court, and, pressing forward impatiently, ran up the stairs, and opened his door.

The sitting-room was dull, and cold, and untenanted.

He hurried through to the bed-room, and looked round. No one there, and everything much the same as when he left it. The bed, as he had lain upon it, covered by the counterpane, with the impression of his head upon the pillow. On the table the papers which he had been sorting scattered about.

He came back to the front room, and looked round. The sofa pulled up close to the fireplace; the fire out; the poker lying across the hearth-rug. A decanter and a glass upon the sideboard; the stopper of the decanter fallen on the floor, and lying there, broken.

"How odd the place looks," he said to himself, somehow a little frightened he didn't know of what.

"What *has* become of Nelly?"

He wandered back into the bed-room, and, throwing open the window, stood looking out at the court without noticing anything. Then he turned round and packed up his papers, walked to the letter-box on his door, of which he had not thought before, and took out one that he found there. It was a lawyer's letter, apprising him that proceedings had began.

He turned hot and cold when he read it, and crumpled it up in his hand. What would Nelly say? Where *was* she?

He rang the bell again furiously, but without getting any answer.

"What the policeman said was true," thought he. "The old lady was a little overtaken last night. I suppose she can't get up this morning."

For want of something to do, he wandered

round the room, looking at and noticing many little things, in the hope that he might get a clue to Nelly's whereabouts.

"I don't see her slippers," said he.

These were a pretty little pair of crimson silk frivolities, embroidered with gold beads, very showy and useless, which Mr. Maurice had squandered a score of shillings upon.

"She can't be out, but yet she must be. I don't see her boots——nor her bonnet," he added, after a pause.

Presently he came upon the note which he had written, lying upon the table—unopened. Ruminating upon this, he turned to the chest of drawers, in which he kept his money, thinking he had better get something to drink, and wait till somebody turned up who could explain matters.

The drawer was open, and—EMPTY.

He stood and stared at it, amazed; then started back, with an oath. He had been robbed—he had been robbed! BY WHOM?

Again he rushed at the bell. This time he tore and dragged at it until it broke, and this time some one came.

It was very hard, at first, to say who the some one was; so unutterably woe-begone and wretched was the individual's appearance, that he could hardly recognise her.

Furthermore was this individual accompanied by a powerful smell of gin, besides being unpleasantly troubled with a hiccup.

"Yoop," said the phantom.

"Where's your mistress?" cried Maurice, with difficulty distinguishing a faint resemblance to Miss Perks. "Has she gone out, and where has she gone to?"

"Yoop."

"Where?"

"Yoop," repeated Miss Perks, making a singular sound something like a sob, with a jerk in the middle.

"Are you dumb, or drunk?" cried Maurice, impatiently. "What is the matter?"

"Oh, deary—deary!" sobbed Miss Perks, falling into a chair near the door, and violently assaulting her eyes and nose with a rag which stood her in lieu of apron. "I do' no' what's a-happened, and what's a-got to everybody. Twisted-his-wrist's a-been a turning of us upside down; and I've been shooked. Oh! Lord a-mercy me, that iver I should a lived for her to shook me like she done!"

"Who shook you?"

"Missus, I tell you. She's been a shooking me because I telled 'em down the court that we'd come into our property, and was all agoing to be lords. Oh, dear, I diddle go for to do no harm; and on'y telled 'em bekase I thought that it 'ud make 'em wild, they was so spiteful to her al'ays. But when old Twisted-his-wrist come in, and talked to you, and told her somethink, she flew at me a good'un. And oh, deary, deary, how she shook me up! My poor bones aches again."

"Do you mean to say," cried Maurice, growing excited, "that the man who came for me last night told Mrs. Cheveleigh something?"

"He must a-told her something; for he says to me as I was coming in—he says, 'Give this to your Missus,' he says. 'She isn't in,' I says. 'She is,' he says; 'I've been a-talkin' to her,' he says."

"What did he give you, then?"

"A bit of writing, folded up. That's it."

She rose as she spoke, and picked up a scrap of paper lying on the floor. It was in Hadget's handwriting, and said, as the reader may perhaps remember, that Maurice was locked-up; but that Mr. Hadget supposed he would get bail, and that she was not to alarm herself. It concluded with, "Do not forget my address."

He read it over twice or thrice. What could she want his address for?

"Did she say anything?" asked Maurice.

"She asked me what I been a saying to you, and then I telled her; and then she shooked me up; and then the gentleman come that come to supper; and then they went away together, and she has never come back. Oh, dear—oh, dear! I don't know what it all can mean."

"What gentleman was it?"

"Him as Missus slapped the head of."

He did not stay to hear another word, but, putting on his hat, went straight to Lyon's Inn, and asked for Hadget.

"Where's my wife?" he cried, fiercely.

"I haven't got your wife."

"That's your writing. Why did you give her your address?"

"Because I want to see her. She hasn't been yet, if that is any consolation to you."

In answer to this, the young man raved and stormed in a mad fashion, until Mr. Hadget, procuring help, he was ejected from the Inn into the street,—there finding himself in the centre of an admiring crowd, he rushed off to Lord Drawler's lodgings. His lordship was out—gone to Paris. Alone? The landlady did not know. Mr. Parsons, his lordship's gentleman, had accompanied him, she believed. Off—off as quick as his legs could carry him to the Apollo. She had not been there. Then back to the court, to wait in the vain hope that she would come.

All day he has neither bitten nor supped. His head is splitting with pain; his bones ache with fatigue and cold, but his hands are hot and feverish. He has no money whatever; Miss Perks takes something to Uncle Attenborough, and makes him a cup of tea.

How pass the next day, and the next, he knows not himself—they wear the semblance of a frightful nightmare. He borrows a paper in the hope that he may find something about Nelly; and in it reads the paragraph about his mother's suicide. The circumstances raise a suspicion in his mind that it is she. He goes, and finds it is. A wretched bastard—homeless, penniless, deserted — hemmed in and overwhelmed by difficulties. His mind and strength give way beneath the shock, and as he lies at death's door on his lonely bed, poor simple-hearted Perks, sitting beside and watching over him, drops her tears upon his wasted hand. He is the kindest, the handsomest, the grandest gentleman that she had ever known; and should he die, to her the world would hold none other!

HERE ENDETH THE FIRST PORTION OF THIS HISTORY.

SECOND PORTION.

ONE OF MR. MOBBLES'S "QUILTINGS."

CHAPTER THE FIRST.

UPON DEATH'S DOOR-STEP.

WEARILY, wearily the hours pass in that ill-lighted second floor in Foot Court, Holborn. But they do pass somehow, growing into days, and lengthening into weeks, until, one day, on looking back, the sufferer finds that it is full three months ago.

How does he live through all this weary

comes a time when there is nothing remaining which Uncle Attenborough will take charg ef.

Now is the door kept locked, and angry voices on the stairs, disputing with the Bony handmaiden, say that they think it "jolly rum as that there gent is never at home." Now do the hook-nosed tribes congregate round the outer door, and keep a watch upon the house; and, whispers getting about in the court, the court agrees that, sooner or later, all profli- time? By small degrees the rooms grow barer and barer—the drawers emptier. At last there

No. 17

gacy must have such an end, and hopes "that hussy" will get her "deservings."

Wearily the hours drag, and the sick man, lying prone upon his restless couch, listens to the murmurs of the crowd below, and sees the day fade out, and gas spring into life, while distant organs, grinding mournfully, bring back to his mind dear memories of happy hours, gone—never to return.

Will he never be able to be about again?— never be strong and hearty, like he used to be? They say that it is beautiful summer weather; and some one who has been by van to Hampton Court, tells old Miss Perks such tales of how the trees are looking (trees to which those in Red Lion Square can't hold a candle), that she is wonder-struck, and brings confused accounts thereof to cheer the invalid.

All-potent Bolusout, M.D., has been to see him, and shaken his head over him, taking the while a bird's-eye view of the apartment, and, seeing nothing there which looks like money, writes his prescription, and calls no more. In future the apothecary's consulted, who, though he stands out for ready money, is not exorbitant in his charges.

When first Maurice fell ill, good Miss Perks suggested that he should try a certain patent medicine, which she pinned her faith upon, and which, according to countless testimonials, is equally good for anything. This he had refused; but when all other medicines failed, or when, weak with protracted illness, he feels unfit for argument, he yields to her entreaties, and gives PROFESSOR HOLLOWAY a chance. I have very little doubt that those famous pills would have cured him, like they have cured so many before, but in his case they have not the fairest trial that they might have given them, for he is in the habit of practising a little jugglery and sleight-of-hand instead of swallowing them, so that they are all found afterwards in corners of the room and underneath the bed, when the time comes for washing the floor, much to the surprise and consternation of Miss Perks.

Do you want to know what Maurice's friends said about him?

Mrs. Falsetto had struck him for ever off her books. She had heard the whole story of his wicked life, with notes and emendations by Messrs. Hadget and Ernest. That woman, Dorcas, had absurdly urged upon her the necessity of doing something for the profligate— advice which the old lady had very properly laughed to scorn.

"I should have enough to do, were I to pension all Sir John's disgraceful connections. A vile old rip, I always disliked him! No— no, my dear. Mr. Maurice can work, I suppose. I can see no reason why his bastardship should live in affluence, and swing his legs, because, forsooth, he has been imposing on us all so long. He's no gentleman, you know. I never thought he was. There always was a *je ne sais quoi* about him that I couldn't bear."

"I thought he was your favourite, madam?"

"Not at all. However did you get such an idea? He has never taken the trouble to pay me any attention, while his cousin has really been quite indefatigable—not that I like him

any more for that—but that's neither here nor there. By the way," continued the old lady, presently, "what did you say had become of the woman he was living with?"

"She's left him," replied Mr. Hadget.

"Of course," said the lady, with a self-satisfied smile, "that's always the case. How young men can be so very infatuated, surprises me."

"According to accounts," said Mr. Hadget, "she was really a very superior person."

"What do you mean by superior——"

"She was an actress, you know, and, I am told, exceedingly clever. She earned a great deal of money."

"Indeed!"

"In fact, I'm sorry to say, from what I hear, it was a most disgraceful connection, the interest being all on his side."

"How very horrible!"

"Quite lived on her, I'm told. Disgusting, is it not? Had he been married to her, of course, it would have been different; but, as it was—I really—no, I don't think I really ever heard of such a case."

"Most disgusting!"

"I'm sure it's false," interrupted Dorcas, stitching at a collar as though it were an enemy, and every thrust of the needle were a stab in some vital part. "It's all that woman, I'm sure. Maurice could never be so base. A nasty wretch, I'm sure she ruined him."

"My dear Dorcas," said the old lady, mildly, "however can you be so absurd?"

Mr. Letchery, the able editor of the *Thirsty Soul* (which I must take this opportunity of advertising as a journal having the narrowest views, and the widest circulation of any religious print in London), met Mr. Charley Bux one afternoon in Piccadilly.

"Seen Cheveleigh lately?" asked the editor.

"Which one?"

"The wrongful heir?" said Letchery, with a laugh.

"Haven't seen him."

"Gone very queer, hasn't he?"

"Infernal blackguard," growled Mr. Bux. "Let me in for a hundred pounds."

"You don't mean that?"

"Egad, I do though. Curse the bills! I shall have to sell out, I expect. That comes of doing a fellow a favour."

"Ah!" said Mr. Letchery, with a sigh, "keep your hands from paper, whatever you do."

There was at that moment a nasty *ca sa* floating about, which caused him a deal of annoyance. He had been doing a little stiff himself, out of which arose the unpleasantness, and so he spoke feelingly.

Many other of Maurice's old friends met together, and thus talked over the mournful state of his affairs. He was not sympathised with over much. There is really so much doing in this busy town of ours, one has not time to fret oneself when Tom goes wrong, and Bill is bankrupt. Our verdict generally is "serve him right;" but when we are compassionate we sigh, and say, "poor fellow," eating our mutton chop afterwards with none the worse appetite.

Of all his friends—at one time you might have counted them by the dozen—one alone came to see him. This was a scene painter from the Apollo, Jack Ochre by name. An uncouth, red bearded, clumsy fellow was Jack. In general, he was taciturn and gloomy. He very seldom did anything to make himself agreeable, and, judging by appearances, had a soul above washing his hands. One of Nature's gems, some authors would have called him, I daresay. Tale writers are very fond of these unpolished Orsons, and make very fine characters of them; but in real life, I am inclined to look upon them as a mistake. What say you, gentle reader?

Jack came to see the invalid in Foot Court, offered him much gratuitous good advice, and lent him a shilling or two.

"I'll be able to get some tin, somehow," said Jack, "that will keep you in physic. You're a deuced deal too weak to move at present."

"But how am I ever to pay you back for so much kindness?" whimpered his sick friend, squeezing his hand. "You'll get yourself into difficulties."

"Bother the difficulties," said Jack; "I like them. There, don't worry yourself any more about it. When I am earning a hundred a-week, I shall never miss it."

His earnings were a long way off that, by the bye.

But one does not like to keep borrowing of one's friends. Indeed, to keep asking favours of your friends, is about the best way to lose them altogether, and so Maurice called in a broker, and cleared out the greatest portion of the furniture.

Now, as he owed three quarters' rent, old Mrs. Perks hearing of the circumstance, told Mr. P that he had better call round and acquaint the landlord.

Acting upon this advice, Mr. P called upon the landlord in the morning. In the middle of the day, the landlord called on Maurice for the money, and, as Maurice had not got it, that very evening a bottle-nosed person looked in, took his position permanently in the easiest chair, and lit his pipe.

He was in possession.

Jack Ochre could raise no more money, and Maurice saw nothing left but to allow the bed to be taken from under him, and retire to the workhouse.

Things being pretty well at their worst, there came a change for the better.

Jack Ochre, you must know, happened somehow to fall across a little paragraph in the paper which turned out to be of the most vital interest to Maurice. It was not one of those one sees in the second column of the *Times*, requesting profligate initials to return to the bosoms of their disconsolate families. (Ah, me! black sheep, ever is there some loving heart which clings to you in spite of all your selfish dissipation and neglect.) It was not one of those informing so-and-so that, upon application at such a place, he or she, as the case may be, would hear of something to his or her advantage. There was nobody in the world, seemingly, who was anxious for Mr. Maurice's society, and nobody had anything they meant to give him. No: the paragraph I mean was in that portion of the paper containing the latest news respecting the British Bureaucracy, Civil Service appointments, etc. There are some persons, I dare say, by whom this sort of intelligence is never missed; like there are people who swallow the Army and Navy news, and the Money Article, as regularly as they do their breakfast. I read none of them myself by any chance, and most probably Mr. Ochre did not, but intently staring at the paper, and pondering deeply the while upon his friend's desperate condition, the sentence caught his eye.

"I say, Maurice," he cried, "you were at the Bad Bargains during the Russian war, weren't you?"

"Yes—what makes you ask?"

"To be sure you were. I remember now, we used to chaff you about starving the horses in the Crimea."

"What makes you ask?"

"I can hardly believe it can be true, but, if is, it's glorious news."

"What is?—speak.

"Why, it says the Bad BargainerGeneral—— He was your head man, wasn't he?"

"Yes—go on."

"The Bad Bargainer General has been for some time endeavouring to obtain a gratuity for those clerks who were discharged at the end of the war, and the Committee of Supply have granted it."

"Good heavens! it can't be true. How much?"

"Twenty pounds."

"Twenty pounds—impossible!"

"Well, so it says—look here."

And he handed the paper to Maurice, who read it for himself.

"Oh! Jack," said he, "what a flutter it has given me. We won't be too sanguine, though. You shall go down, to-morrow, to the office, and see what they say, and whether it includes me. By Jove! only think of twenty pounds. Well, it has not come before it was wanted, that's one thing. Twenty pounds! How shall I spend them?"

He began to calculate what his debts were.

"I really do not think that twenty pounds will cover them," he said, after mature reflection.

At which remark Jack Ochre could not refrain from bursting out a-laughing.

"There—there, old fellow," cried Jack, patting him upon the shoulder, "don't let us be too sanguine, as you very properly observed. Supposing that we have the devilish good luck to find that the money is really going to be paid to you, and it is so much less than what you owe, I don't know that it would not be the best plan to invest the twenty in some way that may bring in a little more, and then you can begin paying off at your leisure. I say, governor," he continued, to the party in possession, "I suppose that it would be against rules for you to go out and fetch some beer, so I'll fetch it myself. A pot among two of us won't hurt any one."

When he returned with the liquor, he found Maurice apparently buried in thought.

"What are you thinking of?" asked Jack.

"I was thinking," he replied, "that if I could only clear myself of my debts, I should throw my whole soul into some work or other, and earn a decent livelihood."

"That's all right, Maurice," said Jack, to humour him. "So you shall—so you shall. Only perhaps we'll do the work to get rid of the debts. Lord bless you, if we stick at it they'll soon be cleared off; and then we'll take care, and make no more, won't we?"

"I'll take good care of that."

"I'm sure you will," continued Ochre. "Had it not been for that infernal woman——"

"Jack!"

Maurice had started up at the last word, and, trembling violently, seized the other's arm, who looked at him in amazement.

"Don't do that!" said Maurice. "Don't mention her again, if you please; or, if you do, don't blame her: I—I—can't stand it, Jack."

"Why, Maurice, what is this?"

"It is—it is because—oh! Jack, I love her still. I love her with all my heart and soul. I'm sure it was not her fault that she left me. She was always so gentle and kind. I say I am certain of it. She must have been reasoned with, and persuaded. Some scoundrel must have told horrible lies about me."

"Some scoundrel probably only told her what we have since read in all the newspapers, Maurice; and, she finding that her scheme of marrying you, and making herself a lady had fallen to the ground, acted like she has—most basely."

"I tell you, Jack, it's a lie! There—there, I beg your pardon, don't let us talk of it any more. I can't bear it; it makes me mad."

"We won't talk of it any more, then. Don't make yourself ill again. Why, Maurice, what's this? Do you feel faint? Shall I open the window? Maurice—Maurice!"

Excited with their conversation, the invalid had fainted. Cold, and pale as death he lay back on the pillow.

Jack ran wildly about the room, seeking restoratives, and cursing his own stupidity.

"Drat you!" said Miss Perks, who had been summoned in the emergency, "what have you been a-doing to him, among you? There! what are you givin' him? I wish you'd leave him alone, sir; he aint your patient, I suppose. Poor dear! how pale he is. Mr. Maurice, look at me. My dear, my dear——Oh! does look at me; it's only your poor old nurse—it's only your Perksy."

With such like childish endearments the simple old creature endeavoured to restore him, bathing his forehead the while with vinegar, and gently chafing his hands between her horny palms.

"And so," thought Ochre, as he walked away that night, "and so he loves her still. Heigho! What a thing it is that some of us should be so foolish. Such a warm-hearted, generous young fellow, to be in love with that cold-blooded hussy! It will be his ruin—it will, by heaven! and I and nobody else can ever prevent it. Poor fellow!"

Verily is Maurice upon the very threshold of death's door. The grim old warrior, with the hour-glass and scythe, is at his back, and, with his upraised hand, has grasped the knocker. Shall he knock, and take his victim in? 'Tis quite a toss-up whether he does or not.

Spare him, King Death! there may be yet a happier future in store for him. Who knows? To-morrow Jack will go to the Bad Bargains, where there is perchance a goodly sum awaiting him. With this may he begin his life afresh; and then, with time and change of scene, the recollection of this unhappy passion will fade away, and he perchance love—love some one else as well, but let us hope, more wisely.

And poor old, simple Perks, what thinks she of the departed goddess? In that old muddle-pate of hers I don't believe she ever had half-a-dozen distinct ideas. It is very questionable whether she ever clearly understood how culpable Nelly had been. The circumstances of the case, as regarded Maurice's illegitimacy, were, until the day of her death, a dead letter to her, and no amount of arguing could ever persuade her that he had not been cheated out of his property.

You see, it had never occurred to her that there was anything improper in the connection between Maurice and that yellow-haired woman. They were not married perhaps, but, then, they would be, some day, she had no doubt. Then, again, if Maurice was the finest gentleman of her acquaintance, Nelly was altogether the grandest lady. It was very difficult for an old woman of weak reasoning powers to look upon that splendidly attired and magnificent creature, who reached and surpassed her highest notions of gentility, as being anything she ought not to be.

What matter if the indignant matrons of the court cried out "shame!" upon the well-dressed, bewitching hussy? Listening to them, she might for the moment have sided with them; but when again brought into contact with the yellow-haired slut, how the poor, dingy dames suffered beneath her slashing sarcasm. Nell never lost an opportunity of ridiculing their rags and patches, and sneering at their little makeshifts to be smart and stylish.

Now there was Mrs. Mobbles, at the coal and potatoe "ware'us" round the corner, one of the bitterest of Nelly's enemies,—how that yellow-haired woman had routed her! One day, when the good lady had been more than usually severe upon the actress, and Miss Perks had, in a rambling fashion, repeated to her mistress some portion of the opprobrious epithets the latter, boiling over with rage, but quiet and cool in outer appearance, as it was her wont to be, took old Perks with her, and stepped round the corner to wreak her vengeance verbally upon the potatoe-salesman's wife.

"Good morning, Mrs. Mobbles," she said, smiling sweetly. "Dear me, you've hurt yourself, I see."

"What do you mean?"

"You've blackened your eye somehow. How ever did you do it? It must be very painful."

She knew well enough, the deceitful slut, how poor Mrs. Mobbles had come by it. All the court had heard her screaming the night before, when Mr. Mobbles, in liquor, had come home and, as he styled it, "quilted" her.

"It's nothing," said Mrs. Mobbles, curtly.

"Oh! yes, I'm sure it must be. How very disagreeable, to be sure! These accidents are really most unfortunate. People do stare so, and make such unkind remarks. Have you any asparagus you can recommend?" she continued, without looking at the poor wife, who, panting with rage, seemed more than half inclined to fling a potatoe at her head.

"That bundle will do. How much is it? You need not trouble yourself to send it—you are so very goodnatured and kind—my servant shall carry it. Good morning, Mrs. Mobbles; I hope your black-eye will soon be better."

And she retired smiling, and burst into a loud laugh before she was out of hearing.

How ever Mrs. Mobbles refrained from sending a potatoe after her, is more than I can imagine.

I couldn't.

CHAPTER THE SECOND.

IN THE LAP OF LUXURY.

HOW got on this brazen strumpet in Paris? Let us follow her insolent career a little longer; for surely to goodness, if there is an avenging Nemesis on earth, he must be sharpening his sword to cut her head off.

Oh, happy, happy days! Most beautiful capital in the world! Could anything in fairy land be more enchanting than thy gardens and boulevards, gay streets, sunny skies, and smokeless atmosphere? This is, alas! a story of London life. My feet must not for long together quit my native flag stones. Still must I wend my weary way, growing each day more wily and world-wise. Of what avail the knowledge of all this wickedness, unless it be to warn you, gentle green ones? Why rent aside the covering of costly lace, and show the ghastly death's head grinning underneath, unless the sight's to frighten you, like nurses frighten babes with bogy, and make you for the future promise to be good boys and girls?

For a little while, however, as I am writing the history of "The Woman with the Yellow Hair," I think I ought to follow my heroine's foot steps in Paris.

The writer of this book was himself in the gay capital, at the time of Mrs. Raymond's visit, and he himself has often seen the handsome woman drive by in her splendid carriage, the dandies at the road side twisting round to look after her, and ogling with all their might, "la belle Anglaise."

What shawls—what bonnets—what wondrous skirts, and monstrous crinolines she wore! That frock of hers—it was a sight to see. That prodigious frock, light as gossamer and so voluminous, that it quite swamped my lord and the little black-and-tan terrier, when they went out to take an airing with her.

That mighty frock, it seemed to flow all over them, fill up the entire carriage, and, as it were, boil over the sides. John, with the calves, had quite a job to shut it in at the door, and keep it off the wheels.

Oh! she was very beautiful. I could have wished that OWEN MEREDITH had chosen her as the subject for one of those exquisite poems of his, teeming with life and passion, in which one seems to see the flash, and feel the blood run trickling hot beneath one's touch.

My lord spared neither cash nor credit in attiring his idol, and, furnishing a delightful little palace for her to inhabit, in the Champs Elysees.

He was very proud of her.

Tuesdays and Fridays were her at home nights, and then all the notables of the Parisian *demi monde* thronged her *salons*.

She soon grew very famous.

My lord was not too strong in French. Few Englishmen, even the well educated, distinguish themselves in the language of that nation of frog-eaters. There is generally an honest John Bull twang about their parley vousing exceedingly unmelodious. My lord, I say, was not very strong in French, so he was delighted to find Nelly so proficient. Perhaps her accent at first was not very good, though she had had some practice with Maurice, who naturally spoke well enough, he being the son of a French woman, and educated in France. However, she very soon acquired what was wanting, and, as I say, grew very famous among the fast youth of Paris.

Who was there of any note at that time in the fair city, who did not find the way to her drawing-rooms?

Even some of the heavy respectabilities condescended to visit her *incognito?* The famous Marquis of Crutchingford, among the number, who was then one of Her Majesty's Prime Ministers, and a leading pillar of the State. A shaky old man, with a brown wig and a glass eye, padded calves, no liver, and the most polished manners of any living gentleman.

Besides being famous as a great diplomatist and profound statesman, he had acquired some small notoriety for tricky dealings on the turf, and his reputation as a broken-down old rake has seldom been equalled. You will not be surprised if he was fascinated by the manners and appearance of the English syren.

"Where ever did she come from!" said his lordship. "My dear Drawler, where did you pick her up?"

But Drawler only smiled. He did not think it necessary to enter into particulars.

And so nobody knowing, everybody kept asking everybody else,—

"Who is she?"

"Where did she come from?"

"What has she been before?"

But Nelly did not trouble her head very much about what they might think. She saw that every man admired, and every woman envied and hated her.

What could be more delightful?

Sometimes, it is true, she could not help fancying that all this splendour and magnificence must be a happy dream, from which at any moment she might awaken with a rude shock. At other times, she almost doubted whether those shabby old court days had ever existed at all, or whether they were not but the recollection of an ugly nightmare.

Well, it was all over now—all passed and gone, and had best not be thought about.

You'll say, perhaps, why did she not send back the money she had taken away with her from the drawer in the court?

She could not want it.

A dozen times at least she had made up her mind to do so; then, something had always occurred to prevent her. She had had to dress in a hurry for dinner, or to go to the Opera with my lord, or else, perhaps, she had been obliged to break into the money to buy a pair of gloves, or something or other she took a fancy to in a shop window, which Drawler would not buy her.

So, you see, it was almost impossible.

In Paris the days thus rolled on in one delicious dream of pleasure, although they dragged their course but slowly in that dirty Holborn Court.

One evening—Sunday evening it was—Nelly was sitting with Drawler in a private box at the Theatre of the Palais Royal, when a fat, common-looking man in the pit, sumptuously attired, and bedizened with jewellery, pointed her out to a mincing little Frenchman by his side, and asked who she was.

"Di-dong, Mossoo," he said, "who is that lady, so beautifully dressed, with the light hair?"

"Not so loud!" cried Mossoo, catching his arm; "that is a compatriot of yours, under the protection of the milor who sits beside her, so glum and quiet. Mon Dieu! how you English are droll!"

"Is she living with him, then?"

"Yes, my dear Bullyrag. Kept in magnificent style, too. She gives parties, now and then, which are the talk of the town."

"Oh! indeed?" said Mr. Bullyrag; "she's very lucky."

The worthy manager had come over the water to look up some novelty for the Apollo; and was considerably surprised and annoyed, as you may suppose, at recognising his former friend in such affluent circumstances. Indeed, he could not refrain from informing his companion that he was already acquainted with the lady.

"Truly?" cried the latter, with astonished pantomime.

"True enough."

"Where did you know her?"

"She belonged to my company."

"Indeed!"

"Only a second-rate. I brought her out, and made her."

"A good chance for her to meet Milor."

"I introduced him to her. Ha—ha!"

"What is it?"

"One tires of a pretty face."

"What do you mean?"

"Don't you understand."

Please to imagine wicked looks exchanged by the two gentlemen.

"Ah—rogue!"

"Get along with you."

Here the couple dig each other in the ribs and snigger, and the little Frenchman thinks ten thousand times more of his friend than he did before.

The object of his remarks, be it understood, was perfectly unconscious of his presence. It is not at all likely that she should be noticing a lot of vulgar persons in the pit. Those whom she condescended to observe through that magnificent double-barrelled, white glass of hers, were a few well-dressed men in the stalls and private boxes, who, in their turn, ogled the fair-haired beauty, and fancied they had made a conquest.

My lord meanwhile stared to the right, and to the left, and any where but at the stage, for being, as I say, no great hand at the language, and the fellows in the play, gabbling so quickly, he, poor man, only caught a word now and then, and made but little of it.

"It's cursed slow," he grumbled, presently. "Let's go some where else."

"Do stop a little, George; I want to see the end of this. It's so capital."

"Oh, ah! it's very well for you who understand it. Curse them, they're like a pack of geese, or chattering monkeys. Just like all these beastly foreigners!"

"Well, if you want to go—go, and come back when it's over to fetch me."

"No, I can't do that. Come now."

"You're very disagreeable to-night," said she.

"Perhaps I am. You're not too obliging yourself, at any time. Come, I'm waiting."

There was something so coarse and brutal in his tone, that Nell, though unused to be dictated to, dare hardly contradict him, fearing an immediate rupture. Besides, she was too good a general for that.

"All right, my dear," she answered, rising, with a smile, and taking his arm. "Whatever you like, George, is certain to please me. Where shall we go to?"

"Let's go and have supper," Drawler suggested, considerably mollified.

"There's nothing in all the world," said Nelly, clapping her hands, "that I should like so much. I am as hungry as a hunter."

And as they walked down stairs, she said to herself.

"An ill-conditioned cub! I suppose I'd better let him have his bone."

He would have his bone sometimes, the high-born bulldog, and snarled and snapped over it like a savage as he was.

"That Drawler's a stupid brute," the Marquis of Crutchingford observed one day, to a friend. "That heavenly angel's thrown away upon him."

Is it not curious? Almost a similar observation had been made respecting Maurice. According to popular opinion, she seemed to be too good for anybody. I really should very much like to know what my lady readers would have said about her, had they had the misfortune to know this outrageous minx.

There are of course in Paris, as in London, a great number of ladies whose virtue is far from being their strongest point.

These lived under the protection of the young noblemen and gentlemen of fortune. These formed the society in which Mrs. Nelly shone a star, and were the society most sought after by all that was witty and wicked.

In England we ignore the existence of these gorgeous Traviatas. In France they figure as the heroines of every other play, and every other book. In England, except at the Opera, where a very trashy production achieved immense success, owing to the newspaper press kindly informing the public that it was something improper (not so improper, by the bye, as others which have not had the advantage of newspaper perspicui y), we seldom find them figuring upon the stage. I don't think the Lord Chamberlain would allow it. And in our books,—except in this history, where an attempt has been made to deal with reality instead of romance,—I know of no respectable book which has ventured to introduce them.

These ladies were, as you may suppose, rather jealous of the English beauty. Like the ladies at home, they agreed with one another in wondering whatever the men could see in her.

However, it was quite sufficient for Nelly, I imagine, that they did see something, and, on the strength of it, made a queen of her.

She had a most supreme contempt for the opinion of her own sex, or pretended that she had, and was so ready with her tongue that few ventured to open the battle.

After all, we might find it in our hearts to forgive her for this, but her ingratitude was really awful.

Do you not remember that on that night when Maurice found her sitting on the doorstep in the rain, and took her into the chambers, she told him a long rigmarole story about having been turned out of her home at the instigation of her mother-in-law?

Well, from that time forth she never more alluded to the circumstance.

Was it not odd?

One would have thought that a young girl would not have left her home in that way, without a thought for the old people who had been so kind to her. Perhaps her mother-in-law had not. Well, her father had, I suppose. But perhaps he had not, either, you may say. Unnatural parents are common enough, as the police reports every day inform us. Even if he had not, then, surely in such a case a woman with a good heart would have occasionally, when parted from the old man, thought tenderly of his memory.

Young women (in novels), living with their seducers, are generally devoured by remorse; but I see no signs of such feelings in this creature's bosom. She seems to have gone hammer and tongs at her French lessons and her music lessons, and improved her mind instead of moping.

When Maurice asked her about her home, she used to answer him carelessly, and at random, and never gave him any details.

He did press her much; for he was always fearful lest she might take it into her head to leave him. At the time, you may recollect, he was laying all sorts of deadly schemes to effect her ruin. He behaved like a scoundrel, you can't deny, although she subsequently turned out bad. Indeed, when we come to look at it, what had she to thank him for?

He had taught her two or three twopenny half-penny accomplishments, but had he not robbed her of that priceless jewel—her virtue?

When I come to think of it, we really ought not to be sympathising with him; what he has got are his deserts. It's only the old story—stone the woman, and pat my gentleman upon the back, and if you scold him at all, do it very gently.

With my lord, Nelly had been romancing to a considerable extent; besides assuring him that she was married to Maurice she had told him that her parents were dead, and that they had moved in a much higher sphere than they did in reality.

By a strange accident he found out the truth.

One day Nelly had taken her book to the garden of the Tuileries, and, taking a chair, sat down to wait for my lord, who was playing a game at billiards with a friend in the neighbourhood.

It was a warm, and drowsy afternoon, and scarcely a breath of air stirring. Shaded by her deeply laced parasol, the pretty woman was indolently skimming through M. MURGER's story; her eyes more frequently resting admiringly upon some handsome man passing by, or contemptuously criticising the costume of a lady in her vicinity, than fastened on the book before her, when a shabby person attracted her attention.

She was not in the habit of looking at shabby people. From such unpleasant sights as poverty, and rags, and famine she turned away her proud eyes, as many other ladies turn away theirs,—the only difference being, that they know nothing of the disagreeable subject, but instinctively dislike it; while she, was perfectly acquainted with it from experience, and disliked it in consequence.

But the conduct of this party of mean appearance was really so very eccentric, no wonder if it attracted her attention.

He stood about ten yards off, and was throwing himself into all sorts of conceivable shapes, endeavouring to catch a glimpse of her face underneath the fringe of her parasol.

"What does he want, I wonder?"

She glanced at him, but, in the position in which he stood, could not catch sight of his face; then tossed her head, and went on with her book.

Still he continued his singular pantomime.

"Bless me! who is he staring at?"

Not at her, surely. Like his impudence, if he was!

At whom else, then?

Behind her was an old nurse and two children. By the side of her a governess-looking person, in a green "ugly." English, by the look of her. Yes, she was reading WALTER SCOTT.

On the other side, an old dowager, nursing a poodle, and taking a nap.

Perhaps he wanted to steal the little black and tan terrier.

"Who knows what he may want? He is a very nasty-looking old man."

She took up her dog, and, paying no further attention to the prying glances of the inquisitive stranger, went on with her story again.

When she had read a page, she looked up once more.

He was gone.

"Thank goodness!"

No, he wasn't.

"Good heavens!"

There he was, peeping at her round a tree; and this time she caught a glance of his face.

It was a common face enough—very common indeed, with a nose and an eye that spoke of strong drink. The owner was, as I have said, very meanly attired, though he looked as if he had his "Sunday things" on.

He was a workman, or something of that kind, and evidently an Englishman.

What was more, she recognised him.

Who could it be, think you?

One of those miserable people from the court who used to watch her so? The husband of one of those good dames who were so contemptuous towards her? Had the meanly attired man caught sight of the beauty, and did he think it a good opportunity, now that he was away from his good lady, to pay his addresses to the slut? You know the matrons of the court were always desperately jealous of her, and took it for granted that their husbands paid her attention when their backs were turned.

No, it was none of these.

Nobody from the court—nobody belonging to the Apollo; but yet she recognised him.

Indeed, she knew very few faces better than his, although she had not seen him for a great many months.

IT WAS HER FATHER.

What did she do?—spring from her chair—rush towards him—throw herself at his feet—clasp his aged knees between her palms, and, weeping and repentant, seek for his forgiveness?

Fiddlestick!

She turned her head another way, and placed her parasol in such a position that her revered parent could not catch a glimpse of her face.

He wasn't to be done like that, though.

Presently, turning her eyes, as somehow one involuntarily does turn one's eyes under an earnest scrutiny, towards the person scrutinising, she saw that he had moved round to the other side.

Then his eyes met hers, and he came forward.

She felt ready to faint. Her heart was in her throat, her hand trembled so that the book fell from her fingers to the ground, where the little terrier, springing from her knee, began to bite the leaves, and worry the back.

Meanwhile the mean-looking man approached, and at last, standing right in front of her, said,—

"Nelly!"

What would you have done, I wonder, in like case? It was an awful predicament. Would not anybody in her shoes have shaken in them? To meet a parent's eye under such circumstances, without a blush and a tremble, must require an amount of "cheek" which it is quite appalling to contemplate.

She had it.

"Nelly!" said her father.

She took no notice.

"Nelly!"

"What is it?" she asked in French, raising her eyes in wonder.

If no great actress upon the stage, she was in private life so good a one, I do not think I ever met her equal.

The man stared stupidly a moment; then said, with a laugh,—

"You know me well enough."

"I do not understand you," she replied, in French.

"Pardong—je—that is—dash me, if you aint my daughter, I never had one!"

The governess, on one side, had put down Walter Scott, and was listening with all her ears. The old dowager, on the other side, who did not understand the language, was staring with all her eyes. The people all round seemed puzzled and amused.

"What do you mean?" asked Nelly, rising in a fury. "What do you want? I have nothing to give you. Please go away."

She spoke in French; and, the governess here addressing the troublesome man in his own tongue, translated what Mrs. Raymond had said.

"She's my daughter," stammered the father. "Unless I am asleep. I'm sure she is. She has the same face and voice. Nelly, why don't you own me!"

"What does he say?" cried Nelly. "Is there nobody who will release me from this insolence?"

"Permettez, madame," said a voice, in her ear.

It was the Marquis of Crutchingford, whose sardonic, wrinkled old phiz was leering over her shoulder.

"Can I be of any service to you?"

Now this was something of a fix.

I have before told you that the marquis had a horrible reputation, and that Drawler had a horrible temper.

Upon more than one occasion when the old nobleman had been rather particular in his attentions, Drawler's face had darkened like a thunder cloud.

Well, if she accepted his arm, and while walking away with him, Drawler should come up and meet them (she expected him every moment), what would follow? A scene, to say the least.

However, on the other hand, did she not accept his lordship's protection, what would her father say next? Could she possibly confront him much longer, and deny herself?

No—she chose the former course.

"Thank you, my lord."

She took his arm and moved away, her parent staring after her in stupid amazement.

"She is my daughter," he said; "I'll swear she is. An unnatural child to disown her own father. It's enough to make a man break his heart, and take to drink: it is—it is!"

And he began to blubber.

"You must be mistaken, my good man," said the governess, more because she wanted to know all about it than because she thought so, and wanted to pacify him.

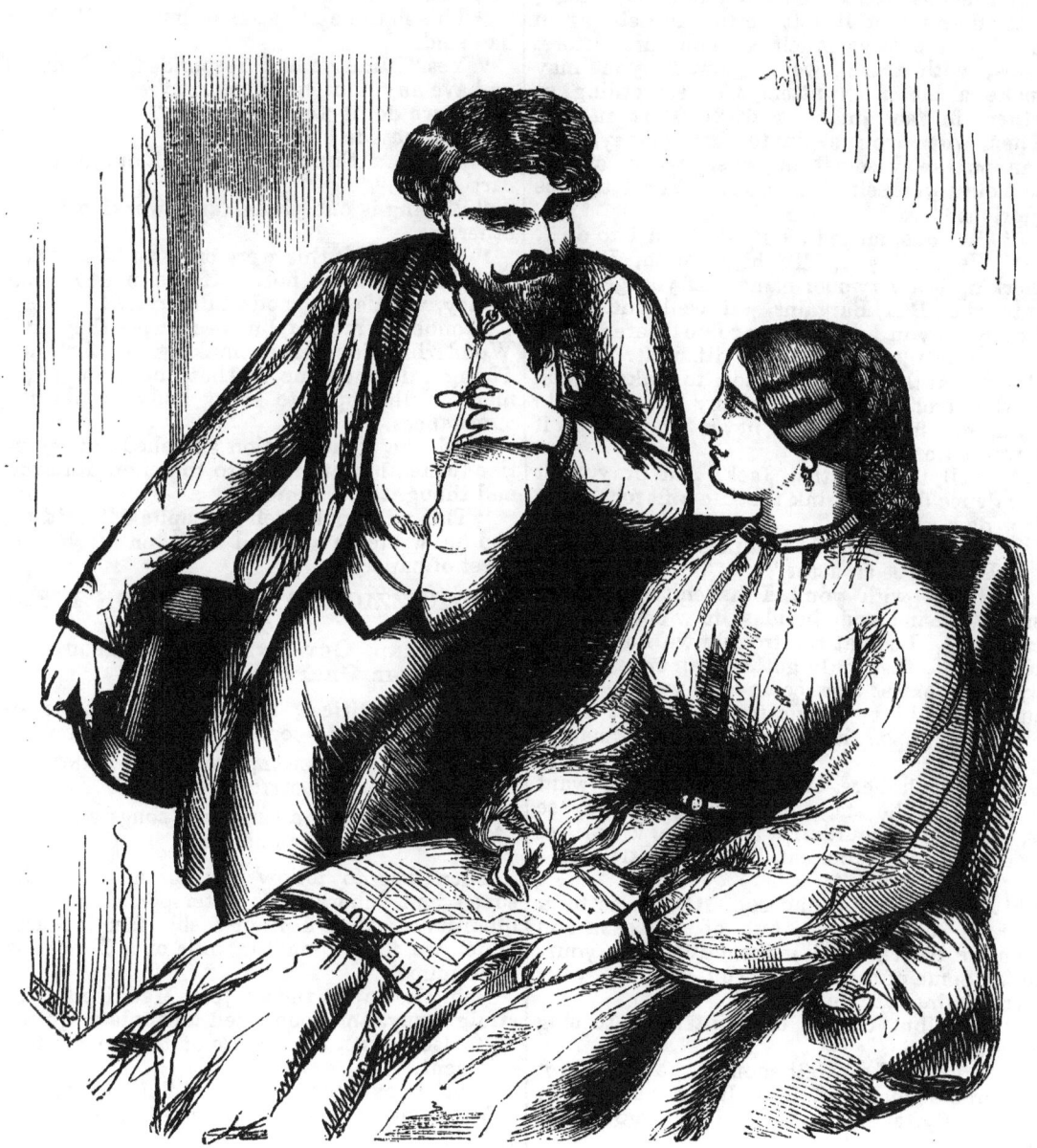

"AND MONSIEUR TURNED OUT TO BE A MOST AGREEABLE COMPANION."

CHAPTER THE THIRD.

A VERY WILD SCHEME.

I DO not wish to make a long story out of nothing. If I were to tell you everything every one of my characters did from morning till night, I should fill a dozen numbers with the history of a day. On the contrary, I only tell you what they do when they do anything interesting—that is to say, interesting for them. Of course, I know as well as you do, a thousand other heroes and heroines in other books, who at all times are much more amusing.

So, to go back to my muttons.

No. 18

Jack Ochre tidied himself up a bit on the next morning after his conversation with Maurice, and, putting on his best clothes, including that awful waistcoat with the sprigs, took himself off to the Bad Bargains' office, and there, to make a long story short, he found that Maurice was entitled to the twenty pounds, and, upon Maurice's signature, obtained the same.

How shall I picture the extravagant joy of the invalid upon hearing the good news?

"What shall we do with it?" he asked of Jack.

"Spend it," said Jack.

"How?"

"I'll tell you."

"I'm all attention."

"Look here, then. Twenty pounds won't pay your debts, nor nearly do so; and if you pay them as far as the twenty pounds will go, I see nothing for it but getting in debt again until you owe as much as you did before. Now, with these twenty pounds you may make a bit of an attempt at something or other—in fact, make a fresh start in life. Then, when you begin to earn money, you can put away something every week, and at last clear yourself altogether. Won't that be glorious?"

"Glorious, indeed; but what am I to do?"

"Well, I'll you. To begin with, I think clerking is a very poor game. If you get back into the Bad Bargains, all well and good. I suppose you had nothing to do there? But in another place it would be different. I don't think you the sort of person to make a good clerk; and, to give you my own private opinion, I for one should never employ you if I wanted one."

"Well, that's settled, Jack. And pray what the deuce do you think that I *am* fit for?"

"Be a vagabond."

"What the devil do you mean?"

"I mean, be an actor."

"Go on with you! I haven't got talent enough, man; and, besides, how could I get engaged? Look at the trouble we had about Nelly, and then only got her an engagement by the luckiest chance in the world. I am sure it would be much more difficult for a man to get upon the stage than for a woman to do so."

"But look here, Maurice, you don't want to get upon the stage at all. What I propose is, that you should try and give a sort of lecture or entertainment, in the country."

"What about?"

"Anything you choose. Comic is best. Pick a lot of pieces out of DICKENS and ALBERT SMITH, and make a little up yourself. Some of those songs you sing are your own writing, are not they?"

"Yes; but they're only intended to sing among friends."

"Oh, they'll do well enough. You've got a tolerable voice, and look like a gentleman. If you only take my advice, it will go off all right."

"What shall I call it?"

"I must leave that to you. You seem a great deal better to-day. Now, to-morrow, or next day, I propose moving you in a cab to my place. There you can write and learn your entertainment. After that we will calculate the expenses. There is nothing particular doing at the Apollo, so I will get a week's holiday, and we will start off for the sea-side. The sea air will make a man of you in no time. We will hire a room, post our bills, and wait till the night comes. What do you say?"

"First-rate!" cried Maurice, with enthusiasm.

Many more suggestions were made. Many more wonderful propositions. More castle-building.

When they separated they had formed a regular plan, and laid down a certain set of rules by which they were to abide. Ochre

was to inquire into the cost of the adventure. Nothing was to be done rashly, or without due consideration.

"This is to be a matter of business," Ochre had said.

"Yes," Maurice had responded, "don't let us have any nonsense about it."

"If we do, it won't succeed."

"Business is business."

"When a thing is begun it ought to be carried out."

"Playing is one thing, and working is another."

"It's not as if this were only an idle lark."

"I should think not. If it's not to make money, what's the good of doing it?"

Wonderful men of business, were they not? Wonderful idea for making a fortune! Though, if you come to that, the same argument would apply to every body in like circumstances.

Well, the plan of action sketched out, Maurice turned his attention to the entertainment, and thought of a name.

"This will look well in capitals," said he, and he wrote in a round hand on his largest sheet of paper,—

THE QUIZZIOLOGY OF LONDON LIFE;
OR,
IN AND OUT AND ROUND ABOUT
THE GREAT METROPOLIS.

A lyrical, satirical, tragical, magical, astronomical, serio-comical discourse upon

THINGS IN GENERAL, AND NOTHING IN
PARTICULAR,

Illustrated by a variety of songs and impersonations.

Then was to follow a programme of the songs and characters, interspersed with a quantity of that kind of feeble facetiousness which we find upon the bills of a Christmas pantomime.

Being hot upon the subject, Maurice fell to straightway, and soon filled a couple of quires of foolscap with the *libretto* of the new entertainment.

By the next evening he had finished it.

Meanwhile the man remained in possession, and it now became a subject for Maurice's consideration whether or not he should pay the rent, and save his goods and chattels.

After consulting seriously with his friend and adviser, it was determined that he should let them go. Acting upon this advice, he quietly pocketed an extra shirt (he had but one left), and, hiring a cab, departed for Jack's lodgings.

Before leaving, however, he thought that it would be best to say good bye to Miss Perks, although he, to some extent, dreaded a parting scene with the old lady.

She had been very kind to him.

During his illness, whenever she could find a spare moment, she was unremitting in her attendance at his bedside. Her relations upstairs were very angry with her on that account.

Sometimes she returned from an interview with Mrs. Perks, snivelling and rubbing her old red nose, in great distress.

"What's the matter?" Maurice would ask.

"They've blowed me up awful for sitting with you."

"Who has?"

"Them up-stairs."

"Who?"

"The o'd 'oman and the o'd man."

It was thus that she spoke of her relatives—if they *were* her relatives. A good deal of mystery enshrouded the matter. Perhaps she was not related to them at all, though all the court agreed that she was. Mr. and Mrs. Perks never by any chance mentioned her name, but used to speak of her as their servant. They were very hard upon her, bullied her, and nagged at her unceasingly.

Old Mrs. Perks said she was not worth her salt.

"And that is why," said Mr. Perks, who fancied himself (I don't know for what) a humourist, "and that is why she gives her pepper."

On this occasion, when Maurice would have said good bye to his humble friend, having rung the bell several times without receiving any answer, he went out upon the landing and called to her.

Nobody replying, he ascended the flight leading to the attics, where the Perkses lived. The sound of angry voices met his ear.

"Where have you been to, you drunken old besom? (It was Mrs. Perks who spoke.) You're always skulking out of the way somewhere or other. You aint worth your victuals."

"I don't eat much," a weak voice replied.

"Don't you? It would puzzle you to earn it. You're always stuffing."

"It's only bits."

"Oh! you're dissatisfied with it, are you? Very well. You'd best suit yourself somewhere else: you don't suit me, I can assure you."

"I don't want to go nowheres," the voice replied, apparently broken by sobs. "You wouln't 'ave the 'art to send me a-ways—a poor, old, broken down think like me? What should I be able to do, and who should I get to take me? I hevn't the cheek for matches, and I suppose theres no crossins as isn't took. It 'ud be the 'ouse I should have to go to, and live on gruel all my born days."

"And serve you right too, you idle old faggot. So get your things ready, and take yourself off."

"Oh! deary! deary! don'tee be so 'ard on me."

"Hard on you, indeed! You deserve it. And so, I tell you, this very day you pack off about your business."

"Oh! deary! deary! what ever shall I do?"

"You'd better get that young man on the second floor to provide for you. He'll be able to, I dare say, when he's paid his rent. Or else go and look for that high and mighty play-acting woman; perhaps she'll take you to be a play-actor too. You'd make a very good witch in *Macbeth*—you would."

Here Mrs. Perks burst out laughing shrilly, and the poor old creature sobbed louder than ever.

Maurice could stand it no longer, and began to call out again for her to come down stairs. She came out hurriedly.

"Lor' bless us and save us!" she cried, on seeing him, forgetting her own trouble in her anxiety for his health, "what ever are you doing out here in the cold?"

"Oh! I'm much better. I'm going away."

"G-g-going away?" she gurgled. "Oh! my poor heart! where to?—where to? *You* ain't a-goin' to leave me, sir?"

"I must," said he; "but never mind—don't cry. I'll come back and see you. As soon as I am able to get about, I'll try and do something for you. If you cannot live here any longer, come to me, and I will help you as much as lies in my power. Here's my address. Take care—there's a sovereign inside. Good bye, my dear Miss Perks, you've been very good to me—I shall never forget you?"

"Oh dear! oh dear! oh, my poor heart! oh, what a soft old fool I am! Oh! Mr. Maurice, God bless and prosper you! May you be rich and happy!—I'm on'y an o'd creeter myself, as 'a nearly lived her time. Don't take no heed on me; I'm right enough, and got as good as I deserves. Good bye, dear Mr. Maurice. How I've loved you—more than if you was my own son. How I've loved you, and *her* too, as is acted so strange to me. You're the on'y two I ever knowed as seemed so different like to all the rest. Good bye. God bless you, dear! You won't mind me shaking your hand. Good bye—God bless you!"

He left her sobbing on the stairs, squatted upon the last step among the dust and rubbish, which, a while ago, she had been sweeping together, and had not finished.

Poor soul, she sat, and moaned, and groaned as though her heart would break. She never knew she had a heart until she felt this bitter sorrow tearing at it.

The day passed slowly on, she heeded not how slowly, for what was there remaining in the world to care about?

If she broke into the pound he left her, which of us shall blame her? Poor, wretched old woman, she never knew that it was a disgrace and sin to stand and guzzle at a public-house bar.

It was her only solace in her sorrow, and so she stood and drank pennyworth after pennyworth in quite a reckless way, which made the landlord at the "Hand and Heart," say,—

"Goodness me! Miss Perks, you've come into your property, haven't you?"

Then he added, to his better half,—

"I hope it's all right, and she aint been robbing any one."

If ever Miss Perks was drunk in all her life, she was that evening.

So was Mr. Perks, for she stood treat to him.

———

CHAPTER THE FOURTH.

ONE OF NELLY'S FIBS.

WHEN Nelly walked away leaning on the Marquis of Crutchingford's arm, the face of the repudiated papa would have made a fine study for a nut-cracker—he pulled such an ugly face.

The sympathising English governess, in the "ugly," had to speak to him twice before he heard her.

"My good man," said she, "what makes you think it is your daughter? She seems to be a person of rank and fashion."

"I tell you she's my daughter, and she's living with some man she ran away with. Her name is Nelly Raymond."

"Whose name is Nelly Raymond?" asked Drawler, who came up at the moment.

"My daughter's, sir. Her with the old swell there, walking up the path."

Drawler turned in that direction, and recognised the couple, with a loud imprecation.

"—— and —— and ——" roared he, in a fury, using very unparliamentary language.

"That's Crutchingford, by all that's holy," he cried. "What does she want with him?"

Then turning to the unwelcome stranger, said,—

"If you have anything to say, come with me, and say it. This isn't the place."

So speaking, he took the mean-looking party by the arm, and they walked some little distance to where the trees and the shrubs hid them from the curious gaze of those who had been spectators of the singular scene which had just been enacting.

"Now, then," said Drawler, turning on the other sharply, "what's all this foolery?"

"Foolery?"

"Aye, what's it mean? Is it a try on?"

"It's no try on, I can assure you. I call heaven to witness what I said was true enough."

"That that lady's your daughter?"

"Yes, sir."

"But suppose her father's dead?"

"Who told you that?"

The man started back amazed; and Lord Drawler, equally amazed at his movement, stared at him.

"Well, if I aint her real father, I'm next door to it."

"What do you mean?"

"I brought her up, and clothed and fed her. When she was a little baby a lady brought her to my wife to nurse, and paid a certain something down. We was living in the country then; and moved to London afterwards by reason of my work, which I'm a working engineer, may it please you, sir, at the present time, employed upon a job here, undertaken by our people on the railway."

"Well—well?"

"The lady never come agin, you see, sir. That is, we moved to London; and I believe she come and couldn't find us out, so the payments stopped. My Missus died then, and I took up with another one. She wanted to turn the little thing out of doors; but I wouldn't stand that, and I put her to get her living at the brush-drawing business, keeping her in clothes, and letting her live at home."

"Well—well," interrupted Drawler, for the man had paused to wipe his eyes.

"My second wife and her couldn't exactly hit it, you see—things didn't go on the square. There was faults on both sides, I daresay."

"What faults?"

"I always liked the gal myself, as much as if I'd been her real father; and I always said I was before my second wife, for fear that she should be jealous of her, like, and make some unpleasantness——"

"Well—well."

"My second wife took a dislike to her from the first, and said that she believed her to be a deceitful, wicked slut. I never thought her so until to-day, when I see how she can behave to me."

"What did she do, then?"

"I don't know what she didn't do. Robbed us over and over again, went out and spent the money along of other bad girls at theatres, and balls, and such like. We could never keep her out of the streets, unless, to be sure, she got hold of a book to read, when there was no getting her away from it. That comforted me, that did——"

"What did?"

"Her being fond of her book. It wasn't story-books only, penny-numbers, and all that sort of trash, but any book she could lay her hand upon."

"What was there to comfort you in that?"

"Why, this. I said to myself, she'll make a fine scholard some day. She was a fine scholard already, much better than I shall be, and I thought, besides—I thought——"

"What?"

"As she couldn't get in no much harm if she liked her book. It would keep her out of it; but I was mistaken."

"How?"

"She went on very bad sometimes. We found her keeping company with young fellows, as was no good at all. I knew no good would come of that, and so I told her to drop it."

"Well."

"She didn't, but went on worse. At last she left us altogether. I heard she was about the streets, in great distress, and I went to look for her. For a long while I could hear nothing of her; and, when I did, some one told me that she was acting at the Apollo Theatre, and I went to see her."

"That's true enough," thought Drawler to himself. "He must know something of her."

"I tried a time or two to get to speak to her, but couldn't. I wrote a letter, but got no answer. I made inquiries about her, and heard that she was in the keeping of a gentleman called Cheveleigh—him that there was the trial about in the papers."

"Well," said Lord Drawler, seeing that the other paused, "what else have you to say?"

"I've nothing more to say, sir," replied the man, rubbing his coat sleeve across his eyes, "except that it's precious hard——"

Drawler tapped his boot with his cane, expecting what was coming.

"Precious hard, indeed—I, as have been as good as half-a-dozen fathers to her—to be treated this ways. The money I've paid for her, too, at different times, and having been out of work for four months, till I got this job——"

"Yes—yes—I understand all that, it's very hard." And Drawler began to move away.

"Do you know my daughter, sir?"

"Only slightly——Good morning."

"If you could do a good turn for a poor but honest man, sir——the smallest trifle."

"There are five francs," said Drawler gruffly; "go and get drunk, and be hanged to you!"

"Well! curse you for an ill-mannered brute," cried the other, when his lordship was well out of hearing.

"Get drunk, indeed—I'm not in the habit of getting drunk. You surly snob, can't you make allowances for a father's sorrow?"

And the bereaved parent took himself off to a neighbouring wine shop, to assuage his wounded feelings.

"Infernal old humbug!" muttered Drawler to himself. "But that doesn't make *her* conduct any the better. What he says is most of it true, I expect. And a nice pack of lies she's been cramming me with, confound her! That's the second I've found her out in to-day."

And he strode along, in no very pleasant temper, I can assure you.

"That damned old rip, Crutchingford, too, what's he purring about her for? and why does she let him? I'll put a stop to this."

He strode on faster, with this resolution, looking so very glum and terrible, that the nursemaids in his path caught up their tender little charges, and carried them out of his way, as though he were a baby-eating giant.

While thus he had been informing himself of Nelly's early history, the wily diplomatist with the glass eye was doing his best to be agreeable and attractive.

"I hope that man had not been long annoying you," said he. "There are some vulgar persons with whom one is by necessity compelled to associate. I know many such—worse luck!—who never know when their presence is most distasteful. They will force their nasty acquaintance upon one."

"My lord, you are quite mistaken," said Nelly, a little haughtily; "I did not know the person, and had never met him before."

"Hadn't you?" said the marquis, fixing her with his real eye, while the other looked in another direction.

"How very odd!"

"What is?"

"That he should have mistaken you for his daughter."

"Did you hear him say so?" asked Nelly, colouring a little.

"I just came up at the time."

"He was mistaken."

"Of course he was—I know that; but it is very singular that he should have made the mistake."

"I should prefer not to dwell longer upon the subject."

Thus rebuked, his lordship adroitly changed it to that general refuge for the embarrassed — the weather, from that to the company in which they found themselves, the toilets of the ladies in general, and Nelly's crape shawl in particular, on which he lavished a variety of pretty compliments.

"So few ladies can wear a shawl," he said insinuatingly. "It requires so much elegance —so much grace, to set it off. Fat, coarse women look horrible in them—*vide* Madame."

And he pointed, as he spoke, to a stout and splendidly dressed female, who came waddling down the path, followed by her footman, and to whom he raised his hat.

"The Bishop of Buttercup's lady," said he, in explanation, when the lady had passed. "Did you ever see anything so atrociously vulgar!"

"Poor thing," said Nelly, in high spirits. She liked a joke at the expense of a respectable married woman. "Poor, podgy thing, she can't help it, can she? Beside, who cares if Buttercup doesn't?"

And the observation set them both a laughing, and quite restored her good temper.

"You seldom go out alone," observed the marquis, after a pause.

"Never."

"I have so few opportunities of seeing you."

"You are always welcome at my house. You know my at home nights."

"I do not think that I am very welcome."

"How do you mean?"

"Drawler isn't very fond of me."

"Dear me! Why?"

"Because I'm fond of you."

"My lord!"

"Shall you be at Madame de la Goutiere's ball to-night? I hope to have the pleasure of meeting you and my lord."

The speaker had raised his voice while saying this, and, taking off his hat, bowed low to the lady he addressed.

She glanced at him in surprise.

Next moment Drawler was by her side.

"Ah! Drawler, how d'ye do?" said the marquis, with a smirk.

He must have noticed him coming. That one eye of his was as sharp as any other person's two.

"How do you do?" said Drawler, glumly. "Nelly, we'll turn back."

"Turn back?"

"Yes."

"So soon?"

"It's late enough. Good morning, Crutchingford."

"Good morning, my dear fellow. Shall I see you to-night at De la Goutiere's?"

"I don't know."

"I hope so. Try, and come."

"I shall see."

"Bring madame, whatever you do."

"She'll go with me, wherever I go."

"Good bye, then, madame. I have the honour——"

Bowing with exaggerated politeness, and smirking till his wicked old face was full of wrinkles, the marquis took his departure, tripping along in a youthful and finnikin fashion, more like seventeen than seventy.

"A charming creature," he thought to himself; "and has to put up with a good deal from that unamiable hound. I cannot say I'm sorry, either. She'll be all the easier conquest."

Thus thinking to himself, he wagged his

naughty old head, and shut up his one eye with a horrible wink, as he chuckled over his villany.

Poor old rake! What good for him to form plans and manufacture schemes? Even as he toddles along among the nursemaids and babies, a cold shiver strikes his frame, a strange dizziness comes over him, so that he is obliged to catch hold of a passer-by to save himself from falling.

With the stranger's assistance he is helped into a passing coach, and carried to his hotel, where the doctor is sent for.

He won't believe that he is ill yet, although the doctor says he is.

Although his speech is broken and indistinct, like it is when his teeth are out at night.

Although his head shakes about, something like a mandarin's.

Although his one eye is at times as fixed and unnatural in appearance as the glass one.

He's all right, he tells them—all right, curse them for staring fools—all right, curse them for babbling idiots—all right, curse them for grimacing apes!

Bring him some wine. He'll dress for dinner. Order the carriage. He was going to a ball—to meet a lady.

"Dobso-you-dog—a charminch creech——"

He would have said "a charming creature," and would have chuckled, only at this point his attack reached a climax. Paralysis had got him in its grip, and, drawing him up into an ugly shape, cocking his mouth on one side, and closing his living eye, left him to glare at his valet with the glass one, in so hideous a manner, that Mr. Dobson was frightened out of his wits, and bawled aloud for help.

CHAPTER THE FIFTH.

ANOTHER OF NELLY'S FIBS.

CARING very little what became of the delapidated old rake, Drawler stalked along by the side of his mistress, and, without saying a word, led the way to where their carriage was waiting for them outside the garden rails in the Rue de Rivoli.

"What has happened, George?" Nelly asked somewhat timidly, judging by my lord's black looks that something unpleasant had occurred; "what has happened to vex you?"

My lord was silent.

"You're not angry with me?" she said.

"I'll tell you presently," he replied.

She walked by his side a few yards without speaking, and by this time they had reached the carriage.

"Drive home," cried Drawler; and away they went.

"George," she said, "you surely are not jealous?"

"Jealous?"

"Jealous of that——that old marquis?"

"Crutchingford?"

"Yes. A stupid old fright—I hate him."

"You act as if you did."

"What are you driving at, George?"

Drawler made no reply, but leant forward with his hands upon his knees, and, looking Nelly straight in the face, said,—

"Did you ever tell a lie?"

"What do you mean?" cried the beauty, turning crimson with surprise and indignation; "how dare you?"

"Nonsense about daring," he replied. "I've just had a letter from Charley Bux. I'll read it to you."

"Very well."

She answered coolly enough, but there was a strange flutter in her heart.

"This is what he says," continued Drawler, reading:—"'We have all been wondering what the devil had become of you. We heard that you had gone to Paris for a few days, and that all letters would be forwarded; but what the deuce made you keep your address so snug?' Oh! that's nothing—it's further on:—'You've been away three months'—no, that's not it. Ah! here it is:—'You recollect that cad, Cheveleigh, who lived in that filthy place out of Holborn, and kept that light-haired woman who acted at the penny theatre——'"

"If you have no other reason for reading that, than to insult me," cried Nelly, in a fury, "perhaps you will spare yourself the trouble."

"I have a reason," said Drawler. "You'll see presently what I mean. Never mind the description, he's just as hard on me, presently."

"I do not wish to hear it."

"But I wish you."

"As you please."

Here she leant back with an air of profound indifference, and he proceeded.

"'Well, there had been great excitement about him in certain circles. You have, perhaps, read it all in the newspapers. He turns out to be illegitimate; and that starchy fool, his cousin, has come into the property. Only the fun of it is, that there is no property to come into. The old fellow, it would seem, sold every mortal thing he could lay his hands on, and was going to make a bolt of it, when he very properly had his throat cut, and the money taken away. The party who did the trick poisoned himself in jail; but what he did with the tin is more than anybody can tell.'"

"Well, my lord, what is all this to me?"

"Nothing yet; it's coming. 'In consequence of his not coming into this property, which was worth nothing, Mr. Cheveleigh, or whatever he calls himself—it is some French name, I think—has been unable to pay his debts; among other things, he has been unable to meet a bill, which I was fool enough to put my name to at his earnest entreaty.'"

Although feigning indifference, she sat and listened to him silently and attentively.

"'Well, you must know that the woman to whom I allude, cut and left him when she found that he wasn't worth a fig. I don't blame her myself. But before she went, she stuffed up every body, right and left, that she was married to this man Cheveleigh.' You stuffed me among others, you may remember," he said, turning towards her.

Nelly was indignantly silent, and he continued,—

"'A painter fellow, at the same theatre, tells me that this Maurice is still very bad about her, and vows vengeance upon the man who has taken her away. A poor fool, who ever he is, who ought to be rich to bear her extravagance. She always struck me as being a false, heartless jade, who would lead any man a deuce of a dance who was mad enough to fall in love with her. You were a little smitten on that quarter once, old fellow, yourself. You may thank your stars, you've had a deuced lucky escape.' What do you think of that?"

"Of what?"

"Of what I've been reading?"

"If you find any pleasure in insulting me, you being my keeper, and I your hired slave and mistress, I suppose there is no law against your doing so?"

"Well, what have you got to say to it?"

"Whatever I have to say, my lord," said she, with bitter contempt, "I shall not trouble myself to say."

"You fancy, perhaps, madame, that you can ride the high horse with me."

"My dear Drawler, you fancy, perhaps, that I am your fool of a wife, and that you can bully me like you do her; but you're mistaken."

"You're damnably mistaken," he roared out, "if you think you can defy me with impunity."

"You seem to me, Drawler, to be seeking an opportunity of picking a quarrel."

"I think I have reason."

"If you think so, there is only one course."

"And that?"

"Is for us to part."

"Let it be so, then."

"As soon as you please, my lord."

Then they were silent, each occupied by their own thoughts, probably neither of them of a very agreeable character.

Drawler spoke first, not being able to contain himself.

"I saw your father this morning."

"Indeed!"

"So learnt the value of another of your statements."

She made no reply, but tapping her fingers on the side of the carriage began to hum a tune.

This made his blood boil.

"Curse your smooth face," he exclaimed, fiercely, clenching his fist; "I'd like to spoil it."

She turned her eyes slowly upon him with a look of such withering contempt, that his lordly ruffianship quailed beneath it.

"You wretched bully and coward," she said, "as soon as ever you dared to lay a finger upon me, I'd scream for help to yonder policeman, and have you locked up like any other blackguard. Coachman!" she cried, "stop the carriage."

Without exchanging another word with him, she alighted, and walked slowly towards the hotel.

"As though," she muttered to herself, "as though there were none other than that brute who would keep me! Am I a fool to quarrel with such a munificent protector? I think not. Not while my lord marquis is to be had for the accepting.

When she reached her villa she sought her own room, and ordered luncheon to be sent to it, resolved not to quit the apartment until it should be time to go to the ball, and she also desired to be left alone.

In the afternoon her maid came up to say that my lord had ordered the carriage to be got ready, and his portmanteau to be packed?

"What is he going to do?"

The maid thought that he was going to England, by what Mr. Parsons said.

Nelly watched the loading of the carriage from the window.

"He surely will not go without speaking to me," she thought.

However, he did go. When he was gone, she rang the bell.

"Did his lordship leave any message?"

"None with me, madame. Perhaps he did with Mr. Parsons."

"Is Parsons left behind?"

"Yes, madame."

"Send him here, then."

Mr. Parsons presently appeared. A sleek, well-bred, deferential person, in a suit of spotless black.

"You asked for me, mam?"

"Where has his lordship gone?"

"To England, mam."

"Did he leave any message?"

"He said, mam, if I might make so bold, mam, to tell you, mam, that everything here should be paid for; and that, as soon as it was convenient, mam, we was to move your effects to wherever you should be pleased to point out——"

"That will do——leave the room."

"He said, mam, if I might make so bold, that I should tell you the lease was out in three days from now, and his lordship didn't intend to renew it."

"Has he left you means to pay what is owing?"

"He has, mam."

"I have occasion for fifty pounds, to pay my milliners' bills—give them me."

"Well, mam," said Mr. Parsons, with something almost akin to a wink, "them wasn't my orders."

"I order you."

"And most delighted I should be to take so pretty a lady's commands, mam, but I really can't."

"I shall speak to your master about your conduct, sir. Leave the room."

"Certainly, mam—though, no offence, I hope—you see, you not being any longer my missus, and taking orders only from my lord——"

"Leave the room—menial!"

"Well! as to menials," retorted Mr. Parsons, a little hurt, "let's call no names, or p'raps I may retaliate."

He had got thus far, and might have added more, but Nelly stepping forward with a threatening gesture, he fled precipitately.

When he was gone, she rang the bell for her maid.

" This cannot be endured," she said to herself, pacing the floor with angry steps ; " I cannot remain to be insulted by these wretched dependants. That man, I suppose, has told everybody who did not already know it, what was the nature of my connection with Drawler. Anything will be better than remaining here to be subjected to their coarse sneers. To-morrow I go, unless the marquis takes Drawler's place. To-night will decide all. I shall meet him at the ball, and must play my cards well."

" You rang for me, madame?"

It was the maid. She had come into the room.

" Yes."

" What did you please to want?"

Nelly turned towards her quickly. Yes, she also had a sort of impertinent smirk upon her face—so Mrs. Raymond fancied.

There was no time to be lost.

Like a good general, she pretended not to notice this sign of mutiny.

" Has anybody been here to-day?"

" Three gentlemen, who left their cards."

" Who were they?"

" Colonel Mac Donaldson."

" The others?"

" Lord Dollyvane and Lord Le-Nox."

" Has the Marquis of Crutchingford been?"

" No, mam. His valet was here a little while ago, and said he was ill."

" Ill ! What is the matter?"

" Something serious, I think."

" Did he not say what?"

" No madame."

" Send immediately, and ask how he is."

" Yes, madame."

The servant departed, and Nelly waited impatiently for her return.

She came at last.

" Well, how is he?"

" He is in bed, mam. Two doctors have been sent for."

" What is the matter witn him?"

" A stroke of paralysis."

" Dangerous?"

" He is not expected to recover. His wits are gone."

" Great God !"

She clasped her head in her hands. The servant thought that she was taken ill, and ran forward to assist her.

" Are you faint, madame?"

" No—no. Never mind. Give me a glass of water."

The servant handed it to her, and Nelly seemed to recover herself a little.

" Pack up my clothes," she said presently ; " and send to ask when the next train starts for Boulogne. I shall go to London to-night."

My lord was well upon his way already.

* * * * *

With hardly any pause, the train bore him along rapidly towards the sea-coast. Then the boat carried him across the Channel, and delivered him up again to the railway, which at last deposited him safely in town.

He had more reasons than one for leaving France.

First of all, he wished to break off his connection with Nelly, of whom he had, like a score of others before, grown tired.

In the next place, he had just received the intelligence — the letter had accompanied Charley Bux's pleasing epistle—that Lady Drawler was about to commence proceedings for a divorce. Now, my lord, although he had been spending an immense amount of money at Paris, was by no means in an enviable position —financially speaking—upon the strength of his being the heir to the Cumbersome Estates, and his near relationship to the rich Duke of Doodledum and the millionaire Marquis of Barebones, he had been lately existing upon certain advances from the Jews, which with some people appear to be always obtainable.

Just now there was a tightness in the Money Market, and supplies failing him, he felt far from anxious to support expensive law proceedings on account of his wife.

Ruminating on these disagreeable subjects, he journeyed homewards, and reaching London, drove straight to his chambers in Piccadilly.

There he ordered some dinner to be procured for him immediately, and, changing his travelling clothes for his dressing-gown and slippers, sat down with a bottle of claret to enjoy himself.

" I won't trouble myself about any cursed money business, or law business either," said he. " They don't go well with dinner."

He was right : such subjects interfere with one's digestion.

My lord was one of the most selfish of mortals, and thoroughly understood how to make himself comfortable.

And he meant to do so.

The curtains were drawn, and the lamp lighted, the dinner hot, and the claret cold— everything that could tend to his enjoyment.

" If you please, my lord," said the servant, as she moved away the meat, and brought the cheese and celery, " there's some one down stairs wants to see you."

" Who is it?"

" A gentleman, I think, my lord ; but he said he had no card."

" Didn't he give his name?"

" Cheveling, I think he said."

" Cheveleigh?"

" Yes, my lord."

" Good heavens !—what does he want? And which one is it? What sort of a man?"

" He wore a cloak, I couldn't see much of him, my lord."

" Go down and ask him what he wants."

" Curse me !" muttered Drawler, when the servant was gone, " he wants to fight, perhaps. I don't see why I should fight him, either, now I've given his woman up. He can have her back again if he likes. Confound him, he's a stiffish customer to deal with, too ; and after all, he's in the right. I don't half like it."

Just then the servant returned.

" He says he'll tell you his business himself, my lord. He looks as if he was in a great passion. Here he is, my lord, coming up-stairs."

BOB SAWDER'S MEDICINE.

CHAPTER THE SIXTH.

MAURICE HAS HIS HAIR CUT, AND BEGINS IN EARNEST.

HOW ever that Jack could have suggested such a mad scheme as that lecturing business, is more than I can imagine.

In most matters, I always took him for a man possessing a more than ordinary stock of common sense and intelligence. He was not at all the sort of fellow, I should have supposed, who would originate such a harumscarum expedition.

As for Maurice, of course, it was different.

No. 20

He was just the kind of person who would go heart and soul into any new idea that came uppermost. Only he soon tired of it, and wanted to be doing something fresh.

As for Mr. Ochre, he worked like a horse in endeavouring to ascertain what each article required for the expedition would cost them.

Only the fun of it was, that when the purchases came to be made, every article cost at least double the amount which had been put down in the estimate.

It was decided that it should be an entertainment something after the manner of WOODIN :—comic impersonations, songs, change of voice and character, and so on.

It is curious what a many geniuses there are amongst us, without our ever finding them out.

When some of Maurice's late acquaintance came to hear of it, they literally screamed with laughter.

"What an absurdity!"

"What cheek!"

"How much is it to be?"

"Free admission, I should hope."

"At the very least, and pay the audience's cab hire to the place."

If ever Jack or Maurice were rash enough to consult any great authorities upon the subject, they looked glum, and rubbed their chins in a depreciating manner.

"Entertainment, eh? Overdone, sir. A great deal too much of that sort of thing already. It ought to be good to pay."

"Well, but," cried Jack, warmly (he had most implicit faith in his friend's abilities), "it is to be good, you know."

"Oh!" said the authorities. "Is it? Then, perhaps, you won't lose so much money."

"That's a consolation anyhow," returned Mr. Ochre, trying to look cheerful.

"Yes," repeated the would-be lecturer, with a face like a fiddle, "that's a consolation anyhow."

As it was to be a character entertainment, of course they wanted dresses.

"Old clothes, cut up, will do," said Jack; "and pink glazed lining goes a long way."

"I haven't got any older clothes than those I am wearing," said Maurice, sadly.

"I have," cried Jack; "so we'll drop into them."

They dropped into them accordingly. Several of the impersonations were to be characters in low life. There were "Jack Rag," the crossing-sweeper; "Billy Nutts," the ballad vender and poet; and "Sally Skeggs," the maid-of-all-work: so that the dresses required for these were not of the choicest kind.

The "dropping in" alluded to consisted, for the most part, in making rents with a pair of scissors in old coats and trousers; then, with boots cut open at the toes, a shocking bad hat, and his nose ruddled, Mr. Maurice was quite in character.

When that deluded Jack first saw him so dressed, he leant back in his chair and roared aloud, so excellent he thought it; though, you know, the "get-up" was nothing wonderful, and far from ludicrous.

I really cannot think how Ochre should have been so mistaken in this instance, except that you usually find that these ponderous philosophers are the very first to make fools of themselves. He never thought much of the celebrated Mrs. Raymond. But then he was prejudiced against Nelly, and, when spoken to upon the subject, persisted in saying that he could not understand what the public saw in her, and that to him her acting was exceedingly objectionable.

Well, the next thing, now the dresses were ready—I should say, by the bye, that the entertainment had been written and learnt—was to have a rehearsal.

At the "Blue-spotted Spaniel," in the City Road, just close to Mr. Ochre's lodgings, they had a capital first-floor room, used for goose clubs, and glee clubs, and other social gatherings of that sort.

This, Jack said, was the very thing; and, as he was a personal friend of the landlord's, he got permission to use the room one evening, and invite about twenty or thirty persons to come and attend Mr. Maurice's *debut*, on the condition that a certain amount was to be spent in liquor.

This arranged, they set about finding an audience. When they came to run over the names of all the people they knew, they found so very few of them whom they would have liked to be present, that the list, as revised and corrected, contained only ten.

"Perhaps they can bring some friends," said Maurice. "I don't mind how many strangers are present. I am not ashamed to do it before strangers, but before a lot of fellow-acquaintances, you know, it's awful."

Invitations were therefore issued to the ten persons they decided on, with instructions to bring as many with them as they could.

As the night drew near, Maurice could not help feeling a little nervous, although Mr. Ochre assured him that it would be "all right."

He had not yet quite got over his illness, and, though he fancied himself as strong as ever, he was in reality very weak.

"Don't I look rather sickly?" He asked of Jack, at the same time regarding himself in the glass.

"A little thin, perhaps, and your hair wants cutting."

"To be sure. I had forgotten that. And I must be shaved."

"Shaved, eh? That's a pity."

"Well! it won't do to wear moustachios as Sally Skeggs, will it?"

"Of course not. I didn't think of that."

Maurice went to the barber's, and returned shortly—shaved, cut, and curled.

"Hallo!" cried Jack, jumping up from his teacup with a startled look upon his face, "who's that?"

"Who should it be?" said Maurice.

"Good heavens! what have you done to yourself?"

"What's the matter?"

"Look in the glass."

"He's taken a good deal off, hasn't he?" asked Maurice, doubtfully.

"Taken a good deal off, man? you look like a young sparrow."

He had, indeed, much the appearance of a youthful bird of that species before it is well fledged.

But the worst of it was, he looked so young.

"Hang me if you look more than sixteen at a little distance."

"Do you think that matters much?"

"Well, it won't do you any good. However, it can't be helped."

"Nor remedied?"

"Nor remedied, I suppose."

"Then it's no good saying any more about it," observed Maurice, a little out of temper.

When they had finished tea, during which Mr. Ochre could hardly refrain from again alluding to his friend's youthful appearance, Maurice began to dress himself.

His dress clothes had been taken out of

pledge for the purpose, and well brushed and warmed, to get rid of the creases.

Scarcely anybody looks his best in evening dress; and I suppose, except professionals and mechanics, nobody wears it out of choice. When Maurice put on his suit of black, Mr. Ochre looked at him very grimly——but he didn't laugh.

Maurice was about six and twenty, and as handsome a young fellow as you could well hope to meet with on a long summer's day; although, just at the present moment, he was a trifle pale and thin. But seen at the distance of about twelve feet, without his moustache, and his hair cropped and frizzed, and wearing a dress-coat, which might have been a little bit too short for him, he certainly did look as Mr. Ochre said, "a shaver."

Maurice feeling himself that he had acted foolishly, became indignant at his friend's remarks, as most of us do when called to account.

"What infernal foolery!" he cried. "Because you never had a suit of dress clothes, you fancy them so ugly. All entertainers wear dress when first coming on the stage, and again between the characters; and as for shaving, it would have been an absurdity if I had not done so. How could I have dressed for Skeggs?"

"I don't know that it wouldn't have been wiser to have left Skeggs out."

"Leave Skeggs out? Why you talk like a fool! It's the best part of the whole entertainment."

"Well, I don't agree with you."

I won't bother you with any more of the Skeggs' argument; but there was a great deal of it.

At nine o'clock the entertainment was to commence. Gentlemen were allowed to smoke, and liquors were served to the audience.

It was a very good idea this, of supporting their friends with something strong and warm. It put them in a good temper, and whatever sort of rubbish they were to sit out, they could sit it out without exhibiting their fatigue and weariness in too open a manner.

When everybody who seemed to be coming had assembled—they were in all about twenty—the lecture began.

Maurice appeared at the table with a decanter of cold water, a tumbler, and his libretto. In his hand he held his pocket handkerchief, which, as he stepped upon the platform, he wiped his mouth with, and coughed in after the approved fashion. Then he poured out a table-spoonful of water, and splashed another tablespoonful over his libretto, took a sip, and rattled the glass against his teeth in his agitation, put it down, leant forward in the sort of attitude a polite linen-draper's assistant assumes when he requests the pleasure of knowing what may be the next article. "Ladies and gentlemen," said he, at which there was some applause.

He was a nice-looking young fellow, although he had had his hair cut, and the ladies present took a fancy to him; though, of course, the men knowing he was an amateur, were rather prejudiced at the commencement.

He was a ready-witted young fellow, too, and had some talent in the histrionic line. You may, perhaps, recollect how he was applauded at the private theatre where Miss Nelly made her *debut*.

The little welcome he had received gave him courage, and, with a few words, he put himself upon a comfortable footing with his audience.

He began by telling them that he felt very nervous, and asked them how they would feel under like circumstances, reqested that they would strain a point and laugh if they could, assured them that though he was only an amateur, and did not for a moment expect to be thought otherwise, he would do his utmost to pass away an hour pleasantly, and at the conclusion of the evening, should take it as a great favour if any one would offer him any suggestions for improving his lecture, or point out what might be dispensed with.

It was not very funny or very flat, sometimes there was a joke which made the people laugh; some of his songs he sang well, and others badly. The audience were not such ungrateful wretches as to sit and swill at the lecturer's expense without applauding him.

There was a good deal of applause, and a good deal of swilling. The bill for drink was rather heavy, and some persons must have sadly abused his hospitality.

He was not very rapid as yet in changing his dress, and some tittering occurred at his wig falling off in the middle of a fine speech without his noticing it.

At another time great confusion was created by a drunken ruffian, attracted by the music, coming up-stairs from the tap-room, poking his head in at the door, and, at an unexpected juncture, requesting to be informed who had swallowed the bootjack. A piece of coarse buffoonery which, although it discomposed the entertainer, caused considerable merriment among the audience.

Anyhow, the rehearsal passed over, on the whole, very satisfactorily, and Jack was much delighted.

Of course, at the termination the suggestions showered in wholesale. As almost everybody differed with everybody else, it was rather difficult to tell which opinion to adopt; but as most of the audience seemed to think it a little too long—I believe that is the fault of all amateur productions—it was considered advisable to curtail it considerably.

"I shall be more up in it next time," said Maurice, who was not in great spirits, for, from what he could judge from his audience, though his entertainment might have been a great deal worse, it might still have been a great deal better.

Heigho! it was the old story. Ambitious youths, must you always aspire to gain the topmost rounds of the steep ladder of Fame? Why not content yourselves with some step a little lower down?

It is not meet that we should all be cocks of the walk. Some of us must play the second fiddle. Because Mr. ALFRED TENNYSON can command a guinea a line, shall we other small fry turn up our noses at three-halfpence?

Ever so many three-halfpences in a lump will make a pound. So rattle them off, brother scribblers, the dirty coppers are not to be despised.

"God grant I may succeed!" was Maurice's prayer. "What else is left for me?"

Finding him dull and out of sorts, Jack bade him take some brandy-and-water, and drank success to him in a steaming bumper.

He was a careless dog, that Maurice; and it was his custom, like it is the custom of other careless dogs, to drown his sorrows in the bowl.

The worst of this is, that, like other ugly things that we drown to get rid of, after a while they rise again to the surface, looking uglier than ever.

"We start on our grand expedition the day after to-morrow," said Jack, as they retired to bed that night. "To-morrow I shall have finished all the work I have to do."

"All right, old fellow, and I hope it will answer."

"Answer—of course it will."

"Hurray! Lecturing for ever!"

And they both sat up in bed and cheered.

CHAPTER THE SEVENTH.

SAVOURS OF THE "P. R."

NEXT afternoon Maurice took the omnibus to the Strand, intending to call at the perruquier's, near Drury Lane Theatre, and have one of his wigs changed.

The man was out, and so he sauntered about to pass the time away.

As he stood waiting at a street corner, in an idle, hang-dog, loafing fashion (how soon men get into that sort of listless, sauntering gait when they have turned the fatal corner, and commenced the downward course!)—as he was waiting there, Mr. Parchingby, the chief clerk of the Bad Bargains, passed by, and looked him up and down contemptuously.

Poor Maurice was rather shabby; he was sucking an orange too, and looked, on the whole, very disreputable.

"Thought he'd come to that," muttered Parchingby to himself. "Wonder what he's about now? Picking pockets, perhaps."

This charitable idea he circulated in the office, and the gentlemen there were not surprised to hear it. Some of them had thought all along that that would be the end of him.

"Confound him!" exclaimed Maurice savagely, thrusting his orange, half-eaten, into his pocket. "I wish he had not seen me."

It put him out a good deal. He began to brush the dust off his coat, and fastened up his waistcoat, which had three buttons undone. He had half a mind to have his boots cleaned.

Is it not so with all of us? When the Arabian has been stolen, we immediately begin to think about having the door coated with plate iron.

Was Maurice going to the bad?

He walked along biting his lips in a moody way, savage and thoughtful.

As he was thus walking and thinking, his eye fell upon a ragged poster, partly torn down from some hoarding where it had been stuck, and flying mournfully in the wind.

It had announced Nelly's benefit. Most of it was torn down, but the name still remained intact.

He stood and looked at it sadly enough. Oh! Nelly, Nelly! You had done it all, and then to desert him in this way. How could you have the heart to do it? Is there really no such thing as gratitude to be found in the world? According to everybody's account, I really do not think there is.

The tears welled up in his eyes as he recalled those dear old times now passed and gone. The recollections of his former happiness came upon him so forcibly, he staggered as it were beneath the shock. Why—why—had he ever known her to love her so? Why had he ever loved her so for her to leave him thus?

Foolish young man! You and I who know the whole history, and who are acquainted with her character, wonder how he can be so mad. To the last he clung to the wild notion of her loving him. She had been artfully seduced, he tried to persuade himself. It was that scoundrel Drawler whose devilish tricks had robbed him of her.

He had just such a thought in his head, and, with set teeth, was brooding over his wrongs, when Lord Drawler passed in a hansom cab.

For a moment he doubted his eyes and senses. He had understood from inquiries that his lordship was going to remain away from England for two or three years. Once or twice during his illness, towards the latter part, he had sent messages to the rooms in Piccadilly to ask when he was expected to return.

What had brought him back, and alone? On the top of the cab there was a portmanteau, and by the side of him upon the seat, a large carpet-bag.

All this Maurice saw at a glance in a moment. In a moment he had formed a resolution.

His first idea was to call a cab, and follow the enemy. He looked round—none was near. There was, however, no time to deliberate. He must follow—on foot, if necessary.

The hansom was going at a rapid pace; it had already got some distance ahead. Maurice ran forward, somebody got in his way, he dodged and stumbled, picked himself up, and ran on again. A cab crossing the road, delayed him, somebody else got in his way, he ran full butt against a man carrying baskets on his head from Covent Garden Market, and sent them flying.

Without waiting to apologise—perhaps an apology to such a person would have been a little out of place—he rushed on, making frantic efforts to overtake the vehicle which contained my lord.

He was too late. Detained by one obstacle and another, and still another, by the time that he had got into open ground the cab was nowhere to be seen.

"I have lost him again," said Maurice, to

himself, "unless he has just returned from abroad, and still lives at his old rooms. In that case, I may find him there."

With this idea he again thought of taking a a cab; but, now being a little cooler, he thought he would be in time enough were he to go about the wig, and, after settling his business, walk quietly to Piccadilly.

He did so.

"Has his lordship returned to town?"

"Just returned."

"Is he at home?"

"He is engaged."

"Particularly engaged?"

"Yes. He is at dinner."

"I have got no card. Take up my name to him. Cheveleigh."

"Yes," replied the servant, doubtful whether or not to call the visitor sir.

Left to kick his heels by himself for ten minutes or so, Maurice grew very impatient.

At the end of that time the servant returned, and said,—

"His lordship wishes to know what your business is."

"My business is with him."

"I don't think he'll like to be disturbed, young man. If you'd take my advice, you'll come another time."

"I must see him now."

"I tell you he's having his dinner."

"Go back, and say that I will explain my business myself."

The servant again departed with the message, and Maurice followed quickly up-stairs. Before it had been well delivered, his foot was on the threshold of the room.

"What is the meaning of this intrusion?" cried Drawler, in a passion, though, at the same time, he spoke a little nervously, it seemed.

"I won't disturb you, my lord. I can wait until you have finished."

"It would have been more polite had you done so down stairs."

"There are times when it is difficult to study politeness."

"I suppose that often happens to you?"

Maurice took no notice of this remark.

After a minute or two he said,—

"Will you ask your servant to leave the room?"

"Give me some more wine, and then leave us."

The wine was brought, and the attendant retired. Maurice and Drawler were alone together.

For a time neither spoke. Perhaps they were the least bit in the world afraid of each other, though neither were cowards.

His worst enemy gave Maurice credit for courage. Although my lord could act like a ruffianly bully when a woman was in the case, he was brave enough at other times. In the trenches before Sebastopol, before the deadly Russian shot, he had shown himself a hero.

It is a great mistake to fancy that brave men cannot be bullies, and bullies brave men. One of the fond delusions of the dear old story-tellers,—nothing more, gentle reader of mine, believe me.

What made them feel a little timid, perhaps, was the awkwardness of the situation. These two men had been friends. The last time they had met was at the supper party in the chambers, when one had been host, and the other guest. The meeting of a friend one has found out to be a villain is almost as disagreeable to the injured party as to the injurer—perhaps more so.

"To what am I indebted for the honour of this visit?" asked Drawler presently, sipping his wine, and affecting a coolness he in reality was far from feeling.

"Ask yourself," replied Maurice. "You could hardly think it possible that I should not call upon you for some sort of explanation."

"For what?"

"You know well enough," said Maurice, raising his voice.

"If I knew, I should not ask."

"For the seduction of my mistress, then?"

"The what?"

"You heard what I said."

"You're talking nonsense."

"You want to trifle with me."

"On the contrary, I want to have nothing more to do with you than necessary."

"You shall have very little after this interview——it shall be our last."

"I'm glad to hear it. Though, I must repeat, you're talking nonsense."

For a moment Maurice hesitated. Had he all along been deceived? Was it not with Drawler that Nelly had gone away?

"If I have been misinformed," he said, "I beg your pardon. But the servant at my lodgings told me that it was with you she went away."

"The servant told you true."

"Then what the devil——"

"Stop a moment——I am willing to afford you every reparation in my power. Don't be afraid that I want to shirk out of the question. You spoke of a seduction, and I say you spoke nonsense."

"Why?"

"The seduction was a great deal more on her side than mine, that's all I have got to say. I have no particular reason for trying to appear any more virtuous than I am, only I should like it understood that if there was any seduction in the case, I was the person seduced."

"You lie! you scoundrel, you lie!" roared Maurice furiously.

And, as he spoke, he made a movement as though he would have struck the other in the face, but Drawler warded the blow.

"I will have satisfaction," continued Maurice, in a violent passion. "We must fight—— how and where you choose."

"You mean a duel, by satisfaction, I suppose," replied Drawler. "I hardly see how I can oblige you. I can only fight with my equals."

"You'll fight with me, however much I am beneath you."

"You think so?"

"I do; unless you are as great a coward as you are a scoundrel."

"Curse you, you'll find me ready when you choose!"

"Now, then."

"You talk like a fool. I have no arms."

"Have you no pistols?"

"I haven't got them here. Besides, it would be madness. We should have all the neighbourhood about us."

"Have you no swords?"

"I've only one," Drawler replied, with a slight smile.

"Infernal cad!" he said, to himself. "It is a wonder he does not propose the fireirons."

Is the reader tittering, too? Rather ridiculous this sort of thing, is it not? When you and I get into a passion, we never lose our heads, and make fools of ourselves, do we?

There were, upon reflection, really no deadly weapons to be had upon the premises, though both were desirous of settling the matter at once.

Drawler, I tell you, was as courageous as a lion, and had the other proposed to exchange shots across the table, would have agreed to it as readily as though Maurice had only offered him a cigar.

Added to that he had no wish to make this quarrel more public than was absolutely necessary.

He had, you know, a most thorough contempt for Maurice and all his belongings, and did not feel inclined to get mixed up in what he considered to be altogether a snobbish set out.

"How do you propose to fight," asked he, presently, "Mr.——What's-your-name?"

Maurice's colour came and went at this fresh insult. He was boiling over with fury, and was quite unable to contain himself.

"If we can fight no other way," he shouted, "we will do so with our fists!"

"With our fists? You're drunk!"

"Are you afraid?" the other asked, still at the top of his voice. "You are stronger than I am. I have only just left a sick bed. The advantages are clearly on your side. Are you afraid, I say?"

"No, damn you! I'm not. Help to push away the table. There's, luckily, no one underneath; and so, if you're bent on it, you shall have your way. But I tell you—by God, you'll have a thrashing!"

"If you were a dozen Samsons, I shouldn't care."

"You look like fighting a dozen Samsons!"

"Never mind how I look. You'll see how I act. Are you ready?"

"In a moment or two. Take something to drink; and don't bawl quite so loud."

"I don't want anything."

"Very well."

Drawler moved the lights on to the mantelpiece, and then stripped off his coat and waistcoat, tyeing his neckerchief round his waist in the true P. R. style. Many nights of practice with ALEC KEENE, BEN CAUNT, and NAT LANGHAM, had made his lordship tolerably expert in the use of his "fives."

He was strongly built, and muscular. Late hours, and the practice of all the fashionable vices, had made but small inroads upon his constitution. For a "light-weight" he would have done some execution; and, had he gone into training, walked his four miles before breakfast, and eaten the proper allowance of raw beef steak, I fancy he would have made a rather formidable antagonist.

When in robust health, Maurice would have been a very fair match for him, for he too was young, active, and strong. They were also very much the same in height and build.

But Maurice's long illness had pulled him down, and now, as he stood facing his foe, the difference was very marked.

Drawler, as I have said, had partially stripped for the encounter, the removal of his coat enabling him to have a much freer use of his arms, and to be much more rapid in his movements. He was, besides, cooler than Maurice, and, seeing the weak state of his companion, more confident of success.

Maurice, perhaps, was a little calmer than he had been at the commencement, and eyed his lordship steadily and firmly, but he made no preparation, except to throw down his hat and cape.

The scene was a novel one: rather curious, and a trifle ludicrous.

It was a singular way for two gentlemen to settle their differences; but, if we must believe the advocates of "muscular Christianity," it is the sort of way we should avenge ourselves upon those who have wronged us.

To tell the truth, I feel rather ashamed of two of my heroes thus misconducting themselves. Had not the "noble art" come a little more in fashion lately, I should have been inclined to leave this incident out of the story, or at most only allude to it very distantly.

However, here it is, gentlemen. It's manly, at any rate. Is it not?

Drawler chose his place without any question. He stood with his back to the light, and Maurice faced him.

By selecting this position the former had a great advantage, as, his face being in the shade, the latter could not easily tell by his eyes when he was about to strike.

They now commenced operations. The first few minutes were occupied by a series of feints and dodges on either side, without a blow being struck. Wearied of this presently, and depending altogether upon a sudden assault to carry the day, for he knew he was so weak that he dreaded the effects of a blow, Maurice, without any warning, rushed upon the other, and, breaking down his guard, dealt him so violent a blow in his face, that his lordship staggered back, and the blood spirted from his mouth.

But before he could follow up this feeler with another of the same sort, Drawler had righted himself, and came in upon Maurice's left eye with such effect that in an instant his daylight was darkened.

Then, in a wild fury, and utterly regardless of all science, they exchanged a dozen furious blows, each one telling, more or less, upon their bleeding and disfigured faces; and then, one more unlucky and more violent stroke than the rest knocked Maurice off his legs, and, striking his head violently against the corner of a cheffonier, he lay like dead, welterng in his blood, upon the rich Turkey carpet.

Scarcely had he fallen, and while Drawler was still hanging over him with his hand upraised, doubtful whether or not another blow was necessary to insure his victory, the door was burst open with a crash, and the landlord, and landlady, and servants stood staring in, with white and frightened faces.

"Murder!" screamed the women, in a breath.

"Hold your tongues!" growled his lordship, holding a napkin over his mouth to stop the blood, which was running down his chin.

"Oh! my lord, has he killed you?"

"Not quite."

"Shall we send for a policeman?"

"No: send for a doctor."

"A doctor?"

"Yes, as quickly as you can. He's badly hurt, I'm afraid."

A doctor came in a few minutes. Maurice was laid upon the sofa, and his face and head bathed and bandaged.

"When he recovers," said Drawler, who had managed, in the same way, to improve his appearance, although he, too, was a rueful object, "send him home in a cab. I am going out."

"Will he get over it soon?" he asked, presently, of the doctor.

"It is not serious, my lord, although he has been severely punished."

"The devil take him," muttered Drawler between his teeth; "if they hadn't come in, I'd have finished him. Well, perhaps it's as well I didn't. What could I have said, unless that he had come to rob me? Perhaps it was all for the best."

His lordship put on his coat and hat, and went out, determined to stop away until the other had recovered and departed.

"I wonder whether he will consider that he has had enough," thought Drawler; "or, shall I have to fight him again. Curse him and his woman too! I wish I had never seen either of them."

Maurice was not long before he came to his senses, and then he took his departure in a cab, as Drawler had arranged.

He did not start for the country next day. It was agreed that he should wait a little while until his face lost some of its bruises.

It would not have done to have lectured with a pair of black eyes.

CHAPTER THE EIGHTH.

IN WHICH NELLY'S BOAT PUTS TO SEA IN A STORM.

THE wind blew great guns; the sea rolled mountains high; the fishing smacks in the Calais harbour nestled closely together under the shelter of the pier, and out of harm's way.

The blue-shirted fishermen staggered about before the blast, and rounded the corners with desperate struggles. The short-skirted fisherwomen scudded like birds along the ill-paved streets.

Landsmen clutched tightly at the brims of their hats, and cursed the wind in every imaginable variation of *sacre*.

Those who had a shelter to go to, went, and those who had friends and relations at sea, looked out into the stormy night with swelling hearts, and offered up to heaven fervent prayers for their safe-keeping.

"When does the mail start?" a handsome lady, in a rich travelling cloak, asked of one of the numerous commissionaires touting for a job.

"Paquebot for Dover, madame?"

"Yes."

"It is close at hand."

"Will you see to my luggage?"

"The Paquebot will not start for some time."

"Why not?"

"It is a weather—frightful!"

Here the little man expressed pantomime of horror.

"How long shall we be delayed?"

An hour or two—perhaps more, he could not say; but he could recommend an hotel. Supper ready in less than a moment. Everything of the first quality. Very comfortable.

No; she would go on board at once.

Certainly. Be assured he would take great care of the luggage.

"Be quick, then."

"Be quick, then," he repeated, and ran about shouting to other persons, who were not naturally so quick to be a little quicker.

"What nonsense about rough weather," the beautiful lady exclaimed, impatiently. "I would much rather start at once."

"Rough weather! Who talks of rough weather?" a gentleman close behind her repeated irritably. "Here, you others! what is this story? Can't put to sea in rough weather? Do you mean to say that the mail is to be delayed for two or three hours on account of the timidity of a parcel of chicken-hearted cowards like you are? I am the bearer of despatches of the utmost importance, and must go at once."

"Certainly, monsieur should do as he pleased."

"What did the captain say?"

The captain said, these thirty years or more he'd seen all sorts of weather, and wasn't frightened easy. It was an ugly night according to his reckoning, and, if he went, he expected to have a rough passage; but, if any one wanted to go, it shouldn't be said that he held back.

Monsieur, who was the bearer of despatches, wanted to go.

Who else?

Madame.

The captain would not advise her. There certainly was danger.

Madame liked danger, and was not afraid of a capfull of wind.

"That's hearty!" the captain cried; "and we'll put out, however hard it blows. Who else goes with us?"

There were a good many who would have liked to have gone, but did not like the weather.

Those who are acquainted with the admirable qualities of CHURCHWARD's mail packets, would perhaps have less fear of encountering a storm in one of them than in any other vessel; though few persons, I imagine, like to brave a storm under even the most favourable circumstances.

The mention of Mr. CHURCHWARD's name reminds me that few persons have conferred such substantial benefit on the public as that gentleman has in his particular department, and few persons have been more hardly used by the Government.

After the usual amount of bawling and swearing, banging of boxes, and clanking of chains, the packet quitted the shore, and, with a roll and a lurch, started upon its perilous journey.

The night was pitch dark and bitterly cold, and the two solitary travellers, as they looked back at the fast receding lights of the town, and out again upon the dreary waste of water, felt, in spite of their recent show of bravery, as though they were leaving all hope behind them.

Inclined as I am to look favourably upon our lively neighbours, and to refute with indignation the many calumnies which it is the custom of the bigoted Briton, with smug, self-complacent ignorance, to heap upon them, I really cannot attempt to defend them as sailors. The hopeless, helpless, overwhelming state of "double-up" to which I have seen Mounseer reduced in those two short hours between the French and English shores, when, wrapped up in a wonderfully-fashioned cloak, with a hood like an extinguisher, he hangs—a shapeless mass—over the side of the vessel, limp and wretched, regardless of the spray which splashes him, and the other passengers who sneer at him,—he is truly a pitiable sight.

Though, mind you, I have seen some English passengers as bad, or worse. Indeed, it is all very well for you sea-faring fellows to bounce us about pleasure of a life on the ocean wave. I, for one, see nothing in it to admire. In poetry it is very well; and I believe there was once a poet who wrote enthusiastically about the beauties of the boundless sea, and died himself of sea sickness off the Nore.

To tell the candid truth, there is nobody who troubles the steward more than I do; but that's between ourselves.

The gentleman, with the important despatches, who was in such a hurry to depart seemed to have very little idea of sea sickness.

He laughed contemptuously at the steward's remark, that he hoped Monsieur was a good sailor.

He flung the end of his cloak over his shoulder, bandit fashion, lit a cigar, and paced the deck, keeping his legs in a way that was wonderful for a landsman.

The lady who had also defied the elements remained upon the deck.

She stood in the forepart of the boat, steadying herself with her hand upon the side, and looking straight out to sea. Monsieur who for a long while had been watching her observed, approached her deferentially.

He was a very polite gentleman, and had a well bred and courteous address, which showed that he had been used to good society.

Monsieur raised his hat, and apologised for the liberty he was taking; but Madame's dress was being spoilt, by the sea water. If Madame preferred to remain upon deck, if he might venture to cover her with his cloak.

Madame thanked him distantly, and declined the offer. She would go below.

The boat was rolling and tossing tremendously, and attempting to walk to the companion-ladder, she almost fell. Monsieur rushed forward, and assisted her, she being constrained, under the circumstances, to avail herself of his support.

"I think I have had the honour of an introduction to Madame," the Frenchman pursued. "I think that it was,—though doubtless, Madame has forgotten the circumstance, surrounded as Madame must be by countless admirers,—at the Grand Opera."

"Probably," Madame replied. "I have forgotten."

Of course she had forgotten, though he had not. No, that would be an impossibility. Madame could not be seen and forgotten. He begged humbly to re-introduce himself to Madame. He was the Baron De Vigny.

The lady was more gracious at the mention of the polite gentleman's title. She even took the trouble to regard him more attentively. He was a handsome, well-dressed fellow, with a peaked beard, and a moustache nicely trimmed and pointed.

It had slipped her memory. She said now she came to think of it, she certainly recollected Lord Drawler had introduced her one evening at the Opera.

"They were playing the 'Huguenots,' I think."

Madame was right. They were.

The circumstance is odd when you take it in connection with others, though by itself it was nothing. The "Huguenots" had not been played that season at any theatre in Paris.

The other curious circumstances to which I would allude were these:—

Monsieur had for luggage only a small carpet bag, and this had a name upon it which was not De Vigny.

Monsieur had taken a great interest in the luggage belonging to Madame, and had read through the labels fastened thereto, previous to his claiming acquaintance with her.

Well, perhaps there was nothing very curious in any of these circumstances. We English are so suspicious of any one who is civil to us.

At any rate he was polite and respectful; and as Mrs. Raymond—for that, as you may suppose, was the name of the fair traveller—had nobody else to talk to, and nothing else to amuse herself with, she deemed it wise to cultivate his acquaintance. And Monsieur turned out to be a most agreeable companion.

The boat rolled and pitched; but, as neither of the travellers were sea-sick, it did not much matter. Nelly chose the easiest seat in the saloon; and, throwing on one side her shawl and bonnet, listened to the baron's amusing small-talk with a deal of interest, and thanked her stars that she had fallen in with him.

ONE NIGHT IN THE HAYMARKET.

CHAPTER THE NINTH.

A HORRIBLE PREDICAMENT.

ACCORDING to the baron's account, he was tolerably rich, though still not so rich as he had been. A passion for high play had helped him to get rid of the vast wealth his poor father (here he looked up at the cabin skylight) had left him.

With what remained to him, he continued, shrugging his shoulders. he managed to exist —nothing more.

What was existence? A suite of apartments in the Chussee d'Antin, a dinner at the Trois Freres, a stall at the Opera, a horse,

a servant, a mistress or two, and other little trifles. Expensive luxuries to persons of limited income—say, five or six hundred a-year, for instance.

As Nelly listened she thought to herself, " He's young and not bad-looking. He is rich and well-bred. I should be a baroness."

Oh! the ambition of some scheming women ! How desperately that yellow-haired syren plotted and conspired against the softer sex.

A rich marriage was the object of her life. Once admitted into respectable society, once equal with those wretched women who called themselves respectable, and prided themselves upon the possession of a virtue it had never been to their advantage to part with, then— then she would be happy.

What did Monsieur think about her, I wonder? Had he any matrimonial intentions? If my lord had introduced him, as he said, doubtless he had learnt some particulars of Nelly's position in his lordship's household. According to his own account of himself he led a gay life, and was not over strict in his morals. I should have fancied, from his conversation, that he was not a marrying man.

Whatever his ultimate intentions might have been, his immediate intention seemed to be that of making himself agreeable.

And this he did with a great deal of art; so gradually and cautiously, that Nelly was astounded to find how intimate they were when she arrived, in course of time, all safe and sound at Dover.

"Shall I clear your luggage at the Custom House?" he asked.

"If you please."

She waited at the hotel for him, and, after they had partaken of some tea together, started by the next train for Town.

Arrived there safely at an early hour of the morning, the baron proposed that they should go to an hotel near the London Bridge Station. She had told him that she was travelling to the north of England, but intended to spend a few days in Town.

"I am the bearer of important despatches for the French Ambassador, as I told you, which I must deliver to-day. I shall remain in Town some days, and any service that I can be to you, Madame, I pray you command me."

"You will be at the same hotel, I suppose?"

"If Madame will allow me, I will share her dining-room."

They drove together to the hotel, and the baron saw to everything. At Nelly's request a sumptuous breakfast was ordered, which, after so many hours' fasting,—for they had hardly tasted anything upon the road,—they were both very thankful for.

She was very sleepy, in spite of the unwearied efforts of her lively companion to amuse her, and intended, after the meal, to lie down for an hour or two in her bedchamber, which adjoined the room where they were sitting.

"A glass of wine, Madame," cried the baron gaily, filling her glass with champagne.

She bowed to him, and drank it off.

"A nasty taste," she said it had.

"A nasty taste!" he echoed, astonished. "Was the glass clean? There, let me give you another."

Perhaps champagne, taken so early in the morning, makes one sleepy. Perhaps it was the long journey—the eventful day preceding it? She could scarcely keep her eyes open.

The baron had risen from his seat. What was he doing—not going to ring the bell surely for more wine? What would the people of the hotel think? How long had they been at breakfast?

She had closed her eyes a moment. Had she closed them for an hour? There was a singing in her head, and a humming in her ears. What was the matter—was she tipsy?

"Madame is ill?"

"No—nothing is the matter," she answered, with a laugh. "The fatigue of the journey——I was a little sleep——"

"Allow me to fill your glass?"

"No—no, thank you."

"The least drop?"

"It must be the least drop in the world."

She drank the wine, or part of it, for he had filled the glass.

It seemed to refresh her for a moment, although, even now, she felt half asleep. How rude she must seem, she thought; and how stupid it was of her. She turned her head towards the baron, who was talking to her earnestly, and in a low tone, though she had not the remotest notion what it was all about.

What on earth was he saying? Making love, perhaps? The idea of making love, when everybody was dying to go to sleep.

"Lovely angel, I adore you."

Who said that? Did the baron? or the captain of the steamboat? or the railway guard? or had she heard it yesterday? or had she dreamt it?

What was this singing in her head? Her senses were going; the room was twisting round; the glasses on the table appeared to be dancing. How could she have been so foolish as to drink that wine?

"I'll go to my room. I don't feel well."

"Not yet."

"What do you mean? Let me go to bed? Oh! my head—Oh! my head!"

What made him hold her back in her seat? How dare he do so? Who was it did so? Could that be the polite and smiling baron, whose face looked so ugly and threatening close to hers, who spoke so savagely, and griped her arms with fingers of iron?

Or was she dreaming? for now she was asleep in earnest.

.   .   .   .   .

When Nelly recovered her senses, awoke from her sleep, or trance, or fainting fit, whatever it might have been, a girl was rubbing her hands, while another, leaning over her chair, was bathing her temples with vinegar.

"Where am I?" she asked faintly.

"You are quite safe, mam. Do not be afraid."

"How long have I been asleep? Where is my watch?"

"Your watch, mam? You haven't one on."

"What have you done with it?"

"Me, mam? I'm sure I know nothing about it!"

Nelly felt round her neck, and at her waist, then put her hand down to her pocket.

"I have been robbed!" she screamed, springing upright in her chair. "My pocket is torn out."

It had been ripped open, as though in haste.

"Where—where is he?"

"Who?"

"That man who was here?"

"Was he not your husband?"

"Husband—no. What do you mean?"

"Well, I'm sure that's what he called himself. We took you for respectable married people."

"How dare you be impertinent! Please to keep your comments to yourself. Answer me. Where is he?"

"He has gone."

"Where?"

"He went away in a cab."

"When?"

"More than two hours ago."

"Two hours!"

"He said we were not to disturb you on any account. You had lain down, and our coming in to clear away might waken you."

"Did he say anything else? Was he coming back?"

"He said he had to take a box to a friend's house, and then he would return."

"A box! What box?"

"One you brought with you. A black one."

"Good heavens! he has taken my dresses and jewels."

She rushed into the adjoining apartment. All the boxes were open, and the contents strewn about.

She searched wildly among them. Little else but her under-clothing remained. All her bracelets, necklaces, ear-rings, coronets, armlets, pendants, brooches, lockets, chains, and rings had vanished.

So had her Genoa velvet dress, her moire-antique, and her organdie muslin. So had yards upon yards of splendid lace, Venetian-point, Bruxelles, Valenciennes, and Honiton.

Everything had been stolen. The rings sucked off her fingers, the diamond ear-rings taken from her ears, her pockets emptied, the solitaires dragged from collar and wristbands.

How had it all happened? How was it? How had she gone to sleep?

Had she been drugged?

Her head ached fearfully, and there was in her mouth the bitter taste peculiar to most opiates. She took up the champagne glasses from the table one after another. In one of them there were the dregs of some dark-coloured fluid. It had been so, then.

The people of the house were talking on the stairs, and the servants peeping in at the door.

The landlord came running in, in a great bustle.

"Wha—at's the matter? Robbery? What robbery? Anybody been robbed? *In my house?* Impossible!"

Nelly explained the circumstances, and how she had become acquainted with the *soi-disant* baron upon the road.

"But," said the landlord, "the foreigner took the apartments as your husband."

"My husband!" cried Nelly, astonished. "He did so altogether without my authority."

Indeed, the polite gentleman had taken all the responsibility of ordering the rooms, and giving directions about the breakfast on his own hands, as he spoke English tolerably well, and Mrs. Nelly, as was her custom when there was any work to be done, had left somebody else to do it, and taken no notice whatever of what was going on around her.

"Well," said the landlord, when he had heard all that she had to say, "it is a very strange case altogether. I am not in the habit of receiving ladies and gentlemen travelling together without being man and wife. Who am I to look to for the payment of my bill?"

"I have no money. I have been robbed."

"Perhaps you had better communicate with your friends."

"My friends are abroad."

"Well, I shall send for a policeman."

"Do as you please, sir. In the meantime, oblige me by clearing the room of your servants."

She spoke calmly and with dignity. Mine host—a fat, fussy little man—was rather awed by her behaviour, and retired with his retinue, abashed.

"She's a lady, I should say," thought he; "but begad I'll keep an eye on her. A breakfast bill of forty shillings! It's lucky this didn't happen after dinner, if the payment's doubtful, and it looks like it."

The policeman came, and heard the story. Then went in and looked at the room.

"What shall I do?" asked the landlord; "Give her in charge?"

"If you like," said the policeman; "though there's no particular evidence against her that I can see."

"I shall give her in charge anyhow, unless she pays the bill."

"But she hasn't any money."

"Let her leave her clothes, then."

"Perhaps she won't."

"Can't I oblige her?"

The policeman considered awhile.

"I don't think it's quite legal."

"Perhaps you'd better speak to her."

"Very well."

Though Nelly was outwardly composed and tranquil, she was in reality in a state of great trepidation. Placed in a position which had never before occurred to her, and, since she had made acquaintance with Maurice, having been accustomed to have somebody to advise her, and relieve her from all responsibility and trouble of all kinds, she scarcely could comprehend the extent of the calamity which had befallen her.

Her first thought was of the loss of her jewels, dresses, and money; but it was the former which annoyed her the most. She had had in her purse about twelve pounds; but when this had been exhausted, she calculated, should she find occasion to do so, that she could dispose of her jewels and dresses for at least ten times that amount.

Perhaps the notion was fallacious; but, judging from the appearance of the gems, and knowing what most of them had cost, she fully expected that they would realise more than a hundred pounds.

Next to the thought of her loss, came the thought of the pleasant position in which she was placed by her injudicious conduct. How absurd her late dream seemed to her? How could she have been deceived by the glib speeches and flashy style of this impostor and cut-purse? Even if he had been what he professed, and had been introduced to her as he said—which, now when she began to reflect, she thought very doubtful—could he have intended anything but an ephemeral *liaison?*

How could she hope, as the cast-off mistress of Lord Drawler,—for who would believe that she herself had broken off the connection,—to get any one to marry her?

If she could only have had, as it were, a fair start, and begun life again respectably—say at some watering-place, where no one would know her—could she not hope, with her personal attractions and accomplishments, to entrap some wealthy swain into the snares of wedlock?

How absurdly she had acted, she thought, now she began to reflect upon her late conduct. This had all come of aiming at such small game, and, in future, what could she hope for? How could she expect to pass for a rich widow, travelling for her pleasure, with only one dress — of ·course she had chosen her worst to have on—and without a shilling in the world?

The predicament was horrible, and one which required a woman of genius to manage properly.

She was at her wits' end.

"This is an awkard job, mum," said the policeman, in a conciliating way, rubbing his hat round with his berlin glove, and keeping his eyes upon the carpet; for he felt a little bashful in the presence of the haughty beauty, and was rather touched, perhaps, by the sight of so much loveliness in distress.

A moment or two ago he had expressed his opinion in confidence to a waiter, and, behind his berlin glove, that she was " an exceeding fine woman. Indeed, he might say he never seed a finer."

Upon which the waiter, on most occasions a meek person of noiseless approach, and suppress demeanour, had leered at him, and winked his eye, remarking under his breath, but with exceeding warmth,—

"She's plummy!"

Meaning perchance that she came up to his idea of female superlativeness.

"A very awkard job for all parties, aint it mum?" the policeman continued.

"It is extremely unpleasant. What would you advise me to do?"

"These things will occur you see, mum," said the officer, having, by the way, no particular suggestion to make, but rubbing his hat, and speaking in a mysterious whisper,— "these things will, and do occur every day almost. But it's a great pity if any unpleasantness should arise. Mr. Jones, here, I'm sure, would ask nothing that was unreasonable, and I'm sure you would do the same."

"I ask nothing but to be allowed to depart."

"Certainly, mum, and quite right, too. So, as I was a-going to remark, if any amicable arrangement could be come to, how much better it would be for all parties."

"What arrangement do you suggest?"

"Well, suppose you paid half, mum," said the constable.

"I tell you I have no money. Every halfpenny I had has been taken from me."

"Well, there's enough of this!" stormed Mr. Jones. "I give that woman in charge."

"In charge!" screamed Nelly, starting up in a fury. "What do you mean?" What do you accuse me of?"

"I shall state my case at the police-court," replied the landlord, buttoning his coat, and snorting like a grampus. "I won't be done by any one."

He was one of a numerous class of pig-headed Britons who, when they have said an absurdity, commit the further absurdity of sticking to it. You find them by scores in vestry-rooms and public meetings,—all very red in the face, and noisy, and bumptious, laying down the law with a thump of their leg of mutton fists which sends the dust a flying.

I should like to kick all such.

"Call a cab!" he roared. And a cab was called, and came.

"If we could only come to an arrangement——" began the policeman.

"Arrangement be bothered! I'm not going to be done."

Determined upon this, the landlord got into the cab, followed by the policeman and Nelly, that latter, speechless with' terror and indignation, and the three started for the Mansion House, followed by a few idlers who had heard a little of the affair, and were anxious to see the end of it.

The night charges were then being heard; and almost immediately Nelly was brought before the Lord Mayor.

Lord Mayor Grub is not the wisest man in the world, according to the newspapers. Most likely he has been shamefully caluminated by a low, carping penny press; but he never has been quoted as a Solomon, and some of his decisions have been from time to time a good deal ridiculed.

Now upon this particular occasion, his lordship had been a good deal worried one way and another.

That morning's paper had contained an attack upon him of an insulting character, and he had just been chaffed by a young pickpocket.

He was not in the best of tempers.

I have heard from the best authority—in short, from a person who has been " committed,"—that the law of Lord Mayor Grub, was a good deal influenced by extraneous circumstances,—

"If he's peckish, and you keeps him off from his wittles, or he's been put out at all before your turn comes, he lets you have it, I can tell you."

This information I received from a young gentleman who is now passing his fourth of seven years' expatriation, unless he has returned before the allotted time by virtue of a ticket-of-leave; and as he had had some experience, we may take his opinion as a valuable one.

It is not often that the mayorality has fallen into the hands of one who has shown such promise of future excellence as the present Lord Mayor CUBITT.

They had the misfortune to come before his lordship under peculiarly disadvantageous circumstances.

He has, as I have said, been a good deal put out. The cases that morning had been long and tedious; and he was, by chance, more peckish than usual, and, in consequence, rather harder than usual upon those who kept him away from it.

Just at the very moment that he was rising for the third time to go to lunch, Nelly was brought into Court.

Grub looked as black as thunder, and fell down into his cushioned chair with a bump like a battering-ram.

CHAPTER THE TENTH.

BEFORE THE BEAK AND BEHIND THE BARS.

"WHAT'S this, in goodness name?" cried the Lord Mayor, with an expression of countenance which seemed to say, "I'll make a short job of it, whatever it is."

Then he caught up a newspaper lying in front of him, and pretended to read something; in reality, feeling so savage at being again disappointed about his meal, that he could not trust himself to speak.

"If you please, my lord," began Mr. Jones, bustling forward, "the state of the case is this——"

"Hold your tongue, sir!" roared his lordship. "How dare you!"

At which rebuke Jones sank into insignificance, and his lordship went on with his paper.

After a couple of minutes his lordship looked up.

"What is this, policeman?"

The policeman stated the case.

"Where's the complainant?"

"Here, my lord," replied Jones.

"Oh, you are, are you? Now, you'd better take care what you're about, sir!"

Mr. Jones, a good deal crestfallen, said he would.

"Don't be impertinent," roared his lordship.

"I wasn't."

"You were. Don't give me the lie, sir."

"Oh! well," said Jones, fretting and fuming under the insults he was receiving, and the knowledge that two of his waiters were cracking their sides at his discomfiture, "if I'm not to be allowed to open my mouth, there's no good in my attempting."

"If you don't take care what you're about, sir, I shall commit you," thundered the mayor, and buried his head in the paper.

"Now then," he roared again, still louder, "are not you going on? What have you got to say?"

The unfortunate Jones made a gulp, and began.

"The prisoner came to my hotel——"

"Begin at the beginning, will you? What's your name?"

"John Jones——"

"You keep a public-house, do you?"

"I keep a family hotel and tavern."

"Do you mean to say you do not keep a public-house?"

"No: only I thought you meant——"

"You'd better take my advice now, Jones, and mind what you're about, or I shall make an example of you. I really shall."

Jones, perfectly purple, continued:—

"I keep the —— Hotel, in —— Street. This morning, the prisoner, in company with a Frenchman, came to my house in a cab. The Frenchman engaged some rooms, saying that the prisoner was his wife, and ordered breakfast. After breakfast, at which they had Sauterne, Hock, and Still Champagne, the foreigner came out, bringing a black trunk with him, which he told a servant to place upon a cab, as he was going to take it to a friend's house, and that he would be back shortly. He also added that the prisoner was lying down, and that no one must go into the room for fear of disturbing her."

Mr. Jones then went on to say that almost two hours having elapsed, a servant opened the door cautiously, found Nelly insensible in a chair, and, alarmed by her extreme pallor, endeavoured to waken her, and called for assistance.

He also added, that upon her recovery from the swoon, real or imaginary, the prisoner had called out that she, too, had been robbed of her watch, money, and jewels.

"Well," said the mayor, "and what on earth do you mean by occupying my time by such a story? There is no evidence whatever against this lady."

Then, turning to Nell, he asked for her account of the transaction.

Here my lady was in a trifling fix. What account should she give of herself? Did she state who she was, most probably the case would be reported in the newspapers, and then Drawler, or Maurice, or some of the people at the Apollo might see it. Worse than all, it might come to the ears of the Marquis of Crutchingford, on whom she had laid some deep schemes, to be carried into effect when she next came across him.

No, it would never do for this business to transpire. She therefore said that she was a widow lady, of the name of Howard; that she had just returned from India, where all her living friends and relations resided; that she had met the foreigner upon the boat, and, as he had claimed acquaintance with her, and she firmly believed him to be a gentleman, she was glad to accept of his company and protection through the dangers of the road.

To this his lordship listened most affably, and, as he had made up his mind to snub Jones, would have dismissed the case at once, had not the clerk whispered to him to ask her for her card.

Nelly said her card-case had been stolen.

"Certainly, that's quite sufficient," said his lordship.

Nelly bowed, and was going to withdraw.

"Ask for her passport," whispered the clerk.

This, too, had been stolen.

"No, it isn't," broke in the indignant Jones. "The policeman has it, and the name isn't Howard. No more is the name on the boxes."

"The passport does not properly belong to me——" Nelly began.

"How is it you are travelling with it?"

"It was changed in a mistake at the Calais Custom House, by a Commissionnaire."

"Certainly—certainly, such things often happen," said his lordship. "I shall dismiss this charge."

"I'm afraid, my lord," whispered the clerk, "that it looks rather suspicious."

"Do you think so?"

"I certainly do."

"What would you do, then?"

"Question her."

"Question her yourself, then. We musn't do anything rash, or those confounded cheap papers will be at us again."

"Very well, my lord."

"Take care what you're about."

"Yes, my lord."

"And be sharp about it. I'm dying for something to eat."

"Certainly, my lord."

When this conference was ended, the clerk turned towards Nelly.

"Your passport was changed, you say, madam, at the French Custom House? Had you no opportunity of restoring it to its owner on board the boat, and receiving yours back again?"

"I did not see the owner."

"Was not the owner on board the boat?"

"There were only two passengers on board—the Frenchman and myself."

"That's rather unlikely," whispered the Lord Mayor. "Ask her how that was."

"How was that?"

"On account of the storm. The other persons who intended to have come over were afraid to do so."

"That's quite likely," whispered his lordship. "There was a storm, you know. It blew one of my chimney-pots off. I'd better dismiss the case."

"I should not yet, my lord."

"Well, go on—only my lunch is waiting."

"How is it then, madam," continued the clerk, "that if your name is not Raymond, as it states upon this passport, the name of Raymond is on your luggage?"

"I changed the labels, being afraid that I should have some difficulty in passing the Custom House at Dover."

That was a thumper, was it not?

There are some people who make lying an art. The worst of it is, that want of memory usually accompanies this talent, which more ordinarily reaches perfection in the inventive faculty of lovely woman, than in the clumsier efforts of the inferior animal.

For a minute or two the clerk was staggered, at a loss for a reply; and as his lordship was all the while nudging him with his knuckles in the back, he was scarcely able to think.

Meanwhile Nelly stood at the dock, placid and calm, as she generally was, and with a slight smile of contempt twitching the corners of her pretty mouth.

"Do you wish to question me any further, my lord?" she asked, looking right over the clerk's head at the Lord Mayor, and totally ignoring the former personage.

"No—no, certainly, Mrs. Howard. I'm quite satisfied."

Nelly bowed, and was again about to retire, when the clerk interposed.

"One moment, madam."

"Really, sir," unless his lordship wishes it——" cried Nelly, in a fury.

"Yes—yes, madam," he said. Then whispered to the clerk, "What do you wish to ask? Be quick, for heaven's sake. I'm positively sinking."

"Might I be allowed to look at your handkerchief, madam?"

In spite of all her presence of mind the artful hussy changed colour, and started when she heard the request.

She steadied herself with her hand upon the rail, and stared at him with wide open eyes; but said nothing.

"Might I be allowed to look at your handkerchief?"

Her tongue clove to the roof of her mouth.

Again he repeated his request.

"Really," said she; "so very extraordinary a demand. I cannot understand you."

"No, nor I either," thought the Lord Mayor; and he whispered eagerly,—"What are you up to?"

"All right."

"Don't be foolish, you know. Think of the papers!"

"Will you allow me to look at it?" repeated the clerk, extending his hand for the daintily embroidered cambric, which Nelly now held crushed up in her hand.

"Am I obliged to do so, my lord," she asked.

"Well," said his lordship, in a fog, "Really, I don't know—that is — yes, of course. Let me look at it."

Without a word she handed it to him by the crier.

The Court was intensely quiet and anxious. His lordship more and more puzzled.

He spread the little belaced frivolity out before him, held it close to his nose, and sniffed the *Ess Bouquet* upon it with a relish; but was no wiser.

"What am I to do with it?" he whispered, to the clerk. "It is very pretty, is it not?"

"Look at the corner, my lord."

"Which corner?"

"For the name."

"The name!"

"Yes. See what name it is."

"Oh, ah, to be sure. Let me see. Oh, that's the wrong way up. Hum—hum—ah. No, that was right, I suppose. Bless me, these ornamental letters are so puzzling! What's this? N—e—l—l—y Nelly R—a—y—m—o——Why, it's Raymond! How's this? Have you got Mrs. Raymond's clothes as well as her passport?"

But Nelly made no reply. This fresh discovery quite overwhelmed her. However could she have been such a fool?

"Well, madam," said the mayor, "please to explain, and as quickly as possible."

"I have nothing to explain," said Nelly, after a pause. "I do not know how I came by the handkerchief. It is not mine."

This was rather a shallow explanation of a very suspicious circumstance, and could hardly be passed over.

On the other hand, his lordship was quite

frantic for his food. "What shall I do?" he asked of the clerk.

"Remand," whispered the clerk.

"Well, really," said his lordship, "I don't think her guilty: though I see nothing else for it, if I'm to have anything to eat to-day."

And so he remanded Mrs. Nelly until some inquiries could be made about her. And she was removed from the dock, a prey to many varied emotions, in which, however, rage, shame, and despair predominated.

"And now for lunch," cried Lord Mayor Grub.

But again was he doomed to disappointment, for another case was brought into court at the very moment.

I don't know what it was about, and, what is more, I don't believe his lordship did.

Anyhow, it was settled in about three minutes. Sentence—Three months, with hard labour.

Nelly had nobody to offer as bail, even if his lordship would have taken it, which, like all his magisterial decisions, is somewhat doubtful.

Later on in the afternoon the van carried her on to the House of Detention. Still later on, she was alone in her cell.

What an awful change from her life, scarcely forty-eight hours ago, in Paris!

Pretty state of affairs, was it not? Oh! you wicked ones, do you suppose that there is no punishment in this world because you see vice triumphant and virtue at a discount?

"But," says a wicked one, of an argumentative turn, "she was not punished when she deserved it, and she is punished for a crime of which she is innocent. What moral are you pointing?"

Disputative Party, don't ask questions, but go on with the story. Don't imagine you have got the best of it though.

I could reply to you at some length, only my publisher tells me that moralising does not pay in penny numbers.

CHAPTER THE ELEVENTH.

SPIDERS.

EVER busy spiders, spinning and spinning! Cobweb upon cobweb choke up the corners of Dudley Craven's dingy office, yet to it comes no fly of any sort. Why should they go on wasting their labour for naught?

Round the corner, in Drury Lane, the steaming window of the pudding-shop is full of flies. With legs and wings heavy with greasy moisture, they crawl in myriads upon the glass, leaving their trails behind them, much like a serpent marks its progress through long grass.

And in the grocer's window, among the figs, and raisins, and moist sugar, they literally swarm. There are some places black with them, and when the shopman puts his arm in among them to reach a pot of jam, or other article there displayed, they rise in a cloud, and fill the air almost as thick as turtle-soup.

None go in to Lyon's Inn to feed the hungry spiders lying in wait for them.

Ever wakeful, watchful, and patient, they lurk in their dark corners, waiting for them; and so do the human spiders bide their time, hungry and cruel.

Is Dudley Craven such a spider? We know that Hadget is. These two are very busy with their webs. Spinning and spinning; deserting the old, useless, and broken, and sitting down patiently to manufacture new in more tempting places.

One summer's day Mr. Hadget turned out of Newcastle Street, and, traversing the covered passage and the dreary yard beyond, opened the office door, and found Dudley Craven already at work.

Mr. Hadget was much better dressed than he used to be, when we first made his acquaintance.

His frock coat was of the very best broadcloth, his trousers well shaped, and his hat a new one.

The worst of it was, that no amount of dressing would make a gentleman of him. Nothing could get rid of that nasty twitch in his mouth, and the low cunning look about his eyes.

He carried a cane in his hand, which he swang to and fro as he walked, and amused himself occasionally by striking little boys with, whom he found playing on his path. Those in a stooping posture, with their trousers tight, he usually selected.

"Early at work," said he, cheerfully, as he looked in at the door. "That's what I like to see. You'll have the worm yet, Dudley, depend upon it."

"I hope so."

"To be sure. That's hearty, now. I like to hear it. You've got up a good many mornings without doing it though, haven't you?"

"I've staid up all night very often——"

"And even then not managed it?"

"And even then not managed it."

"He must be a slippery customer, that early worm."

"It would seem so."

"However, there's only one way I see."

"And that's——"

"To stick at it. Have the salt always handy, and pop it on his tail when the time comes."

The other returned no answer; and so Mr. Hadget, after regarding him for a few moments with an inward chuckle, dropped the subject.

This Dudley Craven was a thin, spare, grey-headed man, whose brow was furrowed with care, and whose cheeks were pinched with want.

He was a threadbare, seedy, needy-looking man, with a meek and timid expression, as though he had been accustomed to be ground down and worked hard all his miserable life.

He was working very hard now. So hard was he scribbling away upon a sheet of foolscap before him, that his busy quill chirped like a little bird.

He looked up, after a few minutes' labour, and addressed Hadget, who was opening, and reading one by one, the letters waiting for him upon the mantelpiece.

" Did you look through the papers I gave you yesterday ?"

" No."

" No ?" echoed Craven, in surprise.

" No," repeated Hadget. " What of it ?"

" There's no time to be lost, that's all. The business was pressing. But, I suppose," he added, after a pause, " you had other work to do."

" Well, I can't say I had."

Craven laid his pen down a moment to look at him, then picked it up, and scratched his nose with it, then laid it down again, then said,—

" Hadn't you ?"

And went on writing.

" No. I took a holiday," replied the other, " and got drunk."

" You're joking, Mr. Hadget."

" What do you mean ? Is there anything surprising in it ? Everybody wants a holiday now and then. You had one a year or two ago ; and, if you go on well, shall have another. Then, as to being drunk, I suppose you know what that is. You've been so."

When you came to look at Dudley Craven's face, there were unmistakable signs about it of its owner's partiality for strong drink.

Therein might have lain hidden the secret of his neediness and seediness.

What else had made him this poor scrub of a drudge ? Or, if there had originally been another cause, what else had kept him down ?

" I spent a glorious night down the Haymarket, Mr. Craven," continued Hadget. " Had supper with three of the finest women in London, at Dubourg's, and kept it up till all was blue."

Craven stared ; but was silent.

" And so you see I hadn't time to read any of this rubbish. You were never very wild yourself, were you ?"

" I don't think I was," said Craven, doubtfully, and scratching a bald place on his head with the feather of his pen. " Not that I can call to my recollection."

And he seemed to think about it a while, as though he might have been wild some time without his knowing it. In his sleep, perhaps.

" I suppose you don't," said Hadget, with a laugh. " You married early, didn't you ?"

" I was just twenty."

" And you are now——"

" Fifty-three."

" And your wife's alive ?"

" She is, God bless her."

" Ha—ha ! Well, you've made a nice fool of yourself, anyhow. There, get on with your writing. Damn it ! there's lots to do ; and it's all you're fit for, in my opinion."

Of a sudden his manner had changed from a jocular one to his usual savage, surly way, and he pursued his task of opening and reading letters, silently and rapidly.

" It's infernally cold, here !" said he, presently, with a shudder. " Take this shilling, and order a quarter-hundred of coal. Tell them to bring it directly. You needn't come back for an hour yourself. I expect a visit. Take something out of the shilling for drink. You can have twopence. Bring the rest of the change back. Do you hear me ?"

" Yes, sir."

" Go."

" I beg your pardon, Mr. Hadget," said the other, nervously, fidgetting at the edge of the table with his fingers, and feeling about, as it were, for words. " I hope you won't think me troublesome."

" Yes, I shall. What is it ?"

" Well, sir, if I must speak——"

" You can do it, or leave it alone, for what I care."

" Ha ! ha !" Craven replied, laughing nervously, and making belief that he thought it rather a good joke.

" I suppose I can ; for it's not likely you could know what I was going to say. Is it, sir ?"

" It wouldn't be the most difficult thing in the world for me to guess, I daresay, if I were to take the trouble ; but I am not going to."

" You're so awfully sharp, Mr. Hadget," said Craven, rubbing his hands and chuckling. " That's the worst of you—that is."

" Is it ? I'm glad to hear it."

Here there was an awkward pause.

" To tell the truth, then, if it's not inconvenient, I should be very much obliged—though I really trust it won't be inconvenient, as it will be of the very greatest service to me —if you will be so good as to so far accommodate me as to advance the whole, or a portion, of my next week's salary ; having a payment to make to-day, or otherwise I would never have ventured to take the liberty of being so bold——"

He was rambling on in this way, when Hadget stopped him.

" Do you want it all ?"

" Well, sir, if you could make it the whole twelve shillings——"

" And, pray, Mr. Craven," asked Hadget, eyeing his companion steadily, " supposing I let you have your money now, what will you do next week ? Borrow it in advance again, perhaps ?"

" Indeed, indeed, sir, I shouldn't ask you, if I were not obliged."

" Yes, that's the old tale. What's up now ? The brokers in ?"

And he turned away and whistled.

" The brokers are in," replied Craven, with a long face : " and my wife is dangerously ill, sir, and not likely to live. If I don't have the money, they'll take the bed from under her. They will, by God !"

" Well, I'll see about it. Go and order the coals ; and you'd better not spend the twopence, perhaps. Take it home with you, instead. It'll go towards the gruel."

At which piece of exquisite humour the lawyer laughed aloud.

Craven, with a woeful countenance, still stood fidgetting at the table's edge.

" Indeed, Mr. Hadget, if you could let me have it before twelve o'clock it would be the saving of me. The landlord promised to wait till then for me, and I said I would ask you."

" Oh, you did, did you ? You made sure of getting it, I suppose. Now, I've a good mind not to let you have it. It would serve you right if I didn't."

MR. OCHRE AT HOME.

CHAPTER THE TWELFTH.

THE GHOST IN THE CELLAR.

"I'M sure, sir, I serve you well," said Craven. "I was all last night working to get those papers done for you. I scarcely ever stirred from that table."

Was it a sudden faintness which seized his companion at that moment, or merely an effect of light and shade; for his face turned deadly pale, and his jaw seemed to fall open.

Craven looked at him amazed.

Hadget made an attempt to speak, but the sound rattled in his throat.

"Did you say——"

No 21

"Say what?"

"Did you say," he asked at last, "that you were here all night?"

"Yes, I was, sir; and very lonely and uncomfortable I felt."

"Why?"

"It's a nasty place to spend your time in. I should think you must have found it so, when you used to sleep here."

"I did not. Why should I?"

"You don't believe in ghosts, you see, and so I suppose you wouldn't feel it."

"Believe in what?"

"Ghosts!"

"Are there," said Hadget, still speaking with great apparent difficulty,—" are there ghosts here? I've never seen them."

"I'll tell you what there are," replied Craven, in a lower tone, and with something of a shudder; "there are the most awful moanings I ever heard, which, if they are not ghosts, I can't tell what they can be."

"Pooh!" observed Hadget, after a pause, "it's your fancy."

"Well, it's a very disagreeable fancy, then, that's all I've got to say; and one that's difficult to shake off."

"Why, what did you hear, pray?"

"I can hardly tell you what it was, or where it came from."

"Very mysterious, I must say."

"I should almost have been led to imagine," said Craven, in a thoughtful tone, "that it came from the cellars."

"The cellars? Nonsense!"

"The cellars belong to you, don't they, sir?"

"Yes; but there's nothing in them."

"Nothing at all?"

"Nothing but lumber."

"Well, I can't make out where it could be, then."

"Take my word for it, it was your own imagination. Don't stop here again all night. There's no occasion for it, and you won't get anything by it, I can tell you."

Thus warned, Craven departed on his errand, and Hadget was left by himself.

"So," said the lawyer, when the sound of the other's retreating footsteps had died out of the yard, "he heard the most awful moanings, did he? I'll soon put a stop to that sort of thing. I'll give him his medicine."

He drew a flask of brandy from his pocket as he spoke, and tasted it.

"It's very hot," said he, wiping the tears from his eyes. "It'll warm him."

Then, taking a candlestick which stood upon a side table, he struck a light, ignited the small end of candle remaining in it, and cautiously descended the stairs leading to the cellars.

All was quiet at first; but when he put a key he carried into the lock of one of the doors, and turned it with a grating scrunch, a low moaning sound within smote upon his ear.

"He wants his medicine," said Hadget, with a grin, "and he shall have it."

Hadget must have been a dare-devil fellow, to go in with a grin to meet this groaning ghost. Don't you think so?

Perhaps he was in the habit of associating with the supernatural personage, and had grown used to him.

He did not seem afraid, although he certainly opened the door with great caution, a little at a time, and glanced round before going any further.

Crossing the first cellar, he took another key from his pocket and unlocked a second door.

But, as the key grated in the lock, the groaning inside was accompanied by a scratching, scrambling sort of noise, as though whatever it was it had been disturbed, and was getting upon its legs.

"He's vicious," muttered Hadget to himself. "Damn him, he's as likely as not to make a spring at me."

To guard as much as possible against surprise, the lawyer placed the candle upon the top of a pile of boxes behind him, in such a way that it threw a stream of light into the cellar he was about to enter.

Then he prepared himself, and threw open the door.

Next moment, somebody or something within came flying towards him with a scream, and clutched him by the throat.

As quick as thought, the lawyer struck his assailant a violent blow upon the head, and, in his turn getting him by the throat, drove him back into the cellar, and pinned him down, panting, on the table.

"Now, then!" cried Hadget, when he had recovered his breath.

"Now, then!" said the ghost.

"What were you trying to do?"

"To get out."

"Were you?"

"I was."

"Then you won't."

"I will."

"We'll see."

And the conversation concluded by a banging sound, which might possibly have been the ghost's head upon the table; and a moaning sound, which might possibly have been the ghost, who didn't like it.

At least so Dudley Craven fancied, who listened with all his ears outside the outer door, upon the stairs leading down to the cellar.

After a while the groaning ceased, and Hadget's voice said,—

"Drink some of this, you old fool, and be quiet, or some day I'll murder you."

"You are murdering me."

"Drink."

"What is it?"

"Your medicine."

"It's—Ugh! Ugh! it's very hot."

"It's cool enough."

Whatever it was, it seemed almost to choke the unfortunate goblin, who was seized with a violent fit of coughing, which lasted for the next five minutes.

"Now, lie down again," said Hadget's voice, "or it'll be the worse for you."

"Let me come out."

"Likely."

"Let me come out!" screamed the voice. "I can't live here. The place is full of devils. They come and prick me in the dark."

"Not they," said Hadget. "They've something else to do, depend upon it."

"I say they do!" the other yelled. "The vault's alive with fiends."

"Black beetles, more likely. There's a cursed lot of them."

"Look at them. See!"

"See what?"

"How their eyes glare at me from the corners.

"Let 'em glare. They'll do instead of candles."

Here the illused goblin sat up so dismal a howling, and commenced so fierce a struggle with his captor, that Dudley Craven thought that he must have broken loose, and was coming out to murder him.

Impressed with which horrible notion, he

fled up-stairs, and shut himself in the office, where he fell upon a chair, and trembled like a leaf.

Then suddenly remembering that it would not do for Hadget to find him here, he came out again upon the stairs to listen, determined the next time he beat a retreat, to run out by the yard, or up-stairs towards the first floor, where he would be hidden from his employer's sight, and could come down again when Hadget had gone back into the office.

"What on earth has he got shut up there?" thought Craven. "There's something wrong, of course. But what reason can he have for keeping a man in the cellar— if it is a man? And what does he give him for medicine? Is he poisoning him?"

Cautiously descending a step or two, he listened for the voices. He, however, heard only one, which was Mr. Hadget's, and it sounded much nearer to him than it had done before.

In fact, he was in the outer cellar, engaged in locking the inner door upon his patient.

"Yes, my gentleman," said Hadget, to himself, "I'll clap you into an asylum before you're a week older."

He went on mumbling to himself; but, Craven fearing that he might be detected, stole away cautiously, and left the coast clear for the other's ascent.

"Who can it be?" said Craven, to himself. "What can he want with him? I'll know more about it before I'm a week older, unless Hadget locks me up, too, which isn't likely."

CHAPTER THE THIRTEENTH.

MAURICE TO THE RESCUE—HADGET TO THE RIGHT-ABOUTS.

AND how gets on our fair penitent? Reading her bible in her neat and orderly little cell in the House of Detention. She would, indeed, have made a beautiful subject for a picture to be called "Hope," "Resignation," or "Oppressed Virtue," according to the artist's fancy.

She did, indeed, look very interesting, and behaved so prettily, that the matron quite took a fancy to her.

"No, no, I never can think that you are guilty," she said. "I thoroughly believe that you are what you represent yourself to be. I am very, very sorry for you."

To some extent, you see, the matron was right. Mrs. Nelly was not a thief, although she was——not what she ought to have been, in other respects.

She had represented, you may remember, that she was a lady—and she looked like one. I regret to have to say it, because you know in novels, your wicked ones, are always, as it were, stamped and labelled. You may tell them at a glance.

In life, people often look what they are not, and so it was Mrs. Nelly looked like a lady, when she was, as I just observed, no better than she ought to have been.

But, although the matron did everything in her power to smoothen down the disagreeable part of Nelly's prison life, my lady was anything but comfortable either in mind or body.

After the luxurious life to which for some time past she had been accustomed, prison fare and prison discipline, were, as you may suppose, irksome.

Ever since she had made Maurice's acquaintance, she had had a very nice time of it. Although Maurice's life was a continual struggle, he was such a jolly dog, such a rollicking, free-and-easy, careless fellow, that his difficulties did not make him ill-tempered to others; and, as he never troubled her about his affairs, it really did not much signify whether he had got his other suit in pawn, or had half-a-dozen drawers full of splendid raiment ready to put on when he wanted them.

She always got what she wanted, and that was enough for her. It ought to be enough for anybody.

When the day came for her re-appearance before his lordship, it turned out that inquiries had been made, and certain trifling variations between her story and the truth came most unpleasantly to light.

We live in an age of newspapers. Her case was rather interesting. It has been reported rather fully.

There are some people in the world who meddle with what does not concern them. There are some who would, I really believe, take any amount of trouble in setting other people's affairs to rights, when they do not gain a hundredth part of a farthing's advantage by so doing. When moved to interference by spite and malice, one can understand it better.

This was Miss Fleshing's case. She and her dear friend, Miss De Courcy, composed a letter—it was on scented paper, and horribly spelt—showing who Nelly Raymond was, minutely describing her appearance, and hinting that Mrs. Howard and Mrs. Raymond were one and the same person.

This letter they sent anonymously to the Lord Mayor.

His lordship looked very blue when he read it, and Nelly was again remanded.

Things did not look very promising. How would it all end? Could she conduct the business without somebody's advice and assistance? Impossible. Who could she ask? Not a stranger. It must be some one who knew the truth. Who then?

She was too proud to seek assistance from Drawler. What of Maurice? No; he might refuse. And she would rather have died in prison than suffer such humiliation as to beg, and be refused by him.

To Ochre the same reasoning applied. It was no good asking Bullyrag. Within the memory of man, he had never done a good action without he thought he might ultimately gain by it. She, too, had so insulted him; and she knew full well that among his other amiable qualities, might be counted that of never forgiving an injury.

Who was left, then? To whom could she apply?

Many days she puzzled her pretty head with the question. At last it struck her all at once. However could she have been so forgetful? How stupid not to think of it before.

She recollected his words, "Should you require my advice and assistance, a note, addressed to my chambers, will meet with immediate attention."

Who had said this? Why, Hadget, to be sure. She did not know his motive for making such a promise. She had no idea that that low pettifogging fellow was smitten by her personal attractions. He was an unpleasant—rather a dirty object to look at in those times. And Mrs. Nelly soared high, it was not likely she should set her cap at him. Lots of other lowly persons were in love with her, of whom she took not the slightest notice. He had offered his advice and assistance. She required them, and, seeing no reason why she should not do so, sent for him.

An hour afterwards he was at the prison.

"I could not be so ungallant as to keep a lady waiting," he said, smirking and twitching his ugly mouth.

"What a hideous brute he is," thought Nelly.

"She's throwing sheep's eyes at me," thought Hadget. "But I won't appear too eager. I'll put her under an obligation to me. She shan't catch me too easily."

See how the deepest of us are sometimes taken in. She had no idea he was anxious to become her protector. His conduct was so very artful, that she could not see through it at all.

Once, it is true, the thought struck her that Mr. Hadget was hardly the sort of man to do much *for nothing*, and she had studied his behaviour to see whether by chance he might be in love with her; but, Mr. Hadget was so very guarded in his conduct—so very wayward and wily—that she came to the conclusion that he had some reason for befriending her, but that, decidedly the tender passion had nothing to do with it.

He did work for her in right good earnest.

"Rather a mistake of yours, to give a wrong name. I see why you did it; but you might have known it would be found out. Always think well when you're going to tell a crammer, and make it a good one while you're about it. Though, you know, the truth has its advantages. It's easier to think of; and if nothing particular is to be gained by telling a lie, one might as well stick to it."

That was the only remark Mr. Hadget made upon the circumstances of her late adventure. He believed her to be quite incapable of attempting such a paltry fraud as she was accused of, and thought it quite as likely as not that she might be telling the truth.

He was a man of the world, was this lawyer, and had made it his business to study the worst side of human nature. Doing so, he had found that there was a good side, too. Therefore, unlike your small philosophers just setting up in business, he did not set everybody down for a scoundrel. "It's quite as likely he's a fool," thought Hadget; "or, though a scoundrel, he may, by accident, be acting like an honest man on this occasion.

There's no knowing. The devil's not so bad as he's painted. Bloodthirsty giants, who have cut off men's heads by the dozens, have kept pet birds, and been moved to tears at the death of a poodle. We've all our tender places."

Hadget promised to leave no stone unturned.

"I'll get you through, depend upon it," said he. "Money will do almost anything."

"But I have not——"

"I have a shilling or two, I've scraped together."

Hadget was as good as his promise. He worked very hard. He had a private interview with the Lord Mayor upon the subject. I don't know what statements he made. He was not very scrupulous about telling the truth when anything was to be gained by lying, as he told Mrs. Nell.

The Lord Mayor was inclined to be severe with the pretty prisoner. Just now the newspapers were attacking him right and left about the way he had treated a female costermonger who had obstructed the thoroughfare vending her ware, and, in deference to public opinion, he had remitted the punishment. (It afterwards turned out, when the *Penny Patriot* had opened a subscription list, and organised a committee of ladies to see what could be done for the unfortunate, that the unfortunate was a most worthless character, and altogether unworthy of their sympathy. But that is not to the point.) Now, there was Nelly's case, about which his lordship had been most unmercifully slanged by the cheap press, and he felt very savage on the subject.

"If what is stated turns out true, I'll give her six months, as sure as she's alive," cried his lordship. "What do you say, Mr. Hadget? What for? I'll let her know what for? What for, indeed! You call yourself a lawyer, and ask such a question."

I expect that she would have had the six months, sure enough, had not something in her favour unexpectedly turned up in the middle of the inquiries.

This was the arrest of a French swindler and forger, for a great fraud upon one of the Paris banks, and who, among other *aliases* had been passing under that of the Baron De Vigny.

Rightly conceiving this to be the man who had robbed Mrs. Nelly, Hadget obtained an interview with him in prison, and as the case of the bank fraud was clearly proved against him, persuaded him by a bribe, to acknowledge that he had committed the theft upon her in the manner Nelly described.

And so, after almost interminable arguments, *pro.* and *con.*, Mrs. Nelly finally obtained her liberty, although she was obliged to retract all her first statements, and own that her name was Raymond, instead of Howard. An admission, which, as you may suppose, forfeited for her all the good feeling of the matron at the House of Detention, and nipped in the bud a little testimonial which some sympathising folks had had an idea of presenting her with.

Upon the day she was liberated, a man, at

the Mansion House, handed her a sealed packet. It contained a five pound note. No letter accompanied it; but the direction was in a handwriting she well remembered. It was Maurice's.

What feelings the receipt of this might have caused, who can say. The tears were standing in her eyes as Mr. Hadget came up smirking and rubbing his bony hands.

"We've got through at last," said he. "Virtue, as usual, is triumphant."

She fancied at the moment, that the grimacing wretch at her elbow was uglier than ever.

"I wish we hadn't had to retract our statements." continued Mr. Hadget. "Supposing that fellow Maurice was to get hold of it, how he would chuckle."

"Perhaps he would. Good morning, sir."

"Hallo, where are you off to?"

"I am going to take some apartments."

"I had better help you, hadn't I?"

"No, thank you, Mr. Hadget. I am very thankful for all the trouble you have taken on my account. I will not further trespass on your kindness."

He was dumbfounded, this scheming pettifogger. His eyes glanced at the bank note she held between her fingers, then at the envelope, which had fallen to the ground without her noticing it.

She bowed, and walked away with the old haughty manner. He let her go without a word, eager to look at the paper at his feet.

He put his foot upon it till she was gone, then snatched it up and read the address.

"Whose writing is this?" said he. "Can it be Drawler's? No, by God! it's that infernal bastard's."

He clenched his fists, and swore a fearful oath.

"That I should have been such a fool, such a wretched fool, wasting my time and money. And she to go back to that simpleton. I thought she had more spirit. Curse her! let her go; if she would do such a thing as that she's not the woman I took her for, and I'm as well without her. But she is very beautiful I do not believe there ever was such another."

Oh, Hadget, you of all men to conceive such a passion!

Oh, Nelly, you of all women to miss such a chance!

But then you did not think him to be as rich as he was. How could you? You no more suspected it, than you suspected him to be the murderous, bloodthirsty assassin that he was.

_____

CHAPTER THE FOURTEENTH.

A SKULL IN A HAT AND FEATHERS.

I AM coming to a part of my story which I would rather leave unwritten.

I feel beforehand that I am getting upon dangerous ground.

I expect the reader will exclaim against me, and ask what good is there in these scenes of vice, even if they exist.

Is it not, as I have said, I don't know how

often, (you must be tired of hearing me say it, by now), is it not agreed by all polite novelists, and by all polite society to ignore those frightful ulcers growing at the heart of civilization?

Now and then the papers make a little stir about the social evil; there are public meetings, midnight tea drinkings, and such like. After a while it dies out.

Nobody comes to any practical conclusion as to what is to be done with the outcast, and so the matter drops.

If you could take all these poor creatures off the streets, and place them in situations, where they would not have to work very hard, and could live very comfortably, I have no doubt but that the well disposed would willingly forsake their old calling.

A great number would go back again very probably, who don't like work. As the supply would then most likely be insufficient to meet the demand, others would come upon the market, some of these, again, might be reformed, and so things would go on as they were. Do you not think so?

After studying the subject attentively in all its bearings, I have come to the conclusion, that if we begin by totally reorganising society, and completely upsetting human nature, we shall be able at last to abolish the social evil altogether.

Till then, boys will be boys, and men will be men, and women must live, and it's a wicked, wicked world, as every body has agreed long ago.

* * * *

Nelly never got back her stolen property. There was some difficulty about recovering the clothes she had left at the hotel, and ignorant of the way she should set about it, and having offended her legal adviser it ended by her never getting them.

She took some lodgings in the gay neighbourhood of Norton Street, (now Bolsover Street, and highly respectable).

Established here, she jobbed a brougham in the park, and ran a bill at the livery stables. She purchased a few articles of clothing, went to the theatre, to the Argyll Casino, to Mrs. Hamilton's, and to some of the best of those mysterious refreshment rooms in Jermyn Street which seem to open about midnight, and where young swells lounge on crimson velvet ottomans, and smoke and yawn till three or four.

Five pounds at this sort of thing cannot be expected to go very far.

She was singularly unlucky.

Why? Who can decide? Perhaps her bearing was too haughty; perhaps the young noblemen and gentlemen mistook her object; perhaps she did not understand her trade.

She ran in debt, ran out of gloves and other little trifles. Her boots got a little too much worn at the soles. Wet weather came on. She could not keep in doors. The landlady grew insulting. She went out wet or fine, and caught cold upon cold.

Matters somehow unaccountably persisted in not looking up. She had to "bilk" her lodgings.

That means, green youth, she shot the

moon, flitted without paying, and left the landlady in the lurch.

It is oftener done than you might suppose, verdant one. As a rule, however, I believe that the landlady is seldom to be pitied.

The wretches who let lodgings, and fatten upon the ill-gotten gains of these unfortunates, and who still have the shameless audacity to hold up their heads unblushingly as respectable married women and mothers of families, are the objects of loathing and abhorrence to all honest, right-thinking persons.

In many cases, where the gay woman has property of her own in the lodgings, and is unable to pay the rent, the same is unjustly seized upon by these harpies, and the poor creature ejected into the street, through their ignorance of the gross illegality of the proceeding. Did they only consult any competent authority, justice would be done them; but, as a rule, these unfortunates submit blindly and passively to every describable tyranny.

When Nelly had left these lodgings, she took others. No reference required by the old beldames who let them.

Here she did as badly. Her cold grew worse, and she fell ill.

Sickness, hunger, and want! The pawnbroker opened his hospitable doors to her. Alas! she had but what she stood upright in to dispose of.

Occasionally she got some money, but it was rare. A curse seemed to be upon her.

If it were a punishment for her past life, it was bitterly hard to bear.

But though she sank, and sank deep, her misery was equalled by her pride.

She would rather have died in the deepest depth of wretchedness, than have applied for help to Maurice, or to Drawler.

One night in the Haymarket she met the latter. She was better dressed than usual, and had half a mind to address him, but he frowned at her, and she passed on without a word.

She instituted inquiries about Maurice, but could hear nothing of him. She fancied she might meet him, perhaps, by accident; but London is a large city, and she never did.

The sort of life this woman led is one which spoils beauty. Without beauty, what chance is there for the unhappy street-walker?

She sank lower and lower.

Great heavens, it is awful to think how women every day sink like this, and go from bad to worse. A year ago, had any one predicted such a change, everybody who knew that glorious golden-haired goddess would have laughed the notion to such a change to scorn.

What was it bore her down? It by no means follows that these women must in this fashion go to the dogs. Did she make no effort to extricate herself? Why not have endeavoured to obtain a situation at one of the theatres? Having once held an engagement, it would surely not have been so very difficult.

Is there such a thing as fate? or, stay, can we find a clue to this woman's fall, in any peculiarity of her character?

Was it pride?

Dear heart, what a life for a proud woman to lead! Can we think of any greater punishment than the degradation of her loathsome calling must have been to this once high-spirited, arrogant, overbearing beauty.

Once so, say you. Through all the wretched scenes of grovelling poverty and vulgar vice, in which hard necessity forced her to play a part, arrayed in her poor threadbare clothes and gaudy tarnished finery, did this unhappy woman, hugging within her breast her pride and hate, stalk cold, inanimate, contemptuous of those around her.

How could she hope to succeed? She tried no blandishments to gain her lovers.

But though her pride was thus the cause of want of success, it, at the same time, sustained her in her distress, sickness, and misery. She would not give in. She would hold on—a change must come. When the fine weather set in, she would get over her cold and recover her good looks. Why should she not meet again with such a lover as Lord Drawler? She saw by the papers that the Marquis of Crutchingford had partially recovered from his attack, and had returned to England. Could she only meet him? Could she only manage to make a good appearance?

She would make an appearance. Something must turn up. She would not be trodden down by Fate in this way. She would live through it.

By heavens, she swore she would yet be a lady!

Little chance of it, Nelly; very little chance of it, I fear.

Respectability has gone to sleep, and virtue, with its night-cap on, is long ago a bed, comfortably tucked up and snoring. They are holding high jinks in the Haymarket.

The gentleman in the fez, outside the Turkish Divan, invites the young noblemen and gentlemen to step inside, and assures them that there is ample accommodation.

At the Cafe de la Regence, and other places of the sort, there is an astonishing run upon the little cups of coffee (a curious refection for two in the morning, however good the quality may be); and there is such a crowd of admirers whispering tender nothings to the seductive *dames du comptoir*, that it is a wonder they can keep such a sharp eye to the sixpences.

At Scott's supper-rooms, Mr. Randal is driven nearly wild by ceaseless demands for oysters, chops, steaks, kidneys, oyster salads, scollops, and pots of stout, and half a mind to cut the business altogether, and retire on his private fortune.

At the Cafe de l'Europe, and Giraudier's, and Dubourg's, heavy swells are doing light suppers, and round about at the various gay hostelries, gooseberry disguised by fanciful labels and leaded corks, sells at high prices, and is quaffed by jolly dogs, to whom still jollier dogs are standing treat. God bless them!

In at the Piccadilly Saloon, green youth, red satin and unlimited ruffianism dance in the same quadrille, shout, sing, and grumble.

swear, quarrel, and fight, in a hot atmosphere, reeking of smoke and dust, and a host of villanous odours.

Out on the pavement. green youth, with pallid cheeks, strolls to and fro, gay-coloured satins whisk, and crush, and rustle. Ruffianism, with beetling brows, and pipe in mouth, looks on, hangs in the wake, gets up a row when occasion offers, and silently helps itself to other people's money when it gets a chance.

Come on, you jolly dog, we're seeing life! Bother the hour! Put up your watch. Youth is the time for enjoyment! Are we not young, and out upon the spree? We won't go home till morning! We, and that simple fluid—the milk, will go in together.

Simple fluid, forsooth! Is it not an artfully contrived concoction of chalk and sheep's brains, and I know not what besides? Is anything simple, virtuous, honest, and what it seems to be? Breathing this polluted air, harkening to conversation around us, seeing the sights which this terrible thoroughfare presents, one almost comes at last to doubt that there is any other life which differs with this, where people are sober and chaste, where women do not rouge, and men have higher aims in existence, than to pass their nights in drunkenness and profligacy.

A wild, jolly, reckless life it seems to you, my young fledglings, does it not? Glorious wine! Lovely women! Vive l'amour! To the deuce with tomorrow.

Ah! me, there is another side. Out of the glaring gaslit street, lead alleys and courts, where poor wretches lie huddled away, and die unknown, uncared for, of starvation and disease. Gaunt phantoms flit by us in the park, or salute us hoarsely at street corners, where they shiver in their scanty clothing. Once, perhaps, they wore silk (the same silk, perhaps). these fair creatures wear, who walk the Haymarket to-night.

Still further in the depths of misery, upon the hospital bed, upon the bank of the river, beneath its murky waters, lie hidden others of the wretched sisterhood.

My friend, it is not all gold that glitters. Beneath that pretty turban hat with a Magenta plume, a death's head leers at us. See, man, through her skirt you can trace the outline of the bones.

Is it not horrible? Yet this is pleasure, my friend. This is the life that they call "gay." We are seeing life, my boy, not DEATH!

Come, let us liquor.

CHAPTER THE FIFTEENTH.

DRAWING TO A CLOSE.

THE old woman in Baker Street yet lingered on her bed of sickness,—clinging with fearful pertinacity to life, and making a stand against the inroads of the enemy, though ever and anon tottering beneath his blows.

Again and again was the kid glove renewed upon the street door knocker, and again and again were the young ladies who passed

the house deceived by the nature of the illness within, and attributed the muffled state of the surly faced lion, to a much more interesting occurrence than the death bed of an ugly old woman; for, I suppose, young ladies do not feel much interest in ugly old people.

The straw had been so frequently laid down, and had drifted round the corner, and the tidy door-steps of the neighbouring houses had so often been littered by it, that the tidy maids had ceased to heed that circumstance, and left it to gambol upon the whitened stone.

But though the outside of the Baker Street mansion were much the same as of old, within the house time and Hadget had wrought great changes.

In the place of Simpkinson departed, was a sleek and meek young man, affecting a flabby jacket of jean, and black cloth trousers, instead of the magnificent plush and embroidery worn by his predecessor.

He never stood a-straddle upon the door step, taking the air and puffing at his like the immortal Simpkinson was so fond doing.

The boys of Baker Street took no heed him, but thought him a second-rate, commonplace person like he was.

The other servants too, had gone away; indeed, Miss Dimples had bettered herself by marriage, and become the wife of a wealthy publican in the neighbourhood, to whose bar her pretty face attracted a host of admirers, and led to the consumption of fabulous quantities of malt and spirituous liquors.

As Dimples had said, there was no living in the place, after that Hadget came into it.

In fact the lawyer took the upper hand, and as his manners at best were far from agreeable, he led the dependants a harassing life.

Not less than the others, Dorcas Abbot.

She still remained faithful to her cruel task mistress. What kept her? Some strange sort of love, perchance, that she bore the wicked old woman, who for the last eleven years and more had bullied and ill used her every day of her life, and forced her to submit to countless small indignities, and petty, paltry insults, which would have broken the heart of any woman less stubborn and proud than the companion.

What else could keep her?

No very strong tie of interest, surely; for the old woman had destroyed the will made in Dorcas's favour. Almost immediately after Hadget had hinted at the possibility of her medicine being drugged, she had told her companion to bring her the strong box in which she kept the document locked up; read her the contents, and burnt it before her eyes, telling her at the same time that she would make her next will when she got better, and watched the dependant's face to see what effect this proceeding would have upon her.

Very little effect it seemed to have. Merely a slight smile of contempt, and a shrug of the shoulders.

"As you please, madam," she had said. "So long as you wish me to stay with you, I will stay. When you are tired of me, say go; and I will go. While I am here, you pay me my wages. It is for that I stop. My wages are not large, and I do not doubt that there are other and better places to be found. Yet, I am content to remain. You have told me a hundred times I serve you well. I know I do. You buy my services, and those I give you willingly; but I have no love for you. I benefit very little by your life. I shall, most likely benefit less by your death. I shall not break my heart when you *do* die."

After which unnatural remark, the old woman had burst into tears, rocked herself to and fro, and sobbed in her usual style.

However, Dorcas's conduct quite allayed all her suspicions; and if it was distressing to find how very little those around cared for her, it was a consolation to know that she need be in no further dread of the dependant poisoning her to come into her property.

After a while, Mr. Hadget, sneaking in and out of her bed-chamber, prying, and meddling, and interfering in everything, managed so to ingratiate himself with Mrs. Falsetto, that she came at last to fancy she could not do without his services. Her illness did not, as you might have supposed, prevent her taking an interest in business matters.

No, the thinner and more gaunt, the weaker and more helpless that she grew, still more attached did she become to her account books and papers.

Mr. Hadget still collected the rents for her, and the poor tenants down the loathsome City courts, where Mrs. Falsetto's houses were situate, found her grow a harder landlady every quarter.

Gradually it got noised about among the old lady's late fashionable acquaintances (one or two of them visited her now and then, but invalids are poor company, and they did not come very often), that Mrs. Falsetto had taken a Mr. Hadget, the son of an elderly sister, to live with her, and look after her affairs, and, that he had, up till now, lived abroad, which accounted for nobody ever having heard of him before.

After that it got noised about that she had made a will in her new nephew's favour, and that he would come into a pretty penny when she died.

A little while afterwards, a faint rumour spread to the effect that she was slowly sinking; and some of the fashionable acquaintance who had visited her, said she was growing childish.

While such statements were in circulation, the life of the old woman, without a doubt, was ebbing fast away.

Almost without a will of her own, when her relation dictated what she should do, yet was the old woman determined upon one point—she would not part with Dorcas.

Constantly was Miss Abbot in attendance upon the old lady. Nearly as faithful in his attendance was Mr. Hadget; and, lynx-eyed, watched her in every movement. What did he expect to find out?

One night he had been out for several hours. It was seldom that he was so long away at a time. All the day the invalid had been sinking in his absence. She grew worse; so much so, that the symptoms alarmed her companion.

The great Bolusout was sent for. Said there was no hope. Advised Dorcas, however, to summon other medical aid.

Another, and still another doctor came round the sick bed.

There was no hope on earth, they said, and, shaking their heads in mournful harmony, retired from the scene.

The old lady, they said, would die that night, perhaps in an hour, perhaps in two hours time—in six hours at most.

Hollow cheeked, and pinched, and terribly like death, the old woman's face lay motionless upon the pillow, conscious of what was passing round, but making no sign that she could speak, or cared to speak.

By the bedside her companion sat, almost as still as her dying mistress. The watch upon the table by her ticked off the seconds as they passed away for ever, and Dorcas, with her eyes fixed upon the pallid face, expected that thus the old woman's life might pass away, and watched for a sign that all was over.

But the time had not yet come for that. It was coming—soon—soon coming. An hour passed, another hour passed. It had come, it was here.

A twitching of the bony hand that lay upon the coverlet, a violent motion of the muscles of the face, a rolling of the eyes, and then a dreadful voice, which was so hollow and unlike in tone to any she had heard before, that Dorcas started at the sound—called to her by her name.

"Dorcas," she said, "lift me up—lift me higher up, I am dying!"

"Not yet," the companion cried, with a gentler voice than she often used, "not yet."

"Not for a few minutes, I think," continued the old lady. "Bring me my box."

"What do you want with papers, now?"

"Bring them me. Don't ask."

The companion obeyed, and placed the box beside her.

"I—I—can't see. Unlock it, dear. The key is under my pillow."

It was done.

"You'll find, at the bottom, a pocket-book. In it, a certificate of my marriage. Find it."

"I have found it."

"Put it in your breast. Now, look for my last will—tied in blue. Do you see it? Be quick. Now, bring the candle nearer. Put down the box. Hush!"

She turned her head in the direction of the door, and listened.

"Do you hear him?"

"Whom?"

"Hadget."

"No. I hear nothing."

"Lock the door, then. Quick—quick!—for God's sake. You don't know how important it is to you."

Amazed at the various requests, Dorcas obeyed, and returned to the bedside.

"Now—now—Dorcas, is it locked? Come here. Hold that will in the candle, and burn it—burn it to ashes. Now, give me that old piece of paper lying by it. There—there—I have done you justice, at last. May God forgive me!"

EXTREMES MEET.

CHAPTER THE FIFTEENTH.

IN WHICH THE OLD LADY DOES TARDY JUSTICE.

AS the flame of the candle caught the edges of the paper, and curled, and twisted them, the old lady seemed to be a little easier in her mind; and when Dorcas had placed the pocket-book in the bosom of her dress, she smiled faintly.

However, her companion was totally at a loss to construe her meaning.

"What do you mean?" Dorcas asked, fancying the old woman's wits were wandering. "You know you destroyed the will in my favour long ago."

"I know I did; but I did not destroy the papers in that pocket-book, nor this paper, either. Often I have meant to — often I have been upon the point of doing so. Thank God, I never did. Forgive me, Dorcas, I have been a sinful wretch! But I can die much easier now I have given you this. They will repay you, in some measure, for the wrongs I have done you."

"How will it repay me, madam? What is it?"

"Oh! Dorcas, oh, do not look at me. I daren't tell you. You will forgive, and will not curse me? The certificate of *your father's marriage with me* is in that pocket-book—the baptismal certificates of your sister and yourself. Find your sister, Dorcas, if she is alive.

Tell her not to curse her mother, Dorcas, —my child! Oh! God, I'm going, Dorcas. See—see—her name is on this paper, and the name of the people I left her with. Oh,. Dorcas, I am a wicked woman!——Snuff the candle. It is going out."

"No—it's burning brightly."

"How can it be burning brightly when I can't see it? Snuff it, I say!"

It was with something of her old impatient manner that the dying woman said this; and Dorcas made a feint of doing what she desired; but was too agitated, and bewildered to know what she was about.

For a few moments, Mrs. Falsetto was silent; and Dorcas tremblingly took her hand.

"Speak to me," she said. "Tell me what you mean?"

"Oh, Dorcas, can you not guess? Oh, my child! Oh, God, how I have wronged you."

"Mrs. Falsetto—madam—mother!" almost screamed the other.

"I could not own you at first; and when the cause was removed, I was ashamed to do so. You will have my property, Dorcas, you and your sister. You will find her?"

"Yes—yes," sobbed Dorcas. "I will try."

"Take this paper, then. You see the names?"

Dorcas looked at the discoloured sheet on which some faint writing was hardly visible. She looked at it, and read the name which the old lady pointed to with a trembling finger,—read it with astonishment—with indignation—with a strange mixture of contending emotions, which deprived her of speech.

Her mother's voice recalled her—speaking rapidly, and almost inarticulately.

"Dorcas, I'm going! Ring the bell. Quick—quick! Have the servants up. Ring the bell, I say! Where are you? Come back. Hold my hand—hold it tight. I'm cold. I'm dying! Dorcas—Dorcas!—say you love me for a moment only. My God, I shall not have time yet!"

The violent ringing of the bed-room bell had brought the servants trooping up; and, Bolusout, who had returned, came in with them.

"Who's here? I can't see," the old woman cried. "Is that Hadget?"

"It is the doctor."

"The doctor? He will do. Doctor, bear witness. Dorcas Abbot is my daughter. She has the proofs. My property I leave to her and her sister. Her name is—the light is going out. Snuff it. Quick—I haven't time. Doctor, is there no hope? There must be hope. I never felt like this before. Dorcas, don't leave me! I shall be better directly. This will be over soon."

It was over very soon.

The sands of life ebbed fast away. The shadow of death crept up the livid face, and, Bolusout, and all the doctors in the world, could do no good for her.

Speechless with horror, Dorcas regarded the parent she had found but to lose. Who can tell what were her feelings? To find that this was her mother—a woman whom she had hated these ten years, and who had used her so badly. To find that this was her sister whom she too had known but to hate!

She trembled as she looked upon the corpse —to think what evil passions had worked recently within her breast—and then her pent-up feelings found vent in a violent burst of grief; and falling on her knees beside the bed, she wildly tore her hair, and moaned, and sobbed, heedless of the servants, who looked on frightened and amazed at the curious drama enacting before them.

A new incident presently added to the excitement of the scene.

Hadget had returned, and came running up-stairs. He seemed furious at finding the room full of people, and glared round at them fiercely.

"What is all this?" he cried. "How is she? What is the matter? Is she worse?"

"She's dead," the doctor replied softly, and pointed to Dorcas.

"What's the matter with her?"

"Hush, she is so much affected by the poor lady's death."

"Affected! why, she had no reason to love her."

"It seems she had."

"What do you mean?"

"If what the lady said was true. It's most astonishing!"

"What did she say?—what has she been doing—why has she had out her papers. Something has been burnt. What is all this mystery?"

"She said that Miss Abbot was her daughter."

"What?"

Hadget staggered back as though he had received a violent blow, and the workings of his ugly mouth were terrible to look at.

"It's a lie!" he cried, "her wits were gone —she was out of her senses—she has no daughters—they are both dead. I've got the proofs. I defy you all—Ha! ha! It's a damned conspiracy!"

"My dear sir—my very dear sir,"-remonstrated Bolusout, quite at a loss to account for the lawyer's extraordinary demeanour, and unwilling to quarrel with the heir-at-law before his bill was settled.

"I quite believe it's as you say; I haven't a doubt of it in fact. I am really grieved that circumstances should have placed me in so unpleasant a position. But my late patient really did make the statement, I assure you she did, and called me as witness. I appeal to these good people to corroborate my words."

A murmur of assent from the servants answered his question, and at the same time, Dorcas, rising to her feet, said, as calmly as she could speak—

"It is true, doctor. I trust that you will not forsake the charge my mother has given you, and that you will protect my interest."

"Where is the will?—where is the will she made in my favour, I know it was in that box. Who has destroyed it?"

"I have," replied Dorcas.

"You hear that," shouted Hadget; "you'll bear witness to that."

"I destroyed it," continued Dorcas, "at the

direction of my mother, you, doctor, heard, and all of you likewise, what my mother's wishes were upon the subject."

"And pray what proof have you got beyond the old woman's delirious wanderings?"

"I have the proofs here," said Dorcas, laying her hand upon her breast.

"The papers you have then you have no right to. Give them up!"

"Nay nay," said Bolusout, interfering. "This will never do, Mr. Hadget, really your conduct is extraordinary."

It was extraordinary that Hadget should so lose his head, something more than usually unpleasant must have occurred, so to discompose him.

He seemed to see all at once that he was acting strangely, and mumbling some sort of apology left the room.

"You must excuse me, doctor; I am so worried by other matters. The grief at my aunt's death,—this absurd attempt of that designing woman to rob me of my rights,—all combined have almost turned my head—I don't know what I am saying. I hope you will forget it."

Words to this effect he had whispered to Bolusout as he left the room.

A loud knock came at the street-door as he descended the stairs, and a servant came up to say that he was wanted. Hadget hurried down into the hall, where two rough-looking men carrying thick sticks were waiting to see him.

"Ah!" said Hadget, "you're here at last. I expected you at my chambers. Come in here."

He led the way into the dining-room and closed the door.

"What news?" said he.

"We haven't nabbed him yet, master.'

"How's that?"

"We've looked high and low, and made every possible inquiry. He's so precious artful."

"What made you let him go when you had him?"

"Well, he's the first that ever did get out of our 'sylum; that's all I've got to say, master."

"What do you mean to do, then—give him up?"

"No, not quite that, I reckon. I think we've spotted him this journey."

"Where?"

"There's a party of the name of Craven—"

"Ah! damnation—I thought as much. Are they together?"

"I rayther expect they are, and that this Craven helped him to give us the slip. But don't you make no mistake, we'll put a plant on the pair of 'em."

"Do so, and quickly. You know what I promised you—I'll double it."

"Consider the thing as done, then. Only we must have your help, I expect."

"When?"

"The sooner the better."

"I'm ready now."

"Come on then, master; we've got the cab a-waiting for us."

CHAPTER THE SIXTEENTH.

COMIC LECTURERS.

YOU can imagine Mr. Ochre's astonishment when Maurice arrived at his lodgings in a cab, all bruised and bloody from his rival's fists.

"What on earth has happened!" he cried. "You haven't been having your hair cut again?"

"I've been fighting," replied Maurice.

"Fighting! Who with?"

"With Drawler."

Ochre pulled a long face, and beat the ashes out of his pipe rather impatiently.

"Who got the best of it?" he asked, after a while.

"He did," Maurice said, sullenly, "this time."

"What do you mean—you're not going to fight again?"

"Who says we're not?"

"Why man, you wouldn't be so foolish."

"Foolish!"

"Yes. I know why you fought, of course. Maurice, do take my advice. She is quite unworthy of you. You will never succeed in anything if your mind is for ever running upon this grievance. Come, my dear boy, listen to me. I am sure some day you will say I was right. Forget her!"

Saying so, Ochre pressed his friend's hand gently in his, and spoke with quite a tremble in his voice.

But Maurice could not agree.

"Forget her!" he cried, springing up, and clutching his forehead in his hands. "While I live I can never forget her. Oh, what did I do that she should have left me as she did? Oh, how I loved her!—how I loved her!"

Mr. Ochre said nothing; but loaded another pipe very tightly, and began to pull at it like a steam engine.

It was three days before Mr. Maurice's face was anything like itself; and even then it bore marks of ill-usage. However, Mr. Ochre suggested at the end of that time that they should start, as it would be necessary to post the town where they were to lecture, at least, three days before the lecture came off.

Not longer than that, Jack said, because people would forget all about it.

"We want to do the thing well, you know." said Jack; "but not to over-do it."

I can't help laughing myself, although I have heard all this story a dozen times before, at the earnest way in which Mr. Ochre—that phlegmatic philosopher—that wholesale dealer in good advice, and pitiless pooh-pooher of all scheming and schemers—went into this ridiculous lecturing expedition.

There are some of you, I daresay, who think that such a matter-of-fact person as that scene painter, would never have done it, and that all this is absurdly unnatural. Upon my word, I think you're wrong. It is just these sort of fellows whose conduct is the most foolish when their turn comes. Just as we know that philosophers have time out of mind been led by the nose by a woman.

But to go back to the subject. Mr. Ochre and Maurice were undecided to what place they should pitch upon for a start. Jack said some large town. Maurice said some little one. He was not quite confident of his own powers as yet, and did not think he had the pluck to face a large audience.

There were a great many arguments upon the subject, and a great many cogitative pipes. It was not until the evening before they started, that they had decided upon CHOKEY-IN-THE-HOLE, which is, as everybody knows, a dull little fishing village, on the Sussex coast.

"We'll give a night there, and, at the same time, have our advertisements up at SHINGLE-SHORE," said Maurice.

"That's the ticket!" said Jack. "So, we'll go to Chokey-in-the-Hole first, and post our bills; then I'll go on to Shingleshore, and have 'em put up there, and then come back to help you with the lecture."

It was all cut and dried, you see, only, unfortunately, it was another example of that popular practice of—reckoning without one's host.

When they arrived, they found that at Chokey-in-the-Hole there was no Lecture Hall. Indeed, it is as it was then, a wretched little place, where nobody in their senses would think of going to stop at unless they were positively obliged to do so.

"Are the're ever any entertainments down here?" Jack asked the landlord of the solitary ale-house.

"I don't recollect hearin' of none."

"That dosen't sound encouraging," said Maurice.

"Nonsense!" said Jack. "We shall be all the more attraction."

"I hope so."

By dint of inquiry, they found that a lecturer on astronomy, last summer, had hired the National School room; and, according to the shoemaker (also fisherman, baker, and linendraper), had made a tidy thing of it.

"What do you call a tidy thing?" asked Jack.

"Well, may be ten or fifteen shillings, when he'd paid his expenses."

"That doesn't sound very encouraging," said Maurice who was a regular damp blanket.

"Why, doesn't it?" cried Jack, furiously. "What could the fool expect, calling his lecture, 'The Heaven's brought nearer,' Why, it sounds like a sermon; and I'm not sure it isn't blasphemous. Why didn't he call it 'Half an 'our with Moon?'" That would have had them. Some people are so infernally stupid!"

"You think the 'Quizziology' will draw them, then?"

"Think? Why, of course it will."

The bills were posted after a little difficulty about the printing. The body of the bills they had had done in London, luckily; so that when a printer *was* found (twelve miles off, by the bye,), the "heads" were soon finished, and posted up on every available wall and paling.

Just when the last bill was nicely up, it commenced raining.

There are some English summers when there is a good deal of rain. This was one of them. It rained steadily all that day, and the next night.

Jack Ochre departed through the rain for Shingleshore, and returned damp, but sanguine. Shingleshore had been posted so as it never had been posted before. He left all the town reading the bills.

All the town, such as it was, read the bills at Chokey, and, if one might judge by the expression of the town's countenance, did not make a great deal out of them.

The rain had made them very damp, and they peeled off easily. A rustic urchin was observed to take down three in succession, and neatly fold, and pocket them; for which, Mr. Ochre, coming upon him unawares, slapped his head.

"Don't you think it's a cut above the clods?" said Maurice.

"Perhaps it is," said Ochre; "but it's the gentry we look to."

The evening of the third day arrived without any change in the weather. Maurice was dressed an hour and a half before there was any occasion for him to be so.

They had had the school-room cleaned out, and the seats arranged—chairs for the reserved seats, and forms for the body of the hall. Then they set up in candlesticks, borrowed from the inn, two pounds of composite candles, lighted them, and got into their places.

Jack was to be the money-taker; and he would have acted his part capitally only——

Only it kept on raining a little harder than ever—only the lecture-room was in such an out of the way place, down a lane full of mud, in fact—only the affair was a great mistake.

"How awfully slow the time goes," thought Maurice, up-stairs.

"Must be some mistake," thought Jack, at the door. "We couldn't have put the time on the bills."

He went outside to look at one by the light of a match. Yes, there it was, as large as life.

"It's most extraordinary," said he. "Perhaps my watch is wrong."

The school-house was a building by itself, and nobody lived in it. Some distance to the next house, too. If his watch was fast it could not be very much so. He would wait a little longer.

Maurice up-stairs was dead beat. For some time he had waited behind a screen. Getting tired of that, he came out, and talked to the musician. Growing hardier, he sat down, and drank up his tumbler of water by sips.

"I'd better go down and see what's the matter," he said, at last.

He was just going down when he heard steps upon the stairs. Rushing frantically behind the screen, he waited with a palpitating heart.

"Hallo!" cried a loud voice. "Hallo! lecturer."

It was Ochre.

"What's the matter?" said Maurice, rather

indignantly, and poking out his head. "Why don't you send 'em up?"

"Send who up?"

"The audience."

"The audience, eh?"

Mr. Ochre made no further remark, but began coolly to blow out all the candles and put the ends into his pocket.

"It's no good wasting them," he said. "Now, then, are you coming?"

"Why, isn't there," asked Maurice, between a laugh and a cry,—"isn't there going to be any Quizziology at all?"

"Not unless you'll give it to me," said Ochre, gloomily. "We seem to be the only two fools out."

They walked home silently through the rain, with their trowsers tucked up. When they arrived at the inn they ordered two shilling glasses of brandy-and-water hot, and sat down before the fire.

"Well!" said Jack.

"Well!" said Maurice, and burst out laughing with all his might.

In which performance Mr. Ochre presently joined him.

"I always said this was a rotten place," observed Jack. He had, by the way, always said quite the contrary. "Shingleshore will make us."

"Hooray for Shingleshore!" cried his companion. "Let's have a pipe,"

That Maurice was always a reckless young vagabond. He asked Jack after a bit whether he had ever had such a lark before in his life.

"It would have been better fun if it had paid," observed Mr. Ochre, who at times was obtuse.

"No, but," argued Maurice, "supposing it had happened to somebody else—supposing we'd read it in a book, shouldn't we have laughed?"

"It's such a dead sell," said Jack. "I shouldn't have believed it."

CHAPTER THE SEVENTEENTH.

MORE COMIC LECTURING.

NEXT day they started for Shingleshore. The day after was the one fixed for the entertainment.

"We made a great mistake," said Mr. Ochre, "by not canvassing. We should have gone round to all the shops and given them orders."

"Ah! that would have been the plan."

So they turned over a new leaf and began to do Shingleshore in a business-like way.

Mr. Ochre knocked at all the private houses and handed in a circular, while Mr. Maurice went round the shops.

"It's not quite the sort of thing I like," said Maurice, to himself. "However, I suppose a lecturer mustn't be proud. Anyhow the people won't insult one."

Won't they. Oh! my poor brothers and sisters, may you never have to supplicate for favours of the arrogant and rich.

You know the story of the doctor canvassing for votes, who called upon the grocer. "Oh, it's you, is it?" asked the paltry fiddler of plums. "Want my vote, do you?"—"No," said Hunter, "I don't: I want a ha'porth of raisins—and look sharp about it."

Maurice many a time felt inclined to act in the same way to the insolent shopkeepers he called upon with his prospectuses.

"What is it," one said. "Put it down," said another. "Take the rubbish away," said a third. "Tickets!" they all cried, as though they were a deadly insult. "We don't want any tickets. Lord bless the man! We can pay if we want to go, which is not likely."

Perhaps you think they had left the rain behind them at Chokey-in-the-Hole. They had not. The lecturing hall was up a lane, too, here. and in an out-of-the-way place.

"This horrible weather will spoil us," cried Ochre; "mark my words if it does not."

It did in some measure, but still there was a slight improvement.

There was a family of five came, one in arms There were a very old man and a very old woman who were hard of hearing, and with whom Ochre had a good deal of trouble, sa they paid in half-pence and were a half-penny short, to convince them of which he had to count the change over twice, and allow them to do the same, and then search on the floor to see whether the missing coin had not been dropped. There was also a very haughty swell with a very stiff collar and an eye-glass, who told Mr. Ochre that he supposed it was "awful bosh," and only came because he wanted something to send him to sleep. To which Mr. Ochre retorted that it was a pity he had not brought two or three more of the same mind, because he had no doubt they could be accommodated.

This gentleman found fault with the hardness of the reserved seats—objected strongly to the youngest member of the family of five, and called the entertainment a swindle before it began.

There were in all about thirty persons, but as the hall was intended to accommodate six hundred, they did not quite fill it.

It was a horrid place, this lecture-room— large, and cold, and damp—with an echo in it which mocked the speaker's voice, and gave a ghostly character to the entertainment.

You know Maurice had had his hair cut. This was not very long ago, and it had not grown much. He still wore a very bird-like aspect.

There was a most distressing light too, in the vault-like room, which made the unfortunate lecturer look like a dead man. Somehow, everything seemed to go against him.

I dare say the reader will think this and what is coming to be grossly exaggerated. I can in reply only say, that it is much truer than the reader thinks for, and I have my own reasons for imparting a certain vagueness to the locale.

The time came for commencing—the overture was played over twice, to give the thirty-first visitor an opportunity of arriving in time, he, however, preferred stopping away altogether.

Maurice rang a little hand-bell behind the screen, and immediately afterwards, in the midst of a death-like silence, stepped upon the scaffold—I meant to say the platform.

The first thing he did was to peg away at the water bottle. The swell in the reserved seats had by this time come to the conclusion that the whole thing was an imposition and made up his mind to hiss at the very first opportunity. The youngest of the family of five was alarmed at the lecturer's spectral appearance, and began to cry, but was shaken quiet. The old couple took no particular notice, but cracked nuts, with reports like small guns.

Could anything be more dispiriting?" Nothing floors an amateur so soon as this kind of reception. Poor Maurice cast his eyes despairingly upon the empty benches and the handful of stragglers, then down at the door, where Jack Ochre was telegraphing in absurd pantomime.

Go on, he seemed to say: what on earth are you stopping for?

There was nothing for it but a bold plunge —a header, as swimmers say—so he took it.

He rattled on with all his might, afraid to stop for fear he should break down. He was so much engaged and so flurried, that he did not notice his audience much, or see how it was going. He did certainly see that one person got up and went out, and that another got up and followed him; but he took no particular note of the circumstance.

It was not until the end of the first song that he saw that things were flat. Somebody hissed—it was somebody at the very back of the sixpenny seats, a gentleman with his hat on, lying across three benches. The reserved swell responded by an ironical "Ha! ha!"

Maurice stopped suddenly as though he had been shot. For some time he could not get on at all. Some of the audience applauded a little, to help him, so he took heart and made another start.

Things did not mend. They grew, if anything, flatter. In course of time he came to an impersonation, and then something awful happened.

In the middle of a song introducing various characters, he was to rush behind the scenes and pop on a cloak, a beard, and a wide-awake, and then rush out again as a bold bandit.

The table at which he lectured stood, as the saying is, very "keggly." A very little would throw it off its balance. Maurice ran at it full tilt, not heeding where he was going, kicked the table with his foot, and sent it and the libretto, the candlesticks, and water-bottle all over that swell in the reserved seat.

I would have liked you to have seen the swell's expression as he rose, and shook himself. After he had shaken himself, he shook his fist at the lecturer, who stood staring at him with a rueful countenance, holding in his hand a candle he had caught at as if fell.

"I'm very sorry, I'm sure," said Maurice, apologetically.

"Damn your sorrow! I shall expect my money back."

"Certainly, sir. But this was quite accidental, I assure you."

"I don't mind the accident—it's the best part of the whole affair. It's an infernal imposition!"

"You shall have your money back," said Maurice; "and as for the affair being an imposition, I appeal to these ladies and gentlemen."

The ladies and gentlemen appealed to, who had been in convulsions of laughter, responded by "Hooray!" and "Go it lecturer!" and "Knock it over again, governor!"

Encouraged by this mirth, the unfortunate lecturer proceeded. Poor entertainer! Poor entertainment!

One by one the audience slunk off. When the old couple had finished their nuts, they went away together. The family of five were divided, — three went, and two remained. The younger was one of those left, and it began to cry.

There was a good deal of talking among the audience, and some coughing and stamping. Once somebody whistled.

It came to an end at last; and, with it Maurice's hopes of earning a living.

Years afterwards the members of that little audience remembered the humour of the thing, and burst out laughing at the recollection. It was rare fun, was it not?—that is to say, for everybody but the lecturer. But, then, we cannot all be happy. Some must be sad, whilst others are merry. It's your turn to-day, and it's my turn to-morrow."

Through the country travelled the lecturer and his staff. Sometimes they filled the room; sometimes they didn't. As a whole the expedition was a failure. Among the various places that they visited was Skearcrows. The Jewish gentleman who had bought the old house had made an inn of it. Maurice had a glass of ale in the parlour.

While he was sitting there, an old man in a Bath chair was wheeled up to the door by a red-faced giant, and Maurice recognised Messrs. Piper, father and son.

He would gladly have escaped their notice; but seeing the old man's eye upon him, Maurice thought it best to speak.

"How do you do, sir?" he said.

"Lord bless me! it's Maurice. How do you do? I'm pretty well myself, thank God. I wish I could say the same of that poor wretch. Don't he look like a ghost?"

"Rather a red-faced one," said Maurice.

"Red face!" cried the old gentleman. "Red face! Ha—ha!—that's not bad. Do you know why he's got a red face? I've found it out. He's appoplectic."

Having thus expressed his opinion, the old gentleman seemed in high spirits, and began to tell all the news.

Kitty had gone to London, and, they did say, was under the protection of a nobleman; but perhaps that was only talk. Old Bob Sawder had gone to London, and never been heard of since, though he had left a suit of clothes behind, and some money in the bank. Hadget had never been down since Sir John's death. Ernest had, but did not stop long. He, too, had gone back to London. In short, everybody was in London.

"I suppose Bob Sawder's been with you?" said Mr. Piper.

"No," said Maurice, "he hasn't. He called upon me to tell me the dreadful news. After that, I never saw him; but I don't think he was examined."

"How was that?"

"Well, I suppose he had nothing important to say."

"Accounts differ," said the old man, shaking his head. "There's been a deal of talk over the business down here; and we've come to several conclusions——"

"And one of them is?"

"That Bob Sawder was kept out of the way."

"What do you mean?" cried Maurice, letting fall his glass. "What are you hinting at?"

"I don't like hinting anything," said the old man; "but if I were you, I'd have my eyes open."

"What, in God name, would you have me believe?"

"The murderer's not dead yet."

"Who do you suspect?"

"What became of all the property? It was sold. By whom? By Sir John? Who got the money? His murderer? Was it found on the cabman? No. Then, who got it? The sailor? Where is he? That's the question. Who was he? That's another. Find the answers."

After thus mysteriously delivering himself of his opinions, Mr. Piper ordered his son to push on the chair, and refused to say another word.

But he had said enough.

"We must go back to London, Jack," cried Maurice. "I have the most terrible suspicions. My brain is on fire! Come—come—at once to London. I will never rest till I find the murderer!"

It is only a few months ago that Maurice had no object in life. He has two now—at least, one is to trace the assassin; the other, to square accounts with my lord.

CHAPTER THE EIGHTEENTH.

EXTREMES MEET.

LONDON by night—the wettest night of a wet autumn. The streets deserted, and lonely. Such few pedestrians who are out per force, but who have homes to go to, making the best of their way through puddle and mire to reach the looked-for shelter. Such who have reasons for remaining out,—the policeman, for instance, waiting to be relieved from his duty,—taking shelter in door-ways, or plodding heavily down the street with extra show of zeal as the time draws nigh for the visit of his sergeant. Others who have other reasons for being out, poor forlorn-looking women, scantily dressed, and ragged and wet, hang about up dark archways, under the lea of houses, or anywhere where they can escape the rain, and where the policeman, made savage by the weather, will allow them to remain.

A mournful scene is Foot Court, Holborn, in its damp desolation. The convivial tailor has come home, and gone to bed an hour ago at least, summoning his Sarah Jane, at the top of his voice, from the attic storey. He has been admitted, has defied the rest of the Court to mortal combat, has laughed, and shed tears, has banged his wife and children, and, finally, been put to bed, and held there after the style of some British husbands who have been out spending a roaring evening, and come home with a little too much drink in their stomachs.

The "Plumes," the "Hand and Heart," and the other public-house are shut up. There is no light in any of the windows, although the poor Court strugglers are not the first people in the world to go to bed. They have not the time, and can't afford it. Everything is quiet and still. The Court is asleep. There is no sign of life.

Yes, one. Upon the doorstep of Cleveland Chambers, in much the same position that Nelly was found by Maurice that other wet night at the beginning of this story, when he took her home with him a lonely woman, cold, and wet, and weary, sits shivering in her rags. Her tattered garments flutter in the wind, and the rain beats down upon her uncovered head. She sits there in her squalid misery, a picture of despair. Through her burst boot one can see her naked foot. Her old wreck of a bonnet has fallen off, and her yellow hair, dank with rain, hangs over her face.

Poor houseless wanderer, what a sad spot to choose for a resting-place! Sitting here, do not the memories of the happy days gone by come thronging thickly back upon your memory? Oh, Nelly! Nelly!—bright, blue-eyed, golden-haired goddess—is it possible that this should be the end of all? Is there no chance for you? Down the hill—down, deeper and deeper. Both you and your scapegrace lover are sinking slowly but surely. Is my story to wind up by your meeting at the workhouse?—what is to become of you?

You have both behaved badly—bad enough surely for a highly moral and conscientious novel writer (as the author of "THE WOMAN WITH THE YELLOW HAIR" wishes to be considered) to make an example of. Yet I do really believe that if that is to be the case, many readers will be discontented and disgusted. I am told that that loose vagabond, Maurice, is a favourite with the ladies; and that disgrace to her sex, Mrs. Nelly, is not without her admirers among the gentlemen.

It is almost time that these questions were answered. My story is drawing to a close, and I hope that everything will be cleared up to your satisfaction (consistent with probabilities, that is to say).

As the bundle of rags, which was once my beautiful heroine, sits crouching on the door-step, another bundle of rags came slinking up the court. An elderly woman this—very bony and spare, much troubled by a hollow cough, and whose eye is covered by a bandage, which also partly obscures the other, and causes her to turn her head on one side to look at anything, in a quaint and curious manner, that gives her the appearance of an inquisitive crow with dilapidated plumage.

This second wanderer arriving, after a long and tedious journey up the court in front of Cleveland Chamber, cocks up her available eye at a certain window on the second floor, and contemplates it for some time, silently and sadly.

After which she sighs deeply, and gathering her rags around it as tightly, as it can, sits down by the side of the other outcast on the door-step, and makes herself as comfortable as circumstances will admit of in the opposite corner—which, by the way, is not very comfortable after all.

At her approach Nelly raises her eyes, expecting it is a policeman come to disturb her. There is something in the old women's appearance which seems familiar to her, and she scans her features earnestly.

"Oh, deary, deary!" the old creature says, with a whine, "Ow my poor bones does ache sure-ly."

"Is that you, Miss Perk!"

"Eh!"

"Is that you?" asked Nelly.

"Oh, lor! oh dear! oh, my! Oh, my bones —oh, my heart! Whose that?"

"Who should it be?"

"It's my missus. It's my dear missus come back to look for me; I know it is. Oh, how good it is of you. I told em, although you did shake me up, you'd a good heart for all that. It don't follow because you shook me you shouldn't have one. People as had got one might yet shake other people as was as stupid as me. I aint surprised a bit that you should shake me, I only wonder you wasn't always at it—I was trying to you, I know. Oh, dear! God bless you! Oh, I am so glad that you've come back!"

The young woman made no reply. With hard, tearless eyes she watched the speaker's face, and bitter, bloodless lips.

Presently, when old Miss Perks had got Nelly within the range of her practical eye, she discovered, by dint of staring, that her late mistress's clothes were very wet and worn.

"Oh! grajus me! Oh, deary, deary! 'Ow wet you are; and, oh!—how thin your dress is —and sitting here this time o'night, you'll catch your death of cold. What does it mean? Why don't you go inside?—why, your boots is in holes. Oh! my poor dear— my love, my lamb—what has come to you?— what has come to Mr. Maurice? Why aint everybody lords and ladies, like they was going to be? I don't know how it's come about, but Twisted-his-wrist is at the bottom of it all, I'm certain sure!"

"It does not matter why," Nelly replied; "you would not understand it if I were to tell you. Circumstances have occurred—I am very poor myself—starving nearly. Thank God it won't be for long."

"Oh, my poor dear mistress! How pale and thin, and worn you look—you, as was so beautiful. There never was nobody a half-quarter so beautiful that ever I see. What ever made you leave us all, and poor dear Mr. Maurice, as was so ill these ever so many months. Oh! how he talked about you; never an hour passed but he mentioned your name, and said he wished you were there, and he wondered what made you go away."

The yellow-haired woman makes no reply. Her eyes are fixed upon the stones on which her feet were resting. Her lips are compressed, and her breast heaves like a troubled ocean.

"But my dear mistress," continued Miss Perks, fingering at Nelly's dress; "what do you mean by starving? Mr. Maurice doesn't know your starving, does he? What are you doing with yourself out in the bitter cold streets at this time of the night? Oh! to think that you should be poor, like other folks, and have to work; I can't—I really can't believe it. You're not made to work; you shan't work. Show me what to do, and I'll work for you till the flesh falls off my bones."

"I don't want you to work for me, thank you; I am not working myself. I don't want anybody to do anything for me. Luck's against me, and I don't care how soon there's an end of it."

"What's luck against you for, poor dear? What have you done to luck that it should spite you?—you, so young and beautiful, and good——"

"There—there!—" cries Nelly, impatiently, 'don't talk about me any more. What are you doing?"

"Don't talk about me, either, then! retorts the old woman, with an effort to be sprightly. "Luck's always been agin me, I suppose. I never got on like others has; but, then, I aint surprised at that. I aint no schollard, you see. I can hardly read, although I'm just on seventy; and as for writing, never dreamt of it. Then, I aint sharp, and active-like. I suppose it is my old bones as has got creaky."

"I suppose it is time that you left off working altogether."

"Who says that? I'm strong enough, I'm sure. Much stronger than many of your young ones. But, oh, oh, oh! I can't get no think to do."

And the old woman begins to whimper.

"Have you left the chambers;" asks Nelly.

"They wouldn't have me no longer," replies the other. They said I was too old for 'em; and Mrs. Perks sent me away. I've been trying to get something to do; but I can't. Sometimes I've slept at the "Hand and Heart," when they've been good enough to let me. Other times, I have slept in the streets. Its dreadful cold and wet these last few days. Its pretty near killed me."

"Cold and wet enough," says Nelly, more to herself than to her companion. "I have found them so."

"Who have you found?" asks the old lady, who was very deaf, being nearly blind. "Talking of finding, you recollect the old lady that came one day to ask for Mr. Maurice, as you sent off again."

"Yes, I remember."

"She has called again twice."

"To see Maurice?"

"No, to see you."

"To see me, impossible! What did she want with me?"

AT HOME.

CHAPTER THE NINETEENTH.

THERE ARE TWO SIDES TO A HALFPENNY.

"INDEED, I don't know, mam! but she wanted to see you very much, indeed she did. She axed a lot of questions about you, she did—whether you had been here since you left Mr. Maurice; where Mr. Maurice was, and whether it was you that there was something about in the papers. The lady said she had put a notice in the paper for you to write to her, but you had never answered. She came about a month ago first, and then again the other night. The other night it was she saw me—about a week was yesterday, and I

was sitting here, as I might be now on this here identical door-step, about one in the morning, when she comes up to me, and lays her hand upon me and says ‘Nelly.’ I jumps up and sees her standing before me, there—See, missus; there—where she stands now."

Looking up, Nelly sees standing before her the dark figure of a woman, which has approached them silently and unobserved, while they have been talking.

"Your name is Raymond?"

"Well."

"I want to speak to you—alone."

"Speak on," replies Nelly, nodding in the direction of Miss Perks. "She's deaf."

"Your tone of voice is angry," the other

woman says. "There should be no anger between us."

"Should there not? Why?"

"There are good reasons."

"Indeed, Miss Abbot; I thought the reasons were all the other way. I fancied that such as you have every reason for hating such as me, and setting your heel upon us when we were at your feet in the mud. Listen to what I say," Dorcas continues, in a deep, low voice, pressing, as she speaks, her hand upon her heart as though to stay its throbbing. "I have reason enough to hate you for being the woman that Maurice loves, in preference to me. I have still further reason for hating you, for being the cause of Maurice's ruin. And were that not even enough, I might hate you for the way in which you have deserted him."

"To be sure," replies Nelly, with a sneer. "In the same way you have reason for loving him for ruining me. That's a good trait in his character, is it not? What is the ruin of a base-born woman like I am, to the insolvency of a fine young gentleman?"

"I say," Dorcas pursues, in the same tone, I have reason enough to hate you."

"Well—and you do. That's settled."

"I must not."

"Must not?"

"No. I am here to rescue you from the streets and from death. Every night for more than a month, I and others have been looking for you. I heard that you had gone down in the world. Only a fortnight ago I heard that you had fallen as low as this; since then, every night I have walked the streets in the hope of finding you. Whenever I have seen the figure of a woman half hidden away in a dark corner, I have gone up and spoken to her. Many awful faces have they lifted up from their laps to look at me when I spoke. I was afraid that you might be like one of these, and that I might not be in time. As I hope to be saved, Nelly Raymond, I swear to you, that every night upon my bended knees I have prayed to God that I might be in time."

The woman she addresses looks up at her, half in astonishment, half in ridicule.

"You're very good to take so much trouble, I'm sure." she says, with something of her old saucy manner.

Beneath those greasy rags and tatters she is still the same cold, proud, insolent woman that she had ever been. An empty stomach and a bare back make not one jot of difference in her style of conversation.

"You're very good, I'm sure. But it's really wasting your time. I don't want to go to a reformatory, I thank you. I've had several kind offers, and I am told that if I really make up my mind to mend my ways and behave well for a year or two, there is an opening for me in the scullery. Thank you very much, but," (this with a savage emphasis) "there is a better opening in the river. Before long it will close upon me."

"Nelly," says Dorcas, sinking upon her knees at the other's feet,—"Nelly, listen to me. You mistake my object. I have come to find you because I promised your dying mother that I would do so."

"How did you know my mother?—she died when you must have been a little child. You are about my age?"

"I am the same age, Nelly, exactly. I have known your mother and have acted as her companion about eleven years. A few moment before she died I learnt that she was your mother—a few moments before she died I learnt *that we were sisters!*"

"Sisters!"

Repeating the word, Nelly has sprung to her feet with an expression of surprise and dismay, and with a half-frightened gesture with her hands, waves the other off, while poor Miss Perks, whom the sudden movement overbalances and topples over, climbs on her legs again, and stares with her practical eye, wide enough open for two of anybody else's.

"Yes, sisters," repeats Dorcas. "And it is to give you that portion or our mother's property which is your share, that I have so long been looking for you. It is not likely," she continues, rising to her feet, "that we, who have known but to hate each other, can, in a moment change our hate to love. Here is money for you, to find a shelter and suitable clothes. Here is also the address of my solicitor, who will, if you choose, also act for you."

"Where do you live?"

"I live in lodgings. If you will come there with me, there is everything prepared for you. To-morrow, if you like, you can leave me again; or, if you like, stay until our affairs are settled."

"You do not think, then, that you can feel like a sister towards me?"

"Like a sister is supposed to feel—never! Do you think you could towards me?"

"I am not of a loving disposition."

"You say truly—you are not. There is that difference in us; it is for me to love hopelessly those who love you as hopelessly in their turn."

"It were better, then, that we did not cross each other's path."

"It matters little now the mischief is done. Come, are you ready?"

Was she then saved from death?—was she again to go back to riches?—had her past life been a lesson to her?—is not all this a little improbable?

There are stranger things happen every day in real life, I am sure. Now, supposing he had not some great hidden reason for doing otherwise, do you suppose anybody who was writing a novel would miss such an opportunity of a grand moral climax? Having brought her down to the gutter, would it not have been poetically just that she should die there? Did she not deserve it?—is it not invariably the end of "all that sort of thing?" Did you not now, reader, fancy to yourself—"Here's the old end coming—the river or dung heap business over again. We might have had something original." I am for the poetical justice myself, but I don't suppose it would please you. I suppose I had better go on as I intended after all. I believe I have previously hinted that I am a person without any imagination, and can only repeat what is told to me, or copy the life I see at the end of my nose. There really is not that triumph of virtue in real life which accompanies the Victorian melo-drama, and I do not intend to paint life a morsel better than I find it, though it would make this story sell double as well as it does.

Besides, after all, was it not quite a toss up whether she was to be lucky or not? It is the same with all the sisterhood.

Up goes Fate's half-penny, cry while it spins.

CHAPTER THE TWENTIETH.

HUMBLE PIE.

THERE are upon record, I have little doubt, many scores of petty meannesses—many score of low rogueries and knaveries, which humanity has been guilty of in endeavouring to annex to their patronymic, what is, in vulgar parlance, termed " a handle." Poor tatter of greatness, what are you without an accompanying pocketfull of dross? So much wind to fill your sails and overturn your cockle shell. You must have ballast.

What! Our aristocratic young friend Sir Ernest Cheveleigh!—the rightful heir to nothing a year—the owner to a proud title that had not a penny hanging to it—what did he do with himself? and what did he do for a living?

That crisis in his affairs had been too much or him. He was a changed man in every respect. When first I introduced him to the reader a more correct, steady, genteel young man I never came across. From his earliest years he had gone in for propriety. Propriety above everything—before everything. Gain the good opinion of the world, bow to the world's opinion, be respectful to your elders, keep your own counsel, and brush your own clothes well. Take those rules to your heart, young man, and if you do not succeed in life, all I can say is that you're very unfortunate.

These had been the rules Ernest had lain down, and strictly adhered to. By these rules had he worked himself up in his office. He was not very clever even as a clerk (I understand that it does not require a genius); but he was very regular, and very steady, kept his nose down to his book, and always had ink in his pen. So he was, in course of time, when his turn came, rewarded by an increase of salary, and put over the heads of Old Quill and Big Bonum, who were geniuses addicted to lax morality and strong liquors—a great weakness with the genius order.

But when he came into his title, supposing that the property was to follow as a matter of course he had thrown up his situation at the Bad Bargains, and, at the same time, said good-bye to his most rigid notions of decorum.

Why should he any longer go on cringing, and bowing, and scraping, and licking of spittal? Was not he, himself a great man, whose shoes small men must come to lick? He had done with such dirty work.

Heigho! Not quite. The property turning out a myth, there came the necessity for living. It was very humiliating to be obliged to beg for the place he had resigned. The worst of this world is, that one is sometimes obliged to eat much more humble pie than one fancies.

So he begged to be taken back; and was taken back after a great deal of begging, only he was obliged to begin again at the bottom of the ladder, and again go over all the ground he had gone over before.

He thought it a very hard case, as did also many others. His salary now was not more than a quarter of what it had been. His wants were, at least, four times as many as they used to be.

Government manages somethings badly, I am told. The office Ernest filled was a most responsible one; and one in which a dishonest person might easily, and without fear of detection, have committed immense frauds.

Ernest wanted money very badly.

CHAPTER THE TWENTY-FIRST.

PROVOCATION.

THERE was only one way that the needy baronet could hope to retrieve his fortune, and that was to find a rich wife.

One may, however, in the ordinary course of events, spend a tolerably long time in looking for such a commodity.

He saw his way, or fancied that he did. I have told you how he had loved Margaret, otherwise Lady Drawler, and how she had loved him before her mamma stepped in and separated the young couple.

As far as he was capable of such a passion —it is possible that there exist human creatures who are not—he loved Lord Drawler's wife.

Did she love him? That was the question. If she did, was her love stronger than her duty? That must be tried. Once having fallen, she would be in his power.

Her father had lately died, and had settled a handsome income upon her, which my lord could not touch. What if she were divorced from him, and Ernest married her? It was his only chance.

But, then, Margaret would not sue for a divorce. She thought it wicked. Some women have strange notions.

In a systematic and wily manner, Sir Ernest Cheveleigh commenced proceedings, and, though he could not triumph over her virtue, succeeded in blackening her character with the world.

He knew that Lord Drawler was eager to get rid of her, and fancied that by this plan he would be induced to commence the suit himself. He even wrote anonymously to his lordship, intimating that his wife had begun to do so; and it was this news which had, in fact, caused Drawler to return so hastily from Paris.

Arriving in London, he found the intelligence to be false.

Everybody—it is true—(of course, I mean by everybody, a limited number of the select few) was gossiping about the apparent intimacy of Sir Ernest and Drawler's wife; but Drawler's friends were rather shy of alluding to it to the Guardsman, who had in his time, acquired a character as a fire-eater that made people careful.

At last it came out; and his lordship behaved in a way which Sir Ernest hardly expected.

One night Charley Bux and Drawler had been having dinner at the Newton Hotel, in St. Martin's Street Leicester Square. It was about ten o'clock, and they were almost alone. Only one straggler remained besides themselves, and he was, apparently, going to sleep in the corner over the newspaper.

They were in the inner room on the right-hand side as you enter, and sat in one of the centre boxes. The individual reading the paper was almost hidden from their view, and had his back towards them. As they had had a bottle of wine, and felt satisfied with themselves, and the world at large, they talked loudly, like men under such circumstances usually talk, paying no particular attention to the stranger, who might have been awake, and overheard them for what they cared.

"By the way," said Bux, "have you seen that light-haired party you took to Paris with you? Oh, you sly dog, to keep it so quiet!"

"Well, I did not want to be bothered by her man. And you see at the time, I thought it was her husband. She was a most awful liar."

"So I understand. By the bye, you had a regular mill with the fellow who used to keep her, didn't you?"

"I gave him a thrashing; but he is little better than a maniac. I expect every day to meet him again, and have another fight in the street."

"What a savage he must be. Why don't you give him into custody?"

"He wanted to call me out, you know. It's damned absurd; but if he annoys me any more, I really think I must, and then break his arm for him. That'll quiet him, perhaps."

"It's to be hoped so. An infernal cad! Did you say you *had* seen his woman lately?"

"I met her one night in the Haymarket. She was on the streets, I was told. Of course, I cut her. It's a great mistake to renew old connections."

"Certainly."

"The other day, too in the park, I saw her again. She was got up a great swell, and was in a brougham. She bowed to me; but I did not take any notice. She wants to pick me up again, I suppose. Do you know if she's in keeping?"

"She's come into some property—you ought to have known that—at the death of your old friend, Mrs. Falsetto. She was her daughter it turned out. A deuced mysterious case altogether."

"By Jove you surprise me!"

"Egad it surprised me, too, when I heard the particulars. It was supposed that that fellow Maurice, and the baronet, and a man called Hadget, a lawyer—I don't think you know him—were to come in for something. However, it is all divided between the two daughters, Nelly, and Charity, I think the other's called. You see, the old woman committed bigamy, among other little trifles. She married on the quiet a betting-man, or jockey, or horse-stealer, called Burgoyne, and was deuced unhappy with him. So, the old banker, Falsetto, turning up, she married him, and said nothing about the jockey, or the two babies she'd had by him. These were put out to nurse, and then left with the nurses. One of them she took as a companion, and the other was your late mistress. Quite a romance, isn't it?"

"Well," said Drawler, with a curse, "I should have spoken to her if I had known that. And though I'm not very happy to hear of her good luck, I'm pleased to think those cursed Cheveleighs haven't come into anything."

"I thought the baronet was a friend of yours?"

"Friend of mine? He's as conceited a prig as the other fellow is a low blackguard."

"Do you know, Drawler," said Charley, out of whose head the wine had driven the wisdom. "If I were you I'd give that fellow a worse hiding than his cousin."

"Why, pray?"

"Well; there's a very good reason I should think."

"What do you mean?"

"It's all talk though, I suppose!"

"What is?"

"This scandal about him and your wife."

"My wife!" roared Drawler, with a fearful oath. "What scandal? Tell me what you know?"

Thus called upon, and rendered incautious by the liquor he had imbibed, Charley repeated the damning stories current at the clubs, and got on from bad to worse, until his lordship, black in the face with passion, dashed his fist upon the table, and swore by everything in heaven and hell that he would have Ernest's blood.

"I'll go to the Windbags now," he roared, "and before the room-full give him the the damnedest thrashing he ever had."

"No, no!" cried Bux, "that won't do. They'll interfere, and the cur will have you locked up. He has no pluck. Challenge him in the proper way, and lame him."

"Very well. I'll go and write the letter at once, and you shall take it. You offer to be his second and see he does not escape. By God, I'll murder him!"

"Hush!" cried Bux, observing that the stranger in the corner had risen from his seat. "Not so loud."

They rose at the same time to leave the room when the stranger turned round and faced them—

It was Maurice!

"Stop," he said. "Before you settle affairs with him, my lord, you must with me."

"Go to the devil," roared Drawler, in a fury. "I've something else to think of."

"Most probably. But you'll please to think of what I'm saying. You had the best of our last meeting. I want my revenge. If you are not as great a coward as you are a scoundrel, you will give me a gentleman's satisfaction."

"Fine gentleman, forsooth. A bastard."

"Silence, you blackguard!" cried Maurice, seizing a knife which lay by his hand. "It is a safe insult you think; but, by heavens, if you repeat it, I will have my revenge here, on the spot!"

"I told you he was mad," said his lordship. "Here; I'll fight you if you like, and if I've any luck, I'll make a short job of both of you. I'll fight you when and where you like. Arrange the matter with Bux. Only one condition, mind, that I fight your cousin first. I want to make sure of him in case of accidents."

"Hush!" said Charley Bux. "Here's the waiter coming. Don't talk any more about it. Here, Charles, tell us what there is to pay."

CHAPTER THE TWENTY-SECOND.

VENGEANCE.

DON'T you believe what the early bird says about early rising, before you have heard all that the early worm has to urge against it.

"Use is second nature," says the proverb, and I suppose you can get used to anything; but most certainly to us lie-a-beds, it's a fearfully uncomfortable thing to get up an hour or two before the proper time—that is to say, half-an-hour after the time the hot rolls come.

It has always struck me as being one of the great drawbacks to duelling. Think of what the most courageous of us must be like at daybreak, and before breakfast.

Bux was right when he said that Ernest was not courageous—indeed, he almost fainted when he received the challenge.

Never for a moment had he anticipated such a proceeding. He thought that it would have been all comfortably settled by SIR CRESSWELL CRESSWELL. He did not care how they took away his character, he had no fancy for losing his life.

Besides, who ever heard of fighting a duel in these days? was it not ridiculous? Fight, indeed!—he should do nothing of the kind.

He would immediately have given information to the police had not Bux prevented him. This gentleman assured him that, did he not fight, he could never hold up his head again in society, and that Drawler was the sort of man who would horsewhip him whenever they met.

"But, my dear fellow," cried Ernest, almost in tears, "I assure you I am innocent."

"Well, if you are," retorted Bux, "you're a greater fool than I took you for."

It was all settled. On the next day but one after Maurice had challenged Drawler, the double duel was to take place on Hampstead Heath, in a hollow, concealed from the thoroughfare, not far off "The Spaniards" public-house.

In anybody else in the world but that lawless dog, Maurice, I should have thought it strange that he should not be in time, seeing how eager he was for the meeting. But there is nothing extraordinary about Maurice's being a few minutes late. He knew the spot that had been chosen, well, and walked towards it. As he approached, he heard the report of firearms, and next moment was upon the ground.

Then he saw Bux, and an army-surgeon leaning over a prostrate form upon the grass, and another figure with its back towards him looking on.

"The scoundrel has killed him," thought Maurice, as he ran towards them.

It is questionable which of the combatants was intended by the word scoundrel, though I should think he did not expect to find what he found.

It was my lord who lay upon the grass. Lord George Drawler, the heir to the Cumbersome Estates, and the nephew of the great Duke of Doodledum, lay there very quiet and bloody.

The story was soon told. Ernest had done all he could to avoid the duel. As he could not do that, he had thought that the next best thing he could do was to preserve his own life by taking my lord's. He had, in his time, had a good deal of practice with partridge, pheasant, and snipe, treating my lord like one of these, he took his aim, and shot him—dead.

Aye, dead enough he lay there among the innocent buttercups and daisies. With his handsome scoundrel's face, white and rigid, with a bullet through his dastard's heart, this ruiner of women, breaker of hearts, bully, and coward, and liar, lay dead and very bloody.

He was a gallant soldier, and a polished gentleman, his biographer tells us. His comrades mourn his loss; and there is a beautiful marble tombstone erected to his memory in a certain churchyard—where rest the ashes of a generation of Drawlers.

He was a hero in the trenches before Sebastopol, a hero in the night-houses of the Haymarket. He will be remembered for his good and his bad deeds long after this novel has sunk into the limbo of oblivion.

"I'm afraid you have been cheated of your turn," said the army-surgeon, gravely, as Maurice stood looking on.

"There's nobody else you would like to fight, I suppose?"

"No, thank you," said Maurice, with something of a shudder. "I have had ample satisfaction."

CHAPTER THE TWENTY-THIRD.

PURSUIT.

TIME and tide waiteth for no man: not even for a novel-writer.

Therefore, while I have been attending to some of the *dramatis personæ* in this polite history, I have been obliged to leave the others for a while to shift for themselves, and they have not been idle.

Hadget, for instance.

We left him upon the point of getting into a cab to go in search of some party, or parties, mysteriously alluded to by the gentleman with the thick stick.

The ingenious reader, from whom I have no secrets, must long ere this have discovered who the party or parties are; but, for the gentle reader who has not taken the trouble (and very properly, for I shouldn't, in his place) to think about the matter, I must explain.

To make a short story of it, one of the parties was Bob Sawder, the other Dudley Craven.

By what you have seen of Hadget's behaviour towards his old clerk, you may suppose that the latter bore him no particular good will.

To snub, browbeat, and trample upon a dependant, is not the way to make him love you. Many years had Craven borne his master's insults and ill-usage. Formerly a solicitor with a large connection, he had, by dabbling in Stock Exchange ventures, lost every halfpenny, and been obliged to accept employment where he could get it. Having, during his stay in Her Majesty's Prison for debt—the Bench—a house of entertainment where spirituous liquors are strictly prohibited —acquired intemperate habits— you cannot be surprised if Mr. Craven gradually sunk in the social scale.

Drunken clerks are not likely to rise in an office. Dudley sank to the bottom—drank deeper, and got worse.

It was, he thought, a very lucky chance for him when he fell in with Mr. Hadget, who had recently been struck off the rolls for certain felonious practices connected with title deeds and other property deposited in his safe keeping.

The proposition which Mr. Hadget made to the shabby, hungry person who solicited employment, was, that Craven's name should appear at the head of the establishment in Lyon's Inn, and that he should nominally be the master, and Hadget the clerk, though in reality, Craven was to work under the other's direction.

Much work, dirty and otherwise, did the two do together. Much money crept into Hadget's pockets by the same. The hardest and the dirtiest part of the work fell to Craven's share, and he kept his nose to the wheel, and the bottle to his lips, muddling on anyhow, upon an errand boy's wages, and trusting to Hadget's promise that better times were coming.

He wearied of this at last. There are limits even to human credulity. The simpletons who flocked into the Haymarket theatre, expecting to see the conjuror cork himself down in a quart bottle, began to think they had been taken in, after they had waited for an hour, and there were yet no signs of the commencement of the extraordinary performance.

Thus was it that Dudley Craven, finding, as time rolled on, that he was still in the same poor position, and that there seemed to be but a very poor chance of his ever bettering himself, resolved to put a watch upon his master, and endeavour to glean some particulars concerning him which he might use as the means of extorting a small increase in his wages.

But Hadget was too wide-awake to give him the opportunity he sought for. Though Craven felt certain there existed some mysterious connection between his master and the murder in the cab, still he never for a moment suspected that Hadget was the murderer.

He thought that Hadget had, somehow or other, benefitted by Sir John's death, but could not exactly tell how. He seemed to have more money lately than he used to have, but then, that was easily accounted for. He must have got it from Mrs. Falsetto. Until he went to live with her, and in the time immediately succeeding the murder, Hadget had been shabbier in attire, and in every way showed more signs than usual of being desperately "hard up."

It was part of his artful scheme to express the deepest regret at the death of the old man, and to profess the most unlimited indignation at the way in which he himself had been cheated.

"I shall never see a halfpenny," he swore, with the roundest of oaths, "of all the money that old scoundrel has cheated me of. Now he is dead, who am I to look to. I have nothing to show for it."

Then again he would say to Craven,—

"Now the old man is dead my only dodge is to help this young humbug, Ernest, to get the property from his cousin Maurice, and trust to him to act honourably and pay me something for my trouble. I may get a hold of him like that and draw him gently."

When it turned out that Sir Ernest came into no property at all, when he came into his title, Hadget pretended to be furious about it.

"I should have thought you knew enough of Sir John's affairs," Craven suggested, "to know that the estate was worth nothing. You helped him to raise money upon it."

"Did *you* know enough?" retorted Hadget.

"No," said Craven.

"Oh!" returned his master, ironically. "I should have thought you would have found it all out with your superior intelligence. Why, you infernal old fool, what do you think I took all the trouble I have taken to get that fellow into his title and drive the other one out unless I should gain something by it."

"Certainly, sir—certainly Mr. Hadget—of course not. I'm sure, I beg your pardon." And Craven was most profuse and humble in his apologies.

Very often the old clerk puzzled his brains, trying to read Hadget's game, but could make nothing of it.

"If Sir John raised so much money," he would argue to himself, "whatever became of it?—what could the cabman have done with it? The body was warm when it was found. The cabman could hardly have had time to dispose of the money. Could he have hidden it somewhere and told Hadget of the place? Then again, Hadget could not be an accomplice of the cabman's, or else he would never have worked so diligently as he has done in tracing home the crime to the unfortunate Taylor's door."

So thought Craven. The unfortunate Taylor had been adjudged guilty, and nobody in the world, except, perhaps, Taylor's wife and children believed a single word of the story he told about the foreign sailor.

However, when he discovered that curious little mystery about the cellar and the mad ghost locked up in it, Craven, without knowing why, connected the incident in some way with Sir John's murder, and determined to investigate the whole business.

The first thing to do was to have an interview with the ghost.

"When shall it be?" said he to himself. "Hadget may stop here all day, or if he goes away, may return at any moment. I had better wait till to-night. At ten o'clock I will return. Should he happen to come in then, which is very unlikely, I will say I came back for some papers. That is how I'll manage."

He returned, therefore, the same evening at ten.

A cab was standing in front of the gate of Lyon's Inn, and, as he approached, four figures came out of the gate way, and advanced towards it.

Craven stood back in the shadow of a doorway, and watched them.

One of the men was Mr. Hadget, two others were thick-set, determined-looking fellows, having very much the appearance of bailiffs. Between them they dragged, or carried a miserable-looking little old man, with grey hair brushed bolt upright on his head, a very red nose, and inflamed countenance, who shrieked and struggled violently upon the way.

"I am not mad!" the little old man cried, wrestling with the energy of despair. "I tell you I am not mad! I'm as sane as any of you. It's an infamous conspiracy! My name's Sawder, and I've been shut up in a cellar full of devils by the murderer of Sir John Cheveleigh, Baronet."

"Make him hold his noise!" cried Hadget, interfering. "Make him hold his noise, can't you? We shall have a mob round us."

"What's the matter with the gentleman?" asked a bystander.

"Nothing pertickler," said one of the men. "Only he's cracked. That's all. We're taking him to Bedlam."

It was not, however, to Bedlam that they took the unhappy Bob Sawder; but to a private Lunatic Asylum, at Hackney, where he soon found himself comfortably shaved, and strapped up in a strait waistcoat.

"Bob Sawder!" repeated Craven, to himself. "Where have I heard that name before? I don't recollect; but by what he says, he must be somehow mixed up in that affair of Sir John Cheveleigh. He can't be the foreign sailor—of course not. But Hadget has got the money out of him, and is having him shut up quietly in a mad house. Perhaps he has made him mad. He was giving the poor wretch something hot he called medicine. What was it, I wonder? If I can only trace anything home to Hadget, I shall always hold him in my power, and screw a little money out of him if he have it. Anyhow, the first thing to be done is to have an interview with this Bob Sawder."

Next day Mr. Craven went to Bedlam, and made inquiries; but found that nobody answering the description had been brought there.

For the present, then, there was an end to the business. Hadget alone could tell him where the man had been taken; but he was not very likely to impart the desired information.

Nothing remained but to wait and watch for something to turn up.

By dint of waiting, and watching, and pouncing upon every scrap and trifle of information, Dudley Craven acquired a certain dexterity, and adroitness in pouncing, that enabled him to pounce upon the truth.

One day when he was hard at work among the spiders, one of the two keepers, who looked like bailiffs, called and inquired for Hadget, and, Hadget happening to be out, Mr. Craven interrogated him artfully.

"Want to see Mr. Hadget, do you?" said he. "You can tell me your business, if you like. I don't expect Mr. Hadget in for some hours."

"My business is with him alone."

"Quite right to be cautious. It does you credit. I'm in Mr. Hadget's confidence. You've come about Sawder. How's the old man getting on?"

The keeper stared at him in astonishment. He had been warned by Hadget not to mention his business to anybody he might find at Lyon's Inn, above all other's Dudley Craven.

"You seem to know all about it," said the keeper.

"I do," replied Craven.

"Then, what is it you do know?"

"What you please to tell me."

"I'm not going to tell nothing to nobody. If you want to know anything, you'd better go to Hackney, and ask the governor, or ask Mr. Hadget."

"I'll do the latter," replied Mr. Craven. "Keep your counsel, my friend, or you'll get yourself into trouble. If Mr. Hadget knew what you had said to me, he wouldn't be best pleased. He asked me to see what sort of a chap you were."

"Well, it's not such a dead secret as all that comes to," retorted the keeper, a little nettled, "or else I daresay I could manage to hold my tongue as well as other folks. The man's mad, and we've locked him up. Where's the harm in it?"

"No harm, that I see. Bob's friends say he aint mad, that's all."

"What friends?"

"Well, the old man's master, for instance."

"How can that be when he's dead? He aint come to life, I suppose."

"Well, it would puzzle him, wouldn't it?"

"It would puzzle anyone who had had their throat cut like he had."

"To be sure. Well, you won't leave your message with me, I suppose?"

"I'd rather not."

"You're quite right, too. The governor will be here directly; and I would suggest to you, that you don't repeat too much of our conversation. I shan't blow on you myself."

When Hadget came, the man delivered a letter, and departed without saying a word about the dialogue he had been having with the old clerk.

"Two things I have learnt," thought

Craven, to himself, with a laugh. "He's at Hackney, and he was the servant of Sir John Cheveleigh. What's he being kept out of the way for? I must see him somehow."

He pondered, and planned, and plotted after this for a very long while without hitting upon any likely scheme.

Had not Hadget helped him, he would probably at this point have stuck fast altogether.

One day Hadget gave him a letter to the proprietor of the private lunatic asylum. He took it there and said as he delivered it that he was told to see Bob Sawder.

As there were in the letter no directions to the contrary, his request was acceded to, and in the interview which followed, Craven came to the conclusion that Sawder was as sane as he was.

He also came to other conclusions with regard to the object of his detention, which filled him, at the same time, with horror and dismay, though, as yet, he could be sure of nothing.

The first thing that he must do, was to enable Sawder to effect his escape. No time was to be lost, for should the people at the madhouse tell Hadget that he had seen the supposed madman, all his plans would be frustrated.

Had he put the matter in the hands of the police, stated his suspicions to a magistrate, and obtained a habeas corpus, the affair might have been easily managed, but that was not exactly what Mr. Craven wanted. His object was to extort money from the lawyer. There had been a reward offered for the apprehension of the accomplice of the cabman. Could he manage, unaided, to find that accomplice, he would get the money.

If he called in the assistance of the great Bucket, or any other sagacious official, the money would find its way into their pockets, and he would not be a penny the better for all his trouble.

Set a rogue to catch a rogue. Dudley Craven had too long studied under his rascally master not to have acquired a little rascality on his own account.

He worked as only those will work who delight in evil doing, and see an opportunity.

It matters very little now—indeed, I cannot spare the space to go into particulars—suffice it is to say, that the escape was effected, and that Dudley Craven conveyed Sawder to a place of safety, where he also concealed himself, and began to hatch his plots.

Quickly in the pursuit followed Hadget, whose fury at Sawder's escape was very great, but when he found that Craven had disappeared also, and had probably assisted him, his rage and terror knew no bounds.

"Trace them!—trace them!" he said. "I will give a hundred pounds for each, if you only get them securely in the madhouse."

The keepers wondered at his words, and nudged one another.

"He don't mean to lock 'em both up, does he?" said one to the other. "That sort of thing won't do you know. That's rayther too strong."

They were not very particular at this private asylum, and did a good deal if they were well paid for it, as I believe they will at other establishments of a similar character, to be found in this land of liberty; but this wholesale kidnapping and incarceration rather startled them.

In hot pursuit they followed. The fugitives fled before them.

They tried every plan to discover their whereabouts, but in vain. When they had traced them to a hiding place, they arrived there only in time to find that the birds had flown.

Months passed like this. In all the newspapers appeared advertisements describing the fugitives. One was termed "an escaped madman;" the other, "a felon."

At any time to a man of such unscrupulous ingenuity, it would have been no difficult matter to trump up a false charge against the absconding clerk; but Craven had saved him the trouble, by appropriating a certain sum of money belonging to his late employer, which he deemed necessary for his current expenses while engaged in making certain inquiries about Hadget's conduct before and after the murder.

Secretly plotting and planning, the two spiders worked at their webs, each keeping in his corner on the look out for the other.

Those who had known Hadget in former times, and saw him about this period, could scarcely believe him to be the same person, such a fearful change had the anxiety and the ever-present dread of discovery worked in his personal appearance. His hair had grown almost white, and his face was lean and furrowed.

Ever on the watch—ever awaiting the dread moment to come—alarmed at the sound of an approaching footstep, dreading to read in every face he looked upon that its owner knew his secret. So Hadget lived a life of intense misery through fear and apprehension.

The crisis was close at hand.

CHAPTER THE TWENTY-FOURTH.

MORE EVIDENCE DESTROYED.

IT'S night in Hadget's office, and the spiders are busy at work silently spinning their webs.

A candle, with a neglected wick, spitting and spluttering unheeded, stands upon the desk at which Hadget sits waiting, his head resting upon his hand.

Some papers lie open before him, and a pen is sticking upright in the inkstand; but he has not been writing, nor has his busy brain been at work upon such matters.

He sits and waits, his restless fingers clawing at the table's edge, and his blood-shot eyes, sunken and dull, through want of rest ever and anon turning slowly towards the door, as he fancies he hears the noise of a footfall without.

While thus engaged, he mutters to himself, in the old mumbling fashion,—

"A little longer—a little longer—and he will come. What could the fool mean by making the appointment, unless he knew all

WITHOUT A HOME.

and felt that I was in his power? In such a case he knew I dare not give him into custody. But what can he know? What can he have found out? If he knows nothing, I will laugh at him; if he knows too much, there is only one way left. The secret will then lie between me and that man Sawder. When I catch him, I'll lock him up again, and take good care he doesn't escape. Ha! ha! Mr. Craven, I'm not foiled yet!"

More busy than ever is that ugly hand scratching at the wood-work. As a distraction, he goes to the fire-place, and, taking up the poker, poises it, and waves it round his head; then takes his place again, and goes on thinking as before.

No. 24

Presently there is a slight noise without—a hand upon the handle of the door.

It turns, and the long expected visitor enters and closes it behind him.

"Well, Craven!"

"Well, Hadget!"

"Are you alone? Why have you not brought Sawder with you?"

"I have left him at home—he is very ill."

"Indeed!" Hadget replies, with a chuckle, which he has great difficulty in repressing. "I'm sorry for that. The old complaint?"

"What is that?"

"Madness."

"There is nothing to be gained by wasting words," says Craven, taking a seat by Hadget's side, and placing his hat carefully upon the table. "Let's understand one another."

"I am willing."

"On the night of Sir John Cheveleigh's murder he visited you here."

Except that Hadget's face grows of a sudden, ghastly pale, and that as it seems to hide the twitching of his lips, he covers his mouth with his ugly hand, and strokes his chin, there is no great change in him, and his voice the same as usual, harsh and grating, as he says—

"Well, what next?"

"If that is the case——"

"Stop," says Hadget. "*If it is*—mind, I don't say it is."

"I *know it is*, and in that case wish to ask you, why, at the coroner's inquest and the trial, you did not state the fact?"

"Well, what next?"

"You have not answered that question."

"Nor do I mean to do so."

"You do not wish to take me into your confidence?"

"I see no occasion."

"I will go on then! You must be aware that Sawder followed his master to town, with the intention of asking to be allowed to go abroad with him. Sir John had told him that such was his intention."

"That's curious, though, is it not?" says Hadget, with a sneer; "when Sir John took such particular pains to keep his destination a profound secret?"

"The most artful of us," replies Craven, "make mistakes. He was drunk when he told his servant."

Hadget eyes the speaker uneasily. The confidence and easy manner his late clerk has assumed is anything but cheering.

"Sir John told his man, Sawder, that he was going abroad," continues Craven, crossing his legs and folding his hands, but keeping his eyes upon the other's face, to watch the effect of his words; "and Bob Sawder came to town. He arrived very late on Sunday night, or rather, early on Monday morning, and went in the direction of the docks, intending to find a lodging about there, so as to be handy to the spot from which the boat started; and it so happened that he was providentially upon the spot when his master's body was discovered and taken into a public-house."

"Well!" says Hadget, hoarsely, and clawing at at his chin as he had clawed at the table. "What next?"

"He therefore recognised him, and the property found in the cab with him."

"There was no property."

"Nothing," says Craven, slowly, taking a small paper packet from his pocket, "nothing but these—*your spectacles!*"

For a moment the two men look at each other without saying a word; and the murderer seems to shrink within himself before the other's earnest gaze.

In vain he tries to say something—the words rattle in his throat, and he grasps the table for support.

But it is not for long—gradually he recovers himself—then he asks—

"What is your object in this?"

"I'm hard up."

"And want money from me?"

"From you or from government. I'm not particular which."

"How much?"

"Five hundred pounds!"

"That's a good deal," says Hadget, with a faint approach to his familiar chuckle. "You and Sawder are two geniuses. Do you know that that lunatic threatened me in this way before?"

"No, I did not."

"He thought it best not to tell you, perhaps. It's a very ingenious plot. You think you have got hold of some nice hanging evidence, and something may be made out of me. Well!"

"Well!"

"I own the evidence is strong. I am anxious that it should not come into a court of justice, for reasons of my own. The money you ask for is a large sum, but if you will give me your written promise never to annoy me more, and give me those spectacles, I will pay you."

"Well!" says Craven, perfectly astounded at the success of his mission. "That's fair enough. Have you the money here?"

"I have it in my pocket, but I shall not pay it now. Read this paper. If you agree to sign it, and your accomplice, or whatever you call him, agrees too, bring him here to-morrow night, and you shall be paid."

As he speaks he lays before Craven upon the table, a paper, which appears to be what he has stated. Then, as the other, off his guard, leans his head over the table to read it by the uncertain light, the lawyer creeps behind him and feels for the poker.

．　　　．　　　．　　　．　　　．

The persevering spiders in their webs work all through the night, spinning and spinning, too busy to heed the dark and dreadful object lying beneath them on the office floor.

No other eyes are there to look upon it, and the murderer has locked it up safe and sound until he has decided how it is to be disposed of.

Safe and sound! When is murder safe? —when is it hidden with sufficient art—buried sufficiently deep that some unforgotten detail is not left exposed to the sight.

"Oh, Mr. Hadget!" the porter of Lyon's Inn says, as the lawyer goes out. "There was a foreigner here asking for you. He said he wanted to see you particularly, but I said you was engaged. You told me to say so, you know."

"Quite right—quite right. I was engaged."

"He was a very ragged person, sir. At first I thought he was a beggar."

"Did he say where he came from, or what he was?"

"He said he would not leave his name, but he came from Lyons."

———

CHAPTER THE TWENTY-FIFTH.

MOSTLY ABOUT ROGUES AND VAGRANTS.

IF all the dear friends who, night after night had drunk and supped at his expense—who had patted him on the back, called him their "dear boy," and assured each other in vociferous and energetic chorus, that he was a jolly good fellow, and that nobody could deny it, who had again and again awakened the echoes of Cleveland Chambers, and driven the indignant lodgers below, near out of their senses—which of them all, I say, gave the poor, ragged, shabby fellow a thought, as he travelled upon his downward course? One alone—a scene painter at the Apollo Saloon, was faithful to him, lent him small sums, recommended him, and endeavoured to get him some employment. Alas! besides being a jolly good fellow, what was this unfortunate young man good for? He had no talent in the scene painting way, and made some frightful messes of the "dells of dazzling delight." Ochre suggested that he should try his hand at writing songs for the music halls. But nothing much came of it—for though he did compose some songs which were a trifle above the average of the wretched doggrel, vended by the hack scribes of those establishments—as the professional *ladies* and *gentlemen*, with a very few exceptions, cheated him out of his words, without paying for them, or when they payed at all, did not give more than a farthing a-line—he did not grow fat upon his literary efforts. Now and then he grew desperately energetic, composing newspaper articles and screaming farces, which might, or might not, have possessed considerable merit. He used to put them into editors' boxes, and leave them at stage doors, and then worry the sub-editors and door-keepers nearly out of their lives, by calling and asking for them. The amiable individual who is usually on guard at the Maiden Lane entrance to the Adelphi, got to know him at last, and used to salute him by name.

But he did no good. The screaming farces were returned tied up in exactly the same fashion as when he left them; and the newspaper articles came back very dusty outside, and clean within, as though they had been lying a long while uncared for, in a pigeon-hole in the editor's room. He had once a notion of writing sermons, of which he advertised shilling copies. I have seen one of them, and can answer for its being strong in the dramatic, though weak in the theological element. I don't think he tried Mr. Spurgeon. Perhaps a shilling is too much. Indeed, I am told fourpence is the usual price. Anyhow, nobody applied for one to "A poor Curate, post office, City Road."

Forsaking the literary business, he turned his attention to clerking, and advertised for a place. There is such a prejudice against the Civil Service among the commercial community, that in spite of the well-known fact that a government clerk must pass the most appalling examination, and convince the Civil Service Commissioners of his efficiency in everything that it is necessary for a clerk to know.

Nothing, however, answered with my unfortunate hero; and, except at Christmas, when he had a "super's" place during the pantomime, at one of the East-end theatres; carried banners, pelted policemen, and did his best towards embodying the British army in a uniform composed of as many incongruous ingredients as the dress of some of our gallant riflemen, he had nothing like regular employment.

I feel certain that there is a sad show of clumsiness in the construction of this story. I notice myself that all my characters seem one after another to be ringing the changes upon the same emotions. They have all a knack of falling ill, and growing well again, getting into difficulties, and getting out of them with ridiculous celerity. The critics, if they condescend to notice me at all, will be down upon these and other little weaknesses of mine, which, were they author, and I critic, I can promise them I should not pass over myself.

Shall I go over the old ground again, like I did with Mrs. Nelly, and show how Maurice sank in the social scale?

I have no time to do so, and had I, it would but try your patience.

What do you suppose would be the likely end of such a scapegrace? What could possibly happen within the limits of probability?

In the first chapter of this story I told you how, upon the night of a general holiday, when the illuminated London streets were as light as noonday—when all loyal citizens and true Englishmen were rejoicing—a man died miserably and alone in a Whitechapel garret, unknown, uncared for: meanwhile the rest of the world went on rejoicing.

What could be a more natural termination for such a ne'er-do-well? Oh, you jolly, good fellows, choice spirits, open-handed young spendthrifts, it is an old, old story. To those amongst us who are born to work, there are two words in the English language we must bear in mind—honesty and industry. Lucky dogs these are who haven't to work (it were not meet that the world should be full of grubs, and there should be no butterflies); but even they must guide their steps, and beware of the dreadful valley of the Shadow of Debt.

It is possible that such a fate as I have described above awaits the hero of my story; but it is not here that I shall record it. To the end, of this volume at least, I hope to carry him alive. That he was at times, between his efforts at earning a livelihood, wretchedly hard up, I cannot deny.

Once upon a time—a fearful time too, in which, at night, hungry and desperate, he crept down to the river's bank—watched the sombre waters creeping sluggishly towards the ocean, and wondered where the body of a wretched outcast who might fling himself into them would come on shore, or whether it would have time to reach the open sea, and so be lost for ever.

At such a time as this, crouching in a corner

upon Waterloo Bridge, bare headed, ragged and woe-begone beyond easy recognition, he looked up, at the sound of approaching footsteps, and there swept by him in rustling silk, in a mantle of costly velvet, in a bonnet of exquisite fabric, in daintily fitting gloves, and little boots which seemed to be glued upon her feet, in the full plenitude of her charms—the same glorious, golden-haired goddess whom he had loved and lost—whom he still loved, and would continue to love until the foolish heart which beat for her was stilled in death.

She did not notice him as she passed upon her way. The lamplight fell full upon her face as she passed, and he thought she had never looked so beautiful. A faint perfume remained in the chilly air when she was gone, an aching pain, too, at his breast——nothing more.

The ragged and hungry, skulking all night in the pitiless streets, seek out, you may be sure, the snuggest doorways, and the warmest of the dry-arches. A good many, in summer, climb over the railings into the enclosure of St. James's Park, and lie upon the grass. This cold spring weather was not suitable to this *al fresco* bed-chamber; and, if a man had a couple of pence to spare for luxury, it would have been as well if he had lain it out in a bed.

Thus thinking one night, during the most miserable period of his vagabondism, Maurice laid out his twopence in a bed, and obtained as near an approach to one as can be had for the money down Whitechapel way.

Here, one night, he made acquaintance with an old Frenchman under these curious circumstances,—

The night being cold, Maurice had covered himself up with some old rags he called his coat and waistcoat. In the morning, when he awoke, he found his next door neighbour deliberately appropriating one of these articles of clothing.

"That's my waistcoat," said the young man laying hold of it.

"I think not," replied the other person, in broken English. "There is my name marked upon the back."

"I tell you it is mine!" repeated Maurice.

One grows careful of one's old rags when there are but few of them.

"I tell you it is mine. Take it off, and look at it. The name of Cheveleigh's on the back."

The old man slowly took off the garment, and turned it inside out. When he had spelt through the name, almost illegible upon the inside, he made an exclamation of astonishment; and catching Maurice by the hand, asked him eagerly in French, whether the name was his. Maurice replying in the affirmative, and in the same language, the old man went on to ask whether he was the son of the late Sir John Cheveleigh.

"I am," said Maurice.

"And your—your mother. She is still alive?"

"No," replied Maurice, gloomily; "dead."

"Dead!" cried the Frenchman. "When and where did she die? Oh, my poor Louise! —oh! my poor sister — after all you have

suffered at my hands, that I should not have been able to see you once more, and ask for your forgiveness. She never spoke of me, I suppose? She used to dance at our circus before she ran away with your father, and I was clown of the ring. She wrote to me to tell me she was married; but did not say to whom. For many years I never heard the truth. Then, an Englishman who was at Lyons, when Sir John and Mr. Hadget were there, told me all the circumstances. Sir John was murdered, I heard, the very next night after I landed in England. They never found the accomplice of the cabman, did they?"

"Never."

"Ah! it is strange how things come about. Do you know, I fancy I saw the murderer."

"What do you mean?"

"That very night the murder was committed, and close to the spot, I saw a man running from the same direction up a narrow alley where I was standing, throw aside a false beard, and a coat, and hat, and then walk quietly on. I was standing in a dark corner where he could not see me; but, as he came by, I stopped him, and asked for alms, more to look at him than anything else."

"Well?"

"He was very much startled at seeing me, and said he took me for a ghost. Then he gave me some money, and I told him I wasn't a ghost, but a poor traveller from Lyons. No sooner had I said so, than he threw the money at me, and made off as fast as he could go."

"Well, what connection is there between this man and the murderer?"

"I'll tell you. When he was gone I went down the alley to look for the things. There was a rough coat something like a sailor's, and a wide-a-wake——"

"Good Heavens!" cried Maurice. "Go on. What else did you find?"

"I found the beard he had taken off, and a piece of string. Nothing more."

"Are you sure?"

"Well, I didn't find anything more then, because it was too dark. I had seen him drop something down a grating; but as it seemed to lead to a sewer, and it was so dark I could not see an inch down, I just took notice of the place, and, at daylight, having passed the intervening time at an adjoining coffee stand, came back and gave a glance down. What do you think I saw?"

"What — what? For God's sake, speak faster!"

"There was a razor which had been thrown down, and stuck on a projecting ledge, just about half a yard from the grating, just out of my reach."

"You left it?"

"No. I fished for it with a stick. I had a good deal of trouble in the fishing, I can tell you. At last I got it up. It had no name upon it. It was an old one, with a tortoise-shell handle, and *it was covered with blood*. So were the coat and the hat."

"What did you do then? Why did you not give information to the police?"

"Because for about a week I did not hear

any of the particulars; when I did, and I heard that an accomplice wearing the sort of clothes I had picked up was advertised, I thought it best to throw them away, which I did."

"And the razor?"

"I kept that, thinking it might come in useful, some day."

"Have you it here?"

"Yes; there it is."

Maurice, with a shudder took the razor in his hand, and turned it over and over thoughtfully, trying to remember whether he had ever seen it before.

"What sort of a man was this?" he asked, presently.

"Middle aged, rather above the middle height, and strongly built; hands very large, and fingers long and bony, and had a habit of twitching his mouth."

"Great God, it is he! There can be no mistake about it. Since you have been in town have you seen this Mr. Hadget you spoke of?"

"No. I don't know where to find him."

"He lives in Lyon's Inn. Go there to-night, and take this razor with you. Ask him if he wants to buy one. Watch his face when you ask. Do not let him take the razor from you, and come back to me again."

"Do you suspect, then——"

"I am sure of it. Before two days are over our head, the murderer of my father shall be in the hands of the police."

CHAPTER THE TWENTY-SIXTH.

ONE MORE CHANCE.

THAT night, two men, very ragged and hungry-looking, came along the Strand from the City, and turning up Newcastle Street, one waited for the other while he went into Lyon's Inn to ask for Mr. Hadget.

The individual left behind wandered slowly back into the Strand, and strolled on by the side of the church, until he came to the cook shop, against one of the window panes of which he glued his nose.

It was an undignified position, I grant you, and one that you and I, who have a wholesome fear of what Mrs. Grundy will say, would not like to be caught in. Perhaps he was standing there unthinkingly; or perhaps he was really, after the manner of small street boys, picking out in imagination the lump of pudding he would most have liked to have had, supposing he had had the money.

For reader, he *was* very hungry, and his pockets were very empty.

While thus employed a hand was laid upon his shoulder, and turning round in some shame and confusion, he saw Dorcas Abbot at his side.

"Maurice," she said, in a mournful voice, the tears welling up in her eyes as she spoke. "Maurice! it is not possible that this is you? Oh, Maurice, Maurice!—what has happened to you?—why did you not apply to me for assistance?"

He was at first going to make some off-hand reply, to misrepresent the case, and pretend that he was not nearly so poor and wretched as in reality he was, but there was something in the tender voice in which the woman spoke, and something in the gentle pressure of her fingers, which touched a hidden chord in his heart, and raising her hand for a moment to his lips, next moment he turned away, and covering his face with his own, sobbed like a child.

"Oh, Maurice! dear, dear Maurice—do not cry like that. It is dreadful to see you suffer so. Oh, Maurice! why did you not apply to me? I have no friend in the world but you. You have none—then why not make a friend of me? Take this money, dear Maurice, and buy what you want in the way of clothes—a good suit and some linen. The shops are yet open, and you will be in time if you are quick. Here too, is my address—but no, that will be no good. To-morrow morning at nine o'clock exactly a ship sails from Gravesend to Australia. I shall be on board. I will take a passage for you. If you consent, there may be a chance in the new country of making a livelihood. Do not be too proud, dear Maurice, to accept of my assistance, and when you are rich, you shall pay me back. Besides, should not a sister help a brother when she finds him like I have found you? There—there! to-morrow morning I shall expect you on board the Gold Digger, at nine o'clock exactly. Good-bye, dear Maurice, till then. I am sure that you will come."

Before he had time to reply, and while he was yet confused and bewildered by the unexpected meeting with Dorcas, and by the startling proposition she had made, she had left him and run across the road, and was out of sight.

The whole affair was so sudden and so surprising, that had he not held the little green silk purse in his hand, and seen the pudding shop just where it had been a moment ago, and the identical lump he had fixed his mind upon lying there as it had then lain, he might have been tempted to believe that it was all a dream.

However, the pudding shop was real enough, and so was the purse, containing, as he found upon inspection, twelve sovereigns and some silver.

The course of action which you would have adopted, Mr. Stars, would have been to have delayed the unfortunate reader with two or three columns of mental argument, as to whether or not he should touch the money. I feel confident that the reader will be obliged to me by sticking to human nature, and dropping the ideal sentimentality.

Here was a man with an empty stomach, next door to starvation, with no prospect of bettering his position, and half a mind to drown himself, got an offer of some money etc., from a girl whom he had been accustomed to look upon as a sister from the time that he and she were little children together. Of course he took the money, and following her suggestion, went straight to Mr. Levy's to get a suit of clothes.

When he was suited to his satisfaction, he

strolled out into the street, intending to look in at the Red Lion, or Mr. Short's, to get something to eat, when he all at once recollected the Frenchman. He ran round as fast as he could go into Newcastle Street, but his late companion was nowhere to be found. He reflected for a while upon the course he should pursue, and at length came to the conclusion that if he went after the Frenchman he would most likely lose the boat. Therefore he gave the business up very easily, and having considered for a moment where he should go to get something to eat, thought that the best place would be the Haymarket, and the sensation of having money in his pocket being too strong for your human nature, he hailed a hansom and rode there like a gentleman.

Oh, that brilliant parade of the Pariahs!—how often I have found the good-for-nothing people I have been writing about, travelling that way.

Quite like a gentleman did Maurice, late of the burst boots and elbowless coat, regale himself upon the very best that Girandler's *cusinier* could offer him.

He sat a long while over it, washing it down with a modest pint of St. George, and cogitating upon his prospects for the future.

Decidedly, of all the places in the world, Australia was the place for him. It was a new field, where his genius and talents would find a market.

Talking of markets, as this was the very last night that he ever hoped to be in this miserable city, he would just walk up and down the crowded side, and smoke the last cigar he ever meant to smoke; for in future, frugality and industry were to be the order of the day.

So, when he had lit his havannah, he sauntered along the pavement with his hands in the pockets of his peg-tops, and puffed the smoke out of the corner of his mouth, as happy as a king.

Who says there are such things in the world as empty stomachs, and pockets with nothing but holes in them. I believe it's all a gross fabrication.

In front of the Piccadilly Saloon, against the door of which he had paused to allow some fair damsel to pass out, a brougham, passing slowly close to the curbstone, suddenly drew up, and a lady, whose hand only he could see, beckoned to him from the carriage window to approach.

He went forward naturally, and, the lady inside, pushing open the door, drew him towards her by the sleeve of his coat.

"Maurice," said a voice that he could never forget, or have forgotten had he lived thrice a hundred years, "come for a ride."

It was a strange welcome after so long a separation. Perhaps it was its very strangeness which deprived him of the power of replying. Had the speaker accosted him in the street, and sought his forgiveness for her past conduct, he might have hesitated when the thought of all that he had suffered on her account came back to his recollection; but she accosted him with a smile as though they had but parted yesterday.

He was at once delighted, and indignant at finding her so lovely—so magnificent:

The sarcasm that he would have liked to have made her writhe under, he had not got at his tongue's end.

Hoping it would come, he stepped into the carriage.

"I'll tell her my mind," he thought. "I'll let her see that I can treat her with the contempt she deserves, and that I don't love her the least bit in the world."

Just as if he did not. Just as if the enchantress could not twist him round her finger as easily as she could twist a curl paper.

* * * * *

The Gold Digger started precisely at nine o'clock in the morning. The ship was crowded fore and aft with emigrants. Fathers, and mothers, and sisters, and brothers, looking tearfully and regretfully at the receding shore of the dear old country they could not make a living in. One lonely woman by the boat side, looked back even more anxiously than the rest. What was she looking for? Whom did she expect?

Oh, Maurice—Maurice!—there were two sisters to choose between—two paths to select. You have chosen—the die is cast! A broken-hearted woman drifts oceanward, to die among strangers in an unknown land, while you are left——For what?

CHAPTER THE TWENTY-SEVENTH.

'TWIXT THE CUP AND THE LIP.

IF Nelly could only have married the Marquis of Crutchingford, she would have achieved her highest ambition.

"*If,*" says the reader, derisively.

If, I repeat. And should she not, she was very near it. When his lordship recovered sufficiently from that paralytic attack, and came to Brighton to recruit his health, did not the fair-haired intriguer just come into her property, quickly follow him, and put up at the same hotel.

What could be more natural than for the gallant marquis to renew their acquaintance? What could be more natural than for him to make certain dishonourable proposals? and what could be more natural than for the lady to refuse them?

"*Natural,*" repeats, the sarcastic reader.

Most certainly. Don't you see, that it was now my lady's game to get a husband just as much as it is the game of any other woman to do the same. The more virtuous they are, of course the greater necessity for doing so. Is it not every woman's grand object in life to get married? The generality of men look upon matrimony from a commercial point of view; but there are some women who rather than not get married at all, would pick up with anything in the shape of a man. If Paul can't be had there is Peter. So better Peter than nothing. Talk of men being the wooers, and women the wooed, I believe there are some desperate spinsters whom it is not safe to know, who lie in wait, pounce upon, and carry off by main force "the poor unprotected he-creature. I read in the paper only yesterday, how, at one of our prlice courts, a chimney sweep, of the age of sixty, was charged with bigamy, and his wives did not wish him to be dealt with severely. I should think not, indeed. Which of the three do you suppose was the victim? There's no doubt about it: it was Chummy.

I will show you what chance our heroine had of becoming a marchioness. It lay in the fact of Crutchingford being an unscrupulous old vagabond. Having set his mind upon the possession of a woman, he would have done anything in the world—*even married her*—te gain his object.

In this instance, after offering her every other temptation that his ingenuity could devise, he proposed a secret marriage as a clincher. Extraordinary as the presumption of this woman must appear to virtuous and beautiful young ladies, who have never had a chance above a retail tradesman or a clerk, she refused it. On only one condition would she surrender—my lord must make an honest woman of her in the eyes of the world.

The paralytic attack must, you will say, have affected the marquis's brain, for he could never otherwise have acted so foolishly. He consented.

They came to London, and a special license was purchased. His lordship's valet asserted that every day his lordship grew deeper in love and weaker in intellect. I am inclined to think that Mr. Dobson was prejudiced, and took great trouble to promulgate this libel upon his lordship's brain.s Let that be as it may, it got about among the clubs. There was a deal of chaff about one of his after-dinner speeches upon political economy, and the cheap press began to ask why he was not pensioned, and put by upon the shelf, and spoke of him derisively, and as poor old grandmamma Crutchingford.

From saying foolish things, his lordship began to do them. Wearing a white hat and waistcoat in the depth of winter might have been a pardonable eccentricity, and surely cannot be taken as a sign of insanity. Then, too, a nobleman has a perfect right, if he so chooses, to purchase herrings at five a-penny, and eat them for his dinner, but that does not prove him to be mad.

He was always notorious for his success and popularity among a certain class of ladies. He was called by persons of an adaptative turn of mind, who had read *Little Dorrit*, "The Father of the Haymarket."

His approaching marriage with Nelly did not prevent him from looking up some of his old haunts of infamy. Indeed, he thought it a good excuse for having his youthful fling before settling down for life. He was not, at the outside, more than seventy-five.

So did it happen that his lordship's fling was one of a character that will be remembered in the neighbourhood of the Haymarket as a fling in which many dozens of champagne were drunk at his lordship's expense, and a prodigious amount of inebriety was had upon the cheap.

So did it happen that upon the morning fixed for the wedding, the future bride was waiting at St. James's church at a quarter to twelve in the forenoon, and wondering why the bridegroom did not come.

So did it happen that Mr. Dobson, my lord's valet, could give no information upon the subject, except that over night, my lord had gone out to have the last of his fling, and had not come home again.

So did it happen that everybody waited, and that he never came at all.

For how could he? There is a corner house with a portico, in a street at the west-end, near a Tennis court, which has a bad name, and is looked at evilly by the churchwardens of St. James's, but which is not indicted for reasons best known to the parish authorities. Here, on the previous night, the noble marquis had finished his fling by dying drunk, and here, upon this morning fixed for the interesting ceremony, my lord lay, without his wig, or teeth, or padding, a very lean and ugly corpse for so great a nobleman.

And so it happened that Nelly was not a marchioness.

CHAPTER THE TWENTY-EIGHTH.

AN OFFER OF MARRIAGE.

YOU do not, surely, expect that I am going to repeat the conversation which took place in Mrs. Nelly's brougham, as it drove rapidly towards Old Brompton, where that lady resided.

Of course Mr. Maurice was very indignant, and sternly demanded an explanation.

Do you suppose, my young Fledgling, that women ever give explanations of questionable conduct, or that men ever get the best of them by argument? Oh! you mighty philosopher of twenty summers! I fancy I see you, with your legs crossed and your pipe lit, laying down the law about the way the inferior animal is to be managed. Your elders by forty years talk differently. They know well enough what it is to try and fight a woman with her own weapons. It is my opinion that a man who is in love with a woman always gets the worst of it in his arguments with her.

That man, Maurice—upon my word, I have hardly patience to speak civilly of him—got the worst of the argument, of course; he was a person without any strength of mind. He had loved this woman with all his heart and soul. She had left him; he had loved her still. She picked him up again; he loved her more than ever.

"Oh, dear Nelly, how beautiful you look! You are not the least changed since—since we parted. You are an angel—a goddess! For your love, Nell, I'd give up everything on earth, and sell my soul to the devil."

These absurd remarks were made over a champagne supper in Mrs. Nelly Burgoyne's villa.

She certainly did look beautiful. There might have been a trifling suspicion of rouge upon her cheek, and her forehead might not have been so smooth as of old, but she was very beautiful, and her beauty had the same effect upon the infatuated simpleton at her side, that strong drink might have had. He was quite maudlin about her. He sat and watched her by the half-hour, as though she were a picture, or something curious in clock-work. He was quite happy to be allowed to touch the hem of her garment, or softly to caress the rich lace upon her sleeves. He secretly hid one of her little gloves within his waistcoat, upon the side where he supposed his heart was situated.

A servant interrupted the happy supper by bringing in a card, and saying that the person to whom it belonged wished to speak to her immediately.

"Dear me," cried the beauty, impatiently. "What an unusual time to make a call. Did you say I was engaged?"

"Yes, madam; but the gentleman said that it was of the greatest importance that he should see you. He is in the next room."

"I will go to him, then," said Nelly. "Go on with your supper, Maurice, till I come back. I won't be long."

She left him; and presently Maurice heard her voice in the next room, which was divided from that in which he sat, only by folding doors. Filling his glass, he leant back upon the sofa, and closed his eyes in a happy dream of love. Busy with his thoughts he took no heed of the passing time. "What a chance it was I met her," he was thinking; "suppose I had not, I should have left the country to-morrow, and been lost for ever. Australia, indeed! as though a fellow could not get his living in dear old England. My native land," said he, draining his glass, "I will never desert thee!"

He forgot at the time that he was more than half a Frenchman.

The sound of some voice in the next room that seemed familiar to him roused him from his reverie.

"That is the reason why I called," it said. "You must decide at once. For a long while you know I have been in love with you. I tell you I cannot live without you. Why should you always treat me with such contempt? I have more than thirty thousand pounds, as here are my bank accounts, to show, while you have only six hundred a-year. Agree to be my wife and we will leave this cursed country to-morrow. I want to go, and if you go with me, you shall live anywhere else you choose, like a princess."

"I could never love you, if I did marry you," replied Nelly, after some hesitation.

"Marry me, and try," the other urged. "I will love you. I do love the very ground you walk upon. I always have since the first time I saw you. You are so unlike, and so superior to any other woman I have ever met with. I will settle every halfpenny upon you. I will be your slave in every way. Come, what do you say?"

"This is so sudden, really. If I consent how can I be sure that what you say is true? Where did you get all this money?"

"Nelly—I may call you Nelly, mayn't I?" supplicated the man, in whining tones,—"I will tell you a secret that is worth my life.

It is to show you how I love you that I do so. Listen to me. Do not shrink. I shall not hurt you."

"I am not afraid. What would you say?"

"This secret I shall tell you will place my life in your hands. Ha! ha! what do I care for life? Without you, life is of no value to me. Twenty-seven thousand pounds of this money belonged to Sir John Cheveleigh. I took it from him."

Maurice started to his feet. He had recognised the voice. It was Hadget who spoke.

"What do you mean?" asked Nelly. "How did you take it?"

"Don't you understand?" the lawyer continued, with a chuckle, and a leer so horribly unnatural, that it made the woman's flesh creep to look at him. "He had it in the cab when the cabman killed him. Ha!—ha! The evidence was strong against the cabman, wasn't it?"

"Stand back, you wretch!" screamed Nelly, springing from him, and twisting herself from his embrace. "Do you mean to say, you monster, that you murdered him? I'm sure you did. Your hands are bloody now. Help! help! Maurice!—Maurice!"

Maurice, flinging open the door, confronted them; and, while Nelly clung to the young man's arm, Hadget, rising from the ground where he had been kneeling, tried to look unconcerned, and to whistle a tune in a manner which was so absurdly out of place, that Maurice thought he was either mad or drunk.

"Who are you?" Hadget asked. "And what's your business? Don't try to frighten me, I'm not to be bounced so easily? It's red ink on my fingers, not blood. And as to Sir John's case, I have got my *alibi* all cut and dried; and I'm ready for my trial."

"Quick!" said Maurice, in a whisper to Nelly. "Run to the door, and call for help, while I secure him."

As she went to obey his directions, Maurice sprang forward to grapple with the other; but, Hadget, with a strength and agility which was as astonishing as it was unexpected, seized the young man round the waist, and flung him to the other end of the room. Then, with a shrill cry, more like a wild beast than a human being, he sprang through the French window, smashing glass and wood-work in the way, and, in another moment, was flying like the wind up the gravel-road, towards Kensington.

In vain the police and Maurice gave chace: he had, for the time, escaped.

For many days they heard no news of him. At last a horrible paragraph crept into the papers, concerning the capture of a raving maniac, in a lonely shed upon the marshes in Essex. A wretched, emaciated object, covered with bruises and dirt, quite mad, and almost dead for want of food. It had, in its insane frenzy, or urged by the awful pangs of hunger, *eaten off three of its fingers!*

.   .   .   .   .   .

And so the ship sailed from old England, and Maurice was left behind. He had given up his last chance for the sake of this yellow-haired woman, whom he still hoped was weak enough to be fond of him.

Dear heart—what a fool the young fellow was! Had he not heard her accept, or almost accept the hand of another, when she had but a moment before told him that he was the only man she ever loved? And still, could he love her?

She ought to have loved him—for was he not willing to be her lover, her shoe-black, or her hired assassin?—she had but to dictate. If I could re-christen my story, I should call it "The Woman without the Heart;" for verily I believe she had not such an article in her composition.

.   .   .   .   .   .

Lend me a magician's wand, or send for a spirit medium, for I should look into the future, In lieu of these I look into my ink bottle, and there I see

Nelly.—Ever beautiful, rich, and beloved, going smoothly through life, giving money in charity, renting a pew at church, and a box at the opera, refusing offers of marriage, and exciting the envy and hatred of all the respectable female Bromptonians.

Maurice.—Ragged, and out at elbows, with a cigar in his mouth, and nothing particular in his stomach.

Dorcas.—Alive still; abroad and in a convent. Much like she ever was, that is—unappreciated. What matters it where she is, and what becomes of her? There is surely nobody who takes an interest in her. Her lot is a very common one: for is no one for ever hearing of broken hearts, and wasted lives, and poor, lone, loveless women, left to pine away and die uncared for? Such is the history of most old maids—and old maids are a capital subject to crack jokes upon. Do you not think so?

Ernest.—Skulking out of the way of the police, who have a warrant to apprehend him, upon a charge of embezzling the public money at the Bad Bargains. Luckily for him, the case is in the hands of the celebrated Bucket, and so, as they both live in the same house, they are not likely to meet.

Jack Ochre.—still scene painter; still in his attic; still ready to prove himself Maurice's friend, should that gentleman give him the opportunity. Still wearing that beast of a spriggled waistcoat. I met him in it, and a tail coat, two or three Sundays ago, in Victoria Park.

Miss Perks.—Poor, dear old simpleton. As bony as ever, and as great a noodle. As great an admirer of Nelly as of yore, and as loud in her praises of her kind benefactress. Nelly has got her into some almshouses, and takes her occasionally a pound of tea, and an ounce of snuff. At other times she is allowed to come and see Mrs. Burgoyne at the villa, and you may be sure she opens her eyes and mouth to the widest extent, when she contemplates the magnificence thereof.

She does not quite understand how it has all come about, but when she goes to see Mrs. Mobbles she says,—

"I told you 'ow it 'ud be. Everythink 'as turned out as I said, exactly. We've come into our property, and is lords and ladies, and hold Twisted-his-wrist is in the 'sylum."

No. 25.

THE LAST CHAPTER.

A SCENE AT THE PUBLISHER'S.

MY publisher said to me the other day— "By-the-bye, Mr. Sm*th, (I have reasons for wishing my name to remain a secret) "there was a lady came here yesterday for all the back numbers."

"Well, sir," said I, "and what of that?"

"She was driving a basket carriage, with a pair of ponies. She was tall, rather stout, and very fair—a deuced fine woman, in fact."

My publisher is a man upon whose taste in these matters one can place dependence.

"Did you know her?" said I.

"No, I didn't; but she asked me to tell her who was the author. She said that she insisted upon knowing, and got quite warm about it. She is going to call again to-day for a number that was out of print, and then— Why, there she is!"

There she was, sure enough.

"I am sure I can rely upon your not divulging the secrets of this office," said I, with my usual dignified politeness. "Were I not pressed for time I should have very much liked to have spoken to this lady, and convinced her of the impropriety of her conduct."

A Turnover-at-Case (which, gentle reader, is a human being, and not a species of summersault, as you might, from the name, be led to suppose) employed upon the establishment, pretends that the writer of this story did not, upon this occasion, speak one word to anybody, but hiding himself behind the door in an ignominious fashion, peeped through a little crevice, at the yellow haired lady who was making a purchase.

When she had made it, she stepped into her carriage, took the reins from the smart little tiger, and drove up Brydges Street, towards Covent Garden Market.

"Is that the woman with the yellow hair?" asked the publisher, when I, having transacted my business, came again into the outer office.

"What do you mean?" I asked. "You see she has yellow hair."

"But is she the heroine of our story?"

"You ought to have asked her," said I, artfully evading the question.

"Who ever she is, she's an awful stunner!" I heard that Turnover-at-Case observing to his companion. Ah! the young men of the present day are not what we used to be. I do not recollect expressing such an opinion at his age, myself. In fact, I am sure I would not have done such a thing. "She's an awful stunner!" repeated the young profligate. "That Maurice was a man of taste."

Did you ever hear the like? After all the writer has said upon the subject, and the awful warning he had intended this history to all evilly disposed young men. I daresay there are some people who even now cannot see the moral he has endeavoured to convey.

"I wonder how Mr. Maurice is going on," said the publisher, presently.

"Well," observed Mr. Letchery, who happened to be in the office at the time. "He's going on much as usual. He writes religious leaders for the 'Thirsty Soul,' at eighteen-pence a-piece. I can tell you they're said to beautiful by the old Tabbies, at Clapham."

"Is he very hard up ?"

"Generally, I believe. But the other day he wanted me to cash a check for him for ten pounds."

"Wherever did he get that from ?"

"I know *where he got it*, but I don't know *why he got it*," replied Mr. Letchery, sar-casticly. "It bore the signature of the party you call THE WOMAN WITH THE YELLOW HAIR. Oh! it's a wicked world, is it not? When I have lived a hundred years, I am sure I shall be heartily sick of it. In the meantime I will go and get my dinner."

FASHION FANCIES.—By Miss Sloper.
No. 61.—"The Gentle Bathist" Costume.

THE PET OF THE PANTOMIME.

DRAWN BY DOWER WILSON.